ROBICHEAUX

ROBICHEAUX

A NOVEL

James Lee Burke

ORION

First published in Great Britain in 2018 by Orion Books,
an imprint of The Orion Publishing Group Ltd,
Carmelite House, 50 Victoria Embankment
London EC4Y 0DZ

An Hachette UK company

1 3 5 7 9 10 8 6 4 2

A CIP catalogue record for this book
is available from the British Library.

ISBN (Hardback) 978 1 4091 7645 9
ISBN (Export Trade Paperback) 978 1 4091 7646 6

Printed and bound by CPI Group (UK) Ltd, Croydon, CR0 4YY

MIX
Paper from
responsible sources
FSC® C104740

www.orionbooks.co.uk

With gratitude to Barbara Theroux and McKenna Jordan for their support of my work over the many years

AUTHOR'S NOTE

THE LITERARY ANTECEDENTS of this novel lie in two earlier works of mine. The unsolved murders in Jefferson Davis Parish formed the backdrop for the Dave Robicheaux novel titled *The Glass Rainbow*, published by Simon & Schuster in 2010. These homicides are often referred to in the media as the Jeff Davis Eight.

The bombing of the Indian village in Latin America happened in 1956. I wrote about this incident in the short story titled "The Wild Side of Life", published in the winter issue of *The Southern Review* in 2017.

ROBICHEAUX

Chapter 1

LIKE AN EARLY nineteenth-century poet, when I have melancholy moments and feel the world is too much for us and that late and soon we lay waste to our powers in getting and spending, I'm forced to pause and reflect upon my experiences with the dead and the hold they exert on our lives.

This may seem a macabre perspective on one's life, but at a certain point it seems to be the only one we have. Mortality is not kind, and do not let anyone tell you it is. If there is such a thing as wisdom, and I have serious doubts about its presence in my own life, it lies in the acceptance of the human condition and perhaps the knowledge that those who have passed on are still with us, out there in the mist, showing us the way, sometimes uttering a word of caution from the shadows, sometimes visiting us in our sleep, as bright as a candle burning inside a basement that has no windows.

On a winter morning, among white clouds of fog out at Spanish Lake, I would see the boys in butternut splashing their way through the flooded cypress, their muskets held above their heads, their equipment tied with rags so it wouldn't rattle. I was standing no more than ten feet from them, although they took no notice of me, as though they knew I had not been born yet, and their travail and sacrifice were not mine to bear.

Their faces were lean from privation, as pale as wax, their hair

1

uncut, the rents in their uniforms stitched clumsily with string. Their mouths were pinched, their eyes luminous with caution. The youngest soldier, a drummer boy, could not have been older than twelve. On one occasion I stepped into the water to join them. Even then, none acknowledged my presence. The drummer boy stumbled and couldn't right himself, struggling with the leather strap around his neck and the weight of his drum. I reached out to help him and felt my hand and arm sink through his shoulder. A shaft of sunlight pierced the canopy, turning the fog into white silk; in less than a second the column was gone.

Long ago, I ceased trying to explain events such as these to either myself or others. Like many my age, I believe people in groups are to be feared and that arguing with others is folly and the knowledge of one generation cannot be passed down to the next. Those may seem cynical sentiments, but there are certain truths you keep inside you and do not defend lest you cheapen and then lose them altogether. Those truths have less to do with the dead than the awareness that we are no different from them, that they are still with us and we are still with them, and there is no afterlife but only one life, a continuum in which all time occurs at once, like a dream inside the mind of God.

Why should an old man thrice widowed dwell on things that are not demonstrable and have nothing to do with a reasonable view of the world? Because only yesterday, on a broken sidewalk in a shabby neighborhood at the bottom of St. Claude Avenue, in the Lower Ninth Ward of St. Bernard Parish, under a colonnade that was still twisted out of shape by Katrina, across from a liquor store with barred windows that stood under a live oak probably two hundred years old, I saw a platoon of Confederate infantry march out of a field to the tune of "Darling Nelly Gray" and disappear through the wall of a gutted building and not exit on the other side.

THE MAN I came to see was Fat Tony Nemo, also known as Tony the Nose, Tony Squid, or Tony Nine Ball, the latter not because he was a pool shark but because he packed a nine ball into a bartender's mouth with the butt of a pool cue. Of course, that was during his earlier incarnation, when he was a collector for Didoni Giacano and the two of them used to drive around New Orleans in Didi's Caddy convertible, terrifying whoever couldn't make the weekly vig, a bloodstained baseball bat propped up in the backseat. Currently, Fat Tony was involved in politics and narcotics and porn and casinos and Hollywood movies and the concrete business. He had also laundered money for the Triads in Hong Kong and helped Somoza's greaseballs introduce crack cocaine to America's inner cities. In terms of territory, he had fingers in pies all over Louisiana, Mississippi, and Florida. If he had any sense of morality or fear about a judgment down the track, I never saw it.

So why would a semi-retired sheriff's detective from Iberia Parish want to make a social call on a psychopath like Tony Squid? Simple. Most investigative cops, often without knowing who Niccolò Machiavelli was, adhere to his admonition to keep your friends close but your enemies closer. Less simple is the fact that we share much of the same culture as the lowlifes, and we are more alike than different, and the information they give us is indispensable.

Fat Tony was sitting in a swivel chair behind his desk when I entered his office. No, that's not correct. Tony didn't sit; he piled himself into a chair or on a couch like a gelatinous heap of whale sperm thrown on a beach, except he was wearing a blue suit with a red boutonniere in the lapel. A sword with a scrolled brass guard in a plain metal scabbard lay across his ink pad. "I'm glad you could come, Dave. You never disappoint. That's why I like you," he wheezed.

"What's the haps, Tony?"

"I'm on an oxygen bottle. I'm scheduled for a colostomy. I couldn't get laid in a whorehouse that has an ATM. My wife tells me I got a serious case of GAPO. Otherwise, I'm doing great. What kind of question is that?" He had to catch his breath before he could continue. "Want a drink?"

"No, thanks. What's GAPO?"

"Gorilla armpit odor. You still on the wagon?"

"I'm still in A.A., if that's what you mean."

"The same thing, right?"

"No."

"Whatever. Take Clete Purcel to a meeting with you."

"What's Clete done?"

"What hasn't he done? He's a fucking cancer on the whole city. He should have a steel codpiece locked on his body so he can't reproduce."

"How can I help you, Tony?"

"Maybe I can help *you*. I heard about your wife."

"I appreciate your concern. I need to get back to New Iberia."

"She got killed in an accident?"

I nodded.

"What, about three months ago?"

"Two years. She was T-boned by a guy in a pickup. I'd rather talk about something else."

He handed me the sword. "I got this at a flea market in Memphis. I asked an expert what it's worth. He said he'd take if off my hands for three thousand. The real value, what is it?"

"I wouldn't know."

"You know about history, what the names of these places on the hilt mean, whether those places make the sword more valuable. What's this Cemetery Hill stuff? Who fights a war in a fucking cemetery?"

The brass on the handle was engraved with the name of Lieutenant Robert S. Broussard, Eighth Louisiana Infantry. The base of the blade was stamped with the initials CSA and the name of the maker, James Conning, of Mobile, Alabama, and the year 1861.

"I did some Googling," Tony said. "The guy who owned this was from New Iberia. It's worth a lot more than two or three thousand dollars, right? Maybe the guy was famous for something."

"You couldn't find any of that on the Internet, with all the Civil War junk that's on sale?"

"You can't trust the Internet. It's full of crazoids."

I couldn't begin to sort through the contradictions in what he had just said. This was a typical Fat Tony conversation. Trying to get inside his mind was akin to submerging your hand in an unflushed toilet. Outside, some black kids were breaking bottles with an air rifle in a vacant lot. There were concrete foundations in the lot without structures on them. A garbage truck was driving down a street, seagulls picking at its overflow.

"Is this about Clete?" I said.

"I got no problem with Purcel. Other people do. It's true he took out that fat dick of his at the Southern Yacht Club and hosed down Bobby Earl's car?"

"I don't know," I lied.

"Two weeks ago he did it again. At the casino."

"Clete did?"

"No, the pope. Earl put his lady friend in the car, and suddenly, she's sitting in a puddle of piss."

"Why did you show me this sword, Tony?"

"Because the family of the guy who owned it lives in New Iberia. I thought maybe they'd want it."

"What does any of this have to do with Clete and Bobby Earl?"

"Nothing."

My head was throbbing. "It was good seeing you."

"Sit down. I know what happened with your wife. No witnesses except the guy who killed her. He says she ran the Stop sign. They had to cut her out with the Jaws of Life?"

I could feel blood veins tightening on the side of my head.

"She died on the way to the hospital and got blamed for her own death?" he said.

"Who told you this?"

"Some cops. You got a dirty deal. Something ought to be done."

"You need to disengage, Tony."

"On top of it, I heard the guy tried to pump the insurance company. Shut the door."

I leaned forward. "Listen carefully, Tony. My wife's death is my business. You stay out of it."

"Mabel, shut the door!" he yelled at his secretary. I raised my finger at him. I was trembling. I heard the door click shut behind me. He spoke before I could. "Hear me out. The guy ran over a kid in a school zone in Alabama. The kid was crippled for life. You give me the nod, this guy is gonna be crawling around on stumps."

"When did he run over a child in a school zone?"

"Ten, fifteen years back."

"Where in Alabama?"

"What difference does it make? I'm telling you like it is. A guy like that has got it coming."

He was like every gangster I ever knew. They're self-righteous and marginalize their victims before breaking their bones. Not one of them could think his way out of a wet paper bag. Their level of cruelty is equaled only by the level of disingenuousness that governs their lives.

"I want you to get this straight, Tony. Go near the man who hit my wife's car, and I'll come looking for you, up close and personal."

"Yeah?" He lit a cigarette with a paper match, cupping the flame. He threw the burnt match into the wastebasket. "So fuck me."

I stood up and pulled the sword halfway from its scabbard, then slid it inside again. The guard was brass, molded like a metal basket with slits in it. It was incised with the names of three battles that took place during Stonewall Jackson's Shenandoah campaign, plus Cemetery Hill at Gettysburg, and extended protectively and cuplike over the back of my hand. The black leather on the grip was both soft and firm, wrapped with gold wire. I replaced the sword on Tony's desk. "I think the Broussard family would be honored and delighted if you gave this to them."

"I'm having a hard time processing this," he said. "I try to be your friend, and you're offended and make threats. If you were somebody else, we'd have a different outcome here."

"So fuck both of us. Tell me something, Tony."

"What? How you should get rid of terminal assholitis?"

"Why do you keep your office in a neighborhood like this?"

"What's wrong with it?"

"It looks like a moonscape. In the next storm, it's going underwater again."

"I like to stay close to the people. On that subject, I'm backing a guy who might end up president of the United States. Want to know who that is?"

"Not really."

"Jimmy Nightingale. People have been talking political correctness in this country for too many years. There's gonna be a change. Fucking A."

"Somehow I believe you, Tony."

And that was probably the most depressing thought I'd had in a long time.

Chapter 2

I PARKED MY PICKUP on Decatur and walked across Jackson Square, past Pirate's Alley and St. Louis Cathedral and a marimba band playing in the shade by the bookstore that used to be William Faulkner's apartment. The day was bright and windy, cool even for March, the flowerpots on the balconies bursting with color, the kind of day in Louisiana that lifts the heart and tells you perhaps spring is forever, that the long rainy weeks of winter were nothing more than a passing aberration, that even death can be stilled by the season if you'll only believe.

Clete's apartment and PI office were located in a grand old building on St. Ann Street, the plaster painted a pale yellow, the ironwork on the balcony dripping with bougainvillea and bugle vine, a dry wishing well in the courtyard. Other than the vintage Cadillacs he drove, the only material possession he ever loved was his building, which may have been owned in the nineteenth century by the same woman who ran the House of the Rising Sun.

When I rounded the corner, I saw not only the building but a moving van at the curb and half of Clete's furniture and office equipment on the sidewalk. Clete was on the sidewalk, arguing with a notorious New Orleans character named Whitey Zeroski, known as the dumbest white person in the city. When he was an independent taxi driver, he thought he'd widen his horizons and run for city council.

He outfitted a pickup truck with loudspeakers and a huge sign on the roof and on Saturday night drove into a black neighborhood, blaring to the crowds on the sidewalks, "Vote for Whitey! Whitey is your friend! Don't forget Whitey on Tuesday! Whitey will never let you down!"

He was stunned by the cascade of rocks, bricks, bottles, and beer cans that crashed on top of his vehicle.

I hadn't seen Clete in weeks, and I missed him, as I always did when we were separated for very long. Oddly, in the last couple of years, Clete had imposed a degree of order upon his life. The scars he carried from an abusive home in the old Irish Channel and Vietnam and the romances that began passionately but always ended badly no longer seemed to be his burden. He didn't drink before noon, laid off the weed and cigarettes, ate one po'boy sandwich for lunch instead of two, and clanked iron in a baggy pair of Everlasts in his courtyard and sometimes jogged from one end of the Quarter to the other. When he'd head down Bourbon, one of the black kids who tap-danced for the tourists would sometimes say, "Here come the pink elephant. Hope he don't crack the cement."

None of this stopped me from worrying about Clete and his swollen liver and his blood pressure, and the violence he inflicted upon others as surrogates for himself and for the father who had beaten him unmercifully with a razor strop. I loved Clete Purcel, and I didn't care who knew it or what others might think of us. We started off our careers walking a beat on Canal and in the Quarter, fresh back from Indochina, the evening sky robin's-egg blue, the clouds as pink as cotton candy and ribbed like piano keys arching over the city. We thought we'd hit the perfecta. The Quarter was alive with music and full of beautiful women and the smell of burgundy and tap beer and bruised mint in a glass of shaved ice and Jack Daniel's. Could the world offer any finer gifts?

Since the death of my wife Molly, I wanted to see more and more of Clete, particularly in those moments when I felt as though the defining moments of my life had little application in the present, that somewhere down a deserted street a bus was throbbing at the curb, the passengers hollow-eyed and mute, unable to assimilate the journey that awaited them. Then the driver popped open the doors with a sucking sound, and I knew with a sinking of the heart that the bus was for me and I wouldn't be returning to the city or the state I loved.

When I have those moments, I say the names of Clete and my daughter, Alafair, over and over. I have done it even in public, indifferent to the stares of others, a napkin held to my mouth or with my chin pointed down at my chest. And that's why I resented Whitey Zeroski and his hired help or anyone else who tried to hurt the noblest man I ever knew.

"How's tricks, Whitey?" I said.

He always looked surprised, as though someone had just stepped on his foot. He also had a habit of jerking his entire head when something caught his attention, like a meth addict or a chicken pecking in a barnyard or a man with a fused neck. He wore coveralls zipped up to his neck, the sleeves cut off at the armpits, his arms covered with hair.

"What it is, Robicheaux?" he said.

"Mind telling me what the hell you're doing?"

"I work for the bank now. They gave me the key to Purcel's building and the paperwork to move his belongings out on the sidewalk. He's got another point of view on that."

"This idiot creeped my house, Streak," Clete said.

"What happened to your cab business?" I said to Whitey.

"Heard of Katrina?" he said.

"Don't do this, Whitey," I said.

"Off my back, Robicheaux. This is a legal action, here."

"Whitey, I try to be kind to dumb Polacks, but I'm about to stuff you in the storm sewer," Clete said.

"How about laying off the ethnic slurs?" Whitey said.

Clete looked at me and opened his hands. A pale red scar ran diagonally through his left eyebrow where he'd been hit with a pipe when he was a kid. "This is like beating up on somebody who was born brain-dead. Whitey, I apologize for calling you a dumb Polack. That's an insult to dumb Polacks."

Whitey's face contorted as he tried to figure out what Clete had just said.

"Let me see the paperwork," I said.

"It's a reverse mortgage," Clete said, his face coloring.

I looked at him blankly. "You didn't?"

"I was jammed up," he said. He had a little-boy haircut and a dimpled chin and green eyes that never faltered unless he was hiding something from me.

"We'll get the furniture off the sidewalk," I said. "We'll work it out."

"Oh, you will?" Whitey said. He had a New Orleans working-class accent, like someone whose voice box had been injected with Novocain. "What, I got nothing else to do but walk behind dick-brain here with a dustpan and a broom?"

"Shoot your mouth off one more time, Whitey, and see what happens," Clete said.

I placed my arm across Whitey's shoulders. "Take a walk with me."

"What for?"

"Your helpers don't seem to speak English. You don't have an inspection sticker on your windshield. Your license plate isn't current. You're parked in a no-loading zone. You don't have flashers. What should we do about that?"

"Give me a break here, Robicheaux."

I took out my wallet, removed all the bills from it, and put them in his hand. "That's about sixty dollars. Tell your boys to put everything back in the building, and buy them a round. I'll call the bank and get this straightened out."

"We're supposed to live on a beer and a shot while you get me fired by the bank? I can't wait to tell my boys this."

"Clete never did anything to you, Whitey, but you're making money off an unrighteous situation that's not Clete's fault."

"I'll make you a counteroffer. Wipe your ass with your sixty dollars. I'll buy the round for the boys, and you and Purcel can haul everything back in the building. Then pour a shitload of Vaseline on it and cram it up your ass. I hope both of you get rich twice and go broke three times. I hope both of you inherit a house with fifty rooms in it and drop dead in every one of them."

I had to hand it to him: Whitey was stand-up. I had tried to use my power wrongly to help a friend, and in so doing, I had probably put an unskilled and poor man at the mercy of an unscrupulous mortgage holder.

Clete and I spent the next two hours dragging furniture back into the building or wrestling it up the stairs into the apartment. It was four o'clock when I sat down heavily on the couch, my head swimming. Clete was in the kitchen, pouring four inches of Scotch into a glass packed with cracked ice. It was not a good moment. My defenses were down, the smoky smell of the Scotch like an irresistible thread from an erotic dream you can't let go of at first light.

"You want a Dr Pepper?" he said, his back to me.

"No, thanks."

"I got some cherries and limes."

"I don't want one."

"Suit yourself."

"I think I pulled something in my back." I got up and went into the kitchen and opened the refrigerator. I took out a Dr Pepper and opened it.

"I thought you didn't want one."

"I changed my mind. Why didn't you tell me you needed money?"

"It was eighty grand."

"How much?"

"What I said."

"You got it from a shylock?"

"I started gambling. I did pretty good at first."

"Here?"

"Everywhere. I had a credit line in Vegas. Google has ruined private investigation. Anyway, I started losing, and I didn't stop until I was broke and borrowing on the property."

He took a long drink from the glass, his eyes on mine, the ice and mint and Scotch sliding down his throat. I felt a twitch in my face. "So the bank owns your place now?"

"It's not a bank, it's a mortgage company. They screw old people. Maybe they're mobbed up."

"Great choice."

He set down the glass. The Scotch was drained from the ice. He dumped the ice into the sink. I felt myself swallow.

"Let's go eat," he said.

"There's something you're not telling me. Tony Nine Ball said you had trouble with Bobby Earl. What's that about?"

"The problem wasn't exactly with Bobby Earl. I almost feel sorry for the bastard. I heard the blacks were loading up on condoms his first night in Lewisburg."

"Tony says you pissed in Earl's car."

"Yeah, years ago. At the Yacht Club."

"Just recently."

"Okay, I'm shooting craps at Harrah's, and in come Bobby Earl and Jimmy Nightingale with this stripper who used to work on Bourbon. Except it was obvious Earl is carrying the stripper for Nightingale, or at least obvious to me, because Nightingale is a bucket of warm vomit who manipulates the subculture like it's his private worm farm. But right now that's not my business, and I'm simpatico at the table as long as these two assholes leave me alone. I've got twenty-six hundred dollars in chips in front of me, and a magic arm, and I'm rolling nothing but elevens and sevens. The broad hanging all over Earl is staring at me with this curious look, then a lightbulb goes off in her head and she says, 'Hey, you're the fat guy who came to my house.'"

Listening to a story told by Clete Purcel was like building the pyramids with your bare hands. I twirled my finger, trying to make him finish.

"Seconds earlier I felt like I owned Fort Knox," he said. "Then I see it all draining away, like dirty water going down the lavatory. I pick up the dice and rattle them once and fling them down the felt. Snake eyes. She goes, 'I'm right, aren't I? You're the guy who came around about that legal problem?'"

"Cletus, try to get to the point," I said.

"Legal problem? She got busted for leaving her kid in a hot car while she was stoned and balling a couple of truck drivers in a motel room. She skipped on her court appearance and left the bondsman on the hook for ten grand. So I pass the dice, and slap Bobby Earl on the back hard enough to rattle his teeth, and say, 'Hey, Bob, I hear you picked up another nail. If you're on penicillin, you shouldn't be drinking. Next time out, wear a hazmat suit or get some radioactive condoms for your flopper.'"

He was sitting at the breakfast table now. He yawned as though just waking up, and put two fingers into his shirt pocket for cigarettes that weren't there. Then he blinked.

"What's the rest of it?" I said.

"Nothing. I left. I saw Earl's wheels. I used my slim-jim to pop his door and took a leak inside."

"No, you've left something out."

"Like what?"

"Why give Bobby Earl a hard time? Like you said, he's pitiful."

"He makes me ashamed I'm from New Orleans. He's a disgrace to the city. He's a disgrace to the planet."

"Does Jimmy Nightingale figure in this?"

"I might have said one or two things I shouldn't have."

"Really?"

"He put his arm on my shoulders like we were old pals. Then he touched my cheek with the back of his wrist. Yuck. I called him a cunt and got escorted in cuffs out the front door. There were only about three or four hundred people watching."

He cleared his throat softly, his eyes shiny.

"He's lucky you didn't drop him," I said. "Those security guys, too."

"Think so?"

"I'm proud of you, Clete."

"Yeah?" He looked at me guiltily.

"What?" I said.

"Nightingale is part owner of the company I took the reverse mortgage from."

JIMMY NIGHTINGALE WAS one of the most unusual men I ever knew. He grew up in Franklin, on Bayou Teche, and lived in a refurbished antebellum home that resembled a candlelit steamboat couched among the live oaks. Like his family, Jimmy was a patrician and an elitist, but among common people, he was kind and humble and an attentive listener when they spoke of their difficulties and travail and Friday-night football games and the items they bought at Walmart. If someone told a vulgar joke or used profanity in his presence, he pretended not to hear or he walked away, but he never indicated condemnation. In a dressing room or a pickup basketball game, his manners and smile were so disarming that it was easy to think of him as an avatar of noblesse oblige rather than the personification of greed for which the Nightingales were infamous.

Please don't misunderstand. My description of Jimmy is not about him or the system he served but a weakness in me. In trying to be a halfway decent Christian, I put aside my resentment of his oligarchic background and accepted him as he was. Actually, it went further than that. I liked Jimmy a lot, or at least I liked things about him. I admired him and perhaps sometimes even envied his combination of composure and ardor, as well as his ability to float above the pettiness that characterizes the greater part of our lives.

He was handsome in an androgynous way, his hair bronze-colored and neatly clipped and perfectly combed, his face egg-shaped, his cheeks pooled with color, his breath sweet. Both men and women were drawn to him in a physical way, and I think many times his admirers could not explain the attraction. He probably wasn't over five-nine and 150 pounds. But maybe that was the key to his likability. He was one of us, yet confident in a locker room or at a boxing match, and he didn't feel a need to contend with criticism or personal insult. Jimmy used to say the only argument you ever win is the one you don't have.

He was our man of all seasons: a graduate of military school, a screenwriter, a yachtsman, a polo player, and a performer at aerial shows. He could speak on any subject and was the escort of women who were both beautiful and cerebral, although he had never married nor, to my knowledge, ever been engaged. His self-contained manner and repressed intensity made me wonder if he didn't belong in a Greek tragedy.

I believed Jimmy had an enormous capacity for either good or evil, and that his spirit was as capricious as a wind vane. F. Scott Fitzgerald once said no one could understand America without understanding the graves of Shiloh. I think the same could have been said of Jimmy Nightingale.

He was about to announce his candidacy for the United States Senate. If elected, he would establish a precedent. Yes, Louisiana has produced some statesmen and stateswomen, but they are the exception and not the norm. For many years our state legislature has been known as a mental asylum run by ExxonMobil. Since Huey Long, demagoguery has been a given; misogamy and racism and homophobia have become religious virtues, and self-congratulatory ignorance has become a source of pride.

I shared none of these thoughts with Clete. Instead, when I returned to New Iberia and my shotgun house on the bayou a short distance from the Shadows, I called Jimmy Nightingale's home in Franklin. A female secretary answered and took a message. Did you ever have a conversation with a professional ice cube?

"Do you know where Mr. Nightingale is?" I asked.

"He didn't say."

"Is he in New Orleans?"

"I'm sure he'll return your call very soon, Mr. Robicheaux."

"It's Detective Robicheaux."

"Thank you for your call, Detective Robicheaux. Is your call in reference to an official matter?"

"I really don't know how to define it."

"I'll tell him that. Good-bye."

The line went dead.

I lit the gas stove in the kitchen and warmed a bowl of frozen crawfish gumbo. The windows were open, the curtains swelling with wind, the house creaking. The light was failing in the oak and pecan trees in my backyard. On the far side of the bayou, a man of color was sitting on a wooden chair, fishing with a cane pole and bobber among the reeds, the late sun splintering on the water. Since my wife's accident, this had become my worst time of day. My home was cavernous with silence and emptiness. My wife was gone, and so were my pets and most of my relatives. With each day that passed, I felt as though the world I had known was being airbrushed out of a painting.

I took the gumbo off the stove and sat down at the breakfast table with a spoon and a chunk of dry French bread and started to eat. I heard a car turn in to my gravel drive, the tires clicking, and come to a stop at the porte cochere.

"Dave?" someone called.

I walked through the hallway into the living room. Jimmy Nightingale stood at the screen, panama hat in hand, trying to see inside. He was wearing beige slacks and a maroon shirt and a windbreaker with a pair of aviator glasses sticking out of the breast pocket. "How you doin', copper?" he said.

"Come in," I said, pushing open the door.

"My secretary called me on the cell." He shook hands, his eyes sweeping through the house, then brightening when they came back to mine. "You look good."

"You, too, Jimmy."

But Jimmy always looked good. He followed me into the kitchen.

"I have some gumbo on the stove," I said. "Or would you like a cold drink?"

"I just ate at Clementine's. You have such a nice place here. The park is right across the bayou, huh? Tell me the truth, did my secretary give you the impression she was blowing you off? She's like that. But she's a class act, believe me."

I had forgotten that Jimmy often spoke in paragraphs rather than sentences. "She was fine," I said.

"Always the gentleman," he said, soft-punching me on the arm. "I bet you were calling about Clete Purcel."

"Clete's sorry about the encounter at the casino."

"Sprinkling his head with ashes? Using a flagellum on his back, that sort of thing?"

"Clete doesn't mean half the things he says."

"Finish your supper while I explain something. Come on, sit down."

That he was inviting me to sit down in my own house didn't seem to cross his mind. He pinched the bridge of his nose and closed and opened his eyes as though fatigued. "I flew a biplane today and got a little sunburned. Ever go up in one?"

I shook my head.

"I wish I could have been in the Lafayette Escadrille. Dancing around the skies of France and Belgium, giving the Red Baron a tap or two with the Vickers."

"War is usually interesting only to people who haven't been to one."

"You should have been a funeral director, Dave."

"Clete says you own the mortgage on his house," I said.

"I own part of a lending company that does. He thinks I'm having him evicted because of a little incident at a craps table?"

"Are you?"

"I forgot it two minutes after it was over."

"People call you a cunt in public with regularity?"

"Wow, you know how to say it."

"Cut him some slack, Jimmy."

Then he surprised me. "I'll look into it. If there's something I can do, I will."

"I have your word?"

"I just gave it to you."

I forgot to mention Jimmy was a very good baseball pitcher, both in the American Legion and in college. His best pitch was the changeup, when you hold the ball in the back of your palm and leave the batter swinging at empty space.

"Thank you," I said.

"You getting along all right? Since the accident?"

"I don't talk about it much."

"I understand."

He gazed through the back window. The lawn was deep in shadow, the air tannic and cold, the ground strewn with yellow leaves spotted with black mold. The door hung open on the hutch that once housed our pet coon, Tripod, the wood floor clean and dry and empty. "I love your place," he said.

"Why?"

"It's out of another era. A more innocent time."

"Why do you pal around with a shitbag like Bobby Earl?"

"The eyes of God see no evil," he replied.

"I've always envied people who know the mind of God."

"I'll call you by the end of business tomorrow on that mortgage situation. Can you do me a favor?"

I waited.

"This novelist who lives up the Teche on Loreauville Road, you know him?"

"Levon Broussard?" I said.

"That's the baby. How about an introduction?"

"You need me for that?"

"I hear he's a little eccentric and his wife got kicked off a spaceship."

"You're the second unlikely person to say something to me today about the Broussard family. The other was Tony Nemo. Is that coincidence?"

"You know what they say at meetings. Coincidence is your Higher Power acting with anonymity."

"I didn't know you were in the program."

"I'm not. I go for the dialogue. It's great material."

"I'll ask Levon if he wants to have dinner with us."

Jimmy made a snicking sound in his jaw. "That's my man. Make it soon, will you? I really dig the guy's work. I'm going to get a shotgun house just like this. See you."

He tapped me on the shoulder with his hat and went out the door. Jimmy kept it simple.

Chapter
3

AFTER SUNSET, I drove to the rural two-lane highway where Molly's car had been struck broadside on the driver's door, knocking her unconscious, pinning her inside. I had revisited the site more than a dozen times, either at night or before sunrise, when there was little traffic. There was a Stop sign at the access road, then nothing but the long curving bend of the two-lane. By flashlight I had looked for the pickup's skid marks, re-created every possibility about the speed of the pickup, and measured the exact distance from the bend to the Stop sign. The speed limit was forty-five miles an hour, the speed the pickup driver said he was traveling when Molly's Toyota had suddenly come through the Stop sign and made a reckless left turn in front of him.

I used a stopwatch to compute the time it would take for the pickup driver to traverse the distance from the bend to the point of impact if he were driving the legal limit. The math led to only two possible conclusions: Either Molly ran the Stop sign, abandoning all reason; or she looked to the left, saw nothing coming, then looked to the right, saw the road was clear, and turned left without looking again and got crushed.

But Molly never ran stop signs. She would never willingly break a law of any kind. The skid marks, now washed away, were no longer than eighteen inches in length, indicating the pickup driver saw her car only seconds before the collision. Everything in me told me that Molly probably failed to double-check the two-lane before she started her turn, and the pickup driver lied and was coming much faster than forty-five miles an hour. The causes of the crash were shared ones.

Like many victims of violent crimes who never find justice, I became obsessed with speculations I could not prove. I told myself that Molly's fate could have been worse, that the Toyota could have burst into flame while she was conscious and trapped inside, that she could have spent the rest of her life as a vegetable or disfigured beyond recognition or left a quadriplegic. I soon began to gaze into space at the office, in the middle of conversation, on a street corner, my hands balling, while others stared at me with pity and concern.

I had never confronted the driver or even spoken to him, because he was part of an official investigation, and my contacting him would have been improper. But the day after I talked with Fat Tony, I drove up the Teche to what were called the Quarters, outside the little town of Loreauville. The Quarters were composed of cabins and shotgun houses that went back to the corporate-plantation era of the nineteenth century. Most of them were painted a yellowish gray and aligned in rows on dirt streets with rain ditches and bare yards where whites and people of color lived in harmony and seemed to enjoy the lives they had. On weekends the residents barbecued and drank beer on their small galleries, washed their cars in the yard, and flew kites and played softball in the streets with their children. I don't mean to romanticize poverty. The Loreauville Quarters were a window into my childhood, a time when few people in the community spoke English and few had traveled farther than two parishes from their place of birth. It wasn't a half-bad world in which to grow up.

I found his name, T. J. Dartez, on a mailbox. I slipped my badge holder and my clip-on holster from my belt and put them under the seat, and stepped across the rain ditch into his yard. An old washing machine converted into a barbecue pit was smoking on the gallery, a chicken dripping in the coals. I heard children's voices in back. I walked up the dirt driveway. A dented washed-out blue pickup was parked in a shed. An unshaved man in work pants and a clean strap undershirt was lobbing a Wiffle ball at two little girls armed with plastic baseball bats. His hair was black and greasy and curly on the back of his neck. He turned around, smiling. The stub of a filter-tipped cigar was clenched in his teeth. I had never seen him before.

"You looking for somebody?" he asked.

"Are you Mr. Dartez?"

"Yes, suh."

I stared at him. I don't know for how long. The little girls looked about six and eight. They had both gone silent. "I need to talk to you."

"About what?"

I glanced at the girls. "A serious matter."

"Y'all go he'p your mama," he said.

His house looked like a boxcar, a poorer version of mine, set up on cinder blocks. The girls went up the wooden steps and let the screen slam behind them.

"You're from the agency?" he said.

"What agency?"

"The bill-collection one."

"No, I'm not."

He looked at nothing. "You're him, ain't you?"

"I don't know who 'him' is."

"The husband of the woman in the accident."

"Yes, that's who I am."

"What you want wit' me?"

"You know who Tony Nemo is?"

"Who?"

"You may not know him, but he knows you. He says you ran over a child in Alabama."

"That's a damn lie."

"It didn't happen?"

"I got a DWI for driving drunk in a school zone there. I didn't hurt nobody. I don't drink no more, either."

"But you were driving faster than forty-five when you hit my wife, weren't you?"

Through the screen, I could see his wife and children staring at us. These were people for whom bad luck was not an abstraction but a constant; a knock on the door, a puff of wind, and their lives could be up the spout.

"You always got your eye on the speedometer when you're driving at night?" he said. "I think I was driving forty-five. I cain't say for sure. She come out of the dark."

"Her lights weren't on?"

He tried to hold his eyes on mine. "I cain't remember."

"Your lawyer told you to say that?"

"Suh?"

"You heard me."

His expression turned into a pout, like a child's. "I ain't got nothing else to say."

"I hear you tried to pump State Farm."

"I missed eight days of work. Who's gonna pay for that? You?"

"My wife was a nun in Central America," I said.

His mouth moved, but no sound came out.

"She was a former sister. She devoted her life to helping the poor."

"She's a farmer—?"

How do you get angry at a man who cannot understand or speak his own language?

"If you were me, what would you do, Mr. Dartez? What would you feel?"

There was a big thickly leafed shade tree by his garage. It was filled with wind, its leaves dark green against an orange sun. He stared at it as though he wanted to hide inside its branches. "This guy you call Tony? He's a dago gangster you using to scare me?"

"How do you know he's a gangster?"

"I know what goes on."

"I'm telling you he took an interest in you. I'm not sure why. I told him to butt out. I'm telling you to learn who your friends are."

"You're my friend? A man who comes to my house and scares my wife and children?"

I stepped closer to him. I couldn't help my feelings, the surge of bile in my stomach, the visceral disgust I felt for his ignorance, my desire to do things with my fists that were ultimately a confession of defeat. He stepped back. "My old lady is calling the cops."

The wind shifted. I could smell his odor, the barbecue smoke on his skin, the grease in his hair. "You lied to the state trooper. Until you admit your part in the accident, you'll never have peace."

"I'm sorry your wife is dead. She come at me. I didn't do nothing wrong. If you won't accept that, go fuck yourself."

"You had your warning," I said.

"My family heard that. What's the sheriff gonna say if I call him and tell him that? Answer me that. Yeah, I didn't think so. Fuck you twice."

I walked away, the sugarcane fields and the horizon tilting, my long-sleeve white shirt peppered with sweat, a war taking place in my chest that I knew I would never win.

CLETE HAD TWO offices, one in New Orleans, one in New Iberia. When he worked out of his New Iberia office, he rented a cottage at the Teche Motel on East Main, down the bayou from my house. When I woke Sunday morning, there were clouds of thick white fog bumping against the tree trunks in the backyard, like cotton on the floor of a gin. I saw a raccoon on top of Tripod's hutch, its coat shiny with dew. I went to the back door and looked through the screen. The coon had climbed into an oak tree and was looking at me from atop a limb. I pushed open the screen. "Tripod?"

Then he was gone. I went outside in my pajamas and slippers and looked up at the branches but saw no sign of him. I went back inside and dressed and ate breakfast and went to Mass at St. Edward's. When I returned home, Clete's metallic-purple Cadillac was parked in the driveway, the top up, his stocking feet sticking out the back window. He was asleep on the backseat with a pillow over his face. He smelled like a beer truck.

I went inside and made coffee and warmed a pan of milk and put four cinnamon rolls in the oven, then went into the backyard

again and looked for the coon. Tripod had died years ago, but I often
dreamed of him in my sleep, as I did my other pets, and I wondered if
animals, like people I've known, have ways of contacting us again. A
half hour later, Clete came through the back door, his face wrinkled
on one side by the pillow, his eyes bleary.

"You just hit town?" I said.

"I'm not sure what I did. I was drinking Jack with a beer back in
Morgan City, then my lights went out. You got a beer?"

"Nope."

"I'll drink kerosene if you've got it." He sat down at the breakfast
table. He was wearing his porkpie hat and the long-sleeve tropical
shirt he had bought in Miami. "You got any uppers?"

"Are you out of your mind?"

"You want me to go?"

"No, I fixed you some breakfast. Just don't get sick on the floor."

"Something weird happened yesterday. I was trying to think my
way through it. That's why I was drinking depth charges. You know,
when you're arguing with yourself and wondering if you're letting
somebody work your crank. My head feels like a basketball."

"What are we talking about, Clete?"

"That douchebag called me."

"Which douchebag?"

"The one who tried to evict me—Jimmy Nightingale. He says we
can work out my problem on the reverse mortgage. I can refinance
and let his company have a quarter-acre lot I own in Biloxi. He'll
also introduce me to a stockbroker who'll let me buy some surefire
winners on the margin. I asked him why he was doing all this. He says
because you talked to him."

"I did."

"You don't think he's trying to shaft me?"

"He wants me to introduce him to Levon Broussard."

Clete looked blank for a moment. "The writer who's got the wife
with outstanding bongos? She jogged by my office a couple of times.
I hear she's nuts."

"Has anyone ever used the term 'arrested development' to you?"

"Yeah, the marriage counselor who was screwing my ex while he was counseling us. You think I should take the deal?"

"What'll happen if you don't?"

"The guys I owe in Vegas and Reno are real shitheads. Guys I used to work with. Use your imagination."

"I have thirty thousand at Vanguard. You can have it."

"That would be like putting a bicycle patch on the rip in the *Titanic*."

I placed the rolls on a plate and set them and a butter dish and a cup of coffee and milk on the table. "Eat up."

"You're the best, noble mon," he replied.

No, Clete was. But no one would ever convince him of that.

CLETE CHECKED IN to his cottage at the Teche Motel, and I called the home of Levon Broussard and his wife, Rowena. Levon had been on the *New York Times* bestseller lists for twenty years, and Rowena's raw-edged paintings and photography were loved by many people in need of a cause and a banner. The only reason I had been given their private number was Levon's admiration for the novels by my daughter, Alafair. The couple lived up the bayou from me in a spacious home built of teardown South Carolina brick, with floor-to-ceiling windows and ventilated green storm shutters and a wide gallery. The house stayed in almost permanent shadow inside a half-dozen live oaks hung with Spanish moss.

Rowena answered the phone.

"Hello, Miss Rowena," I said. "It's Dave Robicheaux. Is Levon there?"

There was a beat, the kind that makes you wonder what kind of expression is on your phone party's face.

"I'll get him," she said, and dropped the receiver on a hard surface.

"Hello?" Levon said.

I told him that Jimmy Nightingale wanted to take us to dinner.

"What's he want with us?" Levon said.

"You're a famous writer. He's written some screenplays. Maybe he wants to do business."

"Isn't Nightingale hooked up with the casino industry?"

"Among other things."

"I don't think this is a good idea."

"He's helping Clete Purcel out of a jam. As a favor, he asked for an introduction."

"So you're being charitable at my expense?"

He had me. "You're right. Forget I called."

"Is Alafair there?"

"She's living in Bodega Bay."

I could hear him breathing against the receiver. Levon was known for his reluctance to say no to anyone when asked for money or to help with a personal problem. In fact, he seemed to live with conflicting voices in his head. "I don't like these casino people, Dave. They put the Indians' face on their operations, but most of them are out of Jersey."

"So is Bruce Springsteen," I said.

"How important is this?"

"Clete has screwed himself financially six ways from breakfast. Jimmy Nightingale can probably get him out of it. We're talking about one hour at a dinner table."

I heard him blow out his breath. "When?"

"Six-thirty tomorrow night at Clementine's. I'll call Jimmy and set it up."

"Give Alafair my best. I love her new book."

Before I could reply, he eased the receiver into the cradle.

HELEN SOILEAU WAS in her third term as sheriff, a period when the Iberia Sheriff's Department and the city police had merged. She had started her career as a meter maid with the NOPD and had worked her way up to patrolwoman, then returned to New Iberia, her birthplace, and worked as my plainclothes partner in our small homicide and felony assault unit. Helen defied all conventions and categorizations. Years ago a smartass told her at our department Christmas party that she had the perfect body for a man. She slapped him off the stool, slammed his head into the bar, then picked him up and propped him on the stool and placed a drink in his hand. "No hard feelings," she said.

She had blond hair cut short at the neck, and she never dyed it; she wore slacks and sometimes makeup and sometimes not. Her love affairs included a dalliance with a female informant (which almost destroyed her career), a circus owner, a male masseuse, a feminist professor, and Clete Purcel.

The silence between her sentences was often louder than her words. She didn't carry a throw-down or jam the perps, and as a consequence, she usually learned more from them than others did with coercion. I believed she had several personalities, one of which was a sexual adventurer whose eye sometimes strayed over me. I didn't care. My feelings about Helen were the same as my feelings about Clete: I believed their virtues were poured from a crucible whose heat couldn't be measured.

Monday morning she called me into her office. Through the window I could see Bayou Teche, the sunlight dancing on the surface, a concrete boat ramp on the far side. Her gaze lifted to mine. She had a ballpoint gripped in her right hand. She clicked it over and over.

"I got a call from T. J. Dartez's lawyer," she said.

"I suspected that was coming."

"He says you threatened his client."

"Not true."

"What were you doing at his house?"

"I told him I thought he was speeding when he hit Molly's car. I told him he wouldn't have any peace until he owned up."

Her thumb pressed and released the button on top of the ballpoint, click-click, click-click. "Those were your words?"

"More or less."

"You know what a good liability lawyer could do with that?"

"I had another reason for being there. Tony Nine Ball offered to do some damage to him, maybe take him off the board."

"You had a conversation with Tony Nemo about killing T. J. Dartez?"

"No, I had a conversation with him about a Civil War sword. On the other subject, I told him to stay out of my business. He said Dartez ran over a child in Alabama."

"This isn't coming together for me, bwana."

"Tony likes to pretend he's in tight with cops. He bought a sword at a flea market. It belonged to one of Levon Broussard's ancestors. He either wants to make some money off it, or he wants to get close to Levon. Tony has been involved with two or three film productions. He's a self-serving, greedy, fat shit. He's not a complex man."

She gave me a look and let the ballpoint drop on the blotter. "Keep clear of Dartez and Nemo."

"I plan to."

She stared into my face, her expression flat. As often was the case, I had no idea what she was thinking or who presently occupied her skin. Her hair looked lighter, sun-bleached, perhaps, thicker and more attractive, as though she had been out on the salt.

"Buy me lunch, Pops, and don't give me any more of your trash," she said.

Chapter 4

JIMMY PICKED ME up in a limo, and we drove up Loreauville Road and turned in to the long driveway of the Broussard home. The carriage lamps on the gallery were lit, the floor-to-ceiling windows glowing from the lighted chandelier in the hallway. The wind was up, and the trees were filled with shadows that seemed to battle one another. Three of his live oaks were registered with a national conservation society and named Mosby, Forrest, and Longstreet, perhaps indicating a tired and old and depressing Southern obsession with the illusion that war is grand. But I had a hard time thinking of Levon in that fashion.

He avoided crowds and formal social situations and conventional thinking, and he had a pathological aversion to people who asked questions about his work. He seldom spoke specifically of his family, but supposedly, they were related to Oliver Hazard Perry, John Mosby, Edmund Burke, and John Wilkes Booth. He said he'd grown up in Galveston, or Lake Charles, or Lafayette, or maybe all three, I'm not sure. He was one of those paradoxical individuals who became notorious for his obsession with privacy. He had lived in the tropics and had known leftists in Mexico and DEA agents in Colombia and CIA operatives who flew for an airline headquartered in Fort Lauderdale. Why he had been drawn into the edges of the New American Empire, no one knew. With his tall frame and genteel manners and kind face and egalitarian attitudes, he seemed to personify virtue.

Strangely, although they looked nothing alike, he and Jimmy Nightingale made me think of bookends that belonged on the same shelf.

I sometimes saw Levon's wife at Red Lerille's Health & Racquet Club in Lafayette, in boxing trunks and a halter, sweaty and dedicated, slamming the body bag hard enough to rattle it on the chain. She was Australian and had dark hair and wide-set blue eyes that stared boldly into your face. She seldom spoke or smiled, and if she had any expression, it seemed to be one of puzzlement or wariness, as though the world were constantly deconstructing and reassembling itself before her eyes.

Before I could get out of the limo and ring the bell, Levon and Rowena came out the front door. Levon put his wife inside the limo, then leaned across the seat and shook Jimmy's hand vigorously. "It's very nice to meet you, sir. This is my wife, Rowena. Thank you for your kind invitation. How you doin', Dave?"

That was Levon, the effusive gentleman no matter the occasion. But his cordiality had no influence on what was about to take place. Jimmy's eyes were glued on Rowena's. The connection was electric and naked to the degree that both of them were obviously embarrassed. She sat down heavily on the leather seat, her gaze never leaving Jimmy's. "You're a screenwriter?" she asked him.

"Not really. I try at it."

"Does anyone have a drink?" she said.

"I started to ice some champagne, but I didn't think we'd be long in getting to the restaurant," Jimmy said.

"We're fine," Levon said.

"I'm starved and dry," she said. "Can we get the bloody hell out of here?"

"Right-o," Jimmy said. He tapped the glass behind the driver.

"Is this your vehicle?" Levon said.

"My vehicle? No, it belongs to the car service," Jimmy replied clearly, not sure what was happening. "I'm not that uptown."

"Hello, Miss Rowena. I'm Dave Robicheaux," I said. "I've seen you at Red's health club in Lafayette."

"You're who?"

"We spoke on the phone."

Her window was up. She stared at her reflection in the dark. Then she turned and looked at Jimmy again, as though seeing him for the first time. Levon leaned forward, interdicting her line of sight. "You keep company with Bobby Earl, Mr. Nightingale?"

"Call me Jimmy. I know Earl, but I wouldn't call him a close friend."

"A friend nonetheless?" Levon said.

"Judge not, lest you be judged," Jimmy said.

"What's to judge? His record is demonstrable, isn't it?" Levon said. "If he had his way, the bunch of us would be soap."

"I think he's paid for his sins," Jimmy said.

"His time in prison?" Levon said.

"Considering the ethnic makeup of the population, I suspect he found himself in the middle of a nightmare," Jimmy said.

"I don't think that's much solace to the victims of the Ku Klux Klan."

"Oh, shove it along, you two," Rowena said. She massaged the back of her neck and rotated her head, glancing sideways at Jimmy.

"Good advice," Jimmy said, reaching for something on the floor.

Rowena rolled down her window, flooding the limo with the smell of night-blooming flowers and the sprinklers spinning on the St. Augustine grass in the dark. "Look at the stars. Did you ever see *Night Has a Thousand Eyes*? When the constellations are out, I always think of that movie. Look, each star is vaporous."

"What do you have there?" Levon asked.

"A sword," Jimmy said, lifting it into the light. "I think it belonged to your great-grandfather. I'd like you to have it."

Levon looked at the name incised on the handle. "My God, where did you get this?"

"Did anybody hear me?" Rowena said. "Has anyone seen *Night Has a Thousand Eyes*?"

"I have," Jimmy said. He pushed the sword away when Levon tried to return it. "It starred Edward G. Robinson and Gail Russell. Did you see her in *Angel and the Badman* or *Wake of the Red Witch*?"

"Yes," Rowena said, her face thrust forward, her wide-set eyes filled with interest.

"How about rolling up the window, Rowena?" Levon said. "The air smells like insecticide."

"If that's what everyone wants," she replied.

"Listen here," Levon said. "I can't accept this gift."

"Maybe we can give it to a museum," Jimmy said. "It needs to be somewhere other than in the hands of its previous owner."

Levon waited for Jimmy to continue.

"I got it from Fat Tony Nemo. He bought it at a flea market," Jimmy said.

"You know Nemo?" Levon said.

"He poured the concrete for a couple of my buildings."

"I forgot. He does that when he's not killing people," Levon said.

"Tony was out of the rackets twenty years ago," Jimmy said.

"Is that right, Dave?" Levon said. "This guy who used to break arms and legs with a baseball bat found salvation?"

"I wouldn't know," I replied, regretting the choices I had made to help Clete.

"Could you tell your driver to go a little faster?" Rowena said to Jimmy. "I'm about to faint."

"No Down Under histrionics tonight," Levon said.

"Oh, balls," she said.

"I need to write you a check for this," Levon said to Jimmy.

"Show me the secret to your novels instead."

"Beg your pardon?" Levon said.

"I'm envious. They're marvelous books. Your prose is magical. I want to know how you do it."

Then Rowena said something I didn't expect, considering the undisguised arousal Jimmy obviously caused in her: "We all have our private cubbyholes, love. Don't be fucking with them."

The chauffeur was a peroxided, crew-cut, steroid-pumped weight lifter with a concave-shaped face whose eyes looked like lumps of lead in the rearview mirror. I wanted to get in the front with him.

* * *

CLEMENTINE'S WAS ON Main Street in a building that once was a saloon and pool hall and betting parlor, with wood floors and a stamped tin ceiling and a long bar and cuspidors and a potbelly stove, in a time when saloon owners one night a week covered pool tables with oilcloths and served free robin gumbo. Now it was a fine restaurant, with a large formally attired staff and sometimes a famous movie actor or musician among the guests.

Unfortunately, none of this was of any comfort to me. The atmosphere at our table was poisonous, the tension unbearable, primarily because there was no way to both acknowledge and resolve the problem, which was raw hatred between Jimmy and Levon and, I suspect, a flicker or two of the green-eyed monster in Levon.

"You understood about my writing a check, didn't you?" Levon said.

"If you want," Jimmy said.

"There's no 'if' to it."

Jimmy smiled. "I think I gave him two thousand for it. Why don't you give that amount in my name to a charity?"

"Why don't I just leave it on the table for the waiter?" Levon said.

Rowena was on her third glass of burgundy. "My grandfather was at Gallipoli. A neighbor tried to give him a souvenir bayonet to cut his hundredth birthday cake. Grandfather told him where to park it."

"Lower the volume, Rowena," Levon said.

"Fuck if I will," she replied.

How about that for conversation in a small city on Bayou Teche where decorum is a religion and manners and morality are interchangeable?

The back of my neck was burning, my scalp drawing tighter each time Rowena had something to say. I went to the restroom, located in a separate building by the patio, and washed and dried my face and went back inside. The bar area was crowded, but in the midst of drinkers, I saw Clete Purcel hunched over a po'boy sandwich and a frosted mug of beer.

When I went to places where alcohol was served, I usually avoided sitting at the bar or at tables where people were there to drink rather than eat. Those distinctions might seem foolish to normal people, but the slip that puts a sober alcoholic back on the dirty boogie usually has innocuous origins. You accidentally eat chocolate cake that has whiskey in it; there's brandy in the plum sauce; two miles from shore, the sun blazing on your head, a friend tosses you a cold can of Miller from the ice chest; or worse, you wake at one in morning, your head full of nightmarish images, and rather than deal with your dragons, you put on your beat-up leather jacket and a wilted hat and find an end-of-the-line dive that has no clocks or windows.

But I wanted to be near Clete, the man who'd carried me down a fire escape when I had two bullets in my back, a man who sought excoriation and feared approval, a blue-collar iconoclast who had to look up the word.

"Can you tell me how to get to Sharkey Bonano's Dream Room?" I said. Sharkey's joint on Bourbon used to feature musicians like the Kings of Dixieland and Johnnie Scat Davis and Louis Prima and Sam Butera, and Clete and I had spent many wasted days and nights there.

Clete jumped when I put my hand on his shoulder. "Jesus, Dave, you know I have a coronary when people walk up on me like that? When did you come in?"

"I'm with Jimmy Nightingale and Levon and his wife."

"You're kidding." He strained his neck to see into the dining room. "Oops, I shouldn't have looked."

"What do you mean?"

"That Australian broad gets to me. My big boy just went on red alert."

"Will you stop that?"

"I know an animal when I see one."

"I mean it, Clete." But what was the point? Clete was Clete. "Join us. I feel like I'm in the middle of a blender."

"I can't take Nightingale. I know he's cutting me a deal, but he's still a bum and a fraud."

"But it's fine for me?" I said.

"Stop pretending. Nightingale hates my guts. I don't know what you see in that prick. Anyway, he's doing a favor for you, not me. He wants something from Levon Broussard. So does Tony Nine Ball."

"Where'd you hear this?"

"From Nig Rosewater."

Nig and Wee Willie Bimstine had run New Orleans's oldest bail bond service, until Katrina drowned the city and FEMA transported their clients all over the United States, never to return.

"Tony thinks he's going to be a Hollywood movie producer," Clete said. "He bought this sword to give to Levon Broussard, except Nightingale took it away from him."

"When did Fat Tony start rolling over for anyone?"

"He's got diabetes and emphysema and cancer in his colon and lymph nodes. He carries a bucket in his car to puke in."

The bartender leaned close to Clete. "Would you like another drink, sir?"

Clete lifted his mug, the shell of ice sliding down the sides, the beer almost to the top. "Do I look like I need one? But since you asked, give Dave a diet Doc with cherries and limes in it."

The man on the other side of Clete left the bar, and I took his stool with no plan in mind other than to delay rejoining the group I'd come with. In seconds I felt at home, the television set tuned to a sports channel, stuffed shrimp I hadn't ordered placed on a paper napkin in front of me, someone talking about the New Orleans Saints. Clete ordered a shot and poured it into his mug. I watched the whiskey bounce on the bottom and rise in a brown cloud.

"Why not just put your brain in a jar and give it to a medical school?" I said.

"I did that five years ago. They gave it back."

He chugged half the mug. I bit into a stuffed shrimp and looked over my shoulder at the dining room, then at the icy cloud rising from the beer box, the bartenders uncorking bottles of Liebfraumilch and dark red wine, fitting an orange slice on the rim of a Collins glass, tipping a jigger of Jack into shaved ice and mint leaves, pouring a creamy-pink gin fizz, setting up a round of Hennessy for everyone, provided by the distributor.

"No?" the bartender said, after setting a shot glass in front of me. I cleared my throat to answer.

"Did he ask for one?" Clete said.

"Sorry, my mistake," the bartender said.

"Give us both a diet Doc. I need a bowl of gumbo, too," Clete said.

"You got it," the bartender said.

"Where you from?" Clete asked.

"California."

"You ever hear of the Bobbsey Twins from Homicide?"

"That's a new one on me," the bartender said. He wore a white jacket, his hair slicked back.

"You're looking at them," Clete said. "You're standing in the middle of history."

"Knock it off, Clete," I said.

"He knows I'm kidding," Clete said. "You, what's-your-name, you don't take people like me seriously, do you?"

"My name is Cedric."

"You knew I was kidding, right, Cedric?"

The bartender wiped the bar. "Two diet drinks coming up."

He walked away on the duckboards, wadding up his bar rag, tossing it into a sink. My face felt small and tight; my eardrums were ringing. "Don't do that again, Clete."

"He's foisting drinks on people. I set him straight."

"Did you hear me?"

"Climb down off it, Streak."

"Off what?"

"You know what I'm talking about."

"No, I don't," I said.

"I gave up trying to pork everything in sight. Why? Because I'm old and I make an idiot of myself. It's called recognizing your limitations."

"See you later," I said.

"Come back here."

But I kept walking, letting the noise in the dining room swallow up my conversation with Clete and the temptations that were as abiding in me as sexual desire and, even worse, that had to do with guns and gambling and the rush of stepping through the dimension into a place I never wanted to go again.

Levon and Rowena and Jimmy were sloshed and had stupid smiles on their faces when I got to the table.

"Sorry, something just came up," I said.

"You're leaving?" Levon said.

"We'll do it another time," I said. "Thanks for inviting me."

"You got your nose bent out of shape?" Rowena said. "Just throw the food to the hogs?"

"*Chacun à son goût,*" I said.

Then I walked out of the dining room and past the revelers at the bar, including Clete, and out the door and into the night. The street was empty, the great looming structure called the Shadows illuminated by floodlights in the yard, a tribute to all the suffering passed down to us by the antebellum era. *What a joke,* I thought.

But my cynicism gave me no release from the fire and the insatiable need burning inside me.

Chapter
5

CLETE CALLED ME at the office in the morning. "I'm sorry about last night," he said.

"Forget it. I had my head on sideways," I said.

"You didn't go home and get wasted, did you?"

"Worry about yourself," I said.

"I'll see you for lunch."

"I've got too much desk work."

"I'll come by tonight. It's about that prick."

"Which prick?"

"That prick Nightingale, who else? I've got to pick up a bail skip in Jennings. I'll see you about nine."

At five-fifteen P.M., I threw my tackle box and rod and reel into the back of my truck, hooked up my boat and trailer, and drove to the Henderson levee, outside Breaux Bridge. Henderson Swamp is part of the vast network of bayous and bays and rivers that constitute the Atchafalaya Basin, the flooded woods a golden green at sunset and so swollen with silence that you wonder if this piece of primordial creation was saved by a divine hand to remind us of what the earth was like when our ancestors grew feet and crawled out of the sea.

The cypress trees were in early leaf, as delicate as green lace, ruffling in the breeze, the water high and black and undisturbed, chained with lily pads, the bream and goggle-eye perch rolling under the pads like pillows of air floating to the surface.

I cut my outboard and let my boat glide silently into a cove lit by a molten red sun, then flipped my plug in an arching loop just beyond a clutch of flooded willows. The western sky was streaked with clouds as pink as flamingo wings. In the distance I heard the Southern Pacific blowing down the line.

But if I had come here for solace, my journey was in vain. The loss of my wife, my inability to accept the suddenness of the accident, the words of a paramedic telling me she was gone and they had done everything they could, his mouth moving like that of someone in a film with no sound track, I carried all these things wherever I went, my blood and mind fouled, the ground shifting, the realization at sunrise that her death was not a dream and she was gone forever, unfairly taken, her dignity and courage and spiritual resolve extinguished by a fool rounding a curve in a pickup truck, the accelerator mashed to the floor.

These thoughts robbed the light from my eyes, the birdsong from the trees, the sound of children playing in a park. Instead of the glory of the sunset, I saw beer cans and Styrofoam cups undulating in the shallows, a rubber tire submerged among the willows, a blanket of debris caught in the cattails, as viscous as dried paint skimmed off the top of a paint bucket.

I retrieved my lure and started the engine and drove back to the levee, the bow scraping on the concrete ramp like fingernails on a blackboard. I stopped into a bait shop and ate a sandwich on the gallery and watched the last of the sun slip beyond the trees. Several men were drinking beer at a spool table next to me. I believed I knew one of them, but I couldn't say for sure. They invited me to join them. I could not get my mind off Molly, her warmth and steadfastness as a companion, her ability to deal with the sorrow and suffering of the world and not be undone by it.

"Everything cool, buddy?" a man said.

"Sure. I look like my gyroscope is busted?" I replied.

"Have a brew."

"I have to be on my way."

"I should, too," he said. "My old lady is going to throw my supper in the backyard. Is yours like that?"

THE SUN WAS only an ember when I drove down the levee. A few minutes later, I was on the two-lane highway outside Breaux Bridge, the sky dark with rainclouds, when a pickup truck got on the back of my trailer and the driver clicked on his high beams, flooding the inside of my truck with light. I tried to see the driver's face in the rearview mirror, but his headlights were blinding. I touched my brake pedal to no avail. I had broken the clamp-on emergency flasher I'd carried in my truck only two days earlier. There were ditches on either side of the road and no shoulder where I could pull off. My eyes were watering from the glare in the mirror.

Like anyone who has been harassed on the road by a tailgater, I felt my anger begin to rise, slowly at first, then build into an emotional straitjacket, and I began to have thoughts I did not associate with who I was. I pressed the brake again, this time hard. But he didn't back off. His headlights were so close they were beneath the level of my trailer. I accelerated. He dropped back a few feet in the mirror, and I saw a pipe bumper welded on the front of his vehicle. Then he came at me again. As I neared the convenience store at the intersection, he roared through the blinking red light and shot me the finger.

The truck was pale blue, one side gnarled with dents, one taillight broken. I saw the driver for only seconds. His hair was black, his face unshaved; he looked like thousands of Cajun men.

I drove home, my wrists throbbing. Clete was sitting on the steps, tossing acorns at nothing, a fedora slanted on his brow.

I PULLED MY TRAILER around his Caddy and parked it on the grass. The leaves crackled under my feet as I crossed the yard. He sniffed.

"You have a cold?" I asked.

"I smell beer."

"I was sitting next to some guys at a bait shop."

His eyes searched my face. I looked away, down the street. The streetlamps were on, rain dripping from the oaks. The sidewalk was arched in the places where the oak roots had broken through the concrete. The only sound was the whir of automobile tires on the street.

"I told Nightingale to stick his deal," Clete said.

"You're not going to work it out with him?"

"You don't work out things with a guy like Nightingale. You park one in his ear."

"When did you get this bright idea?"

"Last night. I couldn't sleep. I felt dirty all over."

"What are you going to do, Clete?"

"Nig and Wee Willie will front me a hundred thousand."

"At what interest rate?"

"I didn't ask."

"How much do you owe?"

"Altogether, with loans all over the city and back interest and my maxed-out credit cards and the vigorish and principle with the shylocks, close to two hundred and fifty thou."

"How'd you do this, Clete?"

"Why don't you try to make me feel bad?"

I sat down next to him. "I'll get a loan on the house."

"Not for me, you won't."

"I'll do it whether you like it or not."

He shook his head, his hands between his knees. "What can they do?"

"You know what they can do."

"I'll go out smoking."

"Why did you change your mind about Nightingale's offer?"

"This skip I had to pick up in Jennings is a pimp and meth dealer. His name is Kevin Penny. Ever hear of him?"

"No."

"This is the third time I've had to go after him. I almost capped him once. In custody. His little boy told the welfare worker what

Penny did to him. I knew what he was going to do to his kid when he made the street." He stopped and tapped his fists up and down on his thighs.

"What is it?" I said.

"I'm not being honest. Earlier, Penny told me about what a sleaze Nightingale was. You think Nightingale is a gentleman or something, but I know better. Nonetheless, I was going to take the deal with him. I didn't want to lose my place in the Quarter. Whatever principles I have, I was willing to sell them out."

"So what did this guy Penny tell you?"

"He delivered coke to Nightingale's house. And a girl or two."

"Every one of these guys has a story like that. They've sold dope to George W. Bush or set up trysts for John Kennedy. Don't buy into this crap, Clete."

"Penny says he's deposited money in a bank account of a company owned by Nightingale. He was even taught how to structure it. To make the deposits in amounts of less than ten thousand so the bank doesn't report it to the IRS."

"I don't buy it."

"Those eight women who were killed," Clete said. "They haunt me."

He wasn't alone. I had worked with a task force on some of those homicides in Jeff Davis Parish. Eight young women, all of them poor, all of them involved with drugs and prostitution, were found with their throats cut, or so badly decomposed in a swamp that the cause of death couldn't be determined. At the same time, there was a series of kidnappings and murders in East and West Baton Rouge parishes. Those victims were also dumped in wetlands areas. We thought we had the killers. In fact, Clete and I helped take them off the board.

We were wrong. The murders in Jeff Davis Parish came out of a culture that many Americans would not be able to understand, an aggregate of corrupt cops, ignorance, greed, misogyny, cruelty, sexual degradation, drug addiction, and ultimately, collective indifference toward the fate of people who have neither power nor voice. I'm talking about a new social class, one that is not racially defined. They come out of the womb addicted to crack and booze, have only a semblance of a family, drift from town to town selling themselves or dealing dope or stealing to buy it. The irony is they're not criminals, not in the traditional sense. They're pitiful, sad, and vulnerable, gathered up in bus stations like grunion at high tide.

"Have you eaten?" I said.

"My stomach's not right," Clete said.

"Come inside."

"Dave?"

"Yeah?"

"Are you back on the sauce?"

"I have some potato salad and cold chicken inside."

"Damn it, damn it, damn it," he said.

I walked ahead of him into the kitchen and clicked on the light. I thought I saw a raccoon on the window ledge, staring through the screen. When I looked outside, the yard was empty and windswept, tormented by shadows.

EARLY THE NEXT morning I got a call I didn't expect.

"Is that you, Robicheaux?"

"Who's calling?" I said.

"How many people got pustules in their throat and sound like a rusty sewer pipe?"

"Tony?"

"Tell the maid to give you a blow job."

"How did you get this number?"

"It cost me a dollar ninety-five on the Internet. I think I got fucked. Speaking of which, you put a posthole digger up my ass."

"In what way?"

"Jimmy Nightingale said he was gonna get that Civil War sword appraised. Now he tells me he gave it to Levon Broussard, but he'll give me ten thousand reimbursement. I told him to change his ten grand into nickels and shove them up his nose. Why'd you do this to me?"

"Do what?"

"Introduce Nightingale to this writer."

"What do you care?" I said.

"I'm on third base. I want to produce one of the guy's books. I'm talking about cable. That's where they're making real art and not this computerized stuff."

I couldn't believe I was having a conversation about art with a man who had chopped up an enemy, freeze-dried the parts, and hung them from a wood-bladed ceiling fan in a family grocery on Magazine.

"I don't know anything about that, Tony. I went to dinner with Jimmy and the Broussards. I also left the dinner."

"I treated you decent. You stabbed me in the back."

"Fire your psychiatrist. He's not helping you."

"I should have known better," he said.

"About what?"

"You're a juicer, the kind that don't ever get cured. You got no honor."

"I'm going to hang up now. Don't call here again."

"Like I want to," he replied.

I WALKED TO WORK. It had rained during the night, and the sky had cleared and the sun had come up bright and hot, and the lawns of the antebellum and Victorian homes along East Main were sprinkled with the pink and red petals of the azalea bushes that bloomed all over Louisiana in the early spring. I passed the grotto and the statue of Jesus' mother next to the library, and walked down the long oak-shaded drive to the huge brick building on the bayou where I made my livelihood. I poured a cup of coffee and went to Helen Soileau's office. The door was open. I tapped on the jamb just the same.

"What's shaking, bwana?" she said from behind her desk.

"Can I close the door?"

She nodded, her face somber, as it always was in enclosed or personal situations. I pulled up a chair. She waited for me to speak.

"Did you ever hear anything about Jimmy Nightingale having ties to dope or prostitution? Around Jeff Davis Parish in particular?"

"No. In fact, that sounds ridiculous."

"I feel the same way."

"Where'd you hear this?"

"Clete got it from a pimp named Kevin Penny."

"Great source."

"That's what I said."

"Then why are you asking me?"

"It bothered me. I just introduced Jimmy to Levon Broussard and his wife."

She picked up her ballpoint and flipped it into the air and let it bounce on her ink blotter. "Why do you get mixed up with these people, Dave?"

"What kind of question is that?"

"I'll answer it for you. Both you and Clete hate the rich but pretend you don't."

"Next time I try to come in your office, don't let me in."

"Okay, maybe that's unfair. But maybe your deeper motivation is even worse."

I got up to go.

"You want to believe people are better than they are," she said.

"Send me a bill for that, will you?"

"Bwana go now. Bwana also shut mouth."

Nobody put the slide or the glide on Helen Soileau.

I'D LIKE TO be humble and say Helen read both Clete and me correctly. To a degree, I guess she did. But there was a larger issue at work. You cannot watch the exhumation of a murdered woman from a bog and ever be quite the same. The degradation by the elements of an unpreserved human body is not a kind one. The earth, the primeval soup, if you will, is tenacious; it clings to the skin, peels it from the arms and face, the hair from the scalp. The eyes remain sunken, sometimes looking at you oddly, like chipped marbles pushed into dough by an insensitive thumb.

The eight women who were killed had no advocate. The cops assigned to the case early on were pitiful if not complicit. Any cop who is honest will tell you there are police officers in our midst who never should have been given power over others. Misogamy is a big part of their makeup. Sexual perversity as well. I've known both male and female vice cops who have the psychological makeup of degenerates and closet sadists. I've also known gunbulls who would have had no problem working in Dachau. That we protect them is beyond my comprehension. The hundreds of cops and firemen who went into the Towers on 9/11 knew they probably would not come out. What are the limits of human courage? The cops and firemen who walked into stairwells that were not stairwells but chimneys filled with flame and smoke, proved that the human spirit is unconquerable, and it is these men and women who define what is best in us.

The eight women who were murdered and dumped like bags of trash in a swamp probably never would find justice. The thought that Jimmy Nightingale was involved in the subculture responsible for their deaths gave me no rest. Plus, I had introduced him in good faith to Levon and Rowena Broussard.

I called him at his home. The same curt secretary answered.

"This is Detective Robicheaux," I said. "Is Mr. Nightingale there?"

"No, he isn't."

"Can you tell me where he is?"

"No."

"Excuse me?"

"He's flying right now."

"Flying where?'"

"I wouldn't know. He's flying his plane. Can I assist you with something?"

"I wanted to ask him about charm schools. Do you have contact with any?"

"I'll certainly pass on the information."

"I didn't get your name."

"Emmeline Nightingale. I'm his cousin."

"It's nice to meet you, if only over the phone."

"Thank you. Good-bye."

Franklin was a short drive down the bayou. I checked out a cruiser, turned on the flasher, and headed down Old Spanish Trail into the past, into the fury and mire of bloodline complexities our ancestors tried to wall up with brick and plaster and mortar, hoping the earth would subsume and cover forever the sins they could not.

JIMMY'S FATHER HAD been known as a hunter of big game in Africa, an archaeologist and mining engineer, a linguist, and a world-traveling swordsman who may have been killed by a British parliamentarian he cuckolded. The mother came from the North and was disdainful and private and, in all probability, very unhappy and consequently very angry. She broke her neck in a steeplechase when Jimmy was fifteen.

I followed Jimmy's driveway through a tunnel of oaks and parked in front of the columned porch on the house. I stepped out on the gravel and looked at the enormity of the house, the immaculate creamy quality of the paint, the wraparound second-story veranda that Southern belles had probably stood on in their finery and watched the boys in tattered butternut march down a long dusty road to defeat and privation or a Yankee prison. I heard the sound of a single-engine plane that had started to sputter, as though out of gas. The plane, one with pontoons, was a dull red and drifted like a leaf out of a deep blue cloudless sky. It touched down on the bayou's surface at the same moment the propeller locked in a stationary position. Jimmy opened the cabin door and threw a small anchor attached to a rope over his dock, pulled the rope until it snugged tight, then brought the plane hand over hand into the shallows. He stepped up onto the dock as though alighting from a pleasure boat.

I walked down the slope, the wind cool, wimpling the water. His egg-shaped face was ruddy, his eyes bright, every hair on his head perfectly in place. "Has a crime wave hit Franklin?" he said.

"You tell me."

"Why you'd leave my table at Clementine's?

"I didn't like the way things were going."

"You mean Rowena's wandering eye?"

"You said it, I didn't."

"She's a young woman. What's the harm?"

"Her husband might have an opinion."

"Dave, you're a Puritan, and you know it. Come inside."

"Do you know a lowlife by the name of Kevin Penny?"

"A lowlife? Let me see. Nope. Who is he?"

"A pimp and a meth dealer. He says he's delivered dope and women to your house."

"Grand. Anything else?"

"He says he makes deposits in a bank account used by your company. He operates around the Jennings area."

"Let's go inside. I have some aspirin in the kitchen. How about a cold washcloth on the forehead?"

"None of this is true?"

He walked ahead of me, looking over his shoulder. "It's good I like you."

"I don't think you get it, Jimmy. This isn't a courtesy call."

"No, it isn't. It's a visitation by a lunatic."

I caught up with him and slipped my hand under his arm. I turned him around. He seemed surprised.

"Lose the attitude, Jimmy," I said.

He looked down at my hand. "All right, I will. My attitude is one of kindness to you. I respect your service to the country and your service to the community. You've been through perfect misery in the last two years. That isn't lost on me or others. Learn who your bloody friends are, Dave."

"Been hanging with the Aussies?"

"That's a cheap shot."

"Tony Nemo says you shafted him."

"Tony has a fried egg for a brain."

"I think Levon Broussard is a decent and honorable man," I said. "I also think he's naive. Nobody is going to use me to hurt him."

Jimmy put his hands on his hips and looked at the bayou, his face cool and handsome and at peace. "I don't know what to say. Come have a cold drink with me. Please."

"This guy Penny is lying?"

"Regarding me, he is. I never heard of the guy."

I looked him in the face.

"As God is my witness," he added.

"Okay."

"Okay, what?"

"I accept your word."

"There you go," he said, and hit me on the back.

We walked up the slope into his backyard, past a gazebo and camellia bushes in full bloom and trellises dripping with roses and wisteria, the St. Augustine grass so thick and dark green and cold and stiff in the shade that it looked and felt like artificial turf.

A woman opened the back door. She wore a black suit and hose; her hair was black, too, pulled straight back, her skin the color of paste, her eyes dark and luminous, as though she had a fever. "I'm Emmeline."

"How do you do, Miss Emmeline? I'm Dave Robicheaux."

"Did you have engine trouble again?" she said to Jimmy.

"Wasn't watching the fuel gauge, I'm afraid. Nothing to be worried about. With pontoons, you can land almost anywhere in Louisiana. What did our local congressman say? 'Half the state is underwater, the other half under indictment.'"

"Would you like a highball or a glass of wine, Detective Robicheaux?"

"No, thank you."

"On the clock, are you?"

"Yes, I must be going. It's nice meeting you in person."

She didn't reply, as though I hadn't spoken. The wind picked up, sprinkling leaves that were as hard as the shells of crustaceans on the grass. It was cold in the shade, the light on the four-o'clocks and caladiums harsh and brittle. We were in the midst of spring, yet I felt a sense of mortality I couldn't explain.

Her face was impossible to read. She was one of those women who seemed to choose solitude and plainness over beauty, and anger over happiness.

"You ever meet a guy named Kevin Penny?" I said.

"Our convict gardener?" she replied. "I fired him."

I looked at Jimmy. He shrugged and turned up his palms. "I don't know the name of every guy who cuts the grass, Dave."

"What is this about?" Emmeline said.

"Veracity," I said.

"I don't care for your tone," she said.

"I don't blame you. It bothers me, too." I pointed my finger at Jimmy Nightingale. "I think you're slick."

"I'm dishonest?"

"Take it any way you want."

"You've got some damn nerve," he said.

"Tell it to the eight murdered women in Jeff Davis Parish," I replied.

"What do they have to do with me?"

"I heard you hung around Bobby Earl because you wanted his mailing list. I never believed that," I said.

"It's politics. This is Louisiana."

"I remember many situations when I said it was just Vietnam."

Jimmy pulled the cork from a green half-empty bottle of wine. "Here's to neocolonialism everywhere."

I wasn't up to his cynicism. I looked at the oaks, the moss lifting in the wind, purple dust rising from a cane field, Bayou Teche glinting in the sun like a Byzantine shield. La Louisiane, the love of my life, the home of Jolie Blon and Evangeline and the Great Whore of Babylon, the place for which I would die, the place for which there was no answer or cure.

I said nothing more and walked to my vehicle, rude or not.

Chapter
6

RECOVERING ALCOHOLICS HAVE ways of setting themselves up. Some get the toxins out of their system and stop attending meetings. Maybe they hang with the old crowd. They drop by a saloon to watch a football game on a Saturday afternoon. They convince themselves their problems had to do with excess rather than compulsion and metabolic addiction and a deep-seated neurosis armor-plated in the unconscious. Or they nurse resentment and fuel their anger on a daily basis, like a primitive fur-clad creature methodically dropping sticks into a fire.

Or maybe they want to cancel their whole ticket but are afraid to lose their soul. If they're in this category, they'll commit suicide in an incremental fashion, one glass or bottle at a time. And if the process isn't fast enough, they will put themselves in dangerous situations involving guns and knives and people who belong in steel cages.

I went to a meeting at the Episcopalian cottage on Center Street, across from old New Iberia High. When the moderator asked if anyone was attending A.A. for the first time, or if anyone was returning from a slip and wanted a twenty-four-hour sobriety chip, I let my face go empty and stared at the floor in the semidarkness. At the end of the meeting, I said little or nothing to friends with whom I had been in the program for years, and drove to my house in a heavy white fog that had moved in from the Gulf, and parked my truck in the porte cochere and went inside and sat in the living room in the dark, the television off, the silence as loud as a scream.

The operative acronym for every A.A. member is HALT, which means don't get hungry, angry, lonely, or tired. I was all of those. I called Clete's cell phone, which went immediately to voicemail. I didn't want the food in my icebox. I woke lifeless and exhausted with every sunrise. My hands opened and closed at my sides for no reason. I deliberately revisited memories of a human face dissolving in a bloody mist when I squeezed off round after round from my army-issue 1911-model .45.

I'm not proud of any of these things. I hated them then; I hate them now. But they live in me like a snake that slowly swallows its prey, compressing it into a canister of despair and pain.

I went into the kitchen and filled a large glass with tap water and drank it to the bottom. In the darkness I heard the claws of an animal scratching at the screen. I set the glass quietly in the sink and went through the mudroom and opened the screen door. A raccoon that must have weighted twenty-five pounds jumped from the windowsill and thumped on the ground, then scampered through the leaves past Tripod's old hutch and disappeared inside the fog.

I walked down the slope, looking for him. The air was cold, the fog hanging in huge clouds on the bayou and in the trees. I heard a splash, like a gator slapping its tail. I took a penlight from my pocket and shone it on the ground. The tracks of a raccoon and probably a possum or an armadillo were stenciled along the mudflat. The tracks disappeared into the cattails. Farther down, inside clouds of fog that rose four feet above the water, I heard a soft knocking sound, like a friend at the door in the early hours. I shined the light ahead of me. The tide was coming in, and an unmoored pirogue had floated up the bayou and lodged against a decayed and collapsed dock at the foot of my property.

I picked up a fallen tree branch and hooked it on the pirogue's bow and scraped it onto the bank. There was a paddle inside, an empty rucksack, a minnow bucket, a newspaper that was two weeks old, and a fish stringer. My earliest memories of my father were fishing with him in a pirogue. There is no more emblematic symbol of life on Bayou Teche than the humble pirogue.

I stepped into the pirogue and steadied my weight, then eased down on the wood seat. The fog was so thick that the lights in the houses along the bayou, even the floodlamps in the backyard of the Shadows and the warning lights on the drawbridge at Burke Street, were hardly more than smudges. I shone the penlight on the rucksack again. A pint bottle of brandy lay in a half inch of rainwater. I touched it with the penlight beam and watched its color flare on my hand and wrist. I pushed with the paddle until the pirogue swung into the current and began to drift toward the bridge and one of the places that had been waiting for me since I was a child, when, in my innocence, I believed the paradisiacal world into which I had been born would always be there for me.

THIS PARTICULAR BAR-AND-GRILL was located on the water, but because of the fog and the intermittent rain, the chairs and tables on the deck had been stacked, and all the patrons had gone inside and crowded into the bar. The windows were lighted, the glass beaded, the patrons happy and warm, safe from the elements. The only problem I had with this place upstream from the drawbridge was that almost everyone there knew me and my history.

When I opened the door, the bartender looked at me without speaking. I pointed at the men's room. He smiled. "Yeah, go ahead, Dave," he said.

I went into the cubicle inside the restroom and shut the door. I waited until I was sure the room was empty, then exited the cubicle and clicked off the light to lessen my visibility and opened the restroom door and went to the end of the bar in the shadows. A young barmaid I didn't recognize was filling the beer box.

"One of those and two shots of Jack on shaved ice," I said. "In fact, make that two doubles. I got a friend coming."

She was pretty and young and had a small red mouth and the amber-colored hair characteristic of many Cajun women. "Aren't you . . ."

"Aren't I who?"

"You know, a policeman. You work in the big building on the bayou. I seen you when I paid a traffic ticket there."

"Yeah, that was probably me. I'm kind of in a hurry."

"Don't set your pants on fire, no."

I stood by the stool. I looked at my hands. I looked down at the bar rail. I could feel a hundred eyes burrowing into my back or the side of my face. When I looked up, no one was paying me any attention. "Miss, I'd really appreciate it if you'd hurry."

"Yes, suh, coming up," she said.

After I finished both glasses of whiskey, chasing each with Heineken, I thought my knees would fold.

"You gonna be all right?" the barmaid said.

"As right as rain."

"You don't look it, no."

"You're an honest lady."

"No, I ain't. I just don't want to have to clean up the flo'."

"See, that's honesty."

She leaned in. "You ain't driving, you?"

"What's your name?"

"Babette Latiolais."

"I wish there were a million like you, Miss Babette. Give me a Heineken for the road."

I pushed a twenty to her with the heel of my hand and left the change on the bar, then went outside into the fog and rain and started walking home. The drawbridge at Burke Street was in the air, a tugboat working its way up the bayou, its running lights on. I waved at the man in the pilothouse. I saw him draw in on his pipe and wave back. I wanted to have a drink with him. I wanted to be on his boat and sail back into time and find a place where there were no clocks or calendars. I wanted to find the vortex that some say is the birth canal and others say is the conduit to eternity. I wanted to find the cowled figure that awaits us all and wrap myself in his cloak.

I remember reaching my front yard and starting my truck with the intention of driving to St. Martinville, the village where the ghost of

Evangeline supposedly waited for her lover, Gabriel, under a spreading oak on the banks of Bayou Teche. My next memory is of headlights in my mirror and the grinding sounds of a vehicle on my bumper.

I WOKE IN MY skivvies, on top of the sheets, the sun in my eyes. When I sat up, a wave of nausea drained through my body. My elbows hurt and my knuckles were scraped, and one fingernail was broken all the way to the cuticle. My clothes were on the floor. The sleeves of my windbreaker looked like they had been raked by barbed wire. I threw up in the bathroom, the backs of my legs shaking.

I got into the shower and turned on the water as hot as I could stand it, filling the room with steam, boiling the grease out of my pores, as though trying to scour an obscene presence from my skin. I touched a painful bump under the white patch in my hair and another bump on the back of my head. I shaved and brushed my teeth and gargled with antiseptic and tried to remember where I had gone and what I had done the previous night. My memory would go no deeper than the blinding glare in the rearview mirror, the smash of a bumper against the rear of my truck, and my head snapping back.

No, I remembered something else. A man's face. His teeth were wide-set, his throat and cheeks patinaed with whiskers that were as stiff as emery-wheel filings.

I looked into the bathroom mirror. My face was bloodless and gaunt and dissolute, my eyes swollen, my hair a tangle of snakes. I scrubbed my face with cold water and looked again and saw an image that could be compared only with the severed head of a Mongol warrior.

I dressed in a long-sleeve red silk shirt and gray tie and gray slacks and oxblood loafers and got to the department at five to eight. I had never felt so sick. I filled a Styrofoam cup with coffee and burned my mouth on the first sip. Helen stopped me in the hallway before I could make it to my office, where I hoped to recover in solitude from my hangover. "Drink up, Pops. We've got a homicide."

"Where?" I said.

"Just this side of the St. Martin line."

"A shooting?"

"Mixed reports. The coroner is on his way. Dump the coffee."

"I've got to use the men's room."

"You don't have one at home?"

"I got a bug."

Her eyes wandered over my face. "I'll bring a cruiser around. Get your shit together."

"Pardon?"

"You haven't been fooling anyone."

She walked away, her back stiff with anger.

HELEN DROVE UP the two-lane toward St. Martinville without speaking, the flasher rippling. I looked out the window at the cane fields flying by, the sun spangling through the canopy of oaks that arched over the highway. "Who's at the scene?" I asked.

"Spade Labiche."

"What's he doing out here?"

"He was investigating a domestic battery charge. He got patched in." She waited for me to reply. "*What?*"

"Nothing."

"You don't like him?"

"I don't have an opinion."

"Dave, what *is* wrong with you? Why not put one in your mouth and be done with it?"

"I'm going to hit a noon meeting."

"What you're going to do is your goddamn job."

"Whatever you say."

"I'll stop the cruiser and stomp the shit out of you."

"I believe you. I'm sorry."

"I don't have words for how I feel. You break my heart."

I knew I would hear that last one in my sleep.

We turned onto a road that made a wide bend through sugarcane fields and cattle pasture, and passed clumps of pecan and oak trees and boxlike farmhouses and trailers and a convenience store that sold live bait. Just past the convenience store, a pale blue pickup truck was parked in knee-high weeds thirty feet beyond a broken wire fence. Both doors were shut. Crime scene tape had been strung from the fence posts to a solitary oak beyond the truck. The tape was bouncing in the wind.

Spade Labiche came from a big family in New Orleans that made a living out of law enforcement and jails. They were either cops, chasers in the Marine Corps, hacks in Angola or Huntsville or Parchman, or bail bondsmen. Without criminals, they would not have had a livelihood. Spade Labiche had worked vice at Miami-Dade and claimed he had resigned because he was homesick for Louisiana.

He had started off in uniform with our department and only recently made plainclothes. Twice, women of color had filed sexual complaints against him, but the complaints were dropped without explanation. Labiche was standing just outside the tape, wearing an ink-blue tie sprayed with tiny white stars and a suit that was as bright as tin. A pair of latex gloves hung out of his side pocket. He lit a cigarette with a match, cupping the flame in the wind; normally, he carried a gold lighter, because there was little he did that wasn't ostentatious. He was blond and trim and worked out every night at Baron's Health Club; his eyes were almost colorless, like glass with a tinge of blue.

"The body is on the other side," he said. "You might check the window on the driver's side first."

"Where's the coroner?" Helen said.

"Taking a whiz in the convenience store," he said.

"Did he examine the body?"

"Yeah," Labiche said.

"What did he say?" Helen asked.

"Nothing. He went blank on me. The way guys like that do."

"Which kind of guys?" I asked.

He fixed his gaze on my face, a curl at the edge of his mouth. "Unusual ones."

Helen and I put on latex gloves. I kept my hands down, out of sight, and tried not to flinch when I pulled the latex over my knuckles. The glass had been knocked out of the window. There was a ragged line of shards sticking out of the jamb, like shark's teeth.

"There's glass all over the dashboard and seat and on the weeds," Labiche said. "There's some pieces in the vic's hair, too."

"Did you run the tag?" Helen said.

"The truck is registered to T. J. Dartez," he said.

I kept my face empty, my arms folded on my chest. The front bumper was made from welded pipes. One taillight was broken. "Where are the paramedics?" I said.

"Fuck if I know."

"How about it on the language?" I said.

I squatted down by the body. Dartez lay on his back, his shirtfront cut and bloodied perpendicularly. His teeth were knocked out; one eye had eight-balled. My head was spinning as though I were in free fall.

Labiche had thrown his cigarette onto the road and stepped over the tape and was standing behind me. The weeds around the body were stippled with blood. The ground smelled sour from either night damp or the blood that had seeped into the soil. The sun was hot on my neck.

"He's the guy who was in the accident with your wife?" Labiche said.

"That's him."

"Tough break."

"What's that mean?"

"It means I think the accident report sucked."

I stood up, my knees hurting. "I didn't hear you say anything about it at the time."

"I'm still a new guy. I don't express every opinion I might have." He turned his head toward the convenience store. "Here comes queer-bait and the paramedics."

"What did you call him?"

"Nothing. It was a joke."

The coroner's name was Cormac Watts. He was a crew-cut likable young guy from Virginia who wore seersucker pants high on his hips, long-sleeve white shirts, and a bow tie without a coat. He looked put together from sticks, with snowshoes for feet. Clete said Cormac made him think of a well-dressed scarecrow stepping over the rows in a tobacco field.

Helen had been on her cell phone. She folded it and stuck it into her pocket. Her breasts swelled against her shirt when she took a breath. "That was admissions at Iberia General. Dartez's wife had to be sedated. The kids are with a social worker."

"Who told her?" I asked.

"Who knows? Maybe we have a witness. Get on it, will you, Spade?"

"You want me to go to Iberia General?"

"No, go to the convenience store first. See if there are any witnesses. Then go to Iberia General."

"I'm assigned the case, though?"

"That's not what's on my mind at the moment."

"Yes, ma'am. Look, I know y'all were a team. I'm not trying to bust up anything."

Helen's fists were propped on her hips, her face pointed at the ground. "You did a good job. Call me from the hospital." She waited until Labiche was out of earshot. "I don't know if I want you on this one."

"You don't think I can be objective?"

She looked toward the convenience store and at Labiche walking to his car; she chewed her lip. "Did you do your drinking at home last night or in a bar? Please tell me a bar."

"I didn't say I was drinking."

"Get cute with me and I'll have you on the desk. Get cute with me twice and I'll have you on suspension."

"I don't know where I went last night. Or what I did."

"Show me your hands."

"They're scraped."

Her lips were crimped, her chest rising and falling.

"I've beaten them against brick walls when I was drunk," I said. "It doesn't matter what the issue is. I always hurt myself."

"And a few others. Shit!"

Cormac Watts walked toward us, the ambulance following him, the weeds whispering under the bumper. Helen turned her back to me. "What do you have, my favorite pathologist?" she said to him.

"The door was locked," Cormac said. "Somebody dragged him through the broken window, then went to work on him. I'd say he died of a broken neck and respiratory failure or maybe massive cranial damage. I don't see any marks characteristic of a weapon, such as a hammer or tire iron."

"You didn't bother to share that with Labiche?"

"I thought I'd save it for y'all."

"How long has the victim been dead?" she asked.

"Nine or ten hours." He paused and exhaled loudly.

"*What?*" she said.

"The guy who did this must have been on meth. My guess is he did it with his bare hands. This is somebody who could eat his own pain while he flat tore somebody else apart. Know anybody like that around here?"

Chapter
7

I DIDN'T GO TO a noon meeting. I went to the bank and applied for a loan against my house. My house was a humble one, built of cypress in the late nineteenth century, but the one-acre lot was located on one of the most scenic streets in the American South. I suspected the total value was around six hundred thousand dollars.

"How much you need, Dave?" the banker asked.

"Around a quarter of a million."

"It shouldn't be a problem. I'll send the appraiser out. You're not headed to Vegas, are you?"

"In a roundabout way."

He looked a bit quizzical, then said, "Have a good one."

I ate a ham-and-onion sandwich at home and brushed my teeth, then headed back to my office, not looking forward to the rest of the day. Helen followed me inside. "You're off the case."

"What?" I said.

"I'm giving the investigation to Labiche."

I sat down behind my desk. "What's going on?"

"Labiche interviewed Ms. Dartez. She says you called her husband last night and arranged to meet him at the convenience store and bait shop by Bayou Benoit."

I stared at her, my scalp shrinking, a pain like a sliver of glass sliding through my bowels.

"You don't remember?" she said.

"No."

"Give me your cell phone."

I handed it to her. She opened it and began clicking through my calls with her thumb. She stared into my face and folded the phone. My heart was in my throat.

"It's clean," she said.

I swallowed.

"You could have deleted the call," she said.

"I didn't."

"How can you say what you did? Did you call the Dartez house on your landline?"

"I don't remember doing that. I remember I was going to St. Martinville to sit on the bench under the Evangeline Oak."

"Do you know how silly that sounds?"

"It's the way I felt at the time."

She picked up my right hand and looked at my knuckles. I pulled my hand away.

"I'm on your side," she said. "Even if you killed that man, I'm on your side. But don't lie to me."

"I don't know what I did, Helen. That's the truth. Does Ms. Dartez have a cell phone or a landline?"

"A cell."

"Did Labiche check it?"

She looked away from me. "Not yet."

"Don't leave him on the case."

"Maybe he's a little hinky, but he came to us with a clean jacket."

"Two black women filed complaints against him."

"The same women have filed complaints against bill collectors and their estranged husbands."

"They're probably telling the truth."

"Get used to seeing him around."

"Thanks for the hand up," I said.

"Piss off, Dave."

She closed the door quietly behind her, sealing me in an airless vacuum, my sweat cold inside my shirt.

CORMAC WATTS CALLED three hours later. "Hi, Dave. I wanted to update you on the Dartez homicide."

"Spade Labiche is handling that."

"Oh."

"What have you got?"

"Cause of death, blunt force trauma. Maybe he was stomped and kicked by someone wearing steel-toes. There was a filter-tip cigar stub lodged in his throat, plus a couple of teeth."

"That's it?"

"He went out hard. What else is there to say?"

IN A.A., WE respectfully refer to normal human beings as flatlanders or earth people. Drunks are space aliens and glow in the dark with phobias and hallucinations and paranoia, at least while they're on the grog. We also believe that blackouts are a violent neurological reaction to a chemical that an alcoholic's constitution cannot process, a bit like a firecracker exploding in the brain. As a rule, a person in a blackout has no more governance over himself than a car crashing through the rail on top of a ten-story parking garage.

After work, I went to Clete's cottage at the Teche Motel and told him everything. He listened quietly, his big hands cupped on his knees. Through the window, I could see chickens pecking in the yard, a family cooking a pork roast on a spit among the oaks on the bayou, ducks wimpling the water. I felt as though I'd been trapped behind a wall of Plexiglas while the rest of the world went about its business.

"You think you did it?" he said.

"Maybe."

"Did you fantasize about doing it when you weren't drinking?"

"No."

"When's the last time you ripped up somebody while you were drunk?"

"Never."

"That's my point. I don't buy this. Who's the last person you talked to before you blacked out?"

"A barmaid."

"At the joint on the bayou?"

"Her name was Babette."

"You walked home? You didn't drive?"

"Right."

"Then you decided to go to St. Martinville?"

"I was thinking about the way things used to be. I was thinking about my mother and father and fishing in a pirogue. It's just the foolish way I get sometimes."

"Listen, big mon. I know your thoughts before you have them. Look at what you just told me. You were thinking about the best times in your life. You weren't thinking about killing a guy. You're not a killer, Dave. Neither of us is. We never dusted anybody who didn't deal the hand. You got that? I don't want to hear any Dr. Freud dog shit."

"Freud was a genius," I said.

"That's why he stuck all that coke up his nose."

"I applied for a loan on the house."

"You did *what*?"

"The banker said it wouldn't be a problem. If any collectors try to lean on you, let me know. I don't have a lot to lose right now."

"I think Jimmy Nightingale is part of this," he said.

"Why Nightingale?"

"Maybe he thinks you're on to him."

"About what?"

"About everything. He's dirty. Maybe you know something about him he doesn't want other people to hear."

"I told him what you said about Kevin Penny. About Penny bringing dope and girls to Nightingale's home."

"That would do it," Clete said.

"Killing someone? I don't believe that."

"When are you going to wake up about that guy?" Clete said. He went to the icebox and took out a quart bottle of beer and began chugging it, then paused. "Excuse me for doing this in front of you, but it's my feeding time. Plus, I can't stand listening to you protect a silver spoon con man like Nightingale."

"I'd like to talk with Kevin Penny," I said. "Where's he in custody?"

"He isn't. The guy he cut across the face decided he doesn't remember who mutilated him. Penny lives in a shithole south of Jennings."

I took a Dr Pepper out of the icebox and sipped it while Clete finished his beer. Outside, I heard raindrops as fat as nickels clicking on the canvas top of Clete's Caddy.

IT WAS STILL raining when Clete and I got off I-10 at Jennings and drove south to an Airstream trailer perched on blocks by a pond dark with sediment and coated with floating milk cartons and raw garbage. A dirt bike was parked in an open-sided shed. Clete cut the lights and took his .38 white-handled snub-nose from his shoulder holster and put it under the seat, then removed a sap and a pair of brass knuckles from the glove box and slipped them into his slacks.

"Leave your piece," he said.

"Why?"

"If it goes down and Penny gets his hand on a gun, he'll kill everybody in the room. When we have time, I'll show you a video of what he did to three black guys on the yard at Quentin."

"He's not your ordinary pimp?"

"Penny is not your ordinary anything."

Clete knocked on the door. I was wearing a raincoat and a rain hat pulled down on my eyes. A man with a complexion like mold on a lamp shade opened it. His expression seemed to shape and reshape itself as though he couldn't make up his mind about what he was seeing. He wore a flannel shirt with the sleeves cut off, his cargo pants buttoned under the navel. The inside of the trailer was a wreck.

"What do you want?"

"A few minutes, Kev," Clete said. "This is my friend Dave Robicheaux."

His eyes seemed to burn into my face. Then his expression lightened. "You a cop?"

"Why do you think that?" I said.

"They walk like their underwear is too tight or they got a suppository up their ass."

"I treated you righteous, Kev," Clete said. "Lose the hostility."

"So what do you want?"

"Jimmy Nightingale's cousin says she fired you. I didn't think that was right. She also said you were a yardman. That didn't ring right, either. Help me out here."

His eyes went from Clete to me and then to Clete again. "That bitch said that?"

"You got it."

"Come in."

He closed the door behind us. "Sit down."

A half-eaten pizza lay in a delivery box on a breakfast table. A television set rested in the sink. A bed against the wall was layered with skin magazines. I tried to keep my expression neutral.

"Why you looking at me?" he said.

"Clete showed me your sheet," I said. "You were in three mainline joints. But you don't have any tats."

"Pencil dicks need tats. Want to find the biggest sissy on the yard? Check the guy with sleeves. What'd that bitch say?"

"Let's back up a little bit," Clete said. "Jimmy Nightingale told Dave he didn't know you."

"He's a liar."

"That's what I thought," Clete said. "I told Dave you were no yardman, either."

"I was the chauffeur."

"You delivered dope and girls to Nightingale's house?" I asked.

"I'm supposed to answer that question? To a cop? What's with all this Nightingale stuff?"

"The Jeff Davis Eight," I said.

"Oh, boohoo time again," he said. "Those whores got themselves killed."

"How do you figure that?" I said.

"They're skanks. They're stupid. They go out on their own. Independence and the word 'whore' don't go together."

"They need a pimp?" I said.

"No, they need plastic surgery. Why you keep looking at me like that?"

"You're an interesting guy."

"What's with this guy, Purcel?"

"Dave is all right, Kev."

"Yeah? This stuff about the cousin? She ain't Jimmy's cousin. She's his sister or half sister."

"Let's stick to the subject," I said. "In your opinion, who killed the eight women?"

"They were in the life, man."

"Why'd Jimmy's secretary fire you?" I said.

"She came on to me. I told Jimmy. Who cares about any of this?"

There was a dull intensity in his eyes that's hard to describe or account for. You see it in recidivists or in lockdown units where the criminally insane are kept, although you are never sure they are actually insane.

"I like your accent," I said. "Did you grow up in New Orleans?"

"I'm from New York."

"Want to give us the name of the company bank account you were using as a drop?" I said.

But I had lost his attention. "What you got in your slacks, Purcel? A blackjack? You're shitting me?"

"I always carry one. Take it easy."

"I'm done talking. I'm gonna finish my dinner."

"You see Tony Squid around?" Clete asked.

"At the aquarium."

"Is Tony doing more than pour concrete for Jimmy Nightingale?" Clete said.

Penny kicked open the door, letting in the rain. "Youse both get out."

"Clete told me you had a son," I said.

I saw the alarm in Clete's face.

"What about him?" Penny said.

"What happened to him?"

"Nothing. He went to a home."

"For irreparably damaged children?" I said.

He pared his thumbnail with the tine of a fork, then raised his eyes to mine. His lips curled as though he were preparing to speak, but he didn't utter a word. Somehow I felt I was gazing into the face of an old enemy.

Clete and I went down the wood steps into the rain. Clete looked back over his shoulder. He took a breath. "He's got a hard-on for you, Dave. If you come out here again, carry a drop."

"He'll cap a cop he's met one time?"

"He's got a brain like flypaper. He doesn't let go."

"I feel like going back in there."

"Let's have a burger and some coffee. Don't argue."

"What'd he do to his son?"

"The kid is too scared to talk. Penny is supposed to get him back in two weeks."

He started the Caddy. We drove slowly past the trailer and the pond blanketed with floating trash.

THE NEXT MORNING, my first visitor in the office was Spade Labiche. He looked energized, glowing with his new assignment, a notepad in his hand. "Got a second, Dave?"

"What's up?"

He sat down without being asked and peeled back his notebook. "I want you to know everything I'm doing. Maybe you can explain a couple of things as we go along."

"Okay."

"We pulled the phone records for calls made to the Dartez number night before last. None were made from your cell or your landline. Except one came in from a pay phone at a filling station in St. Martinville. At just about the time Ms. Dartez says her husband talked to you and said he'd meet you out by Bayou Benoit."

I didn't reply.

"You had a snootful?" he said.

"Who told you that?"

"Helen has to do her job, Robo."

"Yeah, I was loaded."

"I know what you mean," he said, writing in his notebook. "So you were going to iron some things out with Dartez? About your wife's death?"

"I don't remember."

He looked up at me. "Can you give me something to work with here?"

"So you can exclude me?"

"That's one way to look at it."

"Do you have any witnesses?"

"I'm not supposed to discuss that. We've got to tow your truck in. Are you solid with that?"

"What for?"

"An anonymous tipster said he saw a beat-up blue truck slam the rear end of a black truck close to the convenience store. You told Helen you were headed to St. Martinville. So we got to have a look at your truck, Robo."

"I don't know who gave you permission to give me a nickname, but I advise you to stop using it."

"Ease up on the batter, bubba."

"Get out of my office."

He flipped the notebook shut. "Have it your way."

"I plan to."

But I was all rhetoric. The truth is, the backs of my legs were shaking.

THE ELECTRIC TIGER caught up with me at eleven Saturday night. That's what I used to call the heebie-jeebies. I first got them in Vietnam, along with the malaria I picked up in the Philippines. I came home with a hole in my chest and a punji scar like a flattened worm on my stomach and shrapnel in my hip and thigh that set off alarms when I went through metal sensors. The real damage I carried was one nobody saw. I'd hear the tiger padding around the house at three or four in the morning, then he'd sniff his way into the bedroom, glowing so brightly that the air would glisten and warp and my eyes would sting.

The strange phenomenon about alcoholic abstinence is that while you're laying off the hooch and working the program, your disease is doing push-ups and waiting for the day you slip. You can ease back into the dirty boogie or hit the floor running, but I promise you, the electric tiger, or your version of it, will come back with a roar.

My truck was in the pound, but I had a rental parked in the driveway. I drove to a liquor store in Lafayette and bought a pint of vodka, a bottle of Collins mix, a jar of cherries, a plastic cup, a small bag of crushed ice, and drove into Girard Park, next to the University of Louisiana campus, and got serious. The vodka went down cold and warm and sweet and hard as ice, all at the same time. When I closed my eyes, a lantern lit up the inside of my head, as if I had punched a hypodermic loaded with morphine into my arm.

It was an easy slide into the basement. The things I did next were not done in a blackout. I knew exactly what I was doing. I had put a sawed-off pool cue on the backseat before I left home, one that was weighted heavily at the base. I started the engine and got on I-10 and headed west, the speedometer maxed out.

Chapter
8

Maybe penny was sleeping one off. It's hard to say. I knotted a bandana around my face and set fire to the shed with the dirt bike in it, and tapped on the door and waited by the rear of the trailer. There was no reaction inside. A raincloud burst directly overhead, and the fire went out. I smashed on the door with my fist and was standing directly in front of it when Penny jerked it open.

"What's the haps?" I said, swinging the pool cue at a forty-five-degree angle across his face.

He stumbled backward, a hand pressed against one eye and the other eye bulging, so his face looked like it had been sawed down the middle. "Who the—"

I stepped inside, pulled the door shut, and caught him with the weighted end of the cue on the ear. He crashed on the breakfast table, his mouth wide with either pain or surprise. I swung the cue on his neck and back and spine as though I were chopping wood. When he tried to stand, I shoved him onto the floor of the toilet cubicle. He was wearing only his socks and Jockey shorts. Blood was leaking from his ear. "Why you doing this? Who the fuck are you, man?"

I kicked him in the face and dropped a full roll of toilet paper in the bowl and drove his head into the water and kept it there. I could feel him struggling, his forehead wedging the roll into the bottom of the commode, the water rising to his shoulders. I pushed down the handle to refill the bowl. Water was sloshing over the sides. My arm and shoulder were trembling with the pressure it took to keep him down.

I began to count the seconds under my breath. One-Mississippi, two-Mississippi, three-Mississippi. I stepped on his calf so he couldn't get purchase on the linoleum. Four-Mississippi, five-Mississippi, six-Mississippi. I shoved harder and saw bubbles the size and color of small oranges rise to the surface with a gurgling sound. Thirteen-Mississippi, fourteen-Mississippi, fifteen-Mississippi. His arms had turned as flaccid as noodles and were flipping impotently at his sides.

I pulled him dripping from the bowl and threw him onto the floor. He gasped and made a sound like a sheet of tin being ripped out of a roof. He gagged and cupped his mouth.

"When your son comes home, you'll act like a decent father. If you hurt him in any way, I'll be back."

I stomped on his stomach. His mouth opened, and I shoved a bar of soap into it and mashed it down his throat with my shoe.

I got into my rental and drove away. In the rearview mirror, I could see white smoke rising from the shed, as though the fire I had started wanted to have another go at it.

By six A.M., I was teetering on the edge of delirium tremens. By seven they'd passed and I was sound asleep in my skivvies, facedown on the sheets, as though I had gone through a painless evisceration. Strangely, I felt at peace. I had no explanation. I went to Mass that evening in Lafayette and caught a meeting before returning to New Iberia.

HELEN WAS ON my case early the next morning. "You told Labiche to get out of your office?"

"I didn't know he was a snitch."

"He was trying to do his job," she said.

"He's a street rat."

"I'm not going to put up with this, Dave."

"Then don't."

We were standing by the water cooler out in the hall.

"Step inside my office," she said.

I tried to play the role of the gentleman and let her walk ahead of me.

"Get inside!" she said. She slammed the door behind us. "Somebody pounded Kevin Penny into hamburger. The sheriff in Jeff Davis says Penny believes it was you."

"He 'believes' it was me?"

"The assailant had a kerchief on his face."

"Let's see: Penny has been in Quentin, Raiford, and Angola. He was in the AB, but his wife was half black. He's a pimp and a child abuser. Nobody besides a cop would want to hurt him, huh?"

"Where were you early Sunday morning?"

"Helen, I don't blame you because you have to treat me as a suspect in the Dartez homicide. But Labiche is a bum. You shouldn't have put him in charge of the investigation."

"Don't try to change the subject. Did you bust up Penny?"

"Somebody should have done it years ago. End of statement."

"You're going to end up in prison."

"Not because of Penny," I said.

She touched at her nose and sniffed. "Maybe you're right about Labiche."

"Pardon?"

"I'm not comfortable with Labiche's history, either. I never knew a guy in vice who didn't get the wrong kind of rise out of his job. But he caught the case on his own hook, and to give it to somebody else because you don't like him would be obvious bias."

"I know."

"You do?"

"You did the right thing."

"You're a poor liar." She punched me in the chest, hard. "I'm mad at you, Dave."

*   *   *

AT FIVE, I'D left the office and begun walking down the long driveway to East Main, when I saw Levon Broussard turn out of the traffic and park his Jeep under the big live oak by the grotto devoted to the mother of Jesus. He opened the car door and held up his hand. "I need to talk."

"I'm on my way home," I said. "Take a walk with me."

"No, right here."

"It's been a long day," I said.

"It's fixing to get longer."

"If it's business, I'll see you tomorrow at eight A.M."

Just then Spade Labiche came up the drive in an unmarked car. He leaned out the window. "Good news, Robicheaux. A dent on your back bumper, but no paint from the Dartez vehicle. You're clean on the truck. It's at the pound. Catch!" He threw my keys at me. They landed in a puddle of muddy water. "Sorry," he said, and drove away.

I picked up the keys and wiped them with my handkerchief.

"What was that about?" Levon said.

"Departmental politics. What did you want to tell me?"

"My wife has been raped."

The words didn't fit the scene. The wind was blowing through the branches overhead, the moss drifting in threads to the asphalt, votive candles flickering in the grotto.

"Say again?"

"She had a flat tire. Jimmy Nightingale talked her into having a drink and got her drunk." He saw the expression in my eyes. "What?"

"People get themselves drunk," I said. "Where is she?"

"At home."

"Did she go to the hospital?"

"Our doctor came to the house. Why do you ask about a hospital?"

"Can she come to the department?"

"She doesn't want to."

"I can understand that, Levon. But we don't do home calls. A female officer will interview her. The surroundings will be private."

He looked around. "I don't know what to do."

I couldn't be sure if he was talking to himself or to me. "Tell me what happened."

"She was at the grocery last night. She came outside and saw she had a flat tire. Nightingale put her spare on. They went out to the highway and had a drink."

I could already see what a defense lawyer would do with Rowena's story.

"I'm sorry to hear about this," I said.

"You don't believe her?"

"I didn't say that."

"She trusts people when she shouldn't," he said. "She thinks y'all won't believe her. She was doing work among the poor when I met her in Venezuela. She gave her paintings to the Indians, people no one cared about."

He waited for me to reply. I hate to handle sexual assault and child molestation cases because the victims seldom get justice, and that's just for starters. Adult victims are exposed to shame, embarrassment, and scorn. Often they are made to feel they warranted their fate. Defense attorneys tear them apart on the stand; judges hand out probation to men who should be shot. Sometimes the perpetrator is given bail without the court's notifying the victim, and the victim ends up either dead or too frightened to testify. I've also known cops who take glee in a woman's degradation, and it's not coincidental that they work vice.

"I'm in the cookpot these days, Levon. I'll do what I can for y'all."

"You're having some kind of trouble?"

"I'm a suspect in a homicide."

His lips moved without sound.

"Yeah, it's a bit unusual," I said.

He looked up and down the street. "You don't believe Rowena's account, do you?"

"I don't know all the circumstances."

"She's never been unfaithful," he said.

The last statement was the kind no investigative cop ever wants to hear. "Has Jimmy tried to contact you or your wife?"

"*Jimmy?*"

"I've known him most of my life."

"Yes, and you introduced him to us, and now we know him, too."

Sometimes you just have to walk away. And that's what I did.

"I apologize," he said at my back.

THE PHONE WAS ringing as I came through the front door. "Hello?" I said.

It was Alafair. "Clete called. He says you're in trouble."

"I'll get out of it."

"He said you were in the bag."

"No," I said. "I mean I'm not drinking now."

"You stopped going to meetings?"

"I went last night."

"What's this about the guy who hit Molly's car?"

"I was in a blackout. The guy was beaten to death out by Bayou Benoit. Maybe I did it."

The phone went silent. In the backyard, the sun and the smoke from meat fires in the park looked like spun gold in the trees. In my mind's eye, I saw Alafair at age five, after I pulled her from a submerged plane piloted by a Maryknoll priest who was helping illegals escape the death squads in Central America. I thought about the wonderful life we'd had on the bayou.

"You never hurt anyone except in defense of yourself or someone else," she said. "I'm flying into New Orleans tomorrow."

"That's not necessary, Alfenheimer."

"Don't call me that stupid name."

"How's your screenplay coming?"

"I'm writing it for people who think William Shakespeare was too wordy. How do you think it's coming?"

"What time does your flight come in?"

"Don't worry about it. I'll rent a car. Just hold tight till I get back to New Iberia."

"I owned up at a meeting. I'm fine."

"That's when people slip, isn't it? When they say they're fine. Why'd you drink, Dave?"

"The same reason as everyone who goes out. I wanted to." The line was silent. I felt my heart stop. "Alafair?"

"You don't know how much it hurts when you say something like that."

My ear felt as though it had been stung by a wasp.

VICTOR'S CAFETERIA ON Main Street, right across from Clete's office, opened at six A.M. every weekday. It was a grand place to eat and start the day, and usually crowded with businesspeople and tourists and cops and parish politicians. If there was any better food on earth, I hadn't found it. Clete and I went in at seven on Tuesday, and Clete loaded up with his healthy breakfast of four biscuits, scrambled eggs sprinkled with grated cheese, green onions, and bacon bits, a pork chop smothered in milk gravy, orange juice, a bowl of stewed tomatoes, and multiple cups of coffee.

Helen was two tables from us; it was obvious she didn't want to acknowledge us.

"What's wrong with *her*?" Clete said.

"You didn't talk to anyone in Jefferson Davis Parish about an incident there, did you?"

He stopped eating. "Involving you?"

"Involving a graduate of Raiford and Angola and Quentin we both know."

"Something happened to Penny?"

"You could say that."

He took his cell phone from his pocket and looked at the screen. "I've got four missed calls from the Jeff Davis Sheriff's Department."

"Better answer them."

"This isn't funny, big mon."

"Penny didn't think so, either."

He started eating again, then put down his knife and fork and drank his coffee cup empty. "Let's go."

"Where?"

"To the park."

"How about your office?"

"You know how many times I've been bugged?"

We walked to the drawbridge at Burke Street and crossed the bayou and went into City Park and sat in one of the picnic shelters by the water, a few feet from a row of camellia bushes, the petals still wet with dew. I told him everything.

"You almost drowned him in the toilet?"

"Yep."

"He'll come at you."

"No, he won't. He's a gutless shit."

"You're letting your past distort your thinking, Streak. The people who hurt you and me as kids are nothing compared to Penny."

"They're all cut out of the same cloth."

"My old man wasn't. He was just a drunk who figured himself a failure and didn't know where to put his anger."

People make peace with themselves in different ways, sometimes being more generous than they should. But you don't pull life preservers away from drowning people or deny an opiate or two to those who have taken up residence in the Garden of Gethsemane.

"Did you get enough to eat?" I asked.

"No."

I looked at my watch. "We have time for a refill."

CLETE HAD ALLUDED to my childhood experience with a man named Mack. I didn't argue with him about the influence of Mack on my life. In fact, I don't think about Mack anymore. Eventually, he turned into a specter who drifted off into the mist, a dirty smudge not worth remembering. But there was never a man I hated as much, and I carried my hatred to Indochina and put his face on many an enemy solider, none of whom deserved to be a surrogate for this evil man. For that reason alone I did not willingly discuss my experience in the Orient, or the deeds I committed there, or the ribbons and wounds I brought home. Evil is evil, and you don't give the son of a bitch a second life.

Chapter 9

AT 10:41 A.M., Helen came into my office and looked out the window on the bayou. She had a manila folder clamped under her arm. "Rowena and Levon Broussard just left," she said.

"Were they here for what I think?"

"I took her statement. He says he talked with you late yesterday."

"That's right."

"What's your opinion?" she asked.

"I didn't get many details. Alcohol seemed to be involved. No medical report. What'd they tell you?"

"She and Nightingale went to a lounge. They had four rounds of Manhattans. Then he wanted to show her his boat down at Cypremort Point. That's where he did it."

"What time of day?"

"About ten P.M."

When I didn't answer, she said, "Not good, huh?"

"I wonder if it's going to be prosecutable. She's married. It sounds like a tryst."

"I pushed her on that. She said she and her husband had a fight and she used bad judgment."

"Where was her car?"

"At the supermarket."

"How'd she get back to it?"

"Nightingale drove her. Don't make that face."

"The defense will put a scarlet letter on her brow," I said.

"We won't let that happen, though," Helen said. "Will we?"

"We?"

She put the folder on my desk.

"No," I said.

"I've got the video in my office. Let's get started."

"I'm not right for this," I said.

"How about you go on leave without pay instead?"

"I know all the involved parties, Helen."

"Like everybody in this building doesn't?"

I flipped open the folder and flipped it closed again. "What's her emotional state?"

"Like a vase somebody dropped on a concrete floor," she said.

"I never heard of Jimmy Nightingale abusing women."

"His casinos clean out the pockets of pensioners and poor people. He hangs with Bobby Earl. He's business partners with Tony the Nose. Remember when Tony and Didoni Giacano used to stick people's hands in an aquarium full of piranhas?"

"Those were the good old days," I said.

"Time to kick butt and take names, Streak."

"Yes, ma'am."

I WATCHED THE VIDEO. As in most interviews with sexual assault victims, the dialogue, the violation of privacy, and the demeanor of the victim were excruciating. For anyone who has a cavalier attitude about predation, he need only watch its influence on the victims in order to change his attitude. They cannot scrub the stain out of their skin. Over and over again, the assault flickers like a sado-porn film on a screen inside their heads, sometimes for months, sometimes years. This goes on until they turn over the fate of their assailant to a power greater than they are. I've known nine or ten rapists who beat the system. I was convinced every one of them carried an incubus that eventually pissed on their graves.

As I watched Rowena Broussard give her account on the video, I began to wonder if I was possessed of the male bias I never felt myself guilty of. She did not seem to be a person who could be lured easily into a vulnerable situation. She had lived in the third world, where moral insanity, social cannibalism, and violence against the poor are part of the culture. Her paintings were testimony to her anger at dictatorial regimes and imperious personalities and people who sought dominion over others.

I had seen her punch the heavy bag at Red's Health Club with the kind of power and dedication that makes adventurous men think twice. Jimmy Nightingale was not a large man. She said he put a pillowcase over her head and wedged his knee between her legs and worked off her undergarment with one hand. She said she cried out and told him to stop, even begged. I wanted to believe her. I hated cops and judges and prosecutors who sided with a rapist, and I've known many of them. There is no lower kind of individual on earth than a person who is sworn to serve but who deliberately aids a molester and condemns the victim to a lifetime of resentment and self-mortification.

But my uncertainty would not go away.

I called Levon at home. "I need a medical report from your physician," I said. "You and Rowena have to give him permission to release it."

"What good will that do?"

"It will tell us if there was bruising. Or any number of other things."

"Does that have to be public knowledge?" he asked.

"We can't make a case without it."

"Hasn't she talked about it enough? I think there's an element of voyeurism in this."

"Are you serious?" I said.

"What if there are only minor scratches and a small bruise? Dave, the real damage was done in ways I don't want to describe."

"Y'all had better make up your minds."

"All right, I'll call Dr. LeBlanc."

"Thank you." I hung up without saying good-bye.

I used a patrolwoman to call Nightingale's home and find out where he was. I didn't want him prepared for the interview; nor did I want him coming to the department with an attorney. The patrolwoman told the cousin or half sister, Emmeline Nightingale, that she wanted to contact Mr. Jimmy about a contribution to the Louisiana Police Benevolent Association, for which she actually solicited funds.

I headed for his office in Morgan City. It was located not far from the big bridge that spanned the Atchafalaya River, with a view to the south of the shrimp boats at the docks and miles of emerald-green marshland and islands of gum and willow trees.

Jimmy was reading the newspaper, with one leg propped across the corner of his desk, when the secretary escorted me into his inner office. He put aside his newspaper and grinned as though God were in His heaven and all was right with the world. "My favorite flatfoot."

I sat down. "I'm going to turn on my recorder. Okay?"

"What for?"

"Sometimes I can't read my own handwriting."

"You've lost me."

"Rowena Broussard dropped a heavy dime on you, Jimmy. Rape, assault and battery, sodomy, maybe false imprisonment."

"The heck you say."

"She says y'all had some drinks and ended up on your boat at Cypremort Point."

"That's right. But that's all there was to it."

"You didn't attack her?"

"Attack her? I didn't do anything."

"You didn't have consensual sex?"

"I showed her my boat. That woman is nuts, Dave. I was pretty plowed myself. She could have put my lights out."

"She's pretty convincing."

"Send her out to Hollywood. She deserves an Academy Award. I can't believe this."

I couldn't, either, but for other reasons. In most rape cases, the accused immediately claims the act was done with consent. The issue then devolves into various claims about intoxication and the use of narcotics and muscle relaxants, or inability on the victim's part to show sound judgment. I had never caught a sexual assault case involving adults in which the accused claimed to have done absolutely nothing.

Jimmy put a mint into his mouth and looked at me, never blinking. If you have dealt with liars, even pathological ones who pass polygraph tests, you know the signs to look for. The liar blinks just before the end of the lie, or he keeps his eyelids stitched to his brow. He folds his arms on his chest, subconsciously concealing his deception. The voice becomes warm, a bit saccharine; sometimes there's an ethereal glow in the face. He repeats his statements unnecessarily and peppers his speech with adverbs and hyperbole. The first-person pronouns "I," "me," "mine," and "myself" dominate his rhetoric.

Conversely, the truth teller is laconic and seems bored with the discussion, not caring whether you get it right or not.

Nightingale showed none of the traditional characteristics of the liar, and I began to believe him. Then something very strange occurred. For just a second I saw a glimmer in the corner of his eye, like a wet spot. His throat became ruddy; his lips parted slightly, as though he wanted to confide a secret to a trusted friend.

"Did you want to tell me something, Jimmy?"

The moment passed. His eyes were bright, his smile in place. "I don't know what I could add."

"Want to come in and make a formal statement with your attorney present?"

"What good would that do?"

"Do it by the book. Show everybody you have nothing to hide," I replied.

"Said the spider to the fly. Where is this going, Dave?"

"That's up to the prosecutor's office."

"Rowena really said all those things?"

"I'm afraid so."

"I was a fool to take her to the boat. What's Levon got to say about all this?"

"What do you think?"

"I was hoping to put a movie deal together with him. I've got the connections to do it. I guess that's in the toilet, huh?"

"You're being accused of rape and sodomy, and you're worried about a movie deal?"

"I thought Levon and I could make a grand film. He's a bit negative on Hollywood. I thought a down-home touch might be the key."

"A down-home touch?"

"Outsiders don't understand us. Why do we have to depend on Hollywood to make movies about us?"

His presumption and naïveté would probably get him laughed out of Los Angeles or New York, but I couldn't help feeling sorry for him. "Thanks for your time, Jimmy. You're not planning to take a trip anywhere, are you?"

"No, I'm at your disposal. I can't believe this is happening."

I thought about the beating death of T. J. Dartez. "I know the feeling."

ALAFAIR PULLED IN to the driveway late that afternoon. As I looked at her, I had to wonder again at the arbitrary nature of fate and how the most influential events in our lives are usually unexpected and unplanned. On a clear day out at Southwest Pass, I had heard a sputtering sound just before the twin-engine plane came in low on the water, a long black column of smoke stringing behind it. The pilot was gunning the engines, probably trying to reach Pecan Island, where he could pancake in the salt grass. But he'd hit the water and flipped, and the waves had washed over the fuselage, and the plane had gone down in the murk like a deflating yellow balloon.

I still have nightmares in which I swim down to the wreck, my air tank almost empty, while clouds of sand rise from the plane's wings and the bat wings of stingrays flutter by me and a little girl struggles to find an air bubble inside the cabin. My second wife, Annie, and I took her to a hospital and named her Alafair for my mother and began raising her in the Cajun culture in which I had grown up. She forgot her own language and the death squad that attacked her village and became an honor student and went to Reed College. The next stop was number one in her class at Stanford Law.

But as with all parents, when I looked at Alafair, I saw the child and not the adult, as though she were incapable of growing older. I had a footlocker in the attic where I kept her Curious George and Baby Squanto Indian books, her Orca the Whale T-shirt, her Donald Duck hat with the quacking bill that we bought at Disneyland, and her pink tennis shoes embossed with "Left" and "Right" on the appropriate toes.

The leaves were floating from the trees and blowing on the street when I went to greet her. She was tall and lithe and had long Indian-black hair and brown eyes and an IQ that wasn't measurable. Only two people in one million have it.

I carried her things into her bedroom, which I dusted and cleaned every week and kept closed and never let anyone use, not even Clete. After she put her things away, we went to the cemetery and placed flowers in a vase on Molly's grave. I never talked about Molly's death unless I had to, not even at the grave. I don't believe that acceptance of mortality is a situation you resolve by talking with others. The same with personal grief and mourning or loss of any kind. I remember the words of a black ex-junkie musician friend of mine who got clean in a lockdown unit where he beat his head to pulp against a steel wall: "You deal wit' your own snakes or you don't, man. Sometimes you're the only cat in the cathedral. Ain't nobody else can do it for you."

When we got home, I knew Alafair had read my thoughts.

"You bottle up your feelings, Dave," she said. "I think that's why you got drunk again."

"Give it a rest, Alf."

"You kept feeding your anger toward T. J. Dartez. What do they say at meetings? You get drunk *at* somebody?"

"Something like that."

I started taking food out of the icebox. She had just gone to the heart of the matter. Every time I tried to remember what had happened after I'd seen the headlights in my rearview mirror, I reached the same conclusion, and it is the same conclusion every alcoholic reaches after he comes off a bender, sick and trembling and terrified: I had done something my conscious mind refused to accept.

"I haven't quite told you everything," I said. "I went after a guy by the name of Kevin Penny. He's a violent man and a three-time loser who was going to hurt his kid."

"What'd you do?"

"It involved a swimming lesson in the toilet bowl."

Her eyes roved over my face. "What if he takes it out on his kid?"

"I called social services. They're going to make home calls, and so is Clete."

"Why do you have it in for this guy in particular?"

"I don't know. He bothers me. I came within a few seconds of drowning him. I wanted to do it."

I poured a glass of milk and drank it. She watched me silently. "He isn't filing charges?" she asked.

"I had a bandana on my face."

"Did somebody set you up on the Dartez deal?"

"Evidently, I called his house the night he was killed. I asked him to meet me out by Bayou Benoit."

"That's where he was killed?"

"Yes," I said. I showed her my hands. They were scabbed over, the knuckles still swollen.

"Could you have punched a wall?"

"That's what I'd like to believe."

"Clete believes Fat Tony Nemo and Jimmy Nightingale and Levon Broussard may be mixed up in this," she said.

"Clete and I are always trying to find excuses for each other."

"He says you had dinner with Nightingale and Levon."

"Nightingale got ahold of a sword carried by Levon's great-grandfather in the Civil War and gave it to him. Nightingale wants to make a movie from one of Levon's novels. Except Levon's wife and Nightingale hit it off a little too well."

"Nightingale thinks he's going to produce a film with Levon? Where's he been?"

"What do you mean?"

"Everyone knows Levon hates Hollywood. He thinks they screwed up a couple of his adaptations. On CNN he said Hollywood is a potential gold mine for anthropologists because it's the only culture in the world where educated and rich and powerful people have the mind-set and manners of Southern white trash."

"That's not a bad line."

I fixed avocado-and-tomato sandwiches for both of us and we sat down at the breakfast table by the window. I glanced through the screen. "Look yonder."

"What?"

"There's a coon on top of Tripod's hutch."

She leaned forward and peered through the screen. "I don't see him."

"He's right there," I said, pointing. "His tail is hanging down the side of the hutch."

"I guess I need glasses."

Since when? I wondered.

IN THE MORNING, I finally caught Levon Broussard's physician in his office. His name was Melvin LeBlanc. He had been a navy corpsman during the first Iraqi war, and when he came home, he became a Quaker and enrolled in medical school at Tulane. He had the face of an ascetic, thinning, sandy hair, and a stare that gave you the sense that he saw presences others did not. We were sitting in his office with the door closed.

"I'm not keen on this kind of stuff, Dave," he said.

"It's too personal?"

"I don't like to be used. That's what the defense does. That's what you guys do."

"Rowena and Levon gave you carte blanche to tell us everything, didn't they?" I said.

"I can tell you what I found or didn't find. But don't try to put words in my mouth."

"Was there evidence of forced penetration?" I said.

"Around the vagina, no. There was a bruise inside one thigh."

"A recent one?"

"Yes, sir."

"No abrasions?"

"Abrasions where?"

"Wherever they might be significant, Melvin."

"On the hip."

"Scratches?"

"Correct."

"Perhaps consistent with someone tearing an undergarment from a victim's person?"

"I don't know. I didn't use the word 'victim,' either," he said.

"Did you do any swabs?"

"Ms. Broussard showered after she returned home. I recommended she go to the hospital and have a rape kit done. She refused."

"No trauma around the vagina?"

"None other than the bruise on the thigh."

"How about inside?"

"She didn't indicate any discomfort."

"This isn't coming together for me, Doc."

"That's your problem."

"Ms. Broussard says the assailant sodomized her."

"That's a relative word," he said.

"Not in this case."

"If you're asking about bite marks, there were none in the usual places."

"How about elsewhere?"

"On the shoulder."

"A bite mark?"

"What some call a hickey. It could have been put there before she went on the boat."

"Is that why you didn't mention it when I asked about abrasions?"

"Yes, sir."

"Any other reason?" I asked.

"There were only two people on that boat. One is lying, the other is not. That's about all I can tell you."

"You think Rowena Broussard would deliberately put herself through this kind of embarrassment? Would any woman, at least one who's sane?"

"Hell hath no fury," he said.

"Not a good metaphor."

"On the frontier, it was called cabin fever. Levon has a helium balloon for a head. His art comes first. He even tells people that at book signings. Some people want to save the world but don't have time for their own family."

"What are you saying, Doc?"

"The human spirit is frail. People believe whatever they need to believe. I feel sorry for all of them."

THAT AFTERNOON, ALAFAIR was raking leaves in the backyard when she heard a vehicle come up the driveway and park under the porte cochere, as though the driver lived in the house. She walked around the side and saw a trim blond man get out of a red Honda that looked brand-new. He wore loafers and gray slacks and a long-sleeve purple shirt and a shiny black tie with a gold pin. His stomach was flat, his hair stiff with dressing of some kind, his hands big, the knuckles pronounced. He was holding a clipboard. "Hi. I'm Detective Spade Labiche. I work with Dave."

"He's not here right now," she said.

"Yeah, he caught the Broussard rape case, didn't he? Did he see the doc yet?"

"I don't know anything about that."

"I hope you don't mind me parking under your porte cochere. I had my car waxed."

"My car is parked on the street, so we don't need the space right now," she said.

The implication seemed to elude him. "This is a nice spot," he said. "He put you to work? The old man."

"Beg your pardon?"

"I've read a couple of your books. I thought you'd be typing instead of piling leaves."

"Is there something I can help you with?"

"I'm excluding Dave in the situation that took place out by Bayou Benoit." His accent was bottom-of-the-bucket New Orleans.

"Why would Dave be here during work hours?" she said.

"He eats lunch at home some days, doesn't he?"

"It's after two."

"I've never met a famous author. Where do you get your ideas?"

"I've never given it much thought. Do you want to leave a message?"

"Yeah, I could do it that way. You were an ADA in Portland, right? You know the ropes."

"The ropes?"

"Whatever you want to call it. We're all on the same side." He looked away at the bayou, a little dreamy. He scratched at a mosquito bite on his neck and glanced at his fingertips. The day was warm. When the wind changed, his odor touched her face, a mixture of detergent and perspiration.

"We couldn't get any prints off the Dartez door handle," he said. "Maybe somebody wiped them off, or maybe his body was dragged over the handle. I tweezered up some broken glass from the ground and inside the truck. The lab found Dave's prints on a couple of them. I know there's an explanation. I just need to get the explanation into my paperwork." He looked down as he pulled his tie taut on his shirtfront and, at the same time, took her measure from her breasts to her thighs.

"What's your name again?" she asked.

"Call me Spade."

"You're giving me information civilians aren't supposed to have."

"I'm trying to be subtle here. I didn't want this investigation, or at least not one that would cause a colleague problems. Tell Dave I think he was probably out at the Dartez place to talk about the accident, and he had occasion to put his hands on the driver's window of the pickup."

"How long have you been doing homicide investigations?"

"It's not my area. I worked vice and narcotics at Miami-Dade. I was undercover in Liberty City."

"Liberty City is all black."

"I figured that out when they started throwing spears at me from the fire escapes." There was a beat. "Oops. My bad."

"Come back later, okay?" she said.

"If you work the inner city, you have to develop a sense of humor. Ask Purcel. I heard he had a way of dipping into the culture. What a character." He lit a cigarette with a gold lighter, the smoke rising out of his cupped hand.

"Could you not do that, please?"

"You don't let people smoke on your property?" he said.

She tried to crinkle her eyes but couldn't. There was a bilious taste in her mouth that made her want to spit. He flipped his cigarette sparking into a camellia bush and rotated his head as though he had a stiff neck.

"It's good you're raking up all the leaves," he said. "When they get into the bayou, the biodegradation uses up the oxygen and kills the fish."

"Yep, that's what it does," she said. She propped the rake on the ground, her left hand on the shaft. She saw him use the opportunity to glance at her ring finger.

"There's a lot of this area I still haven't seen," he said. "One day I'd like somebody to show me around. I could do the same for them in New Orleans, show them all the things nobody knows about, including where all the skeletons are hid. In the old days, the Mob dumped jackrollers in Lake Pontchartrain because they were bad for tourism. Cops would throw them out of a car at high speed by the Huey Long Bridge. They got things done back then. That was before your time."

"I don't think you're looking for exculpatory evidence about Dave," she said. "I don't think you're a friend. I think you have a lean and hungry look."

"If there's something I haven't done to help your stepfather, tell me what it is, little lady, and I'll get on it."

"He's not my stepfather, he's my father. Call me 'little lady' again and see what happens."

He sucked in his breath, smiling wetly, as though acknowledging his indiscretion. "I don't choose my words very well. That's probably why I've remained a single man."

"I'd better finish my work. I'll give Dave your message."

He snapped his fingers. "Sorry, I forgot to ask you something."

She waited.

"Call it deep background," he said. "It doesn't have anything to do with the case itself. How many times did Dave have to bust a cap on a guy or break his spokes, particularly in a close-quarter situation? Like when he was arresting a guy or the guy got in his face and he lost it? I never met an old-school cop yet who took shit off mutts and pervs. Can you give me a ballpark number?"

Chapter 10

IN THE LIFE, Clete was known as con-wise, even though he had never been a convict. The term in the criminal subculture is laudatory and indicates a level of knowledge and experience that cannot be acquired in a library. You also have to pay dues. A "solid" or stand-up con stacks his own time, does it straight up without early release, work furloughs, conjugal privileges, or snitching off fellow inmates for favorable treatment. It's not easy. Ask anyone who's stood on the oil barrel in Huntsville or chopped cotton inside the system in Arkansas or been thrown into a lockdown unit full of wolves.

Clete went his own way, didn't impose it on others, and asked the same respect. He would not only lay down his life for a friend; he would paint the walls with his friend's enemies. He grew up in the old Irish Channel and palled around with guys like Tony Cardo, who was probably the most intelligent and dangerous and successful old-school gangster New Orleans ever produced. When they were kids, Clete and Tony found a box of human arms outside the incinerator by the Tulane medical school, and hung them from the straps of the St. Claude streetcar just as all the employees from the cigar factory were boarding; one passenger leaped from the window and crashed on top of a sno'ball cart. Except for Tony, Clete's old-time buds went to the can or the chair, and Clete went to Vietnam and came back with the Navy Cross, the Silver Star, and two Hearts, and cruised right back into the Big Sleazy without giving any of it a second thought.

I drove to his cottage at the motor court Thursday afternoon. He was standing amid the trees grilling a two-inch-thick steak, flipping it with a fork. He wore a Hawaiian shirt and a porkpie hat tilted on his brow and a pair of dark blue rayon workout pants that covered his shoelaces. "Big mon. I was just fixing to ask you and Alafair over."

"How you doin'?" I said.

"Not bad."

When Clete was equivocal, you tended to glance at the sky for thunderclouds, dust rising out of the fields, a splinter of lightning on the horizon.

"What's wrong?" I said.

"Have a seat."

I sat down at a picnic table made of green planks and covered with bird droppings and needles from a slash pine.

"I'm worried about Kevin Penny," he said. "I think he's got you on the brain."

"He's not coming after me, Clete. If he does, we'll punch his ticket. He knows that."

"You don't get it. He's an obvious habitual, but he's not on parole, he has no outstanding warrants, and he doesn't have to register as a sex offender, even though he was up on sexual assault charges a couple of times. I don't know how he got out of Raiford, either. They should have welded the door on him and poured concrete on top of it."

"What was he in for?"

"Distribution of cocaine and assault with a deadly weapon. But they couldn't get him for the bigger charge: He and two other guys tortured a dealer in Little Havana for his stash. They hung him from a hoist on a wrecker and put a propane torch on him."

"You're saying Penny is protected?"

"He has to be. Pukes in the projects do life for three street busts involving amounts of money you could steal from bubble-gum machines."

"Who's his protector?"

"I know you don't like this, but I think Jimmy Nightingale is a player in this."

"A player in what?"

"Setting you up."

"Maybe I wasn't set up. Maybe I killed T. J. Dartez."

"This is what Penny just told me—"

"Wait a minute. You just saw Penny?"

"This morning. I saw the social worker who'll be looking after his kid, too. I told Penny I'd be visiting him, kind of like an old friend. Penny says Nightingale is a geek. He says he's AC/DC and humps his sister or half sister or whatever she is."

"This guy has no credibility, Clete."

"Penny says Nightingale is eaten up with guilt. Maybe he killed somebody."

I didn't reply.

"You don't buy it?"

"I don't know. Rowena Broussard says he raped her. He claims he never touched her. When I interviewed him, he almost had me convinced."

"Go on."

"I felt like he wanted to confess. But not to rape. Something else. Maybe Penny is right."

He forked the steak off the flames and laid it on a plate. "Is that what you came by to tell me?"

"No, I got the loan on my house. You're a quarter of a mil richer than you were this morning."

"You actually did that?"

"Why not?"

His eyes were shiny. He wiped them on his forearm. "I've got to get out of this smoke."

"Pay off those bums and get them out of your life."

"You're truly a noble mon, noble mon. I'll brown us some bread."

* * *

THAT EVENING, PUSHING a basket at Winn-Dixie, I saw a young woman with a small red mouth and amber-colored hair and a flush on her cheeks.

"There you are again," she said. " 'Member me?"

I had to think. "You're Babette. From the bar-and-grill."

"You ordered two doubles and a Heineken. You was waiting for your friend, but you drank it all."

"I wish I hadn't."

"Your friend come in afterward. You're a friend of Mr. Spade, ain't you?"

We were in the middle of the aisle, but no one else was around. "Spade Labiche came in the bar after I left?"

"Yes, suh. He left his gold lighter. I run out after him. He was talking to another man, but he drove off befo' I could catch him."

"What'd you do with the lighter?"

"I put it in the drawer for a couple of days. When he didn't come in, I dropped it t'rew the mail slot in the big building wit' a note."

"Did Mr. Spade tell you he was looking for me?"

"He was in the corner. He come over and axed if you'd gone in the bat'room. I tole him you was gone."

"Do you know who Mr. Spade was with?"

Her eyes lingered on mine, as though she were standing on the edge of a cliff. "I seen him once befo'. I don't know his name or nothing about him."

"What's he look like?"

"He's got bad skin. It's thick, like leather. Like his eyes are looking out of holes. I ain't caused no trouble, no?"

"Of course not. You're a nice person, Miss Babette. Did Mr. Spade thank you for returning his lighter?"

"No, suh, he ain't said nothing."

I took a business card out of my wallet and wrote my unlisted number on the back. "If you see that other guy again, give me a ring. Of if you have any problems with anything at all, give me a ring."

I could see the uncertainty, the fear about her job, her paycheck, her relationship with her boss, the prospect of offending people with power and authority over others, the dark figure sitting in the shadows at the end of the bar when it's closing time. I wondered how many people would understand her frame of reference.

She squeezed the card in her fist. "I better go."

"Remember what I said. You're a nice lady."

"T'ank you," she replied.

She pushed her basket to the cashier's counter and didn't look back.

ON FRIDAY MORNING, I went into Labiche's office. It was hardly more than a cubicle, located in a corner without windows. "What's the haps?" I said.

He looked up from his paperwork. He tried to grin. "What's shaking, Robo?"

"Alafair told me about your visit to my house. You found my prints on some broken glass?"

"Like I told her, there's probably an explanation. Maybe you didn't have your latex on at the crime scene."

"No, my gloves were on. Why didn't you come to my office instead of my house?"

"Because you weren't here."

His lighter was on the desk blotter. He picked it up and began clicking the top up and down.

"Nice lighter," I said. "Real gold?"

"A gift. What do you want, Slick?"

"Slick?"

"Get off your high horse."

"I want you not snooping around my house. I want you not looking at my daughter in an inappropriate way."

"I've tried to give you the benefit of the doubt. But that's a waste of time. For arrogance, you take the cake."

"I think you're a Judas and a liar."

"Do you know you smelled like puke at the crime scene? You're a rummy, my friend. I don't know why Helen keeps you around."

I walked closer to his desk. I rested my fingertips on the edge, felt the grain of the wood. "Stay away from my daughter."

He laughed under his breath.

"You're amused?" I said.

"Yeah, by you. I'll make sure I call you Dave from now on. See you later, *Dave*."

I went back to my office, leaving the ceiling lights off, and sat behind my desk and stared through the window, my breath coming hard in my throat, a sound like the ocean whirring in my ears. Then I went downstairs and printed out the rap sheet and mug shots of Kevin Penny on file at the National Crime Information Center.

AFTER THE LUNCH crowd had left the bar-and-grill on the bayou, I parked an unmarked car under a shade tree on the street paralleling the bayou and entered the building through the kitchen. I saw Babette unloading dishes from a washer, her face bright with perspiration in the steam.

"Can I speak with you, Miss Babette?"

She wiped her nose with her wrist. "I'm working, Mr. Dave."

"It'll just take a minute."

She looked around, then followed me out on the deck. The tables were empty, the sky blue, the wind gusting along the bayou; a black kid was flying a yellow kite above the oaks in front of the old convent. I had the photos of Penny in a manila folder. I opened and flattened it on the deck rail. "You know this guy?"

She stared at Penny's face. Her eyes narrowed. "I ain't sure."

"It's important, Babette."

"A lot of people come in here. At night they all look the same."

"I'm not asking you to appear at a lineup or testify at a trial. This guy has nothing to do with your life. I just want to know if you've seen him."

"I need this job, Mr. Dave. I got a little girl. I ain't got no husband."

"This won't have any effect on your job. I give you my word."

"Maybe he was the guy talking wit' Mr. Spade the night you was in."

"Maybe?"

"Yes, suh," she said, nodding.

"Take another look, Babette."

"I don't need to."

"That's the guy?"

"People look different in the daytime than they do at night. Has this guy done some bad t'ings?"

"A few."

"I don't want to lie to you, Mr. Dave. I just don't want to say no more. I don't never talk about people."

I closed the folder and put it under my arm. "You don't need to say any more, Babette."

"What if he comes back?"

"Don't worry about it."

"That's it?"

"That's it." I patted her on the arm.

"I'm all mixed up," she said. "You're giving me your word, ain't you? Ain't nothing gonna happen?"

"You're not involved."

"What do you call this?" she said.

AT FOUR-FIFTEEN THE same day, Jimmy Nightingale was in my office. The top of my desk was littered with photographs from a hit-and-run fatality on the four-lane south of town. There were bags under Jimmy's eyes, a funky smell in his clothes. "You got to help me out, Dave."

I was about to have another lesson on the number of manifestations that can live in the people we think we know best. "Have a seat."

"Can you talk to my cousin Emmeline?"

"I heard she was your half sister."

"I'm not sure what she is. My father's penis roved over five continents. Tell her I didn't do it. You've known me all my life. I don't rape women, for God's sake."

"People do things when they're drunk that they would never do sober."

"I wasn't that drunk."

"You were drinking and took a married woman on your boat, in this case one who obviously had the hots for you. You think things wouldn't get out of hand in a scenario like that?"

"I know what I did and what I didn't do. She was plastered. She fell down outside the lounge. I had to pick her up and put her in the car. I didn't want to take her back to her car; nor did I want to dump her drunk at her house. So we drove down to Cypremort Point, and I showed her my boat and tried to get some coffee down her."

I thought about the bruise inside Rowena's thigh and the scratches on her hip and wondered if Jimmy was providing a fabricated explanation for them.

"I think you ought to get a lawyer," I said.

"I have a half dozen of them. I don't want this going into a courtroom. I want to work it out."

"By denying you didn't do anything wrong?"

"Right now I just want you to talk to Emmeline."

"Why?"

"Because you're a straight shooter."

"Wish I could help you."

"She and I are close."

"I'm not sure I want to hear what you're telling me."

"You're going to hear it whether you like it or not."

I shook my head. "Nope, this has nothing to do with the issue. Talk to a minister or a therapist, Jimmy. This is the wrong place for it."

"She was in an orphanage in Mexico City. You can imagine what kind of place it was. I'm the center of her life."

I got up from the desk and looked out the window, my back turned to him. "I don't know how this one is going to play out, Jimmy."

"Yeah, you do. I'm innocent, and you goddamn well know it."

"But innocent of what? You say you didn't touch Rowena. Maybe you guys got it on and she got caught and you lied. The defendant claiming consensual sex is a cliché. The change of pace is the best pitch in baseball." I turned around. "You were a master at it, Jimmy."

"Talk to Emmeline."

"Adios. Next time come back with your attorney."

He stood up. His lips were gray. A strand of his hair hung over one eye. "You ever do something really bad, something you can't get rid of? It messes up your thinking."

"What are you talking about?" I asked.

"Hell if I know. Sometimes I think life is a pile of shit. Sometimes I feel like putting my grits on the ceiling."

"Bad way to think."

"I try to be the best guy I can. Most people don't believe that. Do you sleep through the night?"

"I killed people I had nothing against, Jimmy. That one doesn't go away."

"Join the fucking club," he said.

He went out the door and didn't bother to close it. I looked at the photos of the hit-and-run on I-10. The homeless man who was killed was run over by not one but two cars, neither of which slowed down as they ground his body into the asphalt. Who were the drivers? Perhaps someone I'd meet on the street or see in church or watch sacking my groceries and never have a clue.

Chapter 11

Mʏ ʜᴏᴍᴇ ɢʀᴏᴜᴘ of Alcoholics Anonymous met in a small frame house on Center Street right across from old New Iberia High. Most of the regulars were provincial and decent and middle-income people who simply wanted to live better lives, free of alcohol and alcoholism. Their histories were seldom dramatic. Few had been arrested for driving while intoxicated or causing a disturbance in public. Sometimes their sensibilities were tender.

At the meeting, I owned up to slipping, or what we call "going out." The room was dimly lit, the street empty of traffic, a freight train creaking slowly through town on Railroad Avenue. As I told the group how I had found the pirogue wedged against the dock at the foot of my property, and how I had drifted up the bayou and under the drawbridge to the bar-and-grill, I felt the oxygen leave the room. I had years of sobriety. I went regularly to meetings and worked the steps and sponsored other alcoholics, and yet I'd chosen to get drunk again and destroy not only my own life but also the faith and trust of my fellows.

Previously, I had told Alafair that I'd gone out because I'd wanted to. It wasn't quite that simple. I've always believed that alcoholism and depression are first cousins. This isn't an excuse. It's part of the menu. No one who has not experienced clinical or agitated depression, coupled with psychoneurotic anxiety, can appreciate a syndrome that, in an earlier time, was treated with a lobotomy. It's a motherfucker, no matter what you call it or how you cut it. There's blood in your sweat; your head feels like a basketball wrapped with barbed wire; you'd eat a razor blade for a half cup of Jack or a handful of reds or a touch of China white. There's another alternative: the Big Exit, with both barrels propped under the chin, the way Hemingway did it.

For me, the presences that the early Celts tried to keep inside the trunks of trees by knocking on wood always came out in the evenings, particularly in spring and summer, when the crepe myrtle and the pale green of a weeping willow seemed at odds with each other. In the croaking of the frogs, the dying of the light, the tide rising along the banks of the Teche, I felt a sensation like spiritual malaria imprisoning my soul. In an instant the sky would turn to carbon. I think that's why I sometimes went out to Spanish Lake at sunset. I would see the boys in butternut sloshing through the flooded stands of cypress and willows, and somehow their loss became mine, allowing me to join the dead and escape the spiritual death I couldn't describe to others.

I didn't try to explain these things to my friends at the Solomon House meeting in New Iberia, Louisiana. As I spoke, their eyes were downcast, their hands folded in their laps. Their embarrassment and pain were palpable. I did not tell them of the blackout, because I had burdened them enough. After the meeting, they shook hands with me and patted me on the back. I didn't deserve to be in their presence, or at least that was how I felt. I also wondered what they would think if I told them they may have been sitting next to a murderer.

ON SATURDAY MORNING, I walked down to our old redwood picnic table by the bayou, where Alafair was typing on her laptop. The trees were quaking with hundreds of robins, and a blue heron was standing in the shallows, pecking at its feathers. I hadn't intended to disturb Alafair, but she heard my footsteps in the leaves. "Hi, Dave. Just the man I want to see. I started a treatment for a screenplay."

"Really?"

"Levon Broussard wrote a historical novel about his ancestor, a

Confederate soldier who taught a slave girl how to read. It's probably one of his best books, but no one pays it much attention."

I knew nothing of screenplays and had not read Levon's book about his ancestor. "Sounds like an interesting story."

"It would make a great independent film."

"So what's the problem?"

"I didn't ask permission."

"Do high school kids have to ask an author's permission to write a book report about the author's work?"

"It isn't a legal problem unless I go to a producer or director with it or pretend that I represent Levon. I just thought he might be touchy."

"Just tell him what you're doing. If he doesn't like it, put the project aside."

"You don't think he'd mind?"

"He's an admirer of your work. He'll probably be happy."

"How you feeling?" she said.

"Fine."

She searched my face. "No, you're not. You didn't sleep."

"I've had worse problems."

"You didn't kill that fellow, Dave."

"How can you be sure?"

"Because I know you. Your war has always been with yourself, not others. I'm going to find out who's behind this."

"Bad idea. And lay off the analysis, will you?"

"There are people who hate you and will do whatever they can to destroy you. It's foolish to pretend otherwise."

"I don't know how my fingerprints got on Dartez's window glass. Outside of the crime scene, I'd never seen his truck except at his house. I didn't touch it."

"I don't care if your prints were on it or not," she said. "You didn't kill him. You get those thoughts out of your head."

She stared at me boldly, as though words and righteous anger could change reality.

*　*　*

THAT SAME MORNING, Clete put down the top on his Caddy, placed his saltwater rod and reel and an icebox load of beer and food into the backseat, and headed for the Gulf by way of Jennings and the trailer home of Kevin Penny. The shed that housed Penny's dirt bike was scorched by the fire I had set; the curtains were closed on the trailer's windows; there was no sound or movement inside. Clete got out of the car and picked up several pieces of gravel and pinged them one at a time against the trailer.

Penny opened the door in his pajamas, his eyes rheumy, his face unshaved. There was a knot above one eye and an angular orange and purple bruise across his face where I had caught him with the pool cue. "What do you think you're doing, asshole?"

"Want to go fishing?" Clete replied.

"Are you off your nut?"

"Have a beer."

Penny stepped out on the stoop, looking both ways. He was barefoot. A young woman hovered in the shadows behind him, peeking over his shoulder.

"Where's your friend?" he asked.

"Which friend?"

"The one who attacked me with a pool cue."

"I don't know anything about that," Clete said. "Kev, did I ever jam you?"

Penny seemed to consider. "No. What about it?"

"I need your help. I'm being honest, here."

"I got company right now."

"I can see that. She'll understand. Right, lady? Can I borrow Kevin for a couple of minutes?"

"You finally fry your mush?" Penny said.

"You got around in Miami. You knew everybody in the life."

"That was then."

"You know who my daughter is?"

"No, I don't know who your daughter is. I don't give a shit, either."

"Her name is Gretchen Horowitz."

"The fuck."

"That's straight up. She's in Syria making a documentary about the refugees."

"The Gretchen Horowitz I knew blew heads for the greaseballs."

"Nobody's perfect."

Penny pushed the woman back inside and closed the door behind him. "What's the angle?"

"No angle. Your son is going to be with you shortly. We come from the same background, Kev. People knocked us around. When we grow older, we want to get even. Then we see somebody who reminds us of ourselves, and we get mad at them because we think they caused the injuries we had to suffer."

Penny stepped closer to Clete, his nostrils flaring. His eyes were red-rimmed and seemed receded beyond the sockets, as though he lived inside a husk. "You think I'm gonna welcome my kid home by beating him up?"

"You hurt him pretty bad before. Don't tell me you didn't."

"I've been to anger management class."

"That's like managing bone cancer. The people who peddle that stuff are douchebags. It's like listening to Pee-wee Herman talk about weight lifting."

"This from you?" Penny said.

"Yeah, because I'm the dumb asshole who messed up his daughter and made an assassin out of her. I owe her a debt. That's why I'm trying to tell you. Get on the square and do right by your kid."

"I'm gonna take to him to Disney World and Six Flags. I've got a job driving over the road. Maybe I'll take him on the road with me."

What about his schooling? Clete thought. What about the loss of friends his own age? What about the fear that probably lived in him every mile on the road? But Clete knew the situation was hopeless. The boy's fate was probably sealed; the blows to the face and head and back would start a short while after the boy came home.

"Who's the woman in the trailer?" Clete said.

"Miss Prime Cut. You want sloppy seconds? She wouldn't mind."

Penny wasn't being sardonic or ironic. He was serious. Clete felt a rubber band pop behind his eyes. "I don't think we're communicating. My vocabulary isn't up to the job sometimes. Where'd you grow up? Where'd you go to school?"

"Yonkers and the South Bronx. Why?"

"What'd your father do?"

"He was a baker. He made bread. My mother was a seamstress. *What,* you think my parents were trash?"

"No, I don't think that," Clete said.

"So what is this about? We're doing family counseling here? If so, mission accomplished."

Clete pointed at a thicket of persimmon trees on the bank of a coulee that meandered into a dry rice field. "The decomposed body of a black girl was found in there. One of the Jeff Davis Eight."

"I wasn't living around here when that happened."

"I think you were, Kev. I dream about those girls."

"My son and I will bring you a souvenir from Six Flags," Penny said. "Don't be mixing in my family life no more, Purcel. It can bounce back on the wrong people. Like you say, maybe I'll lose it again. Then you'd really have some thumbtacks in your head, wouldn't you?"

Penny went back into the trailer. The young woman stared at Clete like a drowning woman watching a lifeboat paddle away. Penny slammed the door.

I HATED THE THOUGHT of interviewing Rowena Broussard. Her story and behavior were of a kind no ambitious prosecutor wants to touch. The particulars that would come out in the trial were a defense attorney's delight; I knew defense and liability lawyers who would drink out of a spittoon. They would be lining up at Jimmy Nightingale's door.

I made an appointment Sunday afternoon at the Broussard home. Normally, I tried to avoid working on the weekends. But I suspected Levon and Rowena already considered me unfocused and preoccupied, since, like most civilians, they had no idea how many open cases a detective has on his desk at any given moment.

I parked my truck in front of their home on Loreauville Road. The yard had just been cut, the oak leaves ground into tiny gold and red and brown pieces on top of the grass. The hydrangeas were blooming in the shade, the bougainvillea bloodred on the trellises, the posts on the wide steel-gray gallery wrapped with Mardi Gras beads.

Rowena answered the door. She was wearing huaraches and faded jeans low on her hips and a workout halter and a bandana twisted around her brow. Her forearms and the backs of her hands were flecked with paint. She didn't speak. At least not to me. "He's here, Levon!" she shouted over her shoulder.

"May I come in, please?" I said.

"Come in."

"Thank you." I stepped inside. "I need to apprise you of your rights about a couple of things, Miss Rowena."

"Where do you want to do it?"

"Do what?" I said.

"Talk to me or whatever."

"Wherever you like," I said. "You can have a lawyer or a female officer present. Anytime you feel uncomfortable, we can take a break or simply discontinue the discussion. Our intention is to give the prosecutor's office the best information available."

I thought I had been as accommodating as I could. Perhaps I wished she would not cooperate and allow me to drop the investigation. I didn't think I had ever seen a woman look more strangely at the world. She made me think of a thick-bodied, frightened bird trapped in a small cage.

"Levon wants to be with us," she said.

"I'd prefer you and I talk first."

"Go tell him that. He's at the end of the hall."

"Didn't you just call him?" I asked.

"Watch the steps."

The center of the house was raised on pilings, the ornate baths and rooms with tester beds and Levon's office on a lower level. The hallway was long and lined with bookshelves and glass cases containing antique firearms. The woodwork in all the rooms was done with restored century-old cypress and radiated a soft, polished glow like browned butter. Levon's office was enormous and filled with light from the floor-to-ceiling windows. Two big fans circulated slowly on the ceiling; there were bamboo mats on the carpet that creaked dryly under my shoes. Outside, windmill palms and banana fronds and chest-high philodendron were threaded with moisture. I felt I had walked into a 1940s Sydney Greenstreet film.

Levon was bent over the keyboard on his desk, which ran the entire length of one wall, with a crucifix at either end. The Civil War sword that had belonged to his great-grandfather lay next to his computer. He saved the material he was typing and turned around. "Sorry to keep you waiting. If I stop in the middle of a paragraph, I can't put it together again." He looked at the paragraph again. I had to wonder about his priorities.

"Miss Rowena said you'd like to sit down with us. I'm afraid that's not the way we need to proceed."

"Why not?"

"It's embarrassing for the victim. The victim is inclined to hide information. Third parties start interjecting themselves into the issue."

"The *issue*? What kind of talk is that?"

"The kind I use when I speak to an intelligent man whom I'm treating as such."

The skin at the corners of his eyes crinkled. No matter how old Levon grew, he always looked young. He was also an innocent, even though he had worked for Amnesty International and had been jailed in Cuba and Guatemala. But I use the term "an innocent" in a different fashion. Like George Orwell, he believed the human spirit was unconquerable. He also subscribed to Orwell's belief that people are always better than we think they are. But sometimes his idealism and innocence led him into arrogance and elitism.

"Take it easy with her, will you?" he said. "She had a hard go of it last night. Nightmares and such. A black hand coming through a window."

"A what?"

"Nothing. She has bad dreams, Dave. What the hell do you expect?"

"I'll let you know when we're finished," I replied.

He looked back at the page on his monitor, his attention somewhere else.

I returned to the living room. Rowena was sitting in front of a giant brick fireplace and chimney, staring at the ashes caked on the andirons. "You'll have to excuse the way I look. I was painting. Can we go up to my studio?"

I followed her upstairs to a spacious room with huge windows that looked down on the bayou and on live oaks that were so huge and thickly leafed that you felt you could walk across their tops. The sun's reflection on the water was like light wobbling in a rain barrel. She sat down at a card table and wiped at her nose and raised her eyes. "So ask me."

I sat down across from her. "You drank about four Manhattans before you left the lounge?" I said.

"I had a couple of drinks earlier, too, before I went to the supermarket."

"Did you fall down outside the lounge?"

"I don't remember."

"I wondered if you hurt yourself."

"Who said I fell down?"

"This isn't a time to hold back, Miss Rowena. The prosecutor is your ally. Don't let him go into court with incomplete information."

"Jimmy Nightingale told you I fell down? You're saying that's how I got the marks on my body?"

"It's the question others will ask."

"Nightingale put those marks on me," she said. "He's salting the mine shaft, isn't he? What a piece of shit."

"Let me be straight up with you. The defense attorney will probably be a woman. Gender buys jury votes from the jump. She'll say you didn't call 911, you accepted a ride back to your car from the man you claim assaulted you, you didn't go to the hospital, you didn't have a rape kit done, and you showered, taking DNA possibilities off the table."

"I told Levon."

"Told him what?" I asked.

"I told him you'd side with that bloody sod whom people around here think so highly of."

"That isn't how we work, Miss Rowena."

"Stop calling me 'Miss.' I don't like your plantation culture. If your ancestors had their way, we'd all be picking their cotton."

"My ancestors were already picking it. What happened on the boat, Rowena?"

"You didn't hear enough on that video? You know what it's like to be filmed while you describe how someone ran his tongue all over you?"

"Tell me again."

"He shoved me on the bunk. I tried to get up. I was stone drunk and couldn't defend myself. I felt his knees come down on me. He ripped off my panties. Then he did all the things I described on that fucking tape."

Her eyes were misting. The blood had drained from her cheeks into her throat.

"You said you 'felt' his knees on you. That's a funny way to put it."

"I couldn't see. The pillowcase was on my head. He was crushing me alive. His mouth was all over me. I can't keep it straight."

"Take your time."

"I don't want to. I've said it over and over."

"The defense will twist your words. They'll make you contradict yourself, they'll make issues out of minuscule details that have no bearing on anything. They'll create a scenario that has nothing to do with reality, thereby forcing the prosecution to prove that the scenario did not happen. The prosecution will have to prove a negative, which they can't do, hence creating reasonable doubt."

She blew her nose into a Kleenex.

"Nightingale said he tried to give you coffee," I said. "When was that?"

"Coffee? He's the gentleman, is he? There was no coffee. There was only his penis and his tongue. Is that a sharp enough image for you?"

"I'm sorry about this, Miss Rowena. I lost my wife Annie to some killers who used shotguns on her in our bed. I've never gotten over it. I never will." Her face seemed to freeze, as though she could not assimilate what I had said. I closed my notepad. "I appreciate your help today."

She didn't answer. She gazed out the window at the live oaks, the wind channeling through the new leaves, the dead ones tumbling on the bayou's surface.

"Ms. Broussard, are you okay?" I said.

Her teeth were showing when she looked in my direction, but I couldn't be sure she saw me. I walked down the stairs and out of the house, closing the door softly behind me. I was old enough to know that insanity comes in many forms, some benign, some viral and capable of spreading across continents, but I believed I had just looked into the eyes of someone who was genuinely mad and probably not diagnosable, the kind of idealist who sets sail on the *Pequod* and declares war against the universe.

Chapter
12

WHEN I GOT home, there were two messages on the machine from Babette Latiolais. I played the first one: "Mr. Dave, I got to talk wit' you. Call me back."

She didn't leave her number. I copied it from the caller ID. The second message was recorded forty-five minutes later: "Mr. Dave, where you at? I t'ink maybe I seen that guy last night. Please call me. Don't come to the bar-and-grill, no. My boss seen us talking and axed if I was in trouble. I cain't lose my job." I called her number and went immediately to voicemail. I tried again that evening, with the same result.

Clete Purcel returned from two days of fishing, sunburned and flecked with fish blood and smelling of beer and sunblock and weed. He told me about his conversation with Kevin Penny.

"You think he's going to treat his boy all right?" I said.

"Probably not. It was like having a conversation with a septic tank."

"You did your best."

"There's only one solution for a guy like Penny."

I saw the look in his eyes. "Negative on that, Cletus."

"If he hurts that boy, I'm going to bust a cap on him."

"And stack his time. How smart is that?"

"If either one of us was smart, we wouldn't be who we are. Maybe we'd be wiseguys. Or stockbrokers. You got to be careful what you wish for."

I had learned long ago to stay out of Clete's head. If you let him alone, his moods usually passed. If they didn't, you got out of his way.

He showered and put on fresh clothes at his motor court, and he and Alafair and I went to a movie. In the morning I called Babette again. There was no answer. I gave up and this time left no message.

Monday night, just after I had drifted off to sleep, the phone rang in the kitchen. I looked at the caller ID and picked it up in the dark. The moon was up, and a light rain was clicking on the roof and the trees. "Babette?"

"I'm sorry I ain't got back to you," she said. "I moved my little girl to my mama's house in Breaux Bridge."

"Has somebody bothered you?"

"No, suh, but like I said on the machine, I t'ink I seen the man again, the one who was taking to Mr. Spade."

"Where?"

"At the Walmart. He didn't have a basket or nothing. He was maybe t'irty feet away, looking at me. He said, 'Hi, you pretty thing. Come have a hot dog.'"

"You're sure it was the same man?"

"He looked a little different, but I'm pretty sure it was the man in the picture you showed me, the one who was outside the bar-and-grill."

"He was different how?" I asked.

"Like he'd been in a fight."

"Say that again?"

"His face was swole up. I called to tell you everything is all right and you don't need to worry no more. I got ahold of Mr. Spade."

"Back up, Babette."

"He ain't in the phone book, but a waitress I know had his number. So I told him about me talking to you and me seeing the guy again and how I don't want no trouble or to be saying anything bad about nobody."

I could feel the floor shifting under my feet. "Listen to me, Babette.

Don't talk any more with Spade Labiche. Stay away from him. He's not a good guy."

"I ain't supposed to talk to the police?"

"The man with the swollen face is a dangerous and violent career criminal. I don't know why he was with Labiche, but I'm going to find out. What happened after you saw the man at Walmart?"

"Nothing. He just walked away."

"What did Labiche tell you?"

"He said not to worry. He said the guy was just axing him directions and he didn't know nothing about him. That ain't true?"

"It could be," I said.

"It *could* be? Oh, Mr. Dave, what I'm gonna do?"

"If you feel threatened, you can stay with my daughter and me."

"That don't sound right. I cain't live off other people."

I didn't know what to say. Who is usually the victim of a criminal? The most innocent of the innocent, and usually those who can least afford the attrition.

"Are you there, Mr. Dave?"

"I'm going to talk to my friend Clete Purcel. He's a private investigator. If you're with him, no one will ever hurt you. Give me your address."

I WENT INTO LABICHE'S office the next morning. "How you doin', Spade?" I said.

He was drinking coffee from a white mug with Wonder Woman on it. "What's on your mind, Dave?"

"You know Babette Latiolais? She works at the bar-and-grill."

"What about her?"

"She call you?"

He set the mug down. "Yeah, she did. What do you want to know?"

"She's a nice lady, don't you think?"

"Yeah. Nice. Good-looking tits. Probably a sweet piece of barbecue. What else you want to know?"

"Why don't you show some respect?"

"I don't know what it is with you, Robicheaux. You've got a two-by-four with nails in it shoved up your ass every time I see you."

"She saw you with a guy who sounds a lot like Kevin Penny. She doesn't know Penny. She has no connection with Penny. She didn't dime you about Penny. She simply described a man who looks like him. You were talking to him in the parking lot outside the bar-and-grill where she works. What about it? Is Penny a confidential informant?"

"Number one, I never heard of this guy. Number two, if he was my snitch, I wouldn't meet him in a public place."

"I'm glad you've cleared all that up, Spade. I heard you were undercover in Liberty City. How'd you get along with the Jamaicans?"

"Fine. They love the color green."

"You ever see their transporters land in the Glades?"

"A few times."

"Did you know the guys transporting coke on I-10?"

"Most of them were blacks the Colombians used like Kleenex."

"They sure did a number on us. In three years this whole area was full of dope. New Orleans became the murder capital of America."

"What's your point?"

"I was just thinking about the systemic nature of the problem. It's like a virus. Those women who were killed in Jeff Parish all had some relationship to the drug culture. The sales are five-and-dime stuff. All those lives were snuffed out for chump change."

He toasted me with his cup before he drank, his fingers spread across Wonder Woman's patriotically dressed body. "Close the door on your way out, will you?"

Be seeing you later, you lying motherfucker, I thought.

BUT LABICHE HAD little to do with the origins of my anger. Maybe he was on a pad, maybe not. I suspected he was a sociopath. Every organization or institution has sociopaths. The objective is always power. People like Labiche function because they're useful idiots.

Prostitution and drug trafficking cannot exist in a community without sanction. Vice is symbiotic and, like a leech, must attach itself to a cooperative host. That's not hard to do. Once it's established, digging it out of the tissue takes years, maybe generations. The majority of victims are people no one cares about. Even though the street sales seem nickel-and-dime in nature, the aggregate can be enormous. The coke is stepped on half a dozen times before it reaches the projects; the skag might have roach powder in it; the speed comes out of labs at Motel 6. But the number of addicts always grows; it never declines. The health and psychiatric problems of the afflicted are pushed off on social services. The big bonus for the dealers is the female trade. They're compliant and easily managed; they provide freebies for corrupt cops; they're never more than one day away.

Since Prohibition, vice on America's southern rim has been run by individuals and families in Tampa, Miami, New Orleans, and Galveston. When Huey Long gave the state of Louisiana to Frank Costello, slot and racehorse machines appeared in every hotel lobby, drugstore, and saloon in the state, followed by an invasion of pimps, hookers, and even commercial fishers (they worked for the Mob in New Orleans and drained the lakes of crappie and sold them by the hundreds of thousands in Chicago). The system was like a pyramid. Everything at the bottom contributed to the top of the structure. In the life, it's called piecing off the action. A working girl who didn't understand that could get a cupful of acid in the face. I knew a black girl who was soaked with gasoline by two pimps and set on fire.

The minions at the bottom of the organization are myriad and need lead shoes on a windy day. But there is always one person at the top, and only one. In this case, the head guy was a steaming pile of gorilla shit known as Tony Nine Ball. All the elements in this story started with Fat Tony and the Civil War sword he planned to give to Levon Broussard, probably to involve Levon in one of Tony's movie productions.

I told Helen I was checking out a cruiser and also where I was going with it.

"What for?" she said, hardly able to conceal the ennui in her voice.

"I think the deaths of the Jeff Davis Eight are indirectly on Nemo. I think the dope in Iberia Parish is, too."

"What you're really saying is somehow he's connected to the murder of T. J. Dartez. That's what you want to believe, isn't it?"

"If you bruise Tony's ego, he never forgets."

"Do what you need to," she said. "Watch your ass. Tony Nemo is a cruel man."

"Does Spade Labiche have any reason for being around Kevin Penny?"

"Not to my knowledge. You know something I don't?"

I told her how Babette Latiolais had tried to return Labiche's lighter to him in the parking lot outside the bar-and-grill and had seen Penny talking with Labiche.

"Did you bring this up with Labiche?" Helen said.

"He denies knowing Penny or having any connection with him."

"Did you tell him the barmaid informed on him?"

"She had already called Labiche. She knows him from the bar-and-grill. I was trying to put out the fire and indicate to Labiche that the girl wasn't conspiring against him."

"Take a breath."

"It's frustrating, Helen. This guy is a son of a bitch, and you're pretending he's not."

"I'll have a talk with him." She got up from her desk and bit a hangnail, avoiding my eyes. "I'm worried about where the Dartez investigation is going. Your prints were on the broken window glass. How do you explain that?"

"I can't."

She cleared her throat. "This is eating a hole in my stomach."

"Then turn everything over to the prosecutor's office. I'll go on leave without pay or resign."

She looked sideways at me, her face so hot it was almost glowing. "The case isn't prosecutable. Not as it stands. A defense attorney would keep you off the stand and present a dozen ways the prints could have gotten on the glass. That makes me glad. It also puts me in conflict with myself. You're not the only person twisting in the wind, Pops."

"I'm sorry you're caught in this."

"There may be another explanation about the prints," she said. "Latents can be transferred. A microscopic examination can detect a forgery, but not always."

"Labiche is manufacturing evidence?"

"He's a mixed bag," she replied. "He's too nice around me. Always with the grin."

"I'd better get going. I'll be back this afternoon."

"Keep Clete out of this. No more Wild West antics at the O.K. Corral."

"You have to admit Doc and Wyatt had clarity of line."

"White man who think with forked brain not speak anymore. White man keep nose clean and not smart off unless white man want slap upside head. White man now get his ass out of my office."

She wiggled her fingers at me.

I HADN'T THOUGHT ABOUT the possibilities with Clete. After I signed out the cruiser, I stopped in the shade by the grotto and called his office on my cell. "Want to take a ride to the Big Sleazy?"

"What for?"

"To share a few oysters with Tony Squid."

"I'll be out front."

Two minutes later, I pulled to the curb in front of his office. He was wearing his powder-blue sport coat and porkpie hat and freshly ironed gray slacks and tasseled loafers shined as bright as mirrors. His eyes were clear, his face ruddy, his youthfulness temporarily restored, as always when he went twenty-four hours without booze.

"Let's rock," he said. When he pulled open the door, his coat was heavier on one side than the other.

"What's in your pocket?" I asked.

"Lint," he replied.

EVERY WEEKDAY AT noon, Tony could be found at one of two oyster bars in the Quarter, primarily because both had accommodations that could seat a gargantuan blob who had to spread his cheeks across a padded bench or two chairs pushed together. The restaurant also had to accommodate his oxygen cylinder and sometimes a nurse and a retinue of hangers-on and, of course, his bodyguards, Maximo Soza and JuJu Ladrine.

JuJu was half coon-ass and half Sicilian and could do squats with a five-hundred-pound bar across his shoulders. He wore blue suits and ties and starched white shirts, regardless of the heat, and in public always seemed embarrassed and popping with sweat and about to burst out of his clothes.

Maximo was another matter. He had a twenty-two-inch waist and the diminutive features of a child; he had been a jockey in Cuba. He wore a flat-topped gray knit cap with a bill and unironed slacks that flapped like rags and a suit coat buttoned tight at the waist and flared on the hips. He took orders from Tony as if there were no moral distinction between chauffeuring a limo and sticking an ice pick into one of Tony's enemies.

I parked the cruiser in a garage on Royal, and Clete and I walked to the oyster bar and went inside. It was 12:05 P.M. Tony was sitting at a long table in a back corner, the checkered tablecloth set with a pitcher of sangria and baskets of sourdough bread. Maximo and JuJu were not Tony's only companions. The man seated immediately next to him was famous for all the wrong reasons. Plastic surgery had transformed him from a homely Ichabod Crane born in the Midwest to a regal and tragic Jefferson Davis in the twilight of the Confederacy. He had been a leader of the Klan and the American Nazi Party and the friend of every white-supremacist group in the country. Then he discovered religion and was born again and wore his spirituality like a uniform. He had served in the Louisiana legislature and run for the presidency and the United States Senate. Then he went to Russia to promote his latest anti-Semitic book. While he was out of the country, the FBI got a warrant on his house and found his mailing list. He had been selling subscriptions to his racist publications and concealing the income from the IRS. Later, the multicultural nature of the prison shower room was not his favorite conversational subject.

Bobby Earl was his name, and manipulation was his game. During the peak of his career, women who affected the dress of Southern belles lined up to be photographed with him. Then the plastic surgeon's handiwork began to soften and deteriorate and slip from the bone, and Bobby Earl's face took on the appearance of wax held to a flame. His hair fell out, too, and he wore a wig that resembled barbershop sweepings glued to a plastic skullcap. While attending an anti-America/anti-Israel convention in Iran, he was interviewed on CNN and reduced by Wolf Blitzer to a raging idiot while spittle flew from his lips.

The hostess started to seat Clete and me at a small table.

"We're with Mr. Nemo," I said.

"Are you sure? He didn't tell me others would be joining him," she said.

Clete waved at Tony. "Sorry we're late, big guy," he said.

The hostess took us to the table and walked away quickly.

"You don't mind, do you, Tony?" I said.

He looked up from his shrimp cocktail. "We're eating, here."

Clete and I opened our menus. Clete turned to JuJu and Maximo. "What do you guys recommend?"

Neither answered.

"You drink your breakfast, Purcel?" Tony said.

"Actually, I did. A protein shake with bananas and strawberries," Clete said. "You ought to try it."

Tony stuck his finger in one ear and wiped it on the tablecloth. "You followed me in here?"

"We were in the neighborhood," I said. "How's it going, Bobby?"

"I'm fine, thank you."

"*The Advocate* says Jimmy Nightingale is trying to distance himself from you," I said. "I think you're getting a dirty deal."

"Yeah, me, too," Clete said. He hit Earl hard between the shoulders, slanting his wig.

I caught the waiter's attention and ordered iced tea and a dozen raw oysters. Clete ordered a po'boy sandwich and a vodka Collins. A black busboy filled our water glasses and took away an empty bread basket and brought back a full one. Tony called the manager over. "That colored kid don't come close to this table again unless he's got white gloves on, clear?"

"Yes, sir, Mr. Nemo," the manager said, bending stiffly.

"What are you looking at?" Tony said to me.

"Nothing," I replied.

He waited for me to go on, but I didn't.

"You being cute?" he asked. "A play on words or something?"

"Not me," I said.

Clete ordered a second vodka Collins.

"If this has something to do with Bobby, I want you two guys to lay off him," Tony said.

I saw Earl's face color, his pale blue eyes looking straight ahead.

"What are you guys here for?" Tony said. "Don't you talk shit to me, either."

Clete took a long drink from his glass. "We were passing by and happened to see you, and thought you could help us with something. See, there's this ex-con named Kevin Penny, and there's speculation that somebody might have sicced him on Dave for messing up a movie deal with Levon Broussard. You got some movie deals hanging, Tony? I hear your films are great."

Tony's eyes seem to cross as he tried to ingest Clete's words. In the meantime, Bobby Earl seemed to be going through an internal melt-down while he picked through the way Tony had marginalized him. He sipped from his water glass and blotted his lips with his napkin. "I'm not the same person I was when I went to prison. I belong to an evangelical reading group now. I'm trying to make amends for my past life. I think, of all people, you would understand that, Dave. May I call you Dave? You treated me harshly once. But I forgave you. Can you do the same?"

Clete drained his Collins. The waiter began putting our food on the table. "Hit me again on this, will you?" Clete said, pointing to his glass. He looked at Earl. "You walk the walk, Bobby. Fucking A."

People at other tables turned in their chairs.

"Are you mocking me?" Earl said.

"Are you kidding? I always thought Jimmy Nightingale was a fraud and a four-flusher. Look how he treated Tony. He takes the Civil War sword Tony bought to give to Levon Broussard and gives it to Broussard himself. Now he's got a rape beef coming down on his head, and he'll probably give up anybody he can to save his own sorry ass."

"What rape beef?" Tony said.

"A well-known lady has brought charges. You can check out the particulars yourself. This guy Penny says Nightingale has got a cut of the action in Jeff Davis Parish. Maybe elsewhere as well. Now that he's in trouble, maybe he'll give up some names. The guy's NCAA, no class at all."

Tony made a wet sucking sound in his throat. "You think you're smart?"

"I was keeping you up-to-date on your boy Nightingale, Tony," Clete said. "I got to hit the head. Don't choke on that oyster."

"Take this thought with you, smart guy. I bought a bunch of your markers, twenty cents on the dollar. Now you owe me, not the shylock."

Clete stared at him in disbelief.

"Yeah, you heard right," Tony said. "Now go piss."

My cell phone rang. It was Helen, but the connection was bad. I went outside on the sidewalk. The air was cool and dank in the shade, and had a winey smell like old Europe. A garbage truck clattered past. "Helen?" I said.

"Where are you?" she asked.

"In the Quarter, eating lunch with Fat Tony and Bobby Earl."

"What's Earl doing there?"

"Cadging favors."

"You need to get back here."

"What happened?" I said. My head was still pounding with the revelation that a man like Tony the Nose had bought part of Clete's debt.

"Rowena Broussard cut her wrists. She's at Iberia General. She says nobody believes her account of the assault. She's putting it on you and me. Levon is yelling his head off."

"About what?"

"He thinks Iberia General isn't up to his standards. He wants his wife transferred to Our Lady of the Lake in Baton Rouge."

"I'll wrap things up here and head back."

"What's going on with Tony Nemo?"

"Trouble." I looked through the restaurant window. Clete was gone from the table. So were JuJu and Maximo. "I'll call you back," I said.

CLETE WAS STANDING at the urinal when he heard Maximo and JuJu come through the door. A man wearing a suit was urinating next to him. The man zipped his pants and began combing his hair in the mirror.

"Go outside, man," Maximo said.

"Why?" the man said.

"We got to unstop a pipe. You need to be somewhere else."

The man took one look at the expression on Maximo's face and went out the door.

Clete turned on the faucet and watched Maximo and JuJu in the mirror. "Don't do this."

"You got to come out in the alley," JuJu said.

"No, I don't."

"Tony says we gotta talk," Maximo said.

"Tell him to boogie, Max," Clete said. "In six months the state of Louisiana will be installing a pay toilet on Tony's grave."

"What happens later don't change nozzing now," Maximo said. "What you got in your coat pocket?"

Clete squeaked off the faucet and jerked two brown paper towels from the dispenser and dried his hands. "Talk to him, JuJu."

JuJu looked like someone had fitted a garrote around his neck. "I got my job to do, Purcel."

"Bad choice of words," Clete said.

"No, bad choice of everything for you, man," Maximo said.

Clete put a hand into his coat pocket for his blackjack, one that was shaped like a darning sock and weighted with lead and attached to a spring and a wood grip. But Maximo had already clicked on the stun gun he held behind his back. He touched it to Clete's spine, and more than fifteen thousand volts flowed into Clete's body.

Clete felt a pain like a bucket of nails tearing their way through his insides, dropping into his genitals, buckling his knees, and making him speak in a voice he didn't recognize. He pulled himself half erect and tried to swing the blackjack at Maximo's head. It flew from his fingers into the toilet stall. Clete stumbled along the wall, knocking over the trash can, his eyes bloodshot and stinging.

"We ain't finished, man," Maximo said. "It don't do no good to run."

Clete felt the sharp edges of a condom machine. He fitted his fingers around it and tore it loose in a cloud of plaster and smashed it on Maximo's head. JuJu was reaching inside his coat for a small five-shot titanium Colt .38 special he carried in a nylon holster under his coat. Clete drove the condom machine like a cinder block straight into his face.

Maximo lay half upright against the wall. JuJu was bent over the sink, teeth and blood and saliva stringing into his cupped hand. Clete wet a handful of paper towels and pressed them to JuJu's mouth. "Jesus Christ, JuJu! Why'd you guys do this? What's the matter with y'all?"

JuJu spat a tooth into the sink, unable to answer. The door swung back on its hinges. Fat Tony stood in the hallway, one hand propped on his cylinder cart, his lungs wheezing. Two uniformed cops stood behind him. "I got your balls in a vise, Purcel. Your new home is Shitsville. How's it feel, Blimpo?"

Chapter 13

MAXIMO AND JUJU went to the hospital, and Clete went to the can. I called Helen and told her I'd be late getting back to New Iberia.

"What happened?" she asked.

I told her. In detail.

"I don't believe this," she said. "Have you lost your mind?"

"New Orleans does that to you."

She hung up.

In the morning I went to Iberia General to visit Rowena Broussard, less out of concern for her than the fact that she had blamed her attempted suicide on Helen and me.

She was out of intensive care and propped up on the bed in a sunny room that gave onto Bayou Teche and live oaks strung with Spanish moss. Her lips were gray, her face pale, her wrists heavily bandaged. A glass of ice water sat on the table next to her. Water had been spilled on the table.

"Levon just left," she said.

"I came to see *you*," I said.

"I forgot. It's a felony to commit suicide in Louisiana."

"How about losing the victim routine?"

"You're a *hard*-nosed wanker, aren't you."

I sat in a chair next to her bed and picked up her water glass. I held the straw to her mouth. She drank from it and laid her head back on the pillow.

"What's a wanker?" I said.

"A fucking Seppo who doesn't know where to plant his bishop."

I thought it better not to pursue any more Australian definitions.

"I heard you put your suicide attempt on Sheriff Soileau and me," I said.

"You're right. That's probably not fair. There was nothing good on the telly, so I thought I'd shuffle off to the crematorium."

"Were you ever treated for depression?"

"Leave the psychoanalysis at the door, if you would."

"I've had a long relationship with depression, Rowena. It eats at you in ways you can't describe to others."

"That's why you're a juicer?"

"I'm a juicer because I chose to be one."

Her eyes held on mine, perhaps with curiosity. Or disdain. I had no idea who she was. I went to the window and gazed down at the bayou. "A Union flotilla came down the Teche in 1863. Twenty thousand Yankee soldiers marched right past the site of this hospital. They raped slave women and set fire to plantation homes up and down the bayou. Thomas Jefferson said, 'I tremble for my country when I reflect that God is just.'"

"Tell me there's a drop of sense in that, because it sounds like drivel."

"I think Jefferson was saying that justice eventually comes about but often in an imperfect way. I'm saying I don't know if you'll get the justice you deserve."

"You're going to let him get away with this?"

"I didn't say that."

"Maybe there're others he's attacked."

"That's not his reputation."

Wrong words.

"I'm the exception? Just out of nowhere he turns into a rapist?"

"At least that we know about."

"That's a grand explanation. You're not responsible for information you're too lazy to find out about. Lovely."

"Jimmy Nightingale has no history of abusing women. His problem is ambition and besting his father."

"Who, I understand, was a walking penis. This gets better all the time. Would you please get the fuck out?"

I left without saying good-bye. I couldn't blame her for her anger, but I wasn't sympathetic with it, either. She seemed to nurse it as a friend at the expense of others. I believed Rowena Broussard might take up residence in a black box for the rest of her life.

Out in the corridor, I heard the elevator door open, then found myself looking at the last person I expected to see at Iberia General that particular day. He looked fresh and radiant, as though he had just wakened from a good night's sleep and was ready to start a new day. A bouquet of flowers in an electric-blue vase was cradled in his arms.

"Are you going where I think you're going?" I said.

"I couldn't find anybody to bring the flowers up, so I brought them myself," Jimmy Nightingale said. "Will you take them the rest of the way?"

"I just got eighty-sixed. I wouldn't advise going in there."

"That bad, huh?"

"What do you expect?" I said.

"She knows what happened or, rather, what didn't happen. I think she's a bit of a thespian. Is Levon here?"

"No!"

"I'll toggle in and toggle back out."

"Leave her alone, Jimmy."

"Sorry." He started to walk around me.

"I'm speaking to you as an officer of the law. You're not going into that room."

"You're showing poor form, Dave."

"If you go in there, you're going to be under arrest."

"Then you'd better get your handcuffs out."

The elevator door opened again. Levon Broussard stepped into the corridor. He remained motionless, staring at us, his lanky frame backlit by a window. His face was as empty as a bread pan. He walked toward us, his eyes never leaving my face, completely ignoring Nightingale. "Why is this lizard standing in front of my wife's hospital room?"

PEOPLE ARE WHAT they do, not what they think, not what they say. But I think we all have moments when we realize we never quite know a person in his or her totality.

"I brought your wife flowers," Nightingale said. "I'd appreciate your not referring to me in a derogatory way."

Levon didn't take his eyes off me. "Get him out of here, Dave."

"Everything is under control here," I said, raising my hand.

"Only a psychopath would do something like this," Levon said.

"Give us a minute here," I said.

"No, I will not," Levon said.

"You don't know how much I admire your novels and your wife's art," Nightingale said. "Drunk or sober, I would never do either of you harm. For God's sake, use reason, man."

Levon watched a black custodian drag a wheeled bucket of soapy water down the corridor. Then he looked at Nightingale and the electric-blue vase and the roses inside it. "Thank you, sir. I'll take care of those."

His fingers were and long and tapered, like a pianist's or a basketball player's. He took the vase from Nightingale and walked to the elevator and pushed the button. When the doors opened, he lobbed the vase inside and watched the doors close again. He walked past us to the custodian and handed him a crisp fifty-dollar bill. "I had an accident in the elevator," he said. "Sorry to make trouble for you."

"It's all right, suh," the black man said.

Then Levon turned around and walked calmly toward Nightingale and me.

"Whoa," I said.

"Woe unto thyself," he replied.

He grabbed Nightingale by the lapels and crashed him into the wall, pinning him against it, staring straight into his eyes. Then he gathered all the spittle in his mouth and spat it in Nightingale's face.

I placed my hand on Levon's arm. "That's enough."

He released Nightingale and stepped backward. I moved between him and Nightingale. "Let's go, Jimmy."

Nightingale wiped his face on his sleeve. His skin was discolored, as though it had been freeze-burned; his eyes were full of tears.

"Did you hear me?" I said. "I'll walk with you to your car."

"Yes, let's do that," he replied.

I rested my hand on his shoulder. "We'll take the stairs."

"That would be fine." He started to look back.

"Step along now," I said.

"It's funny how things can go amiss, isn't it? A wrong word here, a misunderstanding there. I don't think I'll ever quite get over this."

"Let it slide, Jimmy."

"There's nothing like moralizing at the expense of another, is there? I must learn the art of it."

I accompanied him to his car and then went back to the office.

CLETE CALLED JUST before noon. Maximo and JuJu hadn't filed charges. Clete had paid a fine at guilty court and was back on the street. "I'll be in New Iberia this afternoon."

"Did Tony Nemo actually buy your markers?"

"If he did, he screwed himself. I already paid them off."

"I don't think Fat Tony will see it that way."

"He's one step away from worm food and knows it. You know what I think? Every one of these bastards is scared shitless of dying."

The gospel according to Cletus Purcel.

THAT EVENING BROUGHT rain and an ink-wash sky and the throbbing of hundreds of frogs. The air was sweet and cold, and I put on a jacket and opened a can of sardines and poured the juice on top of Tripod's old hutch and set the can inside, next to a bowl of water, careful not to get the smell on my hands or clothes. Then I sat in a big wooden deck chair outfitted with water-resistant cushions and watched the light go out of the sky and the shadows disappear from the bayou's surface and the alligator gars rolling like serpents on the edge of the lily pads.

The house was dark except for Alafair's bedroom, where she was working on her film adaptation of Levon Broussard's Civil War novel. Boys who had been playing softball in the park had left for the evening, and one by one the floodlamps above the diamond clicked off. I felt my eyes closing and a great fatigue seeping through my body, one that I did not argue with, in the same way that, at a certain age, you do not argue with the pull of the earth. In my dream, I saw the boys in tattered gray and butternut brown marching through the trees in the park, a sergeant with a kepi canted on his brow high-stepping and counting cadence. I walked along beside them and spoke to them in both English and French, once again expecting them to pass by without acknowledging me. But this time was different. They were gesturing, waving me into their ranks.

Now? I said.

What better time? the sergeant said. His cheeks were spiked with blond whiskers, his uniform sun-faded and stiff with salt, white light radiating from a hole in his chest.

I have a daughter who needs me.

We all get to the same place. She'll be joining us one day as well.

You wouldn't talk like that if you had a daughter.

I had a son, though. The blue-belly who put a ball through my heart didn't care about him or me.

If God had a daughter, I bet He wouldn't have let her die on a cross.

Then perhaps you belong among the quick. Right you are, sir. Top of the evening to you.

The column disappeared inside the fog. I felt a weight bounce sharply on my lap and tumble off my knees. I thought I had wakened, then realized I was still dreaming, because I saw a raccoon waddling through the leaves, his furry tail flicking like a fat spring. I fell deeper into my sleep, into a place that was cool and warm at the same time, when the year was 1945 and people in my community spoke only

French and on festival days danced under the stars with the innocence of medieval folk.

Someone shook my arm, hard and steady. "Wake up, Dave."

I looked up at Alafair's face.

"Better come in before you get rained on," she said.

I stood up, off balance. "What a dream."

"You were laughing."

"I thought a big coon jumped in my lap."

"Better take a look at your trousers."

The muddy paw prints were unmistakable. There was a gummy smear on one thigh. I touched it and smelled my fingers.

"What is it?" she said.

"Sardines."

"Maybe he got in somebody's trash."

"Coons don't jump in people's laps."

"Tripod did," she said.

"He sure did. How you doin', Alfenheimer?"

"Why are you acting so weird?"

"I'll take weird over rational any day of the week," I said.

THE NEXT DAY, I went to the office of the Broussard family physician, Melvin LeBlanc. "Now what?" he said.

"Rowena cut her wrists right above the palms," I said.

"Yes?"

"If you're serious about going off-planet, you do it higher up, don't you?"

"People are not in a rational state when they try to take their lives," he replied.

"Am I right or not, Doc?"

"They do it here." He drew two fingers high up on his inner fore-arm. He gazed innocuously out the window.

"Is there something else you want to tell me?"

"No."

"Let me rephrase. Is there something else you *feel* I should know?"

"I'd like to have you banned from my office. How about that?"
I held his eyes.

"Rowena had medical training in Australia," he said. "She nursed Indians in South America. What we used to call meatball medicine."

"She wasn't serious about getting to the barn?"

"This doesn't mean she wasn't assaulted."

"Thanks for your time," I said.

Chapter
14

THAT NIGHT, ALAFAIR played tennis with friends at Red Lerille's Health & Racquet Club in Lafayette. The night was black, the lights over the courts iridescent with humidity, the whocking sounds of tennis balls and the huffing and shouts of the players a celebration of spring and rebirth. When Alafair's friends quit for the evening, she wiped herself off with a towel and began hitting on the backboard. A woman in a pleated tennis skirt and a white sweater cut off at the armpits, with black hair pulled back as tightly as wire, walked up behind her, spinning the shaft of a racquet in her left palm. "Like to have another go at it?"

"Pardon?" Alafair said.

"You're Alafair Robicheaux. I recognized you from the photo on your book jacket."

"Yes," Alafair said.

"I'm Emmeline Nightingale."

"Are you—"

"Jimmy Nightingale's cousin and bookkeeper. My partner didn't show. I was hoping to hit a few."

"I was about to head back to New Iberia."

"Maybe another time, then. Your last book was marvelous."

"Thank you."

"I read you graduated at the top of Stanford Law. Look, I didn't mean to do anything inappropriate. I know who your father is, and I know he's talking to Jimmy about some legal matters."

"No, that has nothing to do with my situation," Alafair said.

"Well, anyway, I wanted to introduce myself and tell you how much I admire your writing. Damn it, I wanted to play tonight."

"If you like, we can volley a bit."

Emmeline went to the far end of a nearby court and began dancing on the balls of her feet. Alafair went to the baseline and bounced the ball once, then hit it leisurely across the net. Emmeline returned it in the same way, smiling, showing no sense of competitiveness, making sure the return always went to Alafair's forehand. Then, for no apparent reason, she swung the racquet hard, rolling it with her wrist and top-speeding the ball so it scotched the surface of the court and flew past Alafair's reach.

"Good shot," Alafair said, ignoring the breach of protocol.

"Sorry, I was still thinking about my partner not showing up," Emmeline said.

They stroked the ball back and forth, then Alafair hit to Emmeline's left side and advanced on the net, intending to create a routine pepper game. Emmeline returned the ball with a two-arm backhand that slashed the ball like a BB into Alafair's face.

Alafair lowered her racquet and pressed her wrist to her mouth. Emmeline ran to the net. "Are you all right? I'm sorry. I don't know why I did that."

"I'm fine," Alafair replied. "You didn't know I was coming to the net. It's my fault."

"Here, let me see," Emmeline said. "Your lip is cut. Let's go inside. I'll get some ice."

"It's nothing."

"Let's have a cold drink. Please. I feel awful."

"Really, I'm okay."

"Please," Emmeline said.

Alafair slipped the cover onto her racquet and zipped it up. She looked at her automobile in the lot. Emmeline touched a Kleenex to

Alafair's chin and showed it to her. "Come on, we have to take care of that."

AFTER ALAFAIR WENT to the restroom, she joined Emmeline in the health bar. Emmeline ordered iced fruit drinks for them and put the charge on her bill. "I took a chance: You like strawberries and pineapple, don't you?"

"Sure."

"The ice will stop the swelling. Go ahead. Drink."

Alafair looked at Emmeline's reflection in the mirror. The woman's face was flushed, her breath short, as though from exertion or excitement.

"You seem a little tense," Alafair said.

"I have a confession to make."

"What's that?"

"I recognized you not only from your photo but from the university library. You were asking the reference librarian about Civil War maps and the Union occupation of southwestern Louisiana. You told her you were writing a screenplay."

"That's true."

"Can I ask about what?"

"Reconstruction and the White League and a Confederate veteran who teaches a former slave girl to read and write."

"What's the White League?"

"The Klan were amateurs in comparison. The White League took over New Orleans in 1872 and shot James Longstreet."

"You know what the story sounds like?"

Alafair didn't answer.

"Levon Broussard's Civil War novel based on his ancestors."

"Could be," Alafair said.

"It is, isn't it?"

"In Hollywood, historical stories are called period pieces; they're toxic. Think *Cold Mountain*. I'm doing what's called a treatment. It's a lark more than anything."

"I think Levon Broussard's novel is a great book. The first movies were westerns, weren't they? At some point movies will have to go back to their origins, won't they?"

Alafair pushed her drink back toward the edge of the bar. She touched her lip. "I think I've stopped bleeding."

"Do you have a formal situation with Levon?"

"Maybe you should ask him."

"I would except for that Australian bitch he calls a wife."

Alafair looked at her watch. "I'd better be going."

Emmeline moved her hand on top of Alafair's. " 'Bitch' is kind. She's trying to ruin my cousin's life."

"I'll be leaving now, Miss Emmeline."

Emmeline worked her fingers around Alafair's hand. Her skin felt moist and hot, her fingers squeezing like tentacles. "Hear me out. Regardless of what people say, Jimmy has a tender conscience. He worries over things other people wouldn't give a second thought about. You ever hang around the CEOs in the oil business? They let others do their dirty work."

"I'm not sure what we're talking about. Please release my hand."

"Sorry. Meet this collection of shits and tell me how you like it. You have no idea what they do in the third world."

Alafair couldn't track the sequence. She got off the stool. "Dave worries about me."

"Then call him."

"Be seeing you around, I'm sure."

Emmeline's eyes seem to take Alafair's inventory. "Top of your class at Stanford Law. That's impressive. But somebody has to do it, right?"

"Not necessarily."

Alafair went out the glass doors and didn't look back; she felt a rivulet of blood running from one nostril. When she started her car, her heart was thudding in her ears, as though evil could insinuate its way into a person's life without consent.

*　*　*

IN THE MORNING, I received a call from the coroner, Cormac Watts.

"What's with your colleague?" he said.

"Which colleague?"

"Spade Labiche."

I looked through the glass on my office door. As coincidence would have it, Labiche was passing by. He cocked his thumb and index finger like a pistol and aimed it at me, winking.

"What about him?" I asked.

"I called him twice and left messages he didn't bother to answer. I had additional information to give him on the T. J. Dartez autopsy. Maybe it's insignificant, maybe not."

"What kind of information?"

"I know there's a bull's-eye painted on your back, Dave. I wanted to get all the information right, including the possibility that Dartez was a bad guy and responsible for your wife's death, even though that's not my job."

"Go on," I said.

"The bloodwork showed he was legally drunk when he expired. His wife said he was an epileptic and took anti-seizure medication and wasn't supposed to drink, but he drank anyway, and a lot. She also said he knocked her around. Anyway, I wanted to pass on the info, but the department's affirmative-action homophobe doesn't seem interested."

"You left this on his machine?"

"Enough so he would know it's important."

"I'll get back with you shortly," I said.

I hung up and went into Labiche's office. The message light on his phone was blinking. "Got any problem talking with Cormac Watts?" I asked.

"Not as long as he stays off our toilet seats," he replied.

"How's it feel?"

"How does what feel?"

"Being you. A full-time shithead."

"You're way out of line, Robicheaux."

"Try this: You're ignoring forensic evidence in a homicide investigation. You're queering the prosecution's case before it ever hits the prosecutor's desk."

"Queering?"

"It's the old term for screwing up or delegitimizing."

"I've got to remember that. You're a mountain of information, Robo."

"I'm going to give you five minutes to haul your sorry ass into Helen's office and tell her what you've got."

"I'll think about it."

I walked to his desk and picked up the receiver from his phone. I thunked it into the middle of his forehead and replaced it in the cradle. His cheeks drained; a pink half-moon pulsed under his hairline. "Five minutes," I said.

THAT NIGHT I tried to reach into the blackout where I had disappeared from the world of normal people. Experience had taught me that chemically induced amnesia has no cure. Your memory does not return at a convenient time; you do not walk from an airless black cell in Alcatraz's infamous D block into sunlight and rationality. In all probability, you have permanently destroyed thousands of brain cells, just as though you had struck yourself in the head with a ball-peen hammer. But sometimes the problem is psychological rather than neurological. If so, there is a way you can unspool the nightmare that your conscious mind might not want to accept. Unfortunately, the method is imperfect and dangerous. You can become convinced you have committed horrific acts when in fact you have not.

Your ordinary dreams can contain bits and pieces of a larger event, in my case, an encounter with T. J. Dartez on a narrow two-lane parish road out by Bayou Benoit. The process is like reassembling a sheet of gray and black stained glass fallen from a church window to a flagstone floor. For me, that meant images flashing like a kaleidoscope deep down inside my sleep—the glare of headlights in my rearview mirror, a vehicle gnashing against my bumper, fences and weeds whirling around me, the leering face of an unshaved man with greasy black hair and nails rimmed with dirt, his eyes lit by the fires of stupidity and ignorance and rage.

In none of my dreams, however, was I striking a man with my fists or choking or stomping and kicking him. How could I have killed a man with my bare hands, or with a club, and not have any trace of the crime in my unconscious? I wanted to believe I had set myself free. But I didn't. Another image remained with me, one that had nothing to do with the event by Bayou Benoit. Instead, I saw him behind the wheel of his truck, his tires squealing around the curve that led to the intersection Molly was entering, his face dilated and drunk with the power the pedal transferred up his leg and into his genitals. I wanted to kill him even worse than I had wanted to kill Mack, the man who helped destroy my family. I wanted to break his bones and destroy his face with my fists. I wanted to do other things I will not describe. I harbored emotions that no Christian should ever have. But they were mine. I owned them. And they still lived within me, even though T. J. Dartez was lying on a slab, as cold and bloodless as stale lunch meat.

Was I capable of the homicide out by Bayou Benoit? You tell me.

Chapter
15

SATURDAY MORNING, I put out another can of sardines for our raccoon friend, whom I named Mon Tee Coon. I had not heard Alafair come in from Red's health club the night before. She walked up behind me, a mug of coffee in her hand. She was wearing white shorts and a long-sleeve denim shirt with the tails hanging out. She told me about her encounter with Emmeline Nightingale. "She's a little otherworldly."

"A human icicle?" I said.

"She has dirty eyes."

"You think she hit the ball in your face deliberately?"

"That's what I felt like after I talked with her. She's a controller. She also seems to have an obsession with oil companies. What's the story on that?"

"Jimmy has a degree in geology. He worked in South America awhile. The Nightingales have their fingers in lots of pies."

She sat down in a white-painted wooden chair near Tripod's hutch. The sky was blue and as shiny as silk. Leaves from the live oaks were tumbling on her hair and skin. I couldn't believe she was the little girl I'd pulled from the cabin of a submerged plane.

"She left me with a disturbing sensation," Alafair said. "One I couldn't shake driving home."

"Like what?"

"Evil."

"You think she's going to call you?"

"Probably. She seems interested in the treatment I'm doing on Levon Broussard's Civil War novel."

"Maybe that's a project you should drop, Alf."

"Because of her?"

"Because it's going to drag you into contact with Levon and his wife. I think Rowena Broussard is a sick person."

"You don't believe she was raped?"

"She's an unhappy person who has a tendency to work out her problems on the backs of other people."

"That's two thirds of Hollywood," she said.

"Did you talk to Levon about the treatment?"

"On the phone. He said it was fine with him, but he thought it was a waste of time."

"What do *you* think?"

"It's really good. The battle scenes at Shiloh, the Yankee occupation, the story of the slave girl and her white father who founded Angola Prison."

"Why hasn't someone adapted it?"

"Confederates are the new Nazis. Have you seen the raccoon again?"

"Not yet. He'll be back," I said.

"Are you okay, Dave?"

"You bet."

"Shit," she said. "Shit, shit, shit."

"Don't use that kind of language, Alf."

She put down her coffee mug and stood up and hugged me and pressed her face into my shoulder. I felt the wetness in her eyes.

"What's this about?" I said.

She wiped her eyes on my shirt.

"Answer me, Alafair."

"I hate what they're doing to you," she said. "I'd like to shoot every motherfucking one of them."

"Don't use that language in our home."

She hit me, again and again, her fists bouncing on my chest.

THE SOCIAL WORKER in Jennings was named Carolyn Ardoin. She was a matronly white-haired woman with lovely skin and a blush on her cheeks and soft hands. When Clete's cell phone woke him up at 8:05 on Monday morning, he was surprised by how happy he felt to receive her call. He had met her only once, in her office, to talk about Kevin Penny's eleven-year-old boy. Their conversation had been all business, with little time to speak of anything other than the child's safety. But her perfume and her manner and the freshness of her clothes lingered with him.

"I hope I didn't call too early, Mr. Purcel," she said.

"No, ma'am, I was just about to head to the office."

"I'm probably not supposed to make this call, but you're such a nice man, and I know you want to be apprised of Homer's situation." She paused as though reluctant to continue. "We're reinstating him with Mr. Penny today."

"At the trailer?"

"Yes, a little earlier than I expected. But if not now, we would be taking him there later, and the circumstances wouldn't be any different."

"What time today?"

"At noon sharp."

"This troubles me, Miss Carolyn. Mightily." Why had he used such a strange word?

"Mr. Purcel?"

"Yes?"

The time seemed to drag like a chain down a stairs. "I'm terribly perturbed about this placement," she said finally.

"I'm going to drop by the trailer."

"I know you're a good man. But don't be confrontational with him. You know whom he'll punish."

"I'll call you later," he said. "I promise everything will be all right."

"No, it won't. But you're kind to say that. You're a good man, sir."

He felt a blooming sensation in his chest that he couldn't explain.

Clete drove to Lafayette and made a purchase at a sporting goods store, then got on I-10 to Jennings. Homer Penny had no memory of his mother, a meth addict and an attractive black prostitute whom her husband, Kevin, pimped out to middle-class white men from Lake Charles and Lafayette, including a well-known physician. Homer seldom spoke and always looked uncertain or frightened, as though standing in a canoe or pirogue, about to topple into a bayou filled with snakes. He had big ears and blue eyes and pale gold skin with big brown freckles like human camouflage. Clete could never get him to smile.

Clete pulled up in front of the trailer at 11:45. The dirt bike was gone. At noon a man in a state car came up the track, bouncing in the potholes, the passenger's head barely visible above the dashboard. The passenger wore horn-rimmed glasses and a hand-folded paper hat, and had big ears and a tiny nose and a thin face and slits for eyes and made Clete think of a baby seabird peeping out of a nest. The driver parked and got out. He wore a dark blue coat that had dandruff on the shoulders. "You Mr. Purcel?"

Clete climbed out of the Caddy, a shopping bag in his hand. "I am."

"I'm Herb Smith. With the state. Miss Carolyn said you'd be here. Looks locked up."

"It is."

Smith twisted his wrist to read his watch. "Three minutes to noon." He squeezed his eyes shut and clicked them open again, like the eyelids on a mechanical doll.

"*What?*" Clete said.

"Some days I hope certain people don't show up."

"I brought something for Homer," Clete said. He opened the sack so Smith could see inside. "You mind?"

"No, sir, go right ahead."

Clete removed an Astros baseball cap and a softball and two gloves. "How about it, pal?" he asked the boy.

"I never played," the boy said, his gaze askance.

"We're going to change that. You get over there, and I'll start lobbing them to you. Then you fireball them back."

The boy couldn't catch with a wheelbarrow. He tripped and fell down when he ran after the ball. He couldn't throw thirty feet.

"Tell you what," Clete said. He went back to the Caddy. "I got you a bat. I'll pitch 'em, you hit 'em."

Homer missed the first two pitches, clipped the third, and hit the fourth squarely, ripping it across the grass. The welfare man from the state volunteered as catcher. It was 12:26.

"Do I have to stay here, Mr. Clete?" the boy said.

"For a time. Mr. Smith and Miss Carolyn and I will be looking in on you."

The boy swung the bat at nothing. At 12:37 they heard the whine of a dirt bike. The boy's face drained. Clete saw Smith mouth the words "Son of a bitch."

Kevin Penny cut the gas feed and coasted up to the Caddy. He had a backpack. He pulled on the neck of his T-shirt and wiped his nose with it. "The big three. Or call it the two and a half."

"I need your signature and I'll be gone," Smith said.

"What day of the month does the check come?" Penny said.

"Pardon?"

"It's supposed to be in the agreement. The amount and the date of delivery."

"I think you'll find everything in order," Smith said.

"Oh, hell yes," Penny said. He unslung his pack and walked past his son to the porch, grinding the Astros cap into the boy's scalp. Penny sat on the top step and opened a can of Bud and began tearing apart a rotisserie chicken from his pack and eating it with his hands. "Don't let me stop you."

Clete pitched the ball to Homer, but the boy let the bat stay on his shoulder and watched the ball drop into the dirt.

"Strike one," Penny said.

Clete took off his fielder's glove and walked to the porch. He curled the glove into a cone and tucked it between Penny's thigh and the railing. "There's Little League ball in Jennings."

"Reach me those napkins in my pack, will you?" Penny said.

Clete didn't answer. Penny said something with his mouth full of meat.

"What's that you say?" Clete asked.

Penny cleared his throat and laughed. "I thought that perfumed cunt from the welfare office would be here. Instead I get you."

"I'll be running along now."

"Want a thigh?" Penny raised the chicken and the grease-pooled foil to Clete's face.

Clete walked to the Caddy, a sound in his ears like tank treads clanking or the mewing of barnyard animals caught inside an unbearable flame. He bent down to Homer. "I'll be back to see you, pal. I'm on your side. So are Miss Carolyn and Mr. Smith."

The boy was not listening. His eyes were wide, his bottom lip trembling, as he stared at his father.

Clete could remember little of driving back to New Iberia. Nor could he remember when he'd had a sadder day or a greater sense of foreboding.

That afternoon helen caught me in the corridor. "In my office, Dave."

I followed her inside and shut the door.

"The prosecutor is on my butt about the Dartez investigation," she said.

"He doesn't like how it's going?"

"He thinks you should be on the desk."

"Remind me of that, come the next election."

Helen was silhouetted against the window, her face covered with shadow. I didn't know if I had made her angry or not.

"I made a mistake assigning Labiche to the case," she said. "He wants your job."

Finally, I thought.

"I talked to a couple of people in Dade and Broward Counties. They said he took freebies in Liberty City, but that's about all they knew of."

"Any vice cop who'll take freebies will take money."

"In this instance there's no evidence of that," she said.

"Come on, Helen, if a cop is dirty, he can be blackmailed. He can also be killed."

"All right," she said, giving up.

She had gone to extraordinary lengths for me many times; I took no pleasure in her concession. "Helen, I think everything we're talking about is much bigger than Labiche or me or T. J. Dartez or Jimmy Nightingale. I think it has to do with narcotics, with all the trafficking that starts in Florida and comes straight down I-10 into our midst."

"The crack trade in Jefferson Davis Parish isn't the big score, Dave."

"We're the Walmart of the drug culture. Kids deal dope while they line up to go to a movie."

Her face was still in shadow. "I don't think the Dartez homicide is prosecutable, at least not at this point. I'm telling that to the prosecutor and leaving it in his hands. Prepare yourself."

"For what?"

"We'll be accused of covering up. Look at me, Dave."

I knew what was coming.

"Tell me you didn't do it. Or at least tell me that deep in your heart, you believe you didn't do it."

"I can't do that."

"Goddamn it," she said.

"Don't swear."

She turned her back to me and stared out the window. The wind was blowing in City Park, the boughs of the oak trees swirling, a motorboat towing a water-skier, furrowing the bayou. I wanted to say something of a consoling nature, but I had nothing to offer.

* * *

CLETE PURCEL NORMALLY referred to cop shows on television as "the most recent shit Hollywood is foisting on really stupid people." Clete's intolerance aside, the facsimile has little to do with the reality. Probably one third of cops are dedicated to the job; one third eat too many doughnuts; and one third are people who should not be given power over others. Female detectives do not show off their cleavage. Many cops carry a drop or a throw-down. Cops plant evidence and lie on the stand. In our midst are sadists and racists who taint the rest of us. And the greatest contributor to solving crimes is not the lab but the informant, usually someone who skipped toilet training and couldn't make a peanut butter sandwich with a diagram.

For Clete, at least in the Acadiana area, that man was Pookie the Possum Domingue. Pookie had the eyes and snout of his namesake and walked in the same unsteady, desultory fashion, his head wobbling on his spindle of a neck. Years ago he was a gofer for the Teamsters in Lafayette when they were cheating their own members out of their union books. He also racked balls in Antlers Pool Hall and did scut work for a bail bondsman, shilled for the card dealers in the old Lafayette Underpass area, and washed money with No Duh Dolowitz at Evangeline Downs and the Fairgrounds. But his great talent lay in what he called "research." Though the Internet had put most PIs out of work, Pookie was unfazed. His knowledge of the netherworld could be matched only by the caretakers of the La Brea Tar Pits.

He called Clete at his office on Tuesday morning. "Is that you, Purcel?"

"Who's this?"

"You keeping your plunger under control?"

"All right, wise guy, if this is who I think it is—"

"Dial it down. I got some information for you. I was in Sticks this afternoon."

"*Where?*"

"Sticks Billiards. In Lafayette. We got a bad connection here?"

"I know where you live, Pookie. Smart off one more time, and I'm going to stuff you into a hamster cage."

"I'm only axing for a little respect here."

"I apologize. But I don't need termites in my building or in my head. Now, what do you want?"

"I was shooting some eight ball, taking down this blimp with an ass on him like a washtub, when guess which two clowns come through the door and blow my action. To be more specific, guess which two guys announce to everybody in the place, 'Hey, Pookie, glad to see you're not eighty-sixed no more. Leave us the bones.'"

"Sorry I missed this world-shaking event," Clete said.

"Put the cork in it, Purcel. It was JuJu and Maximo. Both of them look like somebody tried to screw their heads into a fire hydrant."

"That breaks me up."

"Maybe it should. Because the first thing they ax is if I've seen you around. I told them you got an office in New Iberia. So Maximo says, 'No, that ain't what we axed. We don't need nobody to tell us how to use the phone book. We're axing where that fat shit hangs out. Where's he get his knob polished, that kind of thing.'"

"Somebody put you up to this?"

"I'm trying to do a favor here."

"The last favor you did was to talk your mother out of committing suicide because she defecated you into the world."

There was a pause. "I'll say this once. JuJu ain't a bad guy. The tomato picker with him has done eight or nine contract hits. The word is Tony the Nose bought your markers. If that's true, pay him or find an igloo on the North Pole."

"There're no Eskimos on the North Pole."

"You can be the first."

The line went dead.

Clete took his .38 snub from its holster and flipped out the cylinder, rotating it idly with his thumb. What to do? Nothing. Let them come to him. There was nothing like a bullet in the center of the forehead to get your point across.

His thoughts were self-serving, and he knew it. The guy who blew out your wick was always a nasty little hornet like Maximo, a disposable psychopath who watched Saturday-morning cartoons and had a three-hundred-pound mistress whose lap he sat in for a photograph and then put the photo on the Internet.

Clete found the business card that Carolyn Ardoin had given him and dialed the cell number on it. "I thought I'd ring and let you know I'll be checking on Homer as often as I can," he said.

"Mr. Smith told me you bought Homer a ball and glove and bat. That was probably one of the best gifts that boy ever had."

"I happened to see them on sale."

"I don't think you give yourself enough credit, Mr. Purcel."

Clete couldn't remember why he had called. Or maybe he did. It wasn't easy to talk to normal women. "Is the weather pretty nice over there?"

"In Jennings?" she said.

"Yeah, it's a couple parishes over from us. I wondered if the weather was the same."

"I'm pretty sure it's like yours in New Iberia."

"It's a swell day here."

"Are you worried about Homer?"

"I was also wondering, you know, are you a married lady? I mean, I didn't see you wearing a wedding ring."

"You saw correctly. I am not married. I was widowed when I was twenty-three."

"I've enjoyed our talks and meeting you," he said. "Three or four times a year I go fishing thereabouts. South of Jennings, I mean."

"Are you trying to tell me something, Mr. Purcel?"

"I was wondering if you like movies."

"I love them," she said.

"There're some good ones playing in Lafayette. There's a dinner club close by that I'm fond of, too."

"I think I know the place."

"Miss Carolyn, could I motor on by your home this evening?"

"I'd like that very much, Mr. Purcel."

*   *   *

THEOLOGIANS CALL IT the calculated testing of others' charity. By some it's considered a serious sin. But for someone who is manipulative or morally insane, it's not a big obstacle.

Early that same morning, Alafair entered the grounds of the Shadows-on-the-Teche, an enormous pillared twin-chimney two-story brick home built in 1834, and today a National Trust historic site that tourists file through seven days a week. But for Alafair, the Greek revival splendor and the magnificent oaks and gardens and piked fence and bamboo borders had another meaning. Regardless of the time of year—even in spring, when the petals of the azaleas were scattered on the grass and the sunlight was transfused into a golden-green presence inside the canopy of live oaks—the rooms of the house remained cold and damp, the lichen on the trees and flagstones and birdbaths and even the tombs of the original owners a testimony to the decay and slow absorption of man's handiwork on the earth. As Alafair sat on a stone bench in the coldness of the shade, she wondered why the glossy brochures at the entrance said nothing about where the slaves were buried, all 164 of them, nameless souls who at best were spared the lash and fed on a daily basis in the same spirit that one feeds chattel.

The house was occupied by General Nathaniel Banks's command in 1863 and figured prominently in Levon Broussard's novel set during the Civil War and Reconstruction. Farther down Main Street stood the Episcopalian church that served as a battalion aid station for Confederate wounded, then was commandeered by General Banks and the pews pushed together to form troughs for Yankee cavalry. The partial remains of at least two gunboats still lay under the quiet surface of the bayou. The locale was a postcard snipped right out of a history that, for good or bad, you could place your hand on and feel its heart beating.

Alafair looked up from her notebook and saw a woman in a bro-caded white suit and black pumps and an arterial-red necklace walking toward her. She carried a slender box wrapped with satin paper and a purple ribbon.

"I parked between Porteus Burke's law office and the Shadows, and was walking to your house and looked through the gate, and there you were," the woman said.

"Hello, Emmeline," Alafair said.

"May I sit down?"

"To be honest, I'm working right now."

"On the screenplay?"

"That and a couple of other things."

"I'll take just a minute," Emmeline said, sitting on the bench. She put the box in Alafair's lap. "A little chocolate to make up for the tennis ball in your face."

"That's thoughtful of you, but I don't handle sugar very well."

"Oh, Alafair, I do want us to be friends."

"No, I'm sorry," Alafair said, returning the box.

"I understand." She took a breath and smiled self-consciously. "I need a favor. It's about Jimmy. He thinks the world of your father."

"Is this about the rape?"

"No, absolutely not. Jimmy bears terrible guilt for an event that happened years ago, one he had little control over. Your father is a war veteran. He'll understand."

"Dave is investigating your cousin for rape."

"I don't believe a rape ever took place. But that's not why I'm here. You don't understand Jimmy. He wants to be Levon Broussard. Now, thanks to his wife, Levon hates Jimmy."

"What is Dave supposed to do about it?"

"Did Dave see atrocities in Vietnam?"

"He doesn't talk about the war."

"Jimmy was in South America at the same time Levon was, except Levon was working for Amnesty International."

"I'm lost. I also need to go."

"Jimmy is capable of taking his own life."

"Pardon?"

"Levon spat in his face. He might as well have spat on his soul."

"I'm leaving now."

"You tell your father what I said."

Alafair's ears were still ringing when she got home.

Chapter
16

THAT EVENING ALAFAIR told me of her conversation with Emmeline Nightingale. "What's she after?" she asked.

"Money or power or both. Maybe sex is involved," I said. "But that comes automatically with the other two."

"She and her cousin are rich and powerful already."

"They may be brother and sister."

"Then why don't they tell people that?"

"Kevin Penny says they're very close." I let it sink in.

"They're getting it on?"

"The royalty are insular in St. Mary Parish."

"Yuck," she said.

"Tony Nemo wants to produce Levon's book. Jimmy Nightingale not only wants to adapt it but is envious of Levon. If I were a prosecutor, I'd use that as motivation for the rape. He couldn't be Levon, so he'd take second best."

"That's really crude."

"So is rape."

Alafair walked to the kitchen window and bit a fingernail. A tugboat was headed up the bayou, its gunwales hung with tires, the wake sliding into the cypress trees.

"Dave, I know how to make this script work. It could be a great film. The story of the drummer boy at Shiloh could be a film in itself."

"Tell all this to Levon."

"He's an angry man."

"About his wife?"

"I don't think he believes his portrayal of his ancestors is honest."

"In his novels?"

"In everything."

"That could be a problem," I said.

I DROVE UP LOREAUVILLE Road to the Broussard home and rang the door chimes. Tiny black strings of ash were floating down on the lawn and driveway and the steps and camellia bushes. I thought they were from the sugar mill.

Levon came around the side of the house, a leaf rake in his hand. "Back here."

I followed him into the backyard, where he was burning huge piles of blackened leaves in three perforated oil drums. The curds of smoke were drifting into his neighbor's windows and hanging like dirty cotton on the bayou.

"When's the last time you burned your leaves?" I said.

"A couple of years ago. Why?"

"No reason. Emmeline Nightingale has been bugging Alafair."

He hefted a giant sheaf of compressed leaves and dropped them into the flames, his face swelling in the heat. "What does that have to do with us?"

"Maybe nothing. Except Tony Nemo is on Clete Purcel's back and also in my face, directly or indirectly because of a sword your great-grandfather carried. At least that's where all this started."

"So you've come out here to tell me my great-grandfather's sword is the origin of your problems?"

"I didn't say that."

"Then why are you upset?" he asked.

"I'm not upset."

"You could fool me," he said.

"Have you ever been knocked down in your own backyard?"

He began packing more leaves in the barrels, his armpits looped with sweat, ash raining down on his head and bare forearms.

"Levon?"

"Go home."

"I'm an officer of the law. This isn't a courtesy call."

I waited for him to respond. He jabbed the leaves into the flames with the butt of the rake.

"Sir, don't you turn your back to me," I said.

"I'll do what I damn please."

"No, you will not." I put my hand on his arm and turned him around. "This case isn't about just you and your wife. It concerns Tony Nine Ball, and something Jimmy Nightingale did in South America, and a lowlife named Kevin Penny, and something you're not telling me about your wife."

"That's a goddamn lie."

"What is?"

"All your bullshit, Dave. I don't have anything to with gangsters or lowlifes or friends of yours. Rowena was raped. End of fucking story."

"It's just the beginning."

"If it wasn't for your age, I'd pop you one."

"Really? Then you have my dispensation. Forget I'm a cop, too."

He looked away, his hands balling. "Come inside."

"What for?"

"I've got a pitcher of lemonade in my office. Keep it quiet, though. Rowena is asleep."

He unlocked the French doors on the patio and waited for me to walk ahead of him. A pitcher and a glass sat on a folding table by his desk. He filled the glass and wrapped it with a paper napkin and handed it to me, then went to the kitchen and got a glass for himself. For the first time, behind the door, I saw a sun-faded Confederate battle flag mounted on the wall in a glass case. He came back into the room.

"A fourteen-year-old boy carried that up the slope on Beauregard's left flank at Shiloh," Levon said. "They were supposed to be supported by the founder of Angola Penitentiary, but he didn't show up. Forty percent were casualties in fifteen minutes."

I nodded, not knowing what to say. I disliked people who thought war was a glorious endeavor, and I disliked those who enjoyed talking about it. I despised those who had not seen war yet espoused it and lived vicariously through the suffering of others and never gave a thought to the civilians and children who died in burn wards or were buried under collapsed buildings.

Levon was not one of these. He had gone unarmed and with a leftist reputation into El Salvador, Guatemala, and Nicaragua when bodies were dumped off trucks with the morning garbage. Yet here we stood in reverence before an iconic flag that retained the pink stain of a farm boy's blood, and whether anybody would admit it or not, the cause it represented was the protection and furtherance of human bondage.

"You have nothing to say about it?" he asked.

"Rich man's war, poor man's fight. The statement doesn't make the poor man any less honorable or brave."

"You don't give an inch, do you."

"No."

"That's not a compliment," he said.

"I didn't think it was. How's your wife?"

"On painkillers."

He sat down in a swivel chair behind his desk and opened a bottom drawer and removed a pint of brandy. He unscrewed the cap with his thumb and let it drop on top of the desk. "You on or off the grog?"

"No, thanks."

He poured three inches into his glass. I watched the lemonade change color, the ice rise frosty and thick. He took a long pull, watching me, then wiped his mouth. "Nightingale and his sister or whatever she is have one agenda. They want to kill the rape story in the bud. They're using you to do it."

"No, they're not."

"Nightingale is a master manipulator, Dave. He fleeces uneducated and compulsive people in his casinos, pretending to be their friend, when in reality he wouldn't take time to piss in their mouths if they were dying of thirst. This guy might be our next United States senator. He might even end up in the White House. Think about that for a minute."

"What is it you're not telling me about your wife?"

"What makes you think I'm hiding something?"

"Because you're a smart man who allowed his wife to destroy the forensic evidence that would have made the case against Nightingale."

His eyes went away from me. "My wife is bipolar. She's also barren. Occasionally, she does things that are irrational. But none of that alters the fact that she was assaulted by that son of a bitch over in St. Mary Parish."

I was sitting on the couch a few feet from him. "I might be indicted in the death of the man who killed my wife."

"Why are you telling me that now?"

"I know what it feels like to be disbelieved."

"You didn't do it?"

"That's the irony. I don't know. The last person I can trust or believe is me."

He leaned back in his chair. "You should have told me."

"Why?"

"Sometimes I feel like a fraud. That's something no one can ever accuse you of." He drank his glass to the bottom and looked out the window at the three live oaks he had named for Confederate officers. "What a pile of shit."

Then, without saying another word, he left me in his office and went outside and resumed stuffing mounds of leaves in the waste barrels, throwing a jelly glass full of gasoline onto the fire, indifferent to the whoosh of heat that must have singed his eyebrows.

ALMOST TWO WEEKS went by without any change in the status of the Dartez homicide or the sexual assault charges filed by Rowena Broussard. Clete Purcel took Carolyn Ardoin to dinner and a movie in Lafayette. Then the next night to a movie in Lake Charles. Then three days later to a street dance and crawfish boil in Abbeville.

"You're going to wear me out," she said on their way back to Jennings.

"I've been keeping you up too late?"

"It's grand being out with you, Clete."

The top of his Caddy was up, and her skin looked warm and rosy in the glow of the dash lights. He liked everything about her. The way she shook all over when she laughed, the happy shine in her eyes, her manners and all the books she had read. He turned in to her neighborhood, not wanting the night to end.

The houses were small and clapboard with tin roofs, the yards neat and without fences, the driveways nothing more than gravel tracks. If the contemporary automobiles were taken away, the year could have been 1935. He pulled up to the curb. She had not left her porch light on.

He went around to the passenger side and opened the door. When she got out, she looked him directly in the face and smiled. He could smell the gardenias and the two magnolia trees in her yard. She touched his arm when she stood up from the leather seat.

"I'll walk you up to the steps," he said. "I've sure enjoyed the evening."

"As I, Clete." She looked at the sky. There was a rain ring around the moon. "Tomorrow is Saturday."

"Yes," he said.

"With no work obligations."

"Probably a rainy morning, too," he said. "It's a fine time of year."

In the darkness of the gallery, she took her key from her purse. She looked up into his face. "You're a gentleman. You're kind and strong, and you respect women. Those things are not lost on a woman."

"I didn't quite get that."

"If you need to go, I understand. I just want you to know you're always welcome here and that I appreciate your gentlemanly ways."

When he spoke, he felt as though he had swallowed a pebble. "I'd love to come in."

Inside, she closed the blinds and turned on a light in a back hallway. "This way."

In the bedroom, the wood floor creaked under his weight as he approached her. She turned on a lamp. The wallpaper was covered with roses. The quilt on the bed was lavender, the pillows pink. He felt as though he were inside a dollhouse, but in a good way. "Miss Carolyn, I've led a checkered life."

"Who hasn't?" she replied.

He left her house early in the morning, before the neighbors were up, to avoid making Carolyn a subject of gossip. There was not a person on the street. The morning paper lay on people's galleries or walkways. The trees ticked with moisture. At the end of the block, he looked in the outside mirror and saw an SUV swing out of an alley and follow him.

He coasted to the curb, cut the engine, and pretended to look for something in the glove box. The SUV passed him. The windows were charcoaled and rolled up except for a crack at the top, probably for a smoker. Clete wrote down the tag number on a small white pad he kept in the well of the console. At the next intersection, the SUV turned and disappeared down a side street.

Clete drove downtown and ate in a café, stationing himself at a table with a view of the street. Before his food arrived, he saw the SUV park at an angle in front of a hardware store that had gone out of business. After a few minutes, the driver opened the door far enough to drop a cigarette on the asphalt. The driver was wearing a checked sport coat and a gray knit cap with a bill.

Clete ate his breakfast, paid the check, and went outside, his gaze fixed on a black kid skateboarding down the sidewalk. Then he crossed the street and tapped on the window of the SUV.

Maximo Soza lowered the window. JuJu Ladrine was in the passenger seat, his face stretched with tension. Maximo scratched a spot under his eye. "I don't see no envelope."

"Envelope?" Clete said.

"It's Saturday. You got to pay the vig," Maximo said.

"I think I hit you too hard in the head with the rubber machine."

"The vig is the vig, man. It's due on Saturday. If you got to sell your body parts online, you pay the vig."

"You put a Taser on me, Max. But I'm letting that slide. You got to do the same. That means you and JuJu pack up your shit and go back to New Orleans."

Maximo turned his head with the stiffness of a ventriloquist's dummy and let his eyes settle on Clete's. "Tony will hang you on a hook by your asshole. Or maybe somebody else will have to pay the price for what you ain't taken care of."

"You want to clarify that?"

"Nobody can be all places at once," Maximo said. He started the engine. "Step back. I don't want to run over your foot."

Clete felt a sensation like stitches popping loose inside his head. He opened the driver's door and tore Maximo out of the seat, lifting him high in the air, then crashing him on the hood. Maximo rolled off on the asphalt. "Son of a beech, what the fuck, man?"

Clete threw him against the fender and told him to take the position. When Maximo tried to turn around, Clete kicked the man's feet apart and drove his face against the hood, then smashed it down a second time for good measure.

"I ain't carrying, man!" Maximo said.

"What do you call this?" Clete said, holding up a switchblade knife.

"See what I use it for later. I'll be back, man."

Clete turned him upside down and shook him like a rag doll, spilling coins, keys, a rabbit's foot, a pair of dice, a box of condoms, a cell phone, credit cards, and a wallet in the gutter.

"You leave that man alone!" someone called from across the street.

Clete dropped Maximo on the asphalt, then picked him up and threw him back into the driver's seat. He looked up and down the street. No cops yet. He put Maximo's belongings into his cap and tossed it to JuJu. Maximo's eyes were crossed, blood running in two scarlet strings from his nostrils. He was trying to speak. Clete smashed his face into the horn button.

"You got a brain, JuJu," he said. "Tell Tony what happened. Also tell him if he sends you guys after me again, he's going off the board, oxygen bottle and colostomy bag included. That goes for you, too, JuJu."

"It don't work that way, Clete," JuJu said. "Why you making it hard on everybody?"

"Me?"

"It's you went to the shylocks. Not us."

"Get out of here," Clete said.

He slammed the driver's door and walked to the Caddy, burning with shame, eyes straight ahead, trying to ignore the stares of people around him and the knowledge that he had involved a gentle lady in a world she could not have imagined in her worst nightmares.

CLETE CAME BY my house that night. It was raining hard, and he ran from the Caddy through the puddles in the yard to the gallery. I could smell weed on him through the screen. "What happened?" I asked.

"Who said anything happened?" he replied, brushing past me into the living room, his face oily and dilated. He blew his nose into a handkerchief.

"You just get in from Juárez?" I said.

"Cut it out, Dave. I feel bad enough." He told me about Maximo and JuJu.

"Maximo was threatening Miss Carolyn?" I said.

"That's the gist."

"Does she know?"

"She was going to visit her mother in Lake Charles today. I left a couple of messages. What am I going to do? I feel awful."

"Jennings PD might throw a scare into them."

"The same guys who couldn't come up with one suspect in eight homicides?"

"Weed and booze aren't going to help."

"Oh, fuck off."

"Don't use that language in my house, Cletus."

"I'm sorry."

I went into the kitchen and came back with a pair of Dr Peppers.

"I think Tony wants to make movies. I think that's what started all this."

"So what?"

"I'll talk to him."

"You're going to talk reason to that pile of whale shit?"

"He bought a sword that he thought would get him in the good graces of Levon Broussard, and instead he lost the sword and had the door slammed in his face. So being the infantile narcissist he is, he's throwing his scat all over the room."

Clete stared at me. "You think it's that simple?"

"How much time does he have left? Have you been in a closed room with him? He's got the smell of death on him, and he knows it. It's like wallpaper and dead flowers. He wants to see his name in lights before he goes out."

"A guy like that doesn't have a soul."

"That's why he wants his name in lights."

He studied my face. "Where's Alafair?"

"At the grocery."

"She's doing okay? Every time I look at her, I see her as a little girl. That's funny, isn't it?"

I didn't reply.

"What if I treat y'all to dinner at Café Des Amis tonight?" he said.

"I was just about to suggest that."

He grinned, but his heart wasn't in it.

Chapter 17

Sunday morning, I asked Alafair for the names of the ten worst, most mean-spirited, corrupt movie producers or directors in the industry.

"What are you doing, Dave?"

"Stirring up things. Know a few guys out there who are off the wall?"

"Enough to fill the Hollywood Bowl."

"Could you type them up, please?"

After she went on her jog, I called Tony Nemo's office. The office was closed because it was Sunday, but I knew he monitored his voice-mail day and night. Sundays, Thanksgiving, and Christmas might be days of rest or gratitude or celebration for some, but Tony's deity had a dollar sign for a face and gave no days off to his adherents. "Tony, this is Dave Robicheaux," I said. "I think I might have a breakthrough in your movie situation. I need your fax number." I poured a cup of coffee and hot milk, sat at the kitchen table, and outlined the general story of Levon Broussard's Civil War novel. The phone rang seventeen minutes later.

"What's this crap about?" Tony said.

"I knew you were interested in getting together with Levon Broussard, so I thought I'd pass on some info."

"You're a movie agent now?"

"I know a few people out there, Tony. I've heard talk. Your name came up."

"Take the shit out of your mouth."

"I know you're frustrated about not putting a deal together with Levon. But there's a way around that."

"What's the trade-off?"

"Trade-off?"

"Yeah, what are you getting out of it?"

"I want you to give Clete Purcel some slack and quit this bullshit about buying his markers. I paid off those markers, Tony. When you jam him, you're jamming me. I also don't like you sending those two shitheads after him."

"Too fucking bad."

"You want to hear what I have to say or should I bugger off?"

"Should you what?"

"Yes or no?"

There was a pause. "So what breakthrough are we talking about?"

I looked at my outline. "You don't have to pay for the rights to the story line in Levon's novel. The story is based on a real account. His ancestor came home from Shiloh shot to pieces in mind and body, and taught a slave girl how to read and write. The slave girl was the illegitimate daughter of the man who founded Angola Prison. In the meantime, the Confederate soldier fell in love with an abolitionist who nursed him back to health and restored his humanity."

"So I don't got to pay for any of this?"

"Nobody can copyright history."

"Just go make the picture?"

"I've got a list of the names. These are big guys. If you do the pitch yourself, they'll listen."

"Why?"

"You scare the shit out of them."

I could hear him take a hit from his oxygen tank. "They know my name? My work?"

"You bet."

"I'm gonna give you my fax number. You better not be taking me over the hurdles."

"Wouldn't dream of it. Stomp ass and take names, big guy."

The list included a producer who washed heroin money; another who hung prostitutes from ropes and beat them with his fists; and one who put LSD in the food of his Puerto Rican maid and videoed her stumbling around his Beverly Hills home and showed the video to his employees. These were the kind who would be terrified of Tony the Squid and too afraid to ignore his call or put down the receiver once they were on the line. I hoped all of them enjoyed the ride.

HELEN WAS WAITING outside City Hall when I got to work Monday morning, something she had never done before.

"Any problem?" I said.

Two uniformed deputies walked past us and went inside.

"Depends on how you read it," she said. "We've got a witness."

"To the Dartez homicide?"

"A young black guy. He says he was parked in the trees with a girl and saw it."

"Why'd he wait to come forward?" I said.

"The girl is married. But not to him. Also, the girl may not be a girl."

I couldn't get her words straight in my head. "What gave him the change of heart?"

"The minister at his church told him he'd better tell us what he saw or he's going to hell."

I was hardly listening. My heart was gelatin. Sometimes witnesses who come out of the woodwork have had too much time to think and give a distorted account. Minority witnesses are often intimidated and seek to please, particularly when questioned by someone like Spade Labiche. But last and foremost, I might have to accept an unpleasant truth, namely, that I was a murderer.

"Why'd you stop me out here?"

"Because I haven't told Labiche yet. I'm going to interview the kid at his home. I'm taking Labiche with me. I'm giving you the option to come along."

"You'll taint the investigation."

"Hear me out," she said. "You have to stay in the vehicle. The witness will not see you."

"Why are you doing this?"

"Professionally, you don't have the right to be there," she said. "Ethically, you do. I have a photo lineup."

"I'm in it?"

"Big-time," she replied.

HELEN DROVE THE cruiser out to a small frame house by Bayou Benoit, with me in the back and Labiche in the passenger seat. Labiche gazed out the window at the new cane bending in the fields. "What's this guy's name again?"

"Baby Cakes Babineau," Helen said.

"He takes it in the ass?" Labiche said.

"Lose those kinds of references, Detective," she said.

"*Excuse* me," he said.

We pulled in to the dirt driveway. Helen and Labiche got out, Labiche tightening the tuck in his shirt with his thumbs. His badge holder and a holstered .38 hung from his belt. "Not coming?" he said to me.

"I know I'm in good hands," I said.

He leaned down to the window. "Maybe you and me will have a private talk about all this, Robicheaux. I think you've had a free pass too long."

"Do your job and get out of my face," I said.

"Fuck you," he replied.

I got out on the opposite side of the cruiser and walked into the yard, under a pecan tree, and picked up a handful of pecans, still in the husks, and chunked them at the tree trunk, a tuning fork trembling in my chest.

A heavyset older woman with enormous calves and hips came out the back door and began hanging wash. I walked up behind her. "Are you Ms. Babineau?"

She had blue eyes and skin the color of a new penny and features that were Indian and Afro-American. "Who you?"

"Dave Robicheaux."

"Don't y'all be hurting my grandson, no."

"Why would we do that?"

"The one wit' the badge. I seen the look in his face."

"Detective Labiche?"

"Call him what you want."

She picked up her basket and waddled back inside. I could hear voices through the window screen.

"So why were you parked in the trees?" Labiche said.

"To drink a couple of beers wit' my friend," a young male voice said. "I got out to take a leak and seed the truck crash t'rew the fence. Then this guy come running from the road and was fighting wit' the guy in the truck."

"Inside the truck?" Helen said.

"He was messing with the glass, then got mad and busted it and was fighting wit' the guy inside. He pulled him t'rew the window. That's when this other guy come running up. It was dark except for the lightning in the clouds."

"Which guy came running up?" Labiche said.

"Some guy from the road. Maybe all t'ree of them was fighting. I couldn't tell what was going on."

"What's the name of the person who was with you?" Labiche said.

"I cain't tell you that."

"Was it a he or a she?" Labiche said.

"We're just interested in what you saw, Baby Cakes," Helen said. "Let's not worry about this other person right now."

"I was scared," Baby Cakes said.

"Of who?" Helen said.

"People that beat up on people like me."

"Because you're gay?" she said.

"Because I ain't sure what I am."

"Kind of late finding out, aren't you?" Labiche said.

"Wait outside for me, Detective."

"I think I should be here," Labiche replied.

"Now," Helen said.

Labiche came out the front door and walked across the gallery loudly. He leaned against the cruiser and lit a cigarette and scratched at one nostril with a thumbnail.

"I want you to look at these photos," Helen said.

"Who these people?" Baby Cakes said.

"They could be anybody. Do you recognize anyone?"

The seconds passed one tick at a time. "Maybe this one here. Maybe he was the guy who come running from the road."

"Maybe?"

"The lightning flashed. I ain't seen him but a second. He's a big man, ain't he?"

"Tell me what he looked like."

"The man I seen come running was big. Maybe he picked up a rock or a brick. I couldn't see the face of the other man, the one fighting t'rew the window."

"Walk outside with me."

I turned my back to the house as they exited the front door.

"Dave, would you come here, please?" Helen said.

I walked toward the gallery. Even though the day was warm, my face felt cold in the wind, my mouth dry, my ears ringing.

"Know this man?" she said to Baby Cakes.

His hair was peroxided the color of brass, his eyes blue, his earlobes pierced. "He's in the pictures you just showed me."

"This is Detective Robicheaux," she said.

"How you do, suh?" the boy said.

"Have you seen him anywhere besides the photo I showed you?"

"No, ma'am, I ain't seed him before."

"The man you identified is named Kevin Penny. Have you seen him anywhere else?"

"No, ma'am, I ain't."

"Don't talk about this to anyone," Helen said. "Can you do that for me?"

"Am I gonna have trouble? I mean wit' this guy?"

"No, your name will not be given to anyone," Helen said.

"What about at a trial?"

"We'll talk about that later," Helen said.

"I knowed it."

"You knew what?" she asked.

"I'm gonna pay the price."

"Here's my card," Helen said. "Call me if you have questions or trouble of any kind."

I could not count the times I had used a business card to provide solace for people we hung out to dry. That wasn't Helen's intention, but it's what we did with regularity. She and Labiche and I got into the cruiser. Helen started the engine.

"I know when a nigger is lying," Labiche said.

She looked at his profile. "How do you intuit that?"

"They give you that look. Butter wouldn't melt in their mouths."

"You're a reminder from God, Spade," she said.

"Didn't catch that."

"Whenever I hear people talk about white superiority, I have to pause and think back on some of the white people I've known. It's a depressing moment."

She turned onto the two-lane and didn't speak again until we were back at the office. Just outside the back door, she told Labiche to coordinate with the Jefferson Davis Sheriff's Department and arrange an interview with Kevin Penny. Labiche seemed to lose his balance, like a seasick man reaching for the gunwale.

THAT AFTERNOON CLETE got a call from Carolyn Ardoin. "Homer ran away from home. A policeman found him wandering around by I-10."

"Where is he now?" Clete said.

"With me at the office. I'm not going to send him back."

"Can you do that?" he asked.

"I don't care about the rules on this one."

"Go easy with Penny."

"I'm furious."

"What did he do?"

"It's enough that he's his hateful self. I'm furious at our system."

"What if I come over there and get Homer?"

"What about when you're at work?"

"I can pay somebody to watch him."

"He's in school."

"I'll enroll him here."

"I have to think through the paperwork. Sometimes I hate my job."

"Quit and come live with me."

"You're serious?"

"There're probably worse fates," he said.

"This is a lot at one time, Clete."

She was right, but he saw his own face on Homer's and knew what awaited the boy when a social worker took him back to Kevin Penny's trailer.

"Hire an attorney, some guy who's not afraid to make a stink and embarrass local officials," Clete said. "I'll take care of the fees."

"That doesn't work. Right now I have to talk to my supervisor. I'll call you later."

"You've got to think about yourself, Carolyn. Penny's potential has no bottom. Then there're those two rodents who work for Tony Nemo."

"I can handle myself," she replied. "It'll work out. Good-bye."

"Don't hang up, Carolyn."

Too late.

I MENTIONED MY SPECULATION that Helen Soileau may have had several people living inside her, none of them entirely normal. That afternoon, at 4:57, she buzzed my phone and told me to come to her office. I walked down the corridor and went inside.

"Shut the door and sit down," she said.

I took a chair. She walked past me and lowered the blinds on the glass. I waited for her to return to her desk, but she didn't. I felt her standing behind me, saw her shadow fall across mine. There was a lump in my throat. "What's going on, boss lady?"

She placed a hand on each of my shoulders.

"I've wanted to do this all day," she said.

She tucked her elbows in under my chin and pulled my head into her breasts.

"Jesus Christ, Helen!"

"Shut up. I don't know what happened at Bayou Benoit, but you didn't kill T. J. Dartez." She kissed my hair. "Now go home."

Top that.

I LOVE THE RAIN, whether it's a tropical one or one that falls on you in the dead of winter. For me, rain is the natural world's absolution, like the story of the Flood and new beginnings and loading the animals two by two onto the Ark. I love the mist hanging in the trees, a hint of wraiths that would not let heavy stones weigh them down in their graves, the raindrops clicking on the lily pads, the fish rising as though in celebration.

I took great comfort on nights like these, and on this particular night I sat down in a cloth-covered chair in the living room and began reading a novel by Ron Hansen titled *The Kid*, the best story I ever read about the Lincoln County cattle wars. The rain was drumming on our tin roof, pooling in the yard, shining like glass in the glow of the streetlamps. I had opened the front window to let in the cold air. I heard a loud thump and looked up to see a humped silhouette on the screen.

"How you doin', Mon Tee Coon?" I said. *"Comment est la vie?"*

He tilted his head.

"You need a snack, little guy?" I said.

He pawed at the screen. His coat was glistening with water, his whiskers white at the tips.

"I'm going to open a can of tuna and get you a pan of water and set them on the gallery. Hang loose."

Just as I got out of the chair, a sports car turned sharply into the driveway, splashing water into the yard. Mon Tee Coon dropped heavily onto the gallery and was gone. Someone ran from the car with a newspaper over his or her head and twisted the bell not once but three times. I tossed my book onto the chair and opened the door.

"Thank goodness you're home, Dave," Emmeline Nightingale said, wiping the rain out of her hair. "Is Alafair here?"

"No."

"Where is she?"

"She doesn't tell me everywhere she goes."

"I have some important information. I was going to tell her and let her tell you."

Emmeline seemed to lie the way all narcissists do. Whatever they say, regardless of its absurdity, becomes the truth.

"Tell me what?"

"Are you going to invite me in?"

"Yes, please come in," I said.

She stepped inside and blew out her breath. "It's about your friend Levon and his wife."

"Take it to the department."

"Just drop in and chat up the boys in the coffee room?"

"No, talk to me in my office."

"You're getting jerked around, Detective."

She was good. "What's the information on Mr. and Ms. Broussard?"

"She was raped by two black men in Wichita, Kansas. The prosecutor's office wouldn't do anything about it."

"Where'd you get this?"

"I hired a private investigator."

"How long ago did this happen?"

"Twenty years, maybe more. She was a visiting artist at Wichita State University. She was young and maybe drunk when she left the bar with the two black men. Nobody would believe her story."

"You need to bring everything your PI has to the department."

"Did I do wrong coming here?" she said.

Yes, she did. And there was no doubt she had a design. Nonetheless, if the information was true, it presented a problem for the prosecutor and was a gift to the defense. There was a good possibility that Rowena would be victimized by the system again.

"Could I have a drink?" Emmeline said.

"I don't have any alcohol in the house."

"A Dr Pepper, a Coca-Cola, a glass of lemonade."

"Yes, I think I can find something."

"I love the sound the rain makes on a tin roof. Your house is so quaint."

"I have another question for you, Miss Emmeline. What did Jimmy do in Latin America that haunts him? Why are you two always at the center of other people's misfortune when you never seem to pay dues yourself?"

"I think that is the most arrogant and ugly thing anyone has ever said to me."

She was probably right. I didn't like to speak that way to a woman or, for that matter, to anyone. Age does that to you. Sometimes charity toward others is the only respite you get from thoughts about death. And in that spirit, I said, "Let me get you a diet Dr Pepper."

I don't think she had a brain seizure, but close.

Chapter 18

THE RAIN CAME down hard on the house and trees and yard through the night, and in the morning the bayou was running yellow and fast and high on the banks, the eddies frothy and filled with twigs and leaves. I raked a can of tuna for Mon Tee Coon on top of Tripod's old hutch and washed my hands and made breakfast for Alafair and me. I told her about Emmeline Nightingale's visit.

"Jimmy Nightingale's lawyers will make Rowena Broussard look like a meltdown or a slut," she said. "She'll have to convince the jury not only of Nightingale's guilt but also of the guilt of the two black guys in Wichita. That's the place where BTK killed people under the cops' noses for years."

"What do you know about Jimmy Nightingale's activities in Latin America?"

"He inherited his father's company and worked down there awhile, then sold the company."

"Why'd he sell it?"

"I don't know. He likes casinos and attractive women and working people who think he's one of their own." She looked into space. "I remember something a woman said at a party once, like, 'Jimmy would be the perfect man if he hadn't tried to be like his father. He shouldn't have done that to those poor people.'"

"Poor like sad or economic?"

"Your guess is as good as mine. Don't be fooled, Dave. He's a chameleon."

"Can you check out some of this stuff?" I said. "If you're not doing anything else."

"I don't mind. Why don't you copyedit my new book while I do that?"

FROM THE OFFICE, I called Levon's home and was told by the maid that he was at a bowling alley on East Main. It was a five-minute drive. Most of the lanes were empty. Levon was bowling by himself, his sleeves rolled. I walked up behind him and sat down. He curved the ball beautifully into the pocket and exploded the pins with much more force than I associated with him. A bottle of beer was perched next to the score sheet. The time was 9:13 A.M.

"I didn't know you were an enthusiast," I said.

"It beats analysis."

"Emmeline Nightingale came to my house last night."

"Here we go."

"Nope. I'll make it short. She says your wife was assaulted by two men twenty years ago in Kansas."

"She's a charming girl, isn't she? And you're a son of a bitch."

"I didn't make up the information. It's part of the record. Maybe it's time you start dealing with reality."

"How is one assault related to the other?"

"In reality, it's not. The courtroom is a different matter. Why didn't you square with me?"

"Run the tape backward. I told you she has nightmares about a black man's hand coming through a window."

"I asked you about that at the time, and you changed the subject."

He sat down behind the score table and took a swig from the beer bottle. There were no entries on his score sheet. "How bad is this going to hurt us?"

"Nightingale's lawyers will use your wife's history and her suicide attempt or her nationality or her life in Latin America or whatever bogus issue they can think up to bias the jury in his favor."

"You really know how to say it."

"What happened in Wichita?"

"The ADA was going to run for district attorney. She didn't want to be perceived as a dupe for a white woman who willingly left a bar with two black men and went willingly to their house. That she was trusting and young was thrown out the window."

"How's Miss Rowena now?"

"There're mornings I have to be by myself."

He took another hit off the bottle. I clinked it with my fingernail. "If you're depressed, this will screw you up proper."

"I'm glad to hear that from such a great source of wisdom on the subject."

I'd asked for it. "If I were you, I'd get together with my attorney and go to the department and make an addendum to my statement. See you around."

"What does 'see you around' mean?"

"Let the dead bury the dead," I said. "I'm done."

I WENT BACK TO the office and tried to clean out my head. It wasn't an easy job. Being a cop rarely is, at least if you take the job seriously. My in-basket was full of paperwork. There were at least twenty messages on my machine, including two from Clete and one from the Jefferson Parish Sheriff's Department and one from the widow of T. J. Dartez. My first call was to her.

"They say you gonna get off," she said.

"Who did, Ms. Dartez?"

"I know you done it. You gonna lie to God? You gonna tell Him you ain't done it?"

"I'm sorry about your husband's death. But your husband was not sorry about the death of my wife."

"You going to hell, you."

My second call was to a female detective at the Jeff Davis Sheriff's

Department named Sherry Picard whom I'd never met but had heard about. She said, "Kevin Penny says you and your friend Clete Purcel are harassing him. In your case, with a pool cue."

"Penny is a lot of laughs," I replied. "I've never figured out how he stays on the street."

"Is there a second meaning there?"

"How can I be of assistance to you?" I said.

"I doubt if you can. I've run Penny in two or three times. If you've got a problem with him, let us know. In the meantime, stay out of matters that are not in your jurisdiction."

Clete's messages were about the little boy Homer and the possibility that Carolyn Ardoin was in danger at the hands of Kevin Penny or Maximo and JuJu. By the time I had cleaned up my messages, my head was splitting. I went to the water cooler and took two aspirins, then returned to my office and lowered the blinds on the door glass.

Helen believed I was not responsible for Dartez's death, but only because Baby Cakes hadn't identified me and instead had identified Kevin Penny. In other words, I'd caught a break. The only forensic evidence against me was the smudged fingerprints on the broken window glass of Dartez's pickup truck. I could simply say I had been at his house and touched the glass there. Except I would be lying.

In the meantime, I had interviewed Penny and later beaten him half to death with a pool cue and almost drowned him in the commode, apparently without his being completely aware that I was the man he had followed the night Dartez died. Better put, he had probably followed my vehicle rather than me.

I might skate, but Penny might also.

People are shocked when they learn that cops sometimes salt the crime scene and commit perjury. Or maybe they cancel a bad guy's ticket and fold his hand over a throw-down and squeeze off a round with his dead finger to make sure gunpowder residue is on his person. Call it situational ethics, call it murder. It's a big temptation, particularly when it comes to guys like Kevin Penny and perhaps even Spade Labiche.

*   *   *

TWO DAYS LATER, Clete got a call made by a staff member at Lafayette General. Carolyn Ardoin had been transferred from an emergency unit in Jennings and admitted at 4:16 A.M. She was in the ICU and had asked the staff member to call Clete.

"She was in an accident?" Clete said.

"I'm not at liberty to say."

"How bad is she?"

"Sir, we can't give out specific information."

"Can you put her on the phone?"

"That's not possible."

"Is she going to live?"

"Sir, she's getting the best of care. That's all I can say."

"Put someone on with the authority to give out information. Is there a cop there?"

"No. How far away are you?"

"Twenty miles."

"Drive carefully. I'll tell her you're coming. I know that will make her happy."

"Don't do this to me."

"I'm sorry," the staff member said.

Clete took the four-lane into Lafayette, the needle at ninety. He parked illegally and went through the emergency room into the intensive care unit before anyone could stop him. "Where's Carolyn Ardoin?" he asked at the desk.

"Are you a relative?" the nurse said.

"Her grandfather. Where is she?"

The nurse raised her eyes from her paperwork.

"I'm a close friend," he said. "Was it an accident?"

"No," the nurse said. "Follow me."

Carolyn was behind a screen. When he saw her, he tried to keep his face empty, his eyes flat. "How you doin', kid?" he said.

There were streaks of dried blood in her hair. Both eyes were swollen as big as plums. Her bottom lip was stitched. There were finger-shaped bruises on her throat and neck and shoulders.

"Who did this?" he said.

"I was unloading groceries in the driveway. It was dark. Somebody hit me."

"Was Homer with you?"

"He's at my mother's."

"Was it one guy or more than one guy?"

"I just remember a fist hitting me. Then I was on the ground, and the fists kept pounding my face. I tried to speak—" She couldn't finish.

"I'm going to take care of Homer. I'm also going to find out who did this. What did the Jennings cops say?"

"They just asked me questions. One was a woman. Sherry something."

"How'd they treat you?"

"Fine. Everyone has been kind."

"I have to use the bathroom," Clete said. "I'll be back in a few minutes."

"There's one here."

"It's too small for a guy my size."

He went down the hall to a restroom in the waiting area, but not for the reason he had given. An old Technicolor video, one that held interest for fewer and fewer people these days, had begun replaying itself on a screen inside his head. The slick hung in the air above the ville, its rotary blades throbbing. He heard the treads of the zippo track clanking out of the rice paddy and saw an orange flame arch out of its cannon and smelled a stench like burning kerosene and animal hair. People were running, the hooches bursting alight, the ammunition cached under them popping like strings of Chinese firecrackers. Clete cupped water onto his face and dried himself with paper towels, then went to Carolyn's room, the video not finished, a navy corpsman from Birmingham hitting him with a syrette of morphine: "Hang on, gunny. Here comes the dust-off. You're Freedom Bird–bound."

Carolyn had fallen asleep. He stroked her hair and felt a pain in his chest that he had nowhere to put. Two or three faces floated before his eyes like helium balloons with ugly features painted on them.

As he stroked her hair, his left hand curled and uncurled and curled again. He knew where he was going and what he would do when he got there. But there was something else he had do first.

HE CALLED ME on his cell and told me about the assault.

"Where are you now?" I said.

"On the way to Lake Charles. Penny's little boy is with Carolyn's mother."

"Leave him there."

"The mother is an invalid."

"You're not set up to take care of a child, Clete."

"I hired a black lady. Now butt out."

"Don't do what you're thinking about."

"This isn't an act of random violence. It happened in her driveway. Either Penny, Maximo Soza, JuJu Ladrine, or any combination of the three did this."

"You can't be sure of that."

"Are you kidding?"

"Clete—"

"Out," he said.

I CALLED TONY NINE Ball at his office and told the secretary who I was.

"Just a moment," she said. I looked at the second hand on my watch. Thirty-three seconds passed. "I'm sorry, he's still in a meeting."

"Tell him to pick up or I'll be over there in ten minutes and shove that phone up his ass."

One minute later, Tony was on the line. "What'd you say to my secretary?"

"Not to lie."

"So what's so important you got to upset people with bad language?"

"Nothing had better happen to Clete Purcel. We had a deal."

"What deal?"

"I gave you an intro to some producers and agents. That means nobody lays a hand on Clete."

"Those guys in Hollywood like me. Why should I be mad at Purcel or you?"

"Why wouldn't you take my call?"

"I was indisposed. She's leaving now. Out the back door. The best piece of ass in New Orleans. Thanks for ruining one of the few good moments in my current life."

THREE DAYS PASSED with no word from Clete. Then I got a call from Detective Sherry Picard in the Jeff Davis Sheriff's Department.

"What can I do for you?" I said.

"I'm at a crime scene south of Jennings. Can you come over here?"

"In our previous conversation, you told me to stay out of your jurisdiction."

"I'm at Kevin Penny's trailer. The coroner won't get here for a couple of hours. I want you to see this."

"See what?"

"Use your imagination," she replied.

IT WAS RAINING and the sun was shining when I got there. Wildflowers were blooming in a field across the road. The crime scene tape was up; an ambulance and two cruisers were parked by Penny's trailer. A tall woman with jet-black hair, wearing dark slacks and a short-sleeve denim shirt and western boots, the kind with rounded steel tips, stood with an umbrella by the motorcycle shed. She bent over and picked up a Styrofoam fast-food container and put it into an evidence bag. Three cops in uniform lounged in the cruisers, smoking, tipping the ashes outside the windows.

I parked my cruiser outside the tape and put on my rain hat and walked to the shed. She looked at her watch. "Good timing. The coroner will be here earlier than he thought."

"This had better be worth it, Detective," I said.

"Excuse me?"

"Giving parts of information over the phone."

"You're here, aren't you?"

"Because I worry about Kevin Penny's child," I said.

She looked away and then back at me, as though making a reevaluation. She had pale skin and lean features, like an Indian's, and a mole by the side of her mouth. "Get your latex on and be careful where you step. One of the uniforms puked on the porch."

The body was on the floor, dressed only in sweatpants, the naked stomach white and mottled and bloated like a frog's, the wrists pulled taut above the head and fastened to the floor with toggle bolts. There were pools of black blood under both knees and elbows. The left ear was clogged with blood and brain matter. In the corner was an electric drill matted with spray, the extension cord still plugged in the socket.

"Ever see anything like this?" Picard said.

"Overseas."

"Vietnam?"

I shook off her question. "Who found him?"

"One of Penny's chippies. He was supposed to take her shopping today."

"Why'd you want me over here, Detective?"

"You and Penny go back."

"Not a good choice of words," I said.

"He and Clete Purcel go back."

"Clete tried to help Penny's kid."

"Who would you make for this?" she said.

"For a vic like this, half the planet."

"Let's go outside," she said.

The rain had quit. The swaths of flowers in the field looked like twisted rainbows surrounded by green grass. I wanted to walk among them and keep walking, over the edge of the earth. "Why were you picking up trash by the shed?"

"Somebody was eating fried chicken there and throwing the bones on the ground. I don't think it was Penny."

"Penny was a slob."

"The pond is full of trash, but there's none out here. The chrome and paint on the motorcycle are clean."

Not bad.

"Clete's not your guy," I said.

"How about you? The word is you might be up on a murder beef."

"You must know an Iberia detective named Spade Labiche."

"I try to stay upwind from dog shit," she said.

The coroner's car turned off the asphalt road onto the dirt track that led to the trailer.

"You need me for anything else?" I said.

"Nope." Her mouth formed into a button.

"That's it?"

"Yep."

"You haven't bagged anything from inside?"

"Not till the coroner gets here," she said.

"There's a gold cigarette lighter in a corner, right by the mop."

"Yeah, I saw it."

"I'd handle it with special care," I said.

She looked at me blankly.

"You might have to get downwind from dog shit after all," I said.

Chapter
19

I WENT TO HELEN'S office and told her what I had seen at Kevin Penny's trailer. I didn't mention the gold lighter. She leaned back in her chair. "You know what this means, don't you?"

"We lost the one guy who could cut me loose on Dartez's murder."

"Who would have that kind of motivation?" she said.

"Take your choice."

"There's something you're not telling me."

"The person who did it is a psychopath. Penny was tortured for reasons of information or revenge. That leaves lots of possibilities."

"How about Tony Nemo's nematodes?" she said.

"I think Maximo Soza might be a candidate," I said.

"How about JuJu?"

"He does what he's told."

She rubbed her forehead. "I wanted Penny for the Dartez killing. We're going to have trouble with the DA. This stinks."

"There was a gold cigarette lighter on the floor of Penny's trailer."

It took her a second. "Why didn't you say that?"

"I'm not objective about certain individuals."

"Have you seen Labiche?"

"In the coffee room."

"Tell him to get his ass in here."

199

*   *   *

THAT EVENING I went to an A.A. meeting in Lafayette. Sometimes A.A. is a hard sell in South Louisiana. Booze is a big part of the culture. When I was a teenager, nobody was ever carded. Uniformed cops worked as bartenders and in gambling houses in St. Martinville, Lafayette, and Opelousas. The law in Louisiana was never intended to be enforced. Its purpose was to provide a vague guideline that made people feel respectable. New Iberia had the most notorious red-light district in the state. There was a semi-cathouse and bar right around the corner from the Lafayette *Daily Advertiser* in the middle of downtown. Friday was family night, no prostitutes allowed; the boiled crawfish and shrimp were free. What better way to give unto Caesar what is Caesar's?

Drive-through daiquiri windows are open until two A.M. You can get plowed before you go to midnight Mass. Fans get wildly drunk at baseball games. If anyone tells you he's from New Orleans and doesn't drink, he's probably not from New Orleans. Louisiana is not a state; it's an outdoor mental asylum in which millions of people stay bombed most of their lives. That's not an exaggeration. Cirrhosis is a family heirloom.

The meetings I attend are made up of the bravest people I've ever known. Don't let anyone tell you that only victims of war suffer post-traumatic problems. The unconscious of a recovering drunk is filled with images no one wants to have as part of his spiritual cache. They hit you at a red light, shopping in a grocery, talking to a friend, kneeling in church. There are people in A.A. who have killed people with their cars or their bare hands. There are people whose negligence killed their children.

As I sat in the meeting in Lafayette, I felt dishonest and unworthy. I had owned up to my slip but not to the possibility that I was in-volved in a homicide. Nor had I told anyone that the desire to drink was still with me, that pushing a basket down the beer and wine aisle at Winn-Dixie made my throat go dry. A Lutheran minister sat on one side of me, a black hooker on the other. The woman leading the meeting owned a chain of hair salons. Our commonality lay in our addictions and unexplainable chemistry, one that absolutely no one, including us, understands.

Though I don't believe in capital punishment, I don't mourn when someone like Penny gets blown out of his socks. However, no one deserves to go out the way he did. When it was my time to speak, I told the group that I was a police officer and had seen an awful instance of inhumanity that morning. I added that, when drunk and in a blackout, I may have been guilty of inhumane acts myself. After the Our Father, the hooker told me to have a nice evening, the minister asked if I could give his car battery a jump, and the woman who owned the beauty salons stopped washing coffee cups long enough to throw me a dish towel.

As sober drunks say, there are no big deals in A.A.

EARLY TUESDAY MORNING, while I was shaving and Alafair was on her jog, someone twisted the bell on the gallery. I walked into the living room and looked through the window screen. Spade Labiche stood four feet away, staring at a squirrel on the lawn. I resumed shaving. Two minutes later, he was at the back door.

"What do you want, partner?" I said.

"To get something straight."

"See you in my office."

"I know we're not on the best of terms. But I'm going to tell you what I told Helen. You can look at the sign-out sheet. I went to interview Penny. I lost my lighter somewhere. It must have been at his trailer."

"Could be," I said.

"I got a call from this broad in Jennings. She ran my prints. She wants to interview me."

"Sherry Picard?"

"Yeah, that's her name. She sounds like a real cunt."

"You delivered your message, Spade."

"Can't we be friends, shake hands or something? I shoot off my mouth sometimes."

"No problem. I'll see you later."

"Okay. You got it," he said.

I watched him walk away, obviously confident that he had righted the universe. I wondered how much time would pass before he tried to give it to me between the shoulder blades.

THAT AFTERNOON I was just leaving my office when Sherry Picard came up the stairs and walked toward me. Her badge holder and a small holstered revolver were hooked on her belt; a pair of cuffs was pulled through the back. Two deputies at the water cooler couldn't take their eyes off her.

"Got a minute?" she said to me.

"Sure," I said.

Behind her, one of the deputies pretended to draw two pistols and fire at either me or her. I let her walk ahead of me into my office. I closed the door.

"Tell the two needle dicks at the cooler that I heard their comments," she said.

"Report them to Sheriff Soileau. She doesn't put up with that kind of thing."

"There're no helpful prints inside the trailer," she said.

"How about on the fast-food trash you picked up by the shed?"

"They're not in the system."

"What did you get off the drill?"

"The latents aren't in the system."

I twiddled a ballpoint on my desk pad. "Why are you here, Detective?"

"The social worker, Carolyn Ardoin, she and Purcel are an item, right?"

"Anybody who knows Clete will tell you he's not capable of doing something like this. I won't even discuss it."

"Where is he now?"

"I'm not his keeper."

"That's a joke."

She was sitting in front of my desk. She wore starched, Cloroxed jeans and a white snap-button western shirt. Her hair was thick and had the same purplish-black sheen in it as Alafair's. "I've seen Purcel's sheet. He has a way of settling scores on his own."

This time I grinned and said nothing.

She looked away, her frustration obvious. I suspected she didn't get a lot of support from her peers in Jennings.

"I'd start with Fat Tony Nemo and a couple of guys named Maximo Soza and JuJu Ladrine," I said.

"With respect, you don't know shit about this case, Detective Robicheaux. Kevin Penny was a confidential informant for the FBI."

"How do you know this?"

"An agent told me. Penny set up his wife's brother. The brother hanged himself in his cell. The agent told me Penny couldn't have cared less."

"So maybe Tony Nemo is your guy."

"I knew Tony when I was with the St. Bernard Sheriff's Department. He's not stupid enough to torture and kill a federal CI."

"What else can I tell you?" I said.

"Evidently, you worked a couple of the Jeff Davis Eight cases," she said.

"That's right."

"You just shut the drawer on them?"

"Nobody shuts the drawer on a corpse, particularly a young girl's."

"What a laugh."

She got up to go. The two deputies who had made comments about her walked past the door glass. She dropped her business card onto the chair. "I think you're in the right place."

RATHER THAN TAKE overtime pay, I took Wednesday off and went fishing in my boat just north of Marsh Island. The wind was up, and a hard chop was slapping the hull, and few boats were out. I didn't mind being alone. Solitude and peace with oneself are probably the only preparation one has for death. I put the statement in the third person for a reason. I don't believe I ever achieved these things with any appreciable degree of success. But there are moments when we understand that the earth and the sky and the presences that may lie behind them are always with us.

The coastline was a heartbreaking green inside the mist. Flying fish broke from the bay's surface and sailed above the water like pink-gilded, winged creatures, in defiance of evolutionary probability. The salt spray breaking on my bow was cold and fresh and smelled of resilience and the mysterious powers the earth contains. My boat seemed to float on a cushion of air rising from the same primeval soup that gave birth to the first living creatures.

I saw a burnt-orange pontoon plane come in low out of a pale yellow sun, the pilot seated in an open cockpit. The plane swooped by, then circled and set down in the chop, blowing water in a huge cloud. The pilot cut the prop and let his plane drift toward me. He pulled up his goggles with his thumb, smearing grease below his eye, like the World War I aviator he obviously wanted to be. He threw me a rope. "Hope I didn't chase off your catch," Jimmy Nightingale said.

"Lose your way home?" I said.

"Sheriff Soileau told me where you'd be. Can I come aboard?" He jumped onto the bow without waiting for me to answer. "This is the life. You got any coffee or sandwiches?" I pointed to my cooler. He pulled off the lid. "Man, I love fried chicken," he said.

"Fang it down."

He sat on a cushion behind the console and bit into a drumstick. "I'm out here to make a confession."

"I watched you pitch a number of times, Jimmy. You had a nasty habit."

"Like what?"

"Spitting on baseballs."

"Think I'd throw you a slider?"

I didn't answer. He began talking about marlin fishing, Washington politics, benchmark oil prices, everything except what was on his mind. Then he said, "Maybe I did get it on with her. But it was consensual. I had more to drink than I was willing to admit. We were both out of it. I also happened to have a bowl of Afghan skunk on hand. She probably didn't tell you about that."

"You're talking about you and Rowena Broussard?"

"Who else?"

"We've gone from denial of rape, to denial of any physical contact at all, to consensual. It's hard to keep up with you, Jimmy."

"It's the truth."

"You confess but you don't confess."

"You're right. That's not what's on my mind." He stared at the water, the tide slapping against the hull. "You saw some bad things in Vietnam?"

"Can't remember. It's odd."

"Be honest."

"Nope. I'm a total blank on it," I said.

"I did something I'd like to stick in an envelope and mail to Mars."

I didn't want to be the repository for all the evil in the world. Like Clete, I had too many videos of my own. They may not have been of my making, but nonetheless I had to carry them. I was determined not to add Jimmy Nightingale's burden to my own.

"Take your bullshit somewhere else," I said.

He tossed a chicken bone over his shoulder into the water and wiped his hands on his trousers. "You're going to hear it whether you like it or not. It was in South America. We were drilling in jungle that was so thick the wind couldn't blow through it. The temperature was one hundred degrees at ten P.M. and the humidity ninety percent. We all felt like we had ants crawling inside our clothes.

"The Indians claimed the land was theirs and hung bones in the trees as a warning. When that didn't work, they started shooting arrows at us. We built a wooden shell around the derrick. It turned into an oven, maybe one hundred twenty degrees. The floor men were fainting or puking in a bucket. We poured water on everybody every half hour. One guy got hit with the tongs. Then a kid took a blow dart in the neck. It had poison on it."

"I know where you're going," I said, raising my hand. "Don't say any more."

He ignored me. "The crew was going to quit. The alternative was to bring in the army. That meant we'd have them on the payroll. For all I knew, it was the army who stirred up the Indians. What was I supposed to do? Everything was coming apart. There was no reasoning with the Indians. They filed their teeth and mutilated their bodies. The head greaseball said they killed their own children. I had to do something. My father said a leader has to take charge. 'You save lives when you take charge.' That's what he always said."

Jimmy paused in the way people do when they want you to agree with them. I stared at the incoming tide, the orange pontoon plane rocking in the chop, baitfish skittering across the surface as they tried to evade a predator below.

"I got ahold of some satchel charges," he said. "They were old, maybe Korean War–issue. I didn't know if they'd detonate. I was twenty-two years old. Another geologist and I flew over the Indians' village. He took the stick, and I pulled the cord on the satchels and threw them out the window. I thought maybe they'd land in the trees and scare the hell out of everybody. I mean, the plane was banking, I wasn't thinking clearly, that's all I wanted to do, scare them. That's what I was thinking when I got in the plane. Just scare them. I told that to the other geologist. That kid they shot with the blow dart almost died, for Christ's sake."

I reeled in my line and laid my rod across the gunwale. Just off Marsh Island, a sailboat was tacking hard in the wind, waves bursting on the prow. My father used to trap on Marsh Island. He was killed in a blowout on a derrick. Sometimes I would see him standing in the surf, giving me the thumbs-up sign, his hard hat cocked on his forehead.

"You're not going to say anything?" Jimmy asked.

"No."

"*What*, you think I'm geology's answer to Charlie Manson?"

"No."

"Get off it, Dave. What are you trying to do to me?"

"What happened to the Indians?"

"The army went in and cleaned it up."

"Cleaned *it* up?"

"Took care of the injured or whatever."

"Did you go to the village?"

"I had a deadline. We were down eight thousand feet. We should have hit a pay sand at five thousand. Our investors were shitting their pants."

"Answer my question."

"The village was on fire. You could see it glowing all night. In the morning there was a black column of smoke across the jungle for two miles. It smelled like garbage burning. Any white person who went down there would have been killed or tied to a tree, and had the skin stripped off him."

I unscrewed my thermos and filled the cap with café au lait and drank from it. "I'm sorry I don't have another cup. There're some cold drinks in the ice."

"A cold drink? Where's your soul?"

"You've made your statement, Jimmy. My advice is to get rid of the past and get on the square."

"I *am* on the square. That's why I'm running for Senate. I want to do good things for other people. There're people who say I can be president. Look at Clinton and Obama. They came out of nowhere."

"You're in with Bobby Earl," I said. "When he's no longer useful, you'll throw him out with the coffee grounds. Here's a reminder for you. Mussolini was hanged upside down in a filling station by the same people who elected him."

"I'm going to be a dictator?"

I shifted my position on the cushion and flung my line, baited with shrimp, in a high arc over the water. I kept my back to Jimmy Nightingale until I felt the boat wobble as he stepped onto his plane. Then I pulled my anchor and started my twin outboards and headed toward home, eager to see Alafair and Clete and all the others who represent what is good in the human race.

* * *

In my opinion, one of the great follies in the world is to put yourself inside the head of dysfunctional people. The mistake we usually make is to assume there is a rationale for their behavior. In most cases, there is none. Long ago, I came to regard the Mob in New Orleans as I would an infected gland. Most of them had the technical skill of hod carriers. They were brutal, stupid to the core, and had the visceral instincts of medieval peasants armed with pitchforks. Their sexual appetites were a hooker's nightmare. The portrayal of them as family men was a joke. They preyed on the weak, corrupted unions, appropriated mom-and-pop stores, and created object lessons with chain saws and meat hooks. The reinvention of this bunch as Elizabethan men of honor probably would have made Shakespeare and Christopher Marlowe sick.

Tony Nine Ball not only came to New Iberia, his chauffeured Chrysler caught up with Alafair on the paved running track in City Park. He rolled down his tinted window. "How you do, Miss Alafair? I'm Tony Nemo, an associate of your father's."

She thought she was looking at a malignant octopod stuffed into a tailored suit. She sped up and passed the picnic tables and swing sets under the live oaks and circled by the baseball diamond while the Chrysler paced her.

"I just want to explain something," Tony said out the window. "I got the backing for the picture. But I got to tie it down. Hey! How about listening, here? You deaf?"

She stopped and breathed slowly. "Say it."

"Get in. I got coffee, I got beignets, I got cinnamon rolls. I got some chocolates, too."

She had done three miles. She wiped the sweat out of her eyes and tried to catch her breath. "Last chance, Mr. Nemo."

"I got to get out of the car. I can't bend over and talk like this. It pinches off my pipes." His driver helped him out, then walked him to a picnic table. Tony collapsed on the bench, wheezing. "These guys in Hollywood say I got to get the option. It ain't enough to use a historical story. Levon Broussard told me to get lost, that a local person is already doing the treatment. So who's that local person gotta be?"

"I don't have control of the option, Mr. Nemo. I was doing an outline for fun."

"Nobody does anything for nothing in the film business. Look, come in with me on this deal. I checked you out. You're already in the Screenwriters Guild. The state of Louisiana pays up to twenty-five percent in tax exemptions and subsidies for films that get made here. We put some locals in Confederate uniforms and hire a boxcar load of boons, and we're in business." When she didn't answer, he looked her up and down. "I'm not supposed to say 'boons.' They call each other niggers."

"The answer is no."

"Union minimum for a treatment is, what, twenty-two grand? That's for ten pages. I'll write you a check now."

"Sorry."

"How much you want?"

"Talk to Levon."

"He won't talk! That's why I'm here!" He began coughing and spat a wad of phlegm between his legs. He wiped his mouth with a lavender monogrammed handkerchief. His face was dilated, his eyes as big as oysters. "I'm gonna have a heart attack here."

"Levon doesn't think Civil War adaptations have a future."

"He's a snob, and sour grapes is what he is," Tony said. "I ain't a bad man, no matter what everybody says. I didn't invent the rules. I *go* by the rules. I'm a ruthless son of a bitch who always keeps his word. You could do worse in this business."

He began choking again, the handkerchief pressed to his mouth, his face turning purple. His driver spread his gloved hand on Nemo's back.

"You better take him to Iberia General," Alafair said.

Tony waved weakly at the air. "I want you on that script. You've got balls."

"I've got *what*?"

"Balls. You got balls," he said, his voice hardly more than a whisper.

She wondered how so many people could be afraid of such a sick man. The driver held an oxygen cup to Tony's face.

"I hope you're better, Mr. Nemo," Alafair said.

Then she jogged across the green toward the drawbridge at Burke Street, her tanned legs flashing in the sunlight.

Chapter
20

SHE DIDN'T TELL me about her encounter with Tony until that evening.

"Why didn't you say anything earlier, Alf?" I said.

"You were at work. He's a pitiful man. I think we should feel sorry for him."

"Don't tell Clete Purcel that."

"You should have seen him."

"Tony Nemo should have been sent to a rendering plant a long time ago."

"Pretty callous, Dave."

"I'll feel as bad about that as I can."

But you can't get mad at your daughter because she's compassionate, even if you think her feelings are misdirected. I called Levon's house. Rowena answered.

"Could I speak to Levon, please?" I said.

"What for?"

"It's of a personal nature."

"How's this for personal: Why don't you do your job and leave us alone?"

"Where is he, Ms. Broussard?"

"He just went out the door. With his favorite shotgun. Maybe you can catch him."

When I got to the Broussard home, I heard the popping sounds of gunfire from behind the house. It was twilight, the yard deep in shadow, the sky marbled with purple and red clouds. I skirted the house and came out in the backyard. Levon was firing with a twelve-gauge at clay pigeons he launched from an automatic trap thrower, bursting them above Bayou Teche, regardless of the neighbors on the far side of the water.

He took the plugs out of his ears. He was wearing a sleeveless shooting jacket stuffed with shells. His face seemed thinner, his eyes receded, the color of buckshot. "Slumming?" he asked.

"I need a lesson or two about film rights and such. Tony Nemo is on Alafair's case."

"About what?"

"He wants her to write a screenplay or adaptation or whatever you call it based on your novel."

"I've heard from my agent and a couple of producers this character has been pestering. Evidently, you stoked him up."

"I told him he could create a historical piece that wasn't dependent on your novel."

"Thanks a lot for doing that," Levon said.

"He says these guys in Hollywood actually want to go into business with him."

"They probably do. Nemo is wired in to the entirety of the casino culture. He knows how to get around the unions. He launders money. Hollywood is Babylon by the Sea. He's a perfect fit."

"According to Alafair, period pieces are dead on arrival."

"Now they are."

"But someday?"

"What do I know? I don't care, either."

"What writer wouldn't want to see his work on the screen?" I said.

"J. D. Salinger."

"Salinger didn't like to see people, either. That's why he put his name on his mailbox, out on the road."

"You want to shoot?" he asked.

"No."

He ejected the spent shell from the chamber and began thumbing five fresh rounds into the magazine.

"You don't keep a sportsman plug in the magazine?" I said.

"I don't have to. I don't hunt. I shoot only clay targets." He rested the shotgun in the crook of his arm.

"You don't look the same," I said.

"What?"

"Everything copacetic?"

"I'm not the issue. Rowena is."

"I'm sorry all this has happened to you, Levon."

"Actually, I'm surprised you're here. You must not have seen the local news this evening," he said. "You were the lead story. I don't mean to be the bearer of bad news."

AT TEN P.M. Alafair and I watched the replay of the interview with T. J. Dartez's wife. It was hard. Her grief and incomprehension were real. All of her features were round, without corners or angles, her face without makeup, a pie plate full of dough. Her husband was dead, killed, she said, by someone in the Iberia Parish Sheriff's Department, a man who had harassed both her and her husband. She had no income and was about to be evicted from the Quarters outside Loreauville.

Alafair started to turn off the set.

"Let's hear her out," I said.

Mrs. Dartez was crying, her handkerchief twisted between her fingers. The interview had been prefaced with the caption "Justice Denied?" The newsman was obviously moved and had trouble completing the interview. He thanked her for being there, then looked silently at the camera.

"Someone is doing a job on you, Dave," Alafair said.

"Nobody has that kind of beef against me."

"Labiche does."

"He's not that smart."

"At this point you should get a lawyer."

"A lawyer will tell me to shut up and not cooperate with the department. Everything I do will be interpreted as an indicator of guilt."

She couldn't argue with that one.

I had been in the midst of Katrina and its aftermath. Oddly, I wanted to return to those days. There is a purity in catastrophe. We see firsthand the nature of both human courage and human frailty, the destructive and arbitrary power of the elements, the breakdown of social restraint and our mechanical inventions and the release of the savage that hides in the collective unconscious. An emergency room lit only by flashlights and filled with the moans of the dying and feet sloshing in water becomes a medieval scene no different than one penned by Victor Hugo. It is under these circumstances that we discover who we are, for good or bad. And when all this passes, we never talk about it, lest we lose the insight it gave us.

Wars have the same attraction. Rhetoric fades away; truth remains. In my hometown, I was trapped by shadows that had neither substance nor face.

Helen called me in the next morning. "I just got back from the prosecutor's office."

"He watched the news last night?" I said.

"The wire services and networks are on him. I've had three calls myself."

"I see."

"Internal Affairs is taking over."

"Internal Affairs is a joke," I said.

"Let me put you on the desk. All this will pass."

"Not for me it won't. Maybe I killed Dartez. I have dreams I can't remember. I think he's in them. I see headlights shining and hear glass breaking. I see blood coming from someone's mouth."

It was obvious that she didn't want to hear it. "We have a witness who puts Kevin Penny at the scene," she said. "That's reasonable doubt. The prosecutor knows this isn't a prosecutable case."

"Then why doesn't he say that?"

"At some point all of us will. Then a shitload of criticism will come down on our heads, and time will go by, and everybody will forget it."

She was dead wrong, but I let it go. "Tony Nemo is in town."

"Tony Nine Ball is in New Iberia?"

"He wants Alafair to do a film adaptation of Levon Broussard's Civil War novel."

"Lucky her."

"I went to see Levon about it. He talked about his wife's suicide attempt and her depression. I expected him to say something about Jimmy Nightingale not being under arrest."

"So?"

"I thought it was kind of funny, that's all."

"If I ever saw an instance of Southern inbreeding, it's that guy," she said. "The day Levon Broussard makes sense to you is the day you should have yourself lobotomized."

CLETE HAD BROUGHT Homer Penny to New Iberia and placed him during the day with a Creole woman in an Acadian cottage on the road to St. Martinville. According to legend, it was built in the late eighteenth century and was the oldest structure in the parish. Each morning she took him to school, and each afternoon he rode the school bus back to the cottage, where Clete picked him up at five. In the meantime, Clete visited Carolyn Ardoin at her home in Jennings and brought her flowers and candy and baskets of fruit and books from the library, his heart emptying out each time he looked at the damage that her assailant or assailants had done to her. He also launched his own investigation into the attack, starting with Pookie the Possum Domingue.

Clete found him early in the day at an upscale billiard hall in Lafayette, one that had a bar and a mixologist and rows of beautifully maintained tables. Pookie was shooting a game of rotation by himself. He wore an expensive oversize suit and a loud tie and tasseled loafers and a crisp shirt with cuff links. His pointy face shrank when he saw Clete walking toward him.

"Know who Carolyn Ardoin is?" Clete said.

"Maybe I heard the name," Pookie said.

"Wrong answer. She's my lady friend. Know what happened to her?"

Pookie rested the butt of his cue on the floor. He looked at the people drinking and eating at the bar. The free lunch that day was chipped beef poured on crushed beignets. A bowl of it sat on a chair by Pookie's pool table. It looked like cat puke.

"Want me to ask you again?" Clete said.

"There's a shutdown on information in that area."

"Because of Kevin Penny?"

"Cool it, huh?"

"Who did him?"

"I don't know, Purcel. I don't *want* to know."

"Who attacked Miss Carolyn?"

"I warned you about Maximo and JuJu."

"Tony sicced them on Miss Carolyn?"

"I ain't said that. You don't get it. It's the dope, man. That's what all this is about."

"The stuff coming in off I-10?"

"It comes from everywhere. There's legal marijuana farms in Puerto Rico now. The meth labs are gonna take a hit. You know the drugs you can buy in any school yard in this state?"

"I don't care about that," Clete said.

"Nobody does. That's why guys like Tony the Nose are happy. You might pass that on to the broad in the Jeff Davis Sheriff's Department, dresses like she's at the rodeo."

"Sherry Picard?" Clete said.

"Yeah, the one that's got her nose in the air. Here's the word: Stay out of Jeff Davis Parish. Don't mess with any of Tony Squid's people. People should forget any rumors about Jimmy Nightingale."

"Nightingale is a great guy?" Clete said.

"He slept wit' some of those dead girls."

"One of the Jeff Davis Eight?"

"I ain't saying no more."

"What if I spread it around that you've been shooting off your mouth? I might end up being your only friend, Pookie. Give that some thought."

Pookie's skin turned as gray as a dehydrated lizard's, his eyes as tiny as seeds. "This ain't right, no. I always he'ped you out, Purcel."

"Then do it now. There's at least one guy out there who needs to go off the board. Dave Robicheaux saw Penny's body. The man's feet were bolted to the floor. The guy who did him took his time, then pushed an electric drill through his eardrum into his brain."

Somebody power-broke a tight rack, spilling two or three balls onto the floor. Pookie sat down on a felt-covered bench and picked up his bowl of chipped beef and started spooning it into his mouth as though it were wet confetti. He gagged and spat it back in the bowl. "I cain't take this. I got to get out of town."

"Tell me what you know."

"I don't know nothing. That's the point. Ain't nobody gonna believe me, either. Nobody got my back."

Clete went to the bar and bought two long-necks. He sat down next to Pookie and handed him one. "Guys like us are old-school. Drink up and quit worrying, Pook. We're not that important to anybody."

"T'ink so?"

"You bet," Clete said, taking a swig.

Words he would regret.

ON FRIDAY MORNING, I began gathering my notes and writing my conclusions regarding the sexual assault on the person of Rowena Broussard. In many ways, the difficulty lay in the recalcitrant and illogical and contradictory statements and behavior of the accuser. She had not gone to a hospital; nor had she called the authorities or asked for a rape kit. Instead she had showered and destroyed any chance of the prosecution using the kind of forensic evidence that people have learned about from television shows. She had been impaired when the attack took place, if indeed it took place. A pillowcase had been pulled over her head, intensifying her pain and fear but leaving her descriptions muddled. The bruising on her body could have been caused by a fall outside the lounge where she had gotten drunk with the accused.

She said she had been raped by two men in Wichita, Kansas, but the prosecutor had dropped the charges for political reasons. It was possible she had transferred her rage at the injustice done her in Kansas to her current situation in New Iberia. It happens. The family physician had indicated that she may have been a neglected wife. "Hell hath no fury," he had said.

Jimmy Nightingale was a conundrum as well. He had claimed he never touched Rowena except to pick her up when she fell in the parking lot. Then he had indicated he may have had a consensual experience with her, but he could remember no details. He had said they were both swacked out of their minds on hashish and alcohol, which I believed. Other than that, I knew little more than I did when the investigation began.

I've seen cops write off this kind of situation as he said/she said. That's the cliché they use. When we see it in print or in an interdepartmental e-mail, it means the woman is about to get it in the neck. Why?

The situation is not equal. The woman has to prove the existence of an act nobody other than the perpetrator was witness to. Perhaps a year will pass before the case goes to trial. In the meantime, she has to give depositions in front of strangers, accept lewd stares in a courthouse hallway, the hidden smirk in the face of a redneck cop, the muffled laughter among a group of males as she walks by. I once heard a Lafayette cop in the bullpen, right by the dispatcher's cage, tell his colleagues about a man who held a woman down and rubbed his penis all over her body. He thought the story was hilarious.

In my summation, I said I believed the scratches on Rowena's hip, the bruise inside her thigh, the bite mark on her shoulder, and the obvious emotional and psychological trauma visited upon her were consistent with her claim—namely, that while she was impaired, she was raped and probably orally sodomized by James Beaufort Nightingale. I also believed she'd showered and hadn't told her husband about the assault immediately because she was ashamed and felt her drunken state had invited the attack.

What I couldn't put in my report was my dismay at Nightingale's attitude. He was obsessed with guilt for air-bombing the Indians but cavalier about the possibility that he had raped Rowena Broussard in a blackout. Regardless, I did the best I could with the information I had, and I e-mailed it to Helen's computer. Ten minutes later, she opened my door and leaned inside. "Way to rock, pappy."

ON TUESDAY, JIMMY was formally charged. With an attorney by his side, he surrendered at the courthouse, and in under two hours, he was fingerprinted and released on twenty-five thousand dollars bail. That evening he gave an interview to three local television stations in his backyard. He was dressed in golf slacks and a polo shirt and seated by a reflecting pool blanketed with floating camellias. His skin was pink in the sunset, his bronze hair freshly barbered, his expression both calm and humble. Just as the interview began, he set aside a book he had been reading, one that looked like a Bible. His diction was perfect, his accent like the recorded voice of William Faulkner or Robert Penn Warren or Walker Percy. You felt he could recite from the telephone directory and turn it into the Sermon on the Mount.

"I'm disappointed and disturbed by the conduct of some of our officials," he said. "I bear them no ill will, but I believe a small group of individuals have acted politically and done a disservice to their constituency. I promise to be as forthcoming as I possibly can. I love the state of Louisiana, and I love its people. I would never lie to them. Not now, not in the past, not in the future. I say this before the throne of God."

He gazed at the scarlet reflection of the bayou in the moss-hung boughs of the live oaks, his face as chiseled and noble as Robert E. Lee's at Appomattox.

No one could say Jimmy Nightingale didn't have the touch.

Chapter
21

THE MAN WHO got on the flight from Miami to New Orleans and took a seat next to a huge black woman whose rolls of fat seemed to drip into the aisle wore Bermuda shorts, red tennis shoes, a canary-yellow T-shirt with Mickey Mouse's face on it, and big, round sunglasses that were as black as welders' goggles. His skin was the color of powdered milk, his hair like wisps of corn silk on a doll's head, his smile a slice of watermelon.

He stepped on the black woman's foot, tumbled across her body with his drawstring beach bag, and smashed his head on the window. "Owie," he said.

"Are you hurt?" the black woman said.

"Not much," he said, pressing his hand against the red knot on his forehead. He gathered up his sunglasses. "I hope I didn't hurt your foot too bad."

"I been reading my thought-of-the-day book. I don't let nothing bother me."

"My name is Chester Wimple. What's yours?"

"Birdie."

"It's nice to meet you, Miss Birdie." He took two unpeeled peaches from his beach bag and gave one to her and began sucking on the other, like a child finding a teat. "Sometimes people call me Smiley. I can speak Spanish."

She couldn't quite put the two statements together. "Smiley is a very nice name."

"I have a lisp. People think it's because I'm from New Or-yuns. It's because I had a cleft palate that had to be operated on when I was little."

"Don't let nobody be telling you your voice ain't nice. It's nice."

He flipped down the table on the back of the seat in front of him. "Do you like checkers?"

"Our church group plays checkers and Monopoly at the old people's home every Sunday night."

"I love Monopoly," he said. He pushed back in the seat with the thrust of the plane, his face filled with delight, then felt the plane level off and catch hold of the clouds. He could see the city disappearing behind him in the twilight, the condos and palm trees and waves on Miami Beach miniaturizing, the way every stage of his life seemed to shrink and diminish into nothingness whenever he decided to move on to his next adventure. He did not understand why people had trouble with life. Every so often you got on a plane and flew away and let whatever was wrong with that place correct itself. Even the Everglades were shrinking into a tiny pattern of green islands and brown canals and bays that looked like a map rather than a watershed. Distance allowed you to sort things out. Otherwise, there was too much confusion, too many voices bouncing around in your head, too many people who needed correcting.

He opened his folding checkerboard and set out the checkers for his new friend and himself. "You're a lady, so you go first."

SHORTLY, AS THOUGH in a dream, the sun was gone, the sky blue-black as they approached the Louis Armstrong Airport. Chester could see Lake Pontchartrain and headlights streaming across the causeway, the Mississippi winding in serpentine fashion through the wetlands, Algiers shrouded in mist across the river, the revelers dancing in the streets of the French Quarter, as though none of them had to die, the Garden District and Tulane and Loyola Universities up St. Charles

Avenue, all of it streaking past him, about to become real and not as much fun as it was up *here*.

He took a pad from his shirt pocket and wrote on the top page and tore it off and handed it to Birdie. "That's my number. If you ever have any trouble, call me." He always had difficulty with his *r*'s, and "trouble" came out as "twubbel."

Birdie looked at the blinking sign above the captain's cabin and buckled her seat belt. "You have been very courteous to me, Smiley. I'm not fond of flying. But wit' you, I didn't feel no fear. Your father probably wasn't no good. But your mama was."

"How do you know that?" he said.

"Women know these things."

Inside the airport, he retrieved his small wheelie bag and rolled it next to Birdie out the door to the cab stand, which was located in a car tunnel under the building. Two black guys, maybe nineteen or twenty years old, locked on to Birdie and Chester as soon as they saw them, the way school yard and sidewalk bullies always recognize the weak and the vulnerable, the halt and the lame, those born ugly or fat or mentally handicapped or misshapen, those who somehow seemed deserving of torment.

They were probably stealing luggage or shagging change or maybe shagging a country girl new to the city. They were a classic pair: sneering, loud, stupid, cruel, born of a single mother, detested in the womb, raised on welfare, smelling of funk and pomade and rut, users of their roles as victims to cause scenes when confronted with their abuse. They were both chewing gum, smacking it, their eyes bright, the unpredictable glaze you saw in the eyes of meth heads.

"Here come Aint Jemima and the Pillsbury Doughboy," the taller one said. He had one gold tooth and one missing tooth.

"Shut your mouth, boy," Birdie said.

"Big Mama speaks," the other guy said. His pants were so low his pubic hair was showing. "Got her jelly roll ready to rock."

"I'll slap your face," she said.

He responded by tripping Chester. "Sorry dere, boss. He'p massah wit' you bag?"

Chester got up from the concrete, Birdie's face like a hurt child's.

The taller guy was chewing his gum rapidly, grinning. "Go on, man. We didn't mean nothing. Hey, you listening? Get the fuck out of here."

Chester opened the back door of a taxi and helped Birdie in. She looked up at him, a dignified church woman who had probably spent a large part of her life forgiving other people. "We can share the ride if you going near Gentilly."

He shut the door and patted the top of her hand when she placed it on the windowsill. "I got to take care of some business that came up all of a sudden."

"You stay out of trouble."

"Yes, ma'am. I love you, Miss Birdie."

The cab drove away. Chester stood among the crowd on the pavement, the arc lights burning overhead, his knees scraped from the fall. He watched the two black guys walk away and get into an old Honda in the parking lot. Chester grabbed the next taxi in line, one driven by an Arab who had turned his cab into a bead-strung mosque that smelled of burning incense and was filled with yowling sounds. "My name is Chester. What's yours?"

"Mohammed," the driver said.

"Do you see those two black boys?"

"I see them, sir."

"They're friends of mine. I want to go where they go."

The driver turned all the way around to get a full look at his passenger. He had a beard like shaggy black rope wrapped under his nose and scrolled on his cheeks. "I have seen those two men before. They are not good young men, sir."

"They're bad?"

"They are very bad."

"They shouldn't be acting like that," Chester said. "I'll tell them."

The driver started the meter and drove onto I-10, not far behind the Honda.

* * *

THEY CROSSED THE river into Algiers and continued into a neighborhood of empty buildings, alleys oozing trash, bars on windows, rap music blaring from a club, hookers strolling under the neon. Up ahead, the Honda pulled in to the gravel drive of a darkened frame house built up from the street. There were no lights inside.

"Let me out," Chester said.

"Maybe you should let me take you somewhere else, sir," the driver said.

"This is as far as I go. How much is the fare?"

"Twenty-eight dollars."

Chester got out and paid the driver through the window. He added a five-dollar tip. "I like your music."

"Thank you, sir," the driver said. "God is good."

Chester squinted to show that he didn't understand.

"Be careful, sir," the driver said. "There are evil men in the world."

Chester watched the taxi drive away, then began wheeling his bag down the broken sidewalk toward the elevated house. Someone had turned on a light in back, and he saw a shadow move across the kitchen window. There were no streetlamps on the block. He pulled his bag between two cars whose engines had been stripped, and unlocked and unzipped his wheelie bag and removed a nickel-plated snub-nose .357 Magnum from the gun case inside the bag. He walked up the steps of the house, set down his beach bag, and rested his wheelie against the wall, then worked on a pair of thin cotton gloves. The screen and inside door were unlocked. He stepped inside and walked through the living room and into the hallway. The two black guys were eating out of cans at the kitchen table, their cigarettes burning in an ashtray, quart bottles of beer by their elbows.

"Hi, again. My name is Chester. You hurt my knees and made fun of Miss Birdie."

"How the fuck—" the taller guy began.

"A taxi. Some people call me Smiley. Know why?"

They stared at the revolver in his hand and shook their heads. "No," one of them said, so frightened that his mouth did not move and Chester could not tell which one had spoken.

"I like children. They make me happy," Chester said. "You were very bad."

"We didn't mean nothing," the shorter one said. There was dried food on his bottom lip. His fork was trembling on top of an open tuna can.

"Say you're sorry."

"Sure, man," the tall one said, as though he had been released from a bathysphere. "Sit down. You want a beer?" He raked back a chair, his face popping sweat.

"You didn't say it like you meant it," Chester said.

"We mean it, man! Come on, man, don't point that at me. Please."

Just as lightning crashed into someone's yard, Chester shot each of them, one through the throat, one through the chest. They were still alive when he stood over them and shot them again. Then he sprinkled their uneaten food in their faces and turned off the light and retrieved his beach bag and travel case and went out the back door.

A soft rain was falling, the clouds flickering, thunder rolling dully across the wetlands. The wheels on his bag clicked monotonously down the broken sidewalks, past the abandoned buildings that were probably shooting galleries, past the club that shook with rap music. The hookers had gone inside, out of the rain. He stared through the window at the people inside and smiled at the way they danced and seemed to enjoy themselves. The neon glow of the club slid off his body like dissolving watercolor. *See?* he thought. Life wasn't complicated at all. In a minute he would be gone, subsumed inside the great American night, a tiny point of light inside a galaxy that became a snowy road arching into infinity.

He tilted back his head and let the rain fall into his mouth. He licked the drops off his lips as he would sprinkles on ice cream.

CLETE HAD GONE home for lunch. Homer was at private school in the little town of Cade, on the other side of Spanish Lake. Clete had begun splitting a loaf of warm French bread to make a po'boy sandwich when he looked out the window and saw the police cruiser turn in to the motor court and stop in front of his cottage; a woman was behind the wheel. The cruiser had dents and scratches on it, and one headlight hung lower than the other. It was the kind of vehicle that law enforcement agencies often issued to minority members years ago.

A tall brunette woman in jeans and a white shirt and unshined western boots got out and knocked on the door. Clete looked around the room. Homer's baseball bat and glove were on a chair. He threw his raincoat over them and opened the door.

"Detective Sherry Picard," she said. "I need a few minutes of your time."

"I'm about to eat."

"Put it on hold." She stepped inside.

"Why don't you just come in?" he said, shutting the door after her.

"Go ahead with what you were doing." She sat down at a table by the window and took a pad and ballpoint from her shirt pocket. "You have a nice view."

"Look, Miss Sherry—"

"Detective."

"Yes, ma'am. I got to get back to—"

"I'm here for two reasons, Mr. Purcel. We're looking for a missing kid named Homer Penny. Not 'missing' in the real sense but missing from the system, if you get my meaning. Someone went into the crime scene where his father was tortured to death and took his clothes from a dresser. Know who might have done that?"

"Someone who knew the kid needed his clothes. Someone who knew the kid would be better off on the moon than in the hands of the people who returned him to his father."

Her eyes went to the chair where Clete had thrown the raincoat. One flap hung over the tip of the baseball bat.

"The second reason I'm here is about Kevin Penny. We found a gold cigarette lighter in the trailer. It belongs to Detective Labiche. But he's got an explanation. He was sent there by Sheriff Soileau to interview Penny."

"That doesn't mean he didn't go there for other reasons."

"You're not a fan?"

"Labiche is a dirty cop."

"How do you know that?"

"I can smell one. He also has a hard-on for Dave Robicheaux."

"Thanks for telling me that. Who's Labiche on a pad for?"

"Tony Nine Ball. Maybe some meth guys in East Texas. Maybe some greaseballs in Tampa or Miami. Take your choice. We're everybody's punch."

"You know who Maximo Soza and JuJu Ladrine are?"

"One's a psychopath, the other has a triple-A battery for a brain. They both work for Tony."

"You think they're capable of crucifying a man and drilling his elbows and knees?"

"Maximo would do it in a blink. It's not like JuJu."

"What would be the motivation?"

"What motivates these guys to do anything? Half the things they believe don't exist. They're the dumbest shits on earth. That's why they're criminals."

"How about this? Kevin Penny was a federal informant. Maybe Soza and Ladrine were sent to find out if Penny dimed them or Tony Nemo."

"Too extreme, in my opinion."

"So where does that leave us?" she said, looking straight at him as though she knew the answer to her question.

"You got me. I run down bail skips and do other kinds of scut work for Nig Rosewater and Wee Willie Bimstine."

"How about the fact that they were following you around? They even parked their vehicle by the house of your lady friend while you were doing a sleepover."

"How about leaving third parties out of this?" he said.

"Then you had a confrontation with them in downtown Jennings. Then your lady friend got beaten to a pulp. The word is you have some bad markers out. You also gave Kevin Penny a bad time about his kid. Maybe you figured all three of them for the beating of the Ardoin woman, and you started with Penny."

Clete halved the loaf of French bread into two long buns and began layering them with lettuce and sliced tomatoes and chopped onions and deep-fried crawfish and oysters he had taken from the icebox. "Short answer, Detective: I never put a hand on Penny."

"We lifted a lot of prints from the trailer. Most of them were in the computer at the NCIC. Some were not. That bothers me."

"Because people like Penny don't have normal friends?"

"But yours were all over the place. I've seen your sheet. I've known recidivists who would be in awe of your record."

He released the handle of the knife and stared straight ahead. "I'll try again. I was in the Crotch. I did two tours in Vietnam. I saw guys who were skinned alive and hung in trees. I don't torture people." He picked up a small clean brush and began painting mayonnaise and shrimp dip on his sandwich.

"My husband was killed in Iraq," she said.

He turned around. Her face was calm, her eyes clear. She seemed to be looking at a thought or memory inside her head.

"I'm sorry," he said.

"You have to get on the square about the missing boy, Mr. Purcel."

"I *am* on the square. Nothing bad is ever going to happen to that little boy again."

"You committed a felony by deliberately violating a crime scene and taking items from it. You know that, don't you?"

He put the sandwich together and cut it in half. "I'll split this with you."

She got up and walked to the chair where the raincoat was. She tugged it slightly so it covered the bottom of the bat. "No, thanks."

He wiped his hands on a dish towel and watched her. She wore her gun and badge and cuffs on her belt, perhaps as a statement of her own identity and in defiance of male authority. She wasn't aggressive, but she wasn't passive, either. She seemed to live inside a place beyond the fray. She straightened her shoulders and looked out the window at the live oaks arching over the driveway. She turned around, as though asking him *Why the silence?*

"There's a snitch in Lafayette named Pookie Domingue," Clete said. "Sometimes people call him Pookie the Possum. He says the word is out you'd better get your head on straight."

"Or?"

"There're eight dead women who want justice. Somebody out there doesn't want that to happen, Miss Sherry."

"Detective Picard," she said.

"Yes, ma'am. Forget I said anything. I think I really screwed up in a previous incarnation."

Clete sat down at the table and bit into his sandwich.

Then she was standing behind him. "I'm going to cover your ass as best I can. Take care of Homer and Ms. Ardoin. If you shot me a line on any of this, I'll be back."

She dragged a fingernail across the back of his neck as she went out the door. He set down his food and went out on the stoop. He was going to tell her something. He was sure of that. He just didn't know what it was.

THAT AFTERNOON HELEN and I met with the prosecutor, Lala Segretti. He was tall and in his mid-fifties and had freckles and thinning light red hair and wore suspenders and always looked wired. When he was a long-distance runner at LSU and a pretty girl would walk by he would say "Ooh-la-la" to hide that he was afraid of girls because he'd grown up in a fundamentalist church Ayatollah Khomeini could have invented. He was a family man and a straight shooter, but he obsessed over things of no consequence and sometimes translated the Old Testament into a political mind-set that precluded compassion, particularly when it came to capital punishment.

We were in the conference room at a long oak table with him at the head of it, pages from my report spaced out in front of him. He was blinking, his jaw tight. He was obviously agitated, but I didn't know about what. He was one of those men who could eat any kind of food without gaining weight, as though a flame in his stomach burned off the intake the second it came down the pipe.

"Everything all right, sir?" I said.

"We've got a shit storm coming down on us because of the Nightingale indictment," he said. "Plus a lot of criticism about an in-house matter."

He looked at me to make sure I got the point.

"I'm the in-house matter?" I said.

"We'll talk about that later," he replied.

I felt a constriction behind my left eye that caused my eye to water and sent a signal to my brain that has always scared me and that I have never understood.

"Nightingale's constituency thinks we're political," Lala said. "The problem is, to some degree, they're right. He's a demagogue and a liar, and I want to put him out of business before he turns the state into a sewer. We can't let them get away with it."

"Who's 'they'?" Helen said. "Get away with what?"

"His hacks and hucksters. He has an army of them. He's got backers in Vegas. I think they're grooming him for bigger things."

"I don't think this conversation is taking a good turn," I said.

Lala looked at me again. "Rephrase that so I don't get the wrong inference."

"Nightingale is guilty of sexual assault and battery or he isn't," I said.

"Dave is right," Helen said. "We do our job and stay out of the consequences."

"I don't think I've expressed myself very well," he said. "Nightingale and his family are associated with criminals. They've gotten a free pass for years. Iberia Parish voted down casino gambling. That will always be to our credit. We're not going to allow this son of a bitch to besmirch us."

"You're not alone in your feelings," Helen said.

Lala wasn't listening. His attention was fixed on me. "In your report I get a sense of hesitancy," he said.

"There's some elements in the case that aren't clear," I said. "Why would Rowena delay reporting the rape? Why did she destroy evidence? She's educated and intelligent. So is her husband."

"Traumatized people don't behave rationally," he said.

"The family physician indicates she may have been a neglected wife," I said.

"Neglected wives have drinks with another man, or even affairs, but that doesn't mean they invite rape into their lives," he said.

"I'm with you on that."

The room was silent. Helen cleared her throat. A tree limb brushed against the window.

"What are you holding back?" he asked me.

"The last time I talked to Levon, he didn't mention Nightingale not being in jail; that was the kind of thing I expected him to say. It was almost like he didn't care."

"That's perception, not evidence," he said.

"How many sexual assault cases are *not* about perception?" I said.

"Levon Broussard spat in Nightingale's face at Iberia General. Doesn't that tell you something?"

"That was then. This is now."

"You're muddying the water, Dave," he said. "I don't understand why. Helen, could I speak to Dave alone, please?"

"Powder my nose?" she said.

"I didn't mean it that way."

"Your ass," she said, and left the room.

Score one for Helen Soileau.

After she was gone, Lala put the pages of my report back into a folder and leaned forward, his face bladed with color, his nose cut out of tin. "The investigation into the Dartez homicide has been the most unusual in my career."

"Really?" I said.

"Don't be clever with me, Dave. There's a cloud over your head, and nothing we do seems to get rid of it. The department and my office have been taking your weight."

"Then stop doing it."

"It's not a time to be *gallant*. Labiche lifted your prints on the broken glass from the driver's side of the truck. That detail will not go away. Unless you're willing to make it go away."

"What are you hinting at?"

"You were at the Dartez house and could have touched his truck. Or maybe on another occasion." He paused, then said, "Am I right?"

"I could have."

"You did or you didn't?"

I could hear a motorboat on the bayou. I wanted to get up and walk to the window and float away, above the picnic shelters and trees and children playing on swing sets and seesaws. "I did not touch Dartez's vehicle at his home. I cannot explain the presence of my fingerprints on the glass."

I could hear myself breathing in the silence. I counted the seconds. I got up to fourteen, then restarted the count, my heart twisting.

"You think you did it?" he asked. "Just say it. Let's end this crap."

"I think I'm capable of it."

"You truly mean that? You would kill a man with your bare hands?"

"Yes, sir."

"Are you done with your drinking?"

I could feel my control slipping, my old enemy, childhood rage, surfacing once again. "It's not *my* drinking—" I began. I saw a red glow behind my eyes and heard a popping sound in my ears. I started over. "No, sir, I cannot swear that I'm done. No drunk can."

He leaned back in his chair. He shook his head as though in bewilderment. "Best of everything to you."

"Want to translate that?"

"You're an honorable man. But others have to pay your tab."

I have to say, the cut went deep. "Anything else?"

He didn't answer. When I opened the door to leave, he was standing at the window, a hand on his hip, staring at the park, his shirt pinched inside his suspenders.

"I never popped a cap on somebody who didn't ask for it," I said. "Even in a free-fire zone."

"Ooh-rah," he said without turning around.

Chapter
22

Aᴛ ᴏɴᴇ ᴛɪᴍᴇ St. Mary Parish was a fiefdom ruled by an oligarchical family who owned everything and everyone in the parish, bar none. In the 1970s, when a group of activist Catholic nuns tried to organize the cane workers, they found themselves at mortal risk in an area that was more than ninety percent Catholic. Enforcement of the law was situational. Every public servant knew which ring to kiss. The people at the bottom of the pile were not necessarily abused, but they weren't necessarily protected from abuse, either.

Sexual exploitation is not a subject most police departments like to deal with. But it's often there. A cop picks up a hippie runaway hitchhiking. Maybe she's holding, maybe she's got a warrant on her, maybe she's sixteen and her teeth are chattering. It's twilight. She's in the backseat, wrists cuffed behind her, trying to see where they're going as the cop swings around on the shoulder and heads down a two-lane away from town. The cop has already dropped his badge inside his pocket so she won't get his number.

His name was Jude McVane. Before he was a deputy sheriff, he was a chaser in a navy brig, a hack in a women's prison, and a collector for a loan company. He had big hands and smelled of manly odors and was good at his paperwork because he did as little of it as possible. There were never any complaints about him. But his colleagues did not hang out with him after work hours, particularly those who were protective of their wives' sensibilities.

At sunrise Thursday, he was driving his cruiser on a two-lane back road that followed the curves along Bayou Teche. The primroses were blooming on the edge of the cane fields, the sun spangling inside the tunnel of live oaks. He passed two antebellum homes built in the early nineteenth century, then crossed the drawbridge and turned in to a trailer village that belonged in Bangladesh. He stopped in front of a trailer occupied by a young black single mother. Without speaking, she exited the trailer, locked the door behind her, and got into the back of the cruiser.

"Good morning, sunshine," McVane said.

She looked wanly out the window. He drove out of the trailer park and back across the drawbridge and past a closed sugar refinery. Then he hooked back in to the confines of the refinery on a dirt road and parked in the shade of a rusted-out tin shed.

"Nobody does it like you," he said, getting in back.

When she was finished, she walked away from the cruiser and cleared her mouth and spat.

"I always heard it tastes like watermelon rind," he said.

She refused to speak. He drove her back to her home and watched her get out and go inside. He shifted into gear and drove out of the trailer park and back over the Teche and headed toward Franklin. A solitary figure was walking around the edge of the road, dragging a wheeled case behind him, a beach bag hanging from his shoulder. McVane pulled alongside and rolled down the passenger window. "Where you going, partner?"

The man wore red tennis shoes and khakis that probably came from Target and a green T-shirt with Bugs Bunny eating a carrot on the front. "I'm touring the countryside. I got off the bus at the wrong place."

"Where are you from?"

"New Or-yuns, originally. My name is Chester. Sometimes people call me Smiley."

"Chester what?"

"Wimple. What's yours?"

"Get in."

"Why?"

"I'll take you where you're going."

Chester leaned his head in the window and sniffed. "There's been a woman in here."

"Get in the cruiser, please."

"I like walking."

"I guess it's going to be one of those days," McVane said.

"All right. If you want to act like that. I don't want to make anybody mad." The man got inside and inhaled. "Icky."

"What is?"

"Like somebody has been doing something he shouldn't."

"Buckle up," McVane said. He drove down the road until he reached an oak grove. He turned inside it and cut the engine. "I have a feeling you got loose from an institution, Chester."

"I did no such thing."

"Let's see your identification."

"No."

"I'm sorry?"

"You're being impolite and talking to me in a hurtful way."

"I think you're from Crazy Town, Chester. Crazy Town people have to be housed and fed and medicated. They also create shit piles of paperwork. Now get rid of the baby talk and show me your fucking ID."

"I knew people like you in the orphanage. They were bullies and loudmouths and had no manners."

"You're really starting to piss me off. Smart-mouth me again and I'll slap you upside the head, boy."

"I'm going to walk. You need to clean out this car. You should be ashamed of yourself."

"That's it, you little geek. You're under arrest."

"For what?"

"Deliberately creating a dangerous situation on a state highway."

"That's silly."

McVane got out and came around the front of the cruiser and ripped open the passenger door. Chester was putting on a pair of cotton gloves.

"What are you doing with those gloves?" McVane said.

"I don't want to touch anything in your nasty car."

McVane reached for him. Then, for the first time, he saw the absence of light in Chester's eyes. He'd seen it before, once in a lockdown unit at Miramar in the eyes of a female prisoner who had murdered her children; and once in the eyes of a woman he'd sodomized in the back of a liquor store. The revolver was a .357 Magnum, the bullets in the cylinder fat and round and hollow-pointed. The words he wanted to say were trapped inside a gaseous and foul bubble in his throat, the release of his sphincter like wet newspaper tearing apart, his fear so intense he pulled his weapon crookedly from the holster and fumbled it onto the grass.

He tried to smile at his ineptitude, giving up all pretense at manliness, hoping for mercy. The slug hit him in the upper lip like a sledgehammer, and the back of his skull exploded in a gush of bone and brain matter, similar to a grapefruit bursting.

Chester walked around to the driver's side and picked up McVane's hat from the dashboard and put it on, then straightened it in the side mirror. The engine was still running. He climbed in and drove away, remembering the ten-two position on the steering wheel that he had learned in driving school.

My, what a fine morning it was. He hit the whoop-whoop button a couple of times and wondered if he shouldn't apply for the police force somewhere. He'd probably be pretty good at it, he thought. It was time someone did something about the number of criminals and no-goods overrunning the countryside.

THE BODY WAS located right by the St. Mary/Iberia Parish line. The cruiser had been driven through New Iberia, past City Hall and my house and out to Spanish Lake, and left half submerged in the water. The wind was blowing at thirty knots; no fishermen were on the lake.

A black kid who worked in the bait shop said he'd seen the cruiser drive on top of the levee to the north end of the lake, but he'd paid little attention, because sometimes policemen stopped at the lake to eat lunch or take a smoke. He said he'd seen a man walking past the bait shop a half hour later; the man was pulling a small suitcase, but he didn't remember what the man looked like.

Helen and I watched the wrecker pull the cruiser from the cattails, the doors gushing water and mud. We had already been to the crime scene on the parish line, but we had gone in separate vehicles and had talked little among ourselves.

"Somebody shoots a deputy, steals the cruiser, drives through town, and dumps it in a lake in broad daylight?" she said.

"We get them all, don't we?"

I walked down the embankment and looked through the driver's window. A deputy sheriff's hat was floating on the floor. The cut-down twelve-gauge pump was still locked in place on the dash. "You ever meet this guy?"

"McVane?" she said.

"Yeah, you ever meet him?"

"No. What's the story?" she said.

"He had a bad rep with his colleagues."

"For what?"

"Black women didn't always go to jail."

"You think it was one of them?" she asked.

"How many poor black women carry a firearm that can blow a hole the size of a tangerine in a guy's head? Also, he was shot at close range outside the cruiser. There were no other car tracks in the oak grove. Either he met somebody who was on foot, or the person was in his cruiser and the two of them got out and the shooter made his move."

"Our guy didn't see it coming, either," she said.

"Probably not."

"It's your baby, Streak."

"I've got enough on my desk, Helen."

"Sorry, Pops."

"I don't get along well with the guys in St. Mary Parish."

"Boo-hoo," she replied.

She got into her vehicle and drove away. I returned to the crime scene on the parish line. Everyone was gone. I stepped inside the tape. The wind was still up, bending the grass inside the grove, some of it stiff with blood. The spray pattern of the wound pointed toward the bayou. I stood next to the place the body had been and pressed my hands together and formed a V, like the needle on a compass. Then I aimed between my thumbs as though through iron sights, trying to see where the bullet could have gone. The trees were widely spaced, which was not helpful.

I tried to see the shooter inside my head. Nobody likes cop killers, even when they kill a guy like McVane. Most of them go out smoking. Usually, they're almost hysterical with fear and get as stoned and drunk as they can before they check out. Sometimes they take their families with them. A cop killer on the loose is like a tiger prowling a school yard. You're going to hear a lot from him until someone pulls his plug.

The size and character of the entrance and exit wounds indicated the bullet was of large caliber and fired from a serious gun. The round was probably a hollow-point or a dum-dum or a soft-nose that had been notched. The shooter was probably a man, big enough to carry the weapon on his person without McVane noticing it. But why did McVane pull in to the grove? The St. Mary cops said he didn't smoke. The grove was too visible for a tryst or even for harmless goofing off on the job. Maybe he was doing his paperwork when a hitchhiker walked up on him. But why would an armed hitchhiker walk up on a cop he didn't know and shoot him in cold blood?

Maybe the shooter was a fugitive. Maybe he did something suspicious on the road and McVane questioned him. But McVane didn't call in the encounter, and he hadn't been alarmed to the point of drawing his weapon, at least not until it was too late.

I looked at the serenity inside the grove, the wind scudding on the bayou, the moss straightening in the trees. It was the kind of spot you associate with rest, peace of mind, withdrawal from the fray. It was an unlikely place for a violent confrontation, a disruption caused by two disparate personalities trying to kill each other, one succeeding.

Why was McVane late in pulling his gun? He was outside the cruiser, at some point obviously aware that he was in mortal danger. Why did he let his defenses down? This wasn't consistent with the image of a cop who, according to his colleagues, cut suspects no slack and cuffed and searched them roughly and hooked them to a D-ring on the cruiser's floor.

I didn't believe the shooter was local. Aside from two antebellum homes, there were only a few trailers and abandoned shacks spaced along the two-lane, and they were not occupied by the kind of people who would chat up a cop like McVane.

It had to be a hitchhiker. Did McVane pick him up? An armed and dangerous man?

No, he must have known and trusted the shooter. But where did the gun come from? The weather was warm, and a hiker on the road wouldn't have been wearing a coat. Perhaps he was carrying a bag or backpack. He was probably white. Someone so innocuous in appearance that McVane had no fear of him; someone he held in contempt. What kind of person would that be?

I began to see an image of the stroller or hitchhiker, a seemingly harmless character made of Play-Doh, one with a soft mouth and girlish hips and buttocks that waddled, the perfect target for a virile and strong and sadistic male.

Back to weaponry and ballistics. No shell casing had been found. Unless the shooter picked up his brass, the weapon was a revolver. The fatal round had exited the back of McVane's head and had to be somewhere. It was not inside the blood and brain matter on the grass, which meant it may not have fragmented.

I went from tree trunk to tree trunk, running my hands over the bark. I looked down the slope. The Teche was a tidal stream that swelled up on the banks each day and receded with the influences of the moon. The surface was yellow and swollen and churning with mud and leaves and tree branches scattered by the same high winds that had swept through the area earlier in the day. A rowboat was tied to a cypress root a few feet down the bank. On the far side of the bayou was a weathered boathouse with a sagging dock. I got into the boat and rowed across.

Sometimes you get lucky. A bullet was lodged in the door. I opened my pocketknife and eased it out of the wood. The nose was flattened, the sides morphed out of shape, like a piece of bent licorice. The striations were intact. I wrapped the bullet in a handkerchief and wadded up the handkerchief and put it into my pocket, then rowed back across the bayou.

I called Helen and told her what I had found.

"Take it to the lab," she said.

"Want me to check in with the locals?"

"In St. Mary Parish?" she said.

"I may make a stop before I head back."

"Stop where?"

"Maybe the shooter was on an errand and McVane messed up his plan."

"I'm not following you."

"Jimmy Nightingale's place is just down the road. Maybe he was a target."

"Why?"

"Jimmy's predecessors are Huey Long and George Wallace. I think he'll come to the same end."

"It's your case. Talk to you later," she said.

EVEN AFTER JIMMY had told me about the bombing of the Indian village, I did not want to believe he was an evil man. Even though I had concluded in my report that he'd attacked Rowena Broussard, I believed his mind had been addled by booze and hash and driven more by desire than by sadistic intent. Why did I not want to believe these things? Like most of us who subscribe to the egalitarian traditions of Jefferson and Lincoln, I did not want to believe that a basically likable man could, with indifference and without provocation, commit deeds that were not only wicked but destroyed the lives of defenseless people. I also reminded myself that Jimmy was haunted by guilt, which is not the trademark of the unredeemable.

As I pulled up to the Nightingale mansion on the bayou, I did not realize I was about to see a drama that could have come from the stage of the Globe Theatre on the banks of the Thames. I heard shouting on the patio and walked around the side of the house and saw Bobby Earl and Emmeline Nightingale four feet apart, red-faced and hurling invective at each other. Down the slope, Jimmy was calmly whocking golf balls high into the sky, watching them drop into the bayou. His chauffeur, the peroxided one with the steroid-puffed physique and caved-in face, stood by his side, waiting to put a fresh tee and ball on the grass. None of them saw me.

Earl's face was trembling. "He denounced me on national television. Do you know what this has done to me? I went to prison for our cause."

"You went to prison for tax evasion," Emmeline said.

"I gave him my constituency."

"You don't have one. Now get off our property."

"You're a poisonous creature, Emmeline. The Great Whore of Babylon in the making."

"And you're a self-important public fool. Good God, I don't know how Jimmy stands you."

"Hello?" I said.

They both looked at me as though awakening from a dream.

"What do you want, Mr. Robicheaux?" Emmeline asked.

"A word with you and Jimmy," I said. "Bobby doesn't need to hang around."

Earl's face was full of hurt, like a child's. This was the same man who had inflamed the passions of the great unwashed, then disavowed their actions when they burned and bombed and lynched. But I realized that, instead of the devil, I was looking at a moth batting its wings around a light that had grown cold.

He had a pot stomach, like a balloon filled with water; his face was lined, his eyes tired. There was a pout on his mouth. "You remember that time you hit me?"

"I do," I replied.

"It was a sucker punch. I had no chance to defend myself."

"You asked for it, and you were looking me straight in the face."

His eyes were wet. "The Nightingales wouldn't let you clean their bathroom, Dave."

"You're probably right," I said. "And don't call me Dave."

Jimmy walked up the slope, his golf club propped on his shoulder. "I must have missed out on quite a discussion."

"I told Bobby to leave," Emmeline said.

"Better do as she says, Bobby," Jimmy said. "She's tough."

"You've betrayed me," Earl said.

"Two paths diverged in a woods," Jimmy said. "You should have followed mine, not yours."

"A pox on both y'all," Earl said.

"Work on your accent," Emmeline said. "Everyone knows you're from Kansas."

Earl's face seemed to dissolve. He walked away, trying to hold himself erect. When he got into his car, he looked back at the patio. By then Emmeline was removing a pitcher of iced tea and the glasses from the table, and Jimmy was wiping off the mahogany head of his club with a rag. I had the feeling that if there is an invisible hell people carry with them, Earl had found it.

"What puts you at our door, Dave?" Jimmy said.

"A cop was shot and killed not far from your home. We don't know why. Nor do we have anything on the shooter."

"And?"

"You're a famous man," I said.

"I heard the cop didn't have a big fan club."

"The people he abused are not the kind who smoke cops."

"I don't think this fellow's demise has anything to do with me. Want to hit some balls?"

"Listen to him, Jimmy," Emmeline said.

"This is how I feel about death," he said. "I've had a good life. If a stranger walks up to me and parks one in my brain, I'll thank him for waiting as long as he did."

"The cop's name was McVane," I said. "Did you know him?"

"No. Why do you ask?"

"I thought maybe he took a bullet for you. But who knows? Maybe the guy was trafficking. Or maybe an ex-lover got him. You never know."

"There are people out there who want to hurt Jimmy, but not because he's running for office," Emmeline said. "That gangster in New Orleans is actually putting together an adaptation of Levon Broussard's work."

"Tony Nemo?"

"Yes, the same obscene pile you people could never put in jail," she said. "Jimmy had everything ready to go, then you went along with Rowena Broussard's lies and destroyed Jimmy's chances of producing the film. When this is over, I'm going to personally sue you into oblivion."

"Thank you for telling me that," I said. "Unfortunately, I'm mortgaged up to my eyes and not worth suing."

I saw Jimmy laugh silently behind her back.

"What, you think that's funny?" she said to me.

"No," I said, barely able to stifle a grin.

I hated to admit Jimmy Nightingale still had a hold on me. I guess that's just the way it was, growing up in a place like Louisiana, where pagan deities sometimes hide among us and we secretly champion rogues who get even for the rest of us.

THE ROUND WAS a .357 Magnum. We got a priority in processing at the National Crime Information Center because the round had been recovered from a homicide scene. The weapon that had probably killed McVane was an electronic match with six other bullets fired from the same weapon over a seven-year period, most recently in Algiers, where two black men were shot to death in the kitchen of a rented house full of crack paraphernalia.

I spent the next three days talking to cops in Orleans Parish, Tampa, Key West, Fort Lauderdale, and New York. Other than the two crack dealers, the victims were a retired button man from Yonkers, a bartender who shilled for a craps game, a serial pedophile, and a shylock. The obvious common denominator in the victims was criminality. But if these were Mob-connected hits, the usual pattern wasn't there. Button men (so known because they pushed the "off" button on their victims) didn't use the same weapon repeatedly. They also favored a smaller-caliber handgun, because the bullet slowed more quickly and bounced around inside the brain pan. Their classic execution featured one round through the forehead, one in the mouth, and one in the ear. Our shooter seemed spontaneous and left wounds all over the map. He had a way of painting the walls in public, too, without anyone ever getting a good description of him.

For example: He walked into a clam house in Brooklyn and fired point-blank into the face of an infamous gangster who was having a midnight dinner with a beloved television actor. The shooter was so nondescript that no one could remember a distinguishing detail about him. One diner said the man picked up a raw oyster on the way out and sucked it from the shell, and apologized to the diner for disturbing his meal.

I went into Helen's office and told her everything I had.

"This sounds like either an East Coast hitter or a maniac," she said.

"Or both."

"What's he doing here?" she said.

"At least we know it probably wasn't about McVane. But that means the real target is still out there."

"Nightingale?"

"That would be my bet."

"You said Nightingale blew you off."

"His sister didn't. She thinks Tony Nemo wants to take Jimmy off the board because Jimmy wants to produce Levon Broussard's work."

"No wonder most films hurt my eyeballs," she said. She spun her ballpoint on her desk pad.

"Something else bothering you?"

"The prosecutor's office. Lala Segretti thinks you should retire." She kept her gaze straight ahead, not looking at me. "He says the Dartez homicide and investigation will always be a subject of scandal."

"What's your opinion?"

"If you go, I go, too."

"Nobody got me drunk except me."

"The DA has got his head up his ass on this one," she said.

"You're a loyal friend, Helen."

She massaged the back of her neck with both hands, her breasts swelling against her shirt. "And shit goes great with vanilla ice cream."

I didn't try to think through that last one.

Chapter
23

I LOOKED AT THE array of notes, file folders, and photos on my desk. I had cases that had been open fifteen years. Most of them would never be solved. I knew inmates who were innocent of the crimes they were in for but guilty of far more serious ones, including homicides. I knew scores of politicians who sold out their constituencies on a daily basis and were lauded for it. Every cop has a private ulcer about a particular child molester who skates, a victim of sexual assault who's hung out to dry by a misogynistic judge, a greaseball who plays the role of a family man while he extorts and ruins small businessmen, or a racist cop whose behavior puts shooters on rooftops.

How do you handle it when your anger brims over the edge of the pot? You use the shortened version of the Serenity Prayer, which is "Fuck it." Like Voltaire's Candide tending his own garden or the British infantry going up the Khyber Pass one bloody foot at a time, you do your job, and you grin and walk through the cannon smoke, and you just keep saying fuck it. You also have faith in your own convictions and never let the naysayers and those who are masters at inculcating self-doubt hold sway in your life. "Fuck it" is not profanity. "Fuck it" is a sonnet.

In this instance, that meant I had to trust my own perceptions about several open cases I believed were connected. At the bottom of the pyramid were the Jeff Davis Eight. The cultural background was prostitution and narcotics and white slavery. Kevin Penny was a player. He had ties with the Nightingale family, of what kind I wasn't sure. A witness put Penny at the site of the Dartez murder. Why was he there? Had he been sent to follow me and do me harm? Probably, although I had gone to his trailer later and he had seemed unsure of my identity, which meant he had never gotten a good look at me the night Dartez was killed.

Then there was Spade Labiche. Labiche had been seen with Penny right before the Dartez killing. His prints were also in Penny's trailer, though he claimed he had been there to interview Penny and for no other reason.

In the mix were Tony Nine Ball, Jimmy and Emmeline Nightingale, and Levon and Rowena Broussard, and finally, the attack upon Rowena by Jimmy.

Strangely enough, I believed the key lay in the torture death of Penny and the rape of Rowena. The question marks in both cases seemed endless. Who would put Penny through such an ordeal? My guess was Tony Nine Ball. Sherry Picard had said Penny was a federal informant. In his younger years, Tony's logo was a bloody baseball bat. But Tony's victims were either left alive or disappeared altogether. They weren't left at a crime scene with toggle bolts drilled through their limbs.

Another issue was Levon's apparent lack of interest in prosecuting Jimmy Nightingale, the same man whose face he'd spat into. Levon was the kind of idealist you admired but also feared. He seemed to have the inclinations of a pacifist but owned a large number of firearms. He despised dictators and demagogues but revered his ancestors in gray who were authoritarian in their own fashion. He had been a leftist in Latin America, then traveled to Cuba and been picked up by the secret police and confined for a month in a hellish place filled with cockroaches and lice and feces. In my opinion, Levon and Jimmy Nightingale were opposite sides of the same coin. Neither understood himself. And without knowing it, both of them probably served an agenda created for them by someone else, perhaps long dead.

From a professional perspective, my investigation into the rape of Rowena Broussard was over. But I couldn't let it go. Something was wrong. Why the continued coldness or hostility from both her and her husband? Wouldn't they conclude that the wheels of justice were going forward? Jimmy had been charged and indicted and held up in the public eye as a rapist. Maybe his political career would be destroyed. Rowena would probably be a devastating witness at the trial. What more did they want?

I drove to their house on Loreauville Road.

LEVON AND HIS wife were eating at a dining table in their screened-in, brick-floored back porch. Even though we were in the midst of spring, the evening sky was lit incongruously with the colors of a Halloween pumpkin. Rowena's wrists were still bandaged. Levon wore a sport shirt and slacks and Roman sandals without socks. He didn't stand up to shake hands when I opened the screen door. For a man of his background, that message was as blunt as it got.

"Sorry I didn't call in advance," I said.

"What do you need, Dave?"

"You heard about the shooting of the cop in St. Mary?"

"On the roadside, something like that?"

"It happened not far from Jimmy Nightingale's place," I said.

"We're eating," Rowena said.

"I noticed," I replied.

Levon's eyes lifted to mine. "Say what's on your mind."

"Long ago I learned that hostility and fear are first cousins," I said.

"Big breakthrough?" he said.

"It beats cancer and heart disease."

"Let me make it easy for you," he said. "You feel we're ungrateful. We're not. But we're not happy, either. You're too close to Nightingale. You did your job, but you did it grudgingly."

"You're wrong."

I waited for his reply. Or rather, I hoped he might act like the genteel man he was and ask me to sit down. I didn't mention that hostility was also a first cousin of guilt. Again I noticed the leanness in his face, the pinched light in his eyes, as though an illness were taking over his body. Then I said what had probably been in my subconscious for a long time. "You saw the dark side in Latin America."

"So?"

"The use of electrodes. People hung by their wrists with a sack of insecticide pulled over their heads."

"Worse than that," he said.

"How far would you be willing to go yourself?"

He set down his knife and fork and stared at the two candles burning on the table. "I don't think I heard you right."

"Maybe you went looking for evidence on your own. Maybe you used a PI to check out Nightingale's employees and came up with Kevin Penny's name. Maybe you thought he was a guy who'd have some useful information."

"I tortured somebody to death?" he said.

"It's the stuff of the Inquisition."

"I can't take any more of this," Rowena said.

She left the table and went through the kitchen door into the house. I leaned over the table as though to speak to him and let my hand tip his wineglass. It rolled off the table and shattered on the brick. "I'm sorry."

"You can say that again," he said. He got up, wiping his trousers, then went in the house for a broom and dustpan. I used my handkerchief to pick up his butter knife and drop it into my pocket. He came back outside. "You're still here?"

"I always respected you and your wife, Levon. Don't pretend I didn't."

"You pretend about everything, Dave. Jimmy Nightingale has all the trappings of a fascist. Tell me that's not so."

"He shitcanned Bobby Earl."

"That's because he doesn't need him anymore," he said. "Why don't you genuflect before him while you're at it?"

"See you around," I said.

"Not if I have anything to do with it," he replied.

* * *

I WENT TO THE lab early Tuesday morning. They lifted Levon's prints off the knife, and I took them on a card to Jennings and left them with a desk sergeant for Sherry Picard. She called me the next day. I had not given her any directions or information about the source of the latents on the knife, maybe in part because I didn't want to confirm my own suspicions.

"They're a match," she said.

"With what?"

"The latents in Penny's trailer. That's why you sent them, right?"

"Correct."

"Whose are they?" she asked.

"Levon Broussard's."

"The author?" she said.

"Yep."

"They were on two doorknobs. They were also on the drill."

My heart was in my throat. "Were there any others on the drill?"

"Just his."

"I guess you guys better get a warrant."

I don't believe I ever spoke sadder words.

THE NEXT DAY Labiche was not only in my office, he was hooking one haunch on the corner of my desk, flipping a half dollar and catching it. "Good detective work, Robey."

"Which detective work?"

"Bringing down that snooty ass-wipe on Loreauville Road."

"Levon Broussard?"

"Him and his wife both think their shit doesn't stink."

"What did you hear?"

"He's in custody. He'll probably bail out this afternoon. From what I understand, you nailed his dick to his forehead. I guess this might screw up his wife's rape claim, too."

"What does one have to do with the other?"

"Everything?"

Labiche was right. I just didn't want to admit it. "How well did you know Kevin Penny, Spade?"

"Me? Just from the interview. Why would I know him otherwise?"

"You worked vice in Miami. Penny was an active guy thereabouts."

"Where do you come up with these scenarios?"

"I think you're a dirty cop," I said.

He stood up, his face constricting. "I gave you a way out of the Dartez beef. I covered for your drunk ass because I've had problems of my own."

"Good show. No cigar."

"Yeah?" He blew air out his nose and smiled. He caught the half dollar and put it away. "You couldn't carry my jockstrap, Robo."

LABICHE WAS WRONG about Levon making bail that afternoon. Unlike his counterpart Jimmy Nightingale, Levon didn't make friends with authorities or politicians he didn't like. The South has changed in many ways, but beyond the sophistry and hush-puppy platitudes is a core group that is as malignant and hot and sweaty as a torchlit mob flinging a rope over a tree limb. The judge before whom Levon appeared was the Honorable Bienville Tomey. His face had the choleric intensity of a dried squash and the same level of humanity. He wore his irritability like a flag.

"What the hell do you have to say for yourself?" he asked Levon.

"Nothing, Your Honor," Levon answered.

"You're entering a plea of not guilty?"

"Yes, that's correct, Your Honor," Levon's attorney said.

"I didn't ask you. The defendant will answer my question."

"Yes, sir," Levon said.

"Yes, sir, what?"

Levon looked out the window and didn't reply.

"Are you deaf?"

"I don't have anything to say, sir."

"You mean 'Your Honor.'"

Levon continued to stare out the window. "I didn't torture or kill anyone. Interpret that in any way you wish."

"Remanded in custody," the judge said. He snapped down his gavel as he would a fly swatter.

I WAS ALLOWED TO see Levon in a holding cell. It was an old one with a concrete floor that sloped down to a drain hole with a yellow-streaked perforated iron lid. There was no bench or chair to sit on. He stood at the door in an orange jumpsuit, his hands on the bars.

"Why were you in Penny's trailer?" I said.

"Rowena remembered something. Actually, it was in a dream. In her dream, the assault by the two black guys was mixed up with the assault on Nightingale's boat. Then she heard a voice. It was a man with his mouth right by her ear. The pillowcase was over her head, so she couldn't see his face. She thought it was one of the black guys. It wasn't. The voice said, 'Here's a penny for your thoughts.' The voice wasn't Nightingale's, either."

"Go on," I said.

When you question a suspect, you do not offer any information unless you want him to think you know more than you do. In this instance, I wanted Levon to give up details that only a perpetrator would know. Unbeknownst to him, he might also give up details that could set him free.

"When Rowena told me about the dream, I began to think maybe Nightingale wasn't her attacker, or maybe there was more than one attacker, somebody who held her down. I know a guy who used to work for Nightingale. He gave me the names of almost everybody on his payroll. That's how I made the connection between Kevin Penny and Rowena's dream."

"Go on."

"I went to see him. Nobody answered. The door was unlocked. I opened it and went inside. That's when I heard him."

"Heard him?"

"He was alive. Moaning. His wrists were bolted to the floor, above his head, like the hanged man in the tarot deck."

"What did he say?"

"He didn't say anything. He was choking on his vomit. The drill was hanging out of his ear. I removed it and turned his cheek to let his mouth drain. Then he died."

"What did you do next?"

"I left."

"Why didn't you call 911?"

He brushed at his nose. "I don't know."

"Your lawyer will tell you that 'I don't know' is not the way to win people's hearts and minds."

"I told myself Penny had it coming. There wasn't any point in my getting involved."

"You left your prints at the scene. Wouldn't it be better to explain your presence there than to flee?"

"I wasn't thinking, Dave. His eyes were rolled in his head. His face was contorted in a death mask. It was horrible."

"You saw the work of the death squads in El Salvador and Guatemala. I don't think you rattle that easily."

His hands were high on the bars, his head down. "It wasn't my best day."

"You had doubts about Jimmy Nightingale's guilt?"

His gaze remained on the floor. His hair was uncut, hanging in his eyes.

"That's it, isn't it?" I said. "You didn't want to let Nightingale off the hook?"

"He took her to the boat. He got her drunk. He was doing everything he could to get in her pants."

"That doesn't make him a rapist."

"If Nightingale didn't rape her, he knew Penny did."

"Not if Nightingale was passed out."

"Why not join his defense team?"

"I don't have to be here," I said.

Somebody slammed a gate. Somebody else dragged a baton across a row of bars. Another someone was yelling gibberish from a cell. Think hell is just in the next world? Visit your average county bag or rental prison.

"I've written about the Jeff Davis Eight," Levon said. "Look in on Rowena, will you?"

"Sure."

"Tell Nightingale this doesn't change anything. He's a liar and a fraud, and I'm going to prove it to the world. I hate that son of a bitch."

ON FRIDAY NIGHT, Clete took Homer to a movie in New Iberia, then for ice cream. Homer carried the baseball glove Clete gave him on his belt, and never took off his baseball cap. On the way home, his face looked wizened in the dash light, as though it had been freeze-burned or his youth stolen. He was the most isolated and strange little boy Clete had ever known.

"They treating you all right at school?" Clete said.

"Not everybody, but most people do."

"You worried about something?"

"When are they gonna take me back?"

"Who?"

"The people who run the foster program."

"I'm not going to let them do that."

The boy stared at nothing for a long time. "I'm glad my father was killed. And that makes me feel bad."

Clete turned off Main into the motor court, bouncing Homer in the seat. "Your emotions get mixed up in a situation like that," Clete said. "See, what you're glad about is he can't hurt you anymore."

"I feel dirty."

"Your father didn't deserve to have a fine little boy like you."

"I feel dirty all the time."

"Why?"

"Because of what they did."

"Who are you talking about?"

"The men who came to the trailer. His friends. I told him about it, but he didn't care. He called me a liar."

Clete pulled the Caddy under the oaks and cut the engine and lights. "Those things were not your fault. Your father was an evil man. So were his friends. If I catch up with the men who hurt you, they'll never have a chance to hurt anyone again."

"They're gonna take me back. They won't let you keep me. There's got to be both a man and woman in the house."

"Maybe Miss Carolyn and I will work something out."

"I heard you talking to her on the phone. She's moving in with her mother in Lake Charles. Don't pretend."

"I won't, Homer. I promise."

Homer walked ahead of him into the cottage and turned on the light. Clete heard a hiss from the shadows and stared into the darkness. A tug was droning up the bayou, its running lights on. "Who's there?"

"Pookie. I got to talk," a voice said.

Clete removed a penlight from his pocket and shone it into the darkness. "You trying to creep my cottage?"

"I got a flat. Down the street. I got to hide."

Clete shone the light on Pookie's clothes. "Did you wet your pants?"

"A guy was following me. Not *a* guy. *The* guy."

"Make sense."

"Maybe the guy who smoked that cop in St. Mary Parish. He's out of Florida. Nobody knows what he looks like. He's like a cleaner, except he doesn't just clean. He wipes out everything in the environment. I saw JuJu. He said Maximo is missing, down by Morgan City."

"You need to soak your brain in a bucket of Drano, Pookie. I can't begin to follow the crap coming out of your mouth."

"Somebody put the grab on Maximo. He takes his lady on a picnic, then she goes for a whiz, and when she comes back, Maximo has gone into thin air."

"The lady is the haystack from outer space?"

"Show some sensitivity here."

"Maximo is a sadist and a pervert. In case you haven't heard, one of his kids disappeared. The mother thinks Maximo killed him. Did he and JuJu attack Carolyn Ardoin in her driveway?"

"You already said it, Purcel. If it was Maximo, she wouldn't have a face."

"Get out of here, Pookie."

"Listen to me. This guy who was following me wears red tennis shoes and fruity shirts and queer-bait pants. He ain't out to just cap me. He wants information. You know what that means. T'ink about what somebody done to Kevin Penny."

"I can't help you. Don't come around here anymore." Clete went up the stoop and opened the screen door.

"Don't leave me like this, no," Pookie said.

Clete shut the door and turned the bolt and clicked off the porch light. He looked through the window. Pookie's arms were thrashing in rage and frustration, as though he were caught in a wind tunnel.

CLETE COULDN'T SLEEP that night. Forty years ago he had accepted insomnia as a way of life. For a long time the ghost of a mamasan lived on his fire escape. Sometimes he made a pot of tea for her, then put it and a demitasse and saucer and napkin and tiny spoon on the windowsill, regardless of the terror in his wife's face. One day the mamasan moved on, and his wife joined a Buddhist cult in Boulder, one in which the members were made to remove their clothes and humiliate themselves, and Clete was left with a sense of desertion and emptiness no amount of booze or redwings or weed could kill.

At three in the morning he sat up in the bed and looked at the moon. Homer was asleep on the couch, his cap and ball glove by his feet. He had read Clete's situation correctly: Carolyn Ardoin was moving in with her mother. But that was a small part of the problem. Clete and domesticity didn't flush. He had tried it in all its forms. The result was always a disaster. He had even seen a psychiatrist. The psychiatrist had told him to get a vasectomy and never get drunk in Reno or Vegas, where he might accidentally stumble into a marriage chapel.

Clete looked at Homer in the moon glow. His skin was pale and his breath so shallow, his nostrils hardly quivered. Clete thought of the bodies of the people buried alive by the Vietcong along the banks of the Perfume River, the dirt clutched in their hands, the waxy look in their faces.

The world hasn't treated you right, kid. But I don't know what either one of us can do about it. If there's a way, God help me find it.

IN ANY GIVEN twenty-four-hour period, we received a steady flow of reports and complaints about house break-ins, car wrecks, noisy house parties, fights outside bars, domestic disputes, a backed-up septic tank, a water heater that wouldn't light, the garbage that wasn't picked up, a sofa dumped in the bayou, a Peeping Tom, an alligator in a swimming pool, another alligator taking a barbecued chicken off a grill, possums chewing through someone's wiring, a live skunk that kids had put in the high school principal's car, and sometimes the real deal—a homicide or a felonious assault or an armed robbery.

The theft of the ice cream truck was a new one. In the late hours, the driver had gassed up in St. Martinville and entered the convenience store for a cup of coffee. When he came back outside, his truck was gone. We added the theft to our list of bizarre occurrences in Acadiana.

IT WAS SATURDAY. The wind was balmy, out of the south, and smelling of salt and rain, when a man in a Jolly Jack ice cream suit and a white stiff-billed hat stopped the truck by a park in a poor black neighborhood near Bayou Lafourche. Happy tunes jingled from the loudspeakers. The driver stuck his head out the window and waved at the children. There were tiny plastic roses on his coat, like candied flowers on cake icing. "Hi, kids! Who wants some ice cream?"

"We ain't got no money," a little girl said.

"What if I told you the ice cream is free today?" the man said.

"Then you be lying," a little boy said.

The children laughed.

"My name is Smiley," the driver said. "I can make my face look like rubber." He made his face go out of shape.

They laughed louder this time. "Do it again, Smiley!" someone yelled.

He hooked his fingers inside his mouth and stretched it until it was almost splitting. "I can speak Spanish. I bet you can't."

"If we could speak it, there wouldn't be nobody here who could understand it," the little girl said. "So why do we want to speak it?"

"That's pretty good," the driver said. He rose from his seat and opened a locker behind him. "Hang on, you guys. Here it comes."

He was wearing gloves. As fast as he could, he trundled out Popsicles, fudge bars, cups of marbled ice cream, ice cream sandwiches, Eskimo Pies, and frozen sundaes, while more children came running from all over the park. He peeled the paper off the last fudge bar and ate it with them. "How do you like that, kids?"

"Yea!" they shouted.

The little girl stuck her head in the door and looked into the rear of the truck. "What's that sound?" she said.

"Which sound?"

"It goes thump, thump, thump."

"That's my refrigerator unit. It's broken."

"It sound like you got a gorilla locked in there," the little boy said.

"Maybe that's what it is," the driver said.

"No, it ain't," the girl said.

"I got to go," the driver said. "Make sure you clean up your trash. Don't be litterbugs."

"You coming here tomorrow, Smiley?" she asked.

"I got a lot of places to visit. Be good kids." He raised his hand in farewell.

"Hey, everybody t'ank Smiley," the little girl said.

"T'ank you, Smiley!" they yelled.

He shifted into gear and drove away, water streaming off his back bumper, the back end swaying and vibrating.

He stopped at the end of the street and got into the rear of the truck. He opened a large door that gushed with cold. He looked at something on the floor, his jaw tightening. "I told you to be quiet."

He held on to the doorjamb for balance and stomped a mouth-taped figure with his red tennis shoe, then stood on the figure's face for good measure. "You make me very mad. You have been a bad boy. Don't make me come back here again. I do not like bad boys."

On sunday morning I got the call.

"We've got a beaut, Pops," Helen said. "We haven't been able to get inside the ice cream truck yet, but this looks like one for the books."

Chapter
24

AT SUNRISE, A man wearing a Jolly Jack vendor's uniform pulled up to the pumps in the same truck that had been stolen at the same filling station two days previous. He turned off the engine and went inside without buying any gas. He used the restroom, bought a bag of Ding Dongs, and munched them while he read the newspaper in the convenience store. Then he paid for the newspaper and went outside and did something in the back of the truck.

A minute later, the clerk saw him activate the gas pump with what turned out to be a stolen credit card. The clerk had never seen him before and knew nothing of the truck's history. The driver was on the other side of the truck, so the clerk assumed he was gassing up. Someone entered the store and said smoke was rising from the back of the truck. The digital counters were racing on the gas pump. The hose and nozzle had been draped over the driver's window and were sloshing gasoline across the seats and the floor. A flame flickered inside the glass in the rear doors. The driver had disappeared.

The explosion seemed to lift the truck off its wheels, then the fire roared with such intensity that it wilted the roof into carbon paper. One of the customers said he heard the muffled cries of a person inside the flames.

It took me only ten minutes to reach the site. The firemen had finished hosing down the truck, and one of them was prizing open the back doors with a crowbar. Helen was standing by her cruiser, talking into her mic. I waited for her to finish.

"What's that smell?" I said.

"I hate to think," she replied. "A car was reported stolen up the road. That's probably how our man made his getaway."

"What's on the surveillance cameras?"

"The top of a head wearing a cap. It looks like he had gloves on."

"What's the clerk say?"

"The guy talked baby talk, like Elmer Fudd, and has lips that were 'red like licorice.' Fudd ate a bag of Ding Dongs and read the paper before he set the truck on fire."

"This is the same truck that was stolen from here?"

"You got it."

"How do you figure that one?"

"Our guy's a nutcase?" she said.

The fireman was now inside the truck. He used the head of the crowbar to snap loose the handle on the freeze locker and pulled back the door on its hinges. He jumped down from the bumper, the ends of his mustache bouncing. He coughed wetly in his chest. "Y'all better take a look."

The man inside the locker was bound hand and foot with ligatures, a strip of heat-baked tape hanging from his mouth. His eyes were wide, like those of someone holding his breath underwater. His forehead and bare feet were crusted with black blood, his hair and eyebrows singed, his clothes covered with burn holes. His skin had turned to orange marmalade. I hoped he had died of asphyxiation or a heart attack rather than from the burning gasoline that had curled around the bottom of the freeze locker.

"Recognize him?" Helen said.

"It's Maximo Soza."

"That's him? I remember him being larger."

"He was a small man inside and out."

"Who's the guy in the Jolly Jack suit?"

"I think the same guy who shot McVane."

"How do you arrive at that?"

"He commits crimes no one would suspect him of. He does it for reasons that make sense to him but no one else. He builds the gallows and drops the trapdoor before anyone realizes he's not a carpenter."

"Who would want to pop one of Tony Squid's guys?"

"Somebody who wants information about Tony or somebody who plans on popping Tony."

"Mob guys don't get popped without permission," she said.

"That was in the old days. Whoever did this plans to leave a big footprint."

AT 7:38 SUNDAY evening, I got a call from the man himself. "I'm all broken up. What the fuck is going on over there in Mosquito Town?"

"You said you were not going to call here again, Tony," I said.

"Maximo was like a son to me."

"Yeah, he was a great guy. Maybe he tortured Kevin Penny to death or put a kindhearted social worker in Lafayette General."

"My people don't do those kinds of things."

"If the price were right, your people would work at Auschwitz."

"Where's your daughter?"

"None of your business."

"I need to talk to her about the script. You're not gonna believe who I got to play the role of the Confederate soldier."

When he told me, he was right, I couldn't believe him. The actor was well known and respected; he'd received a Golden Globe Award and other nominations.

"I told him Alafair was doing the script," Tony said. "She's gonna love working with him."

"I can't tell quite how I feel at this moment."

"What's wrong?"

"Where do you get off using Alafair's name in your business dealings?"

"I'm giving her a break."

"The only break here is going to be in your fat neck," I said.

"Fuck you."

"Maximo went out hard, Tony. Think about the implications. Ten years ago nobody would have touched one of your guys."

"Put her on the phone."

"Are you listening? My daughter is never going to work with you."

"Yeah? My lawyer already talked with Levon Broussard in the can. He wants Alafair to do the script."

"Levon wants to work with you?"

"Not exactly. But he will. He wants to get even with Nightingale. This is gonna be like a telephone pole with spikes in it kicked right up Nightingale's ass."

"I thought you were going to put him in the White House."

"Nightingale is a Benedict Arnold. I kept the unions off his back, introduced him to people with billions of dollars, got him a girlfriend or two. Then one day I'm the stink on shit."

"A heads-up, Tony: If a guy who talks like Elmer Fudd and has lips like red licorice shows up at your house, don't invite him in."

"I'm supposed to be afraid of a guy who escaped from a Bugs Bunny cartoon?"

"I think he capped two black guys in Algiers and blew a cop's brains out in St. Mary Parish. For a while I thought he might be working for you. Now I think you're a target."

"You know why you're a cop? You're dumb and can't do anything else. For years Maximo had a thing for little boys. One of his victims caught up with him. Fade to black."

"Sounds more like your epitaph, Tony."

"My dork in your ear, Robicheaux," he replied, and hung up.

In the morning, the judge who had remanded Levon Broussard changed his mind and released him on a two-hundred-thousand-dollar bail.

I DIDN'T KNOW WHAT to make of Levon's story about Kevin Penny. Levon had deduced that Kevin Penny had probably raped his wife but had allowed us to continue our prosecution of an innocent man. Then Levon had gone on his own to Penny's trailer, supposedly to confront him, and had left his fingerprints on the electric drill that had taken Penny's life, supposedly while trying to save him from drowning in his own vomit. But he hadn't called 911. Why hadn't he? He wasn't the kind of man who panicked. His account was a hard sell.

Maybe Levon didn't care whether Jimmy was guilty of the actual rape. He blamed Jimmy regardless. As for most of us who seek revenge, his anger and need probably had their origins in the past, and the present situation was a surrogate for an injury that had occurred long ago. Levon's wife had been raped and then abandoned by the system in Wichita, Kansas. I also believed his liberal sentiments and his commitment to civil rights were sorely tested by the fact that the rapists were black.

Two hours after his release from a lockdown unit in Jennings, I found him in his backyard, unshaven, red-eyed, dirty, and still smelling of jail. He was flinging baseballs at a wooden box he had nailed to the side of his carriage house. I had forgotten that he'd played American Legion ball. I had also forgotten that he'd attended a military academy in Mississippi, if only for one year, at the end of which he had been expelled for knocking down an instructor who insulted his family.

The ground was littered with baseballs. A cooler with a corked bottle of white wine pushed down in the ice rested on a picnic table.

"Pretty good forkball," I said.

He looked at me blankly. "There's a soda in the box, if you want one."

"The prosecutor's office is a bit upset."

"Because they'll have to drop charges against Nightingale?"

I didn't answer.

"That's *their* problem." He took a windup and fired the ball into the center of the wooden box, putting his shoulder and hip into it, whipping his wrist just before releasing his fingers.

"You and Jimmy have a lot in common."

"No, we don't."

"You both played ball, and you both went to military school."

"I didn't know that. You know why boys get sent to military school? Their parents don't want them."

"Are you going in on a movie deal with Tony Nemo?"

"If Alafair does the adaptation."

"What you do with Fat Tony is your business. But I don't want you dragging my daughter into it."

He tossed a baseball up and down in his hand, then let it fall to the grass. "Alafair is my friend. You think I'd hurt her?"

"Not intentionally."

"Then give me some credit."

"Nemo is an evil man. Don't darken your life with this guy."

"Nightingale knows how to place his thumb on the pulse of an unhappy electorate. Individuals don't change history. History finds the individual. John Steinbeck said that."

"So let the electorate fall in their own shit."

"I don't doubt Nemo got me sprung. If Alafair will do the first draft, I'm going to make a movie with him. I'll tell you the reason why. My best novel is the least popular of my books. Maybe this is vanity on my part, but I believe we owe the dead a debt. We have to give them breath and voice, even though their mouths are stopped with dirt. If we don't, they allow us no rest. I think they're out there in the mist. Sometimes I see them."

I felt a wind blow through my chest, as though he had pirated my thoughts.

"How's your wife doing?" I asked.

"Not good."

"Can I ask you something straight up, off the record?"

"Shoot."

"Is it fair to say you're still hanging on to the events in Wichita?"

"Events?"

"The rape of your wife by the two black guys."

"No, I let go of that a long time ago."

"I don't believe you. People's emotions don't work like that."

He slid the wine bottle out of the ice and uncorked it and took a drink from the bottle. "One of them was knifed to death in the Alabama state pen. A store owner shot and killed the other one during a robbery. They got what they had coming."

"But they skated in Wichita," I said.

"So that's on the DA's office in Wichita. Fuck them."

"Good attitude. But my experience is that survivors of violent crimes tend to become gun enthusiasts."

He winked. "I throw baseballs."

"Jimmy hits golf balls into the bayou."

"May I visit Alafair at your house?"

"Anytime," I replied.

I walked back to my pickup. Rowena was sitting in a rocking chair on the gallery. "Mr. Robicheaux?"

I tried to keep my face pleasant, but I didn't speak.

"It's my fault," she said.

"Pardon?"

"All of it. I got drunk with another man when I should have been home with my husband. I gave you people the wrong information. I caused Levon to go to Kevin Penny's trailer. These things are all my doing."

"Forget it," I said. "You're a nice lady, Miss Rowena."

There was a smile in her eyes. It's strange how much a kind word can do.

CLETE PURCEL WAS the most thorough and insightful and successful investigative lawman I ever knew. If he hadn't wiped out his career with hooch and pills and weed and strippers and other women who glowed with neurosis, he could have had a job in the Department of Justice. Instead, he ended up working with the Mob in Vegas and Reno. I'll take it a step further. He ended up working for a degenerate killer named Sally Dio, also known as Sally Ducks, who had his boys slam Clete's hand in a car door. Later, Sally was on his private plane with his boys when the engines failed and the plane crashed into the side of a mountain near Flathead Lake. The coroner had to comb Sally's remains from a tree with a rake. The National Transportation Safety Board said the fuel lines were clogged with sand. For unexplained reasons, Clete immediately grabbed a flight to Mexico City with only his toothbrush and a shaving kit.

Clete drove his Caddy down East Plaquemine Street in Jennings to the sheriff's office. The sky was lidded with steel-gray clouds, the air muggy and superheated by the asphalt, the live oaks and palm trees motionless. The building was located in a strange piece of green landscape that had a few small frame houses on it, none of them with fences, like a semirural neighborhood from a simpler time.

He left his .38 snub and holster in the glove box, put on his porkpie hat, locked his car, and went up the walk, touching his face with a folded handkerchief, his collar and his own odor bothering him. The problem did not lie in the weather. Clete could have overcome his reputation for vigilantism and chaotic behavior, but his brief association with the Mob and his accidental shooting of a federal witness followed him wherever he went, in part because he was a better man and a better and more honorable cop than his detractors could ever be. But that was poor consolation. Among those who should have been his colleagues and friends, he was a pariah and a turncoat.

"I'd like to see Detective Picard," he said to the desk sergeant.

"Name?"

"Purcel."

"Ohhh, yeah," the sergeant said.

"What's that mean?"

"It's been that kind of day."

"How about it, top? Is she here or not?"

"Down the hall."

"Would you mind telling her I'm here? I don't have an appointment."

"She'll be glad for the company."

He removed his porkpie hat and ran a comb through his hair and put the comb away. He yawned, his eyes empty. "You got any openings? I'd really dig working in a place like this. It reminds me of El Sal when it was run by the death squads."

"I'll make a note of that," the sergeant said.

Clete went down the hall and tapped on Sherry Picard's half-open door. She was on the phone but waved him in. She smiled when she hung up. "How you doin', Mr. Purcel?"

"Clete."

"How you doin', Mr. Clete?"

He gave her a look. "I want to run a couple of things by you regarding the Penny homicide."

"I'm all ears."

"Am I about to put my head in a bear trap?" he said.

"I was on the phone with social services."

"About Homer?"

"I think maybe they found a good home for him."

He felt a thorn pierce his heart. "He's got one now."

"It's only temporary. You have to accept that."

"Right is right, wrong is wrong. I'm not big on rule books."

"How did you make it through the Corps?"

"The Crotch was a breeze after New Orleans."

"What'd you want to tell me?"

"Remember when we were talking about the latents at the Penny crime scene that weren't in the system? You said it bothered you because a guy like Penny didn't hang out with normal people."

"Right."

"Run everybody who works for Jimmy Nightingale. Also start looking hard at Spade Labiche."

"I can't randomly pull in people and fingerprint them, particularly when they're from St. Mary Parish."

"There're other ways."

"I know your methodology. I want to keep my job. I've got another problem, too."

"Like what?"

"You and Dave Robicheaux have a way of getting into it with rich guys. It doesn't do a lot for your credibility."

"I'll try to explain that. Most rich people here made their money off somebody else's back."

She looked him up and down, biting the edge of her lip. Unconsciously, he put his thumb in his belt and tightened his shirt.

"You got anything on Nightingale?" she said.

"Penny said he made deposits for Nightingale and delivered skanks to Nightingale's house."

"Do you believe him?"

"I don't like Nightingale. I think he's a bum. Not because he's rich. Around here, you screw down and marry up. He doesn't marry up. He just screws everybody. In answer to your question, nothing Penny said was trustworthy. He told me Nightingale's sister came on to him. I have a hard time buying that."

"The feds used him for a long time. They must have believed him."

"Yeah, they did the same with Whitey Bulger. Look, I came here because I thought you could use a friend."

"Why do I need a friend?" she said.

"You work in a shithole."

"You're here to tell me I work in a shithole?"

"It's all relative. Can I sit down?" he said.

"I have a lot of work to do."

"Don't take Homer away."

"It's not in my hands. The system is the system."

"I say fuck the system, Miss Sherry."

"Where has that gotten you, sir?"

He felt his eyes go out of focus and wondered if it had to do with the brightness of the sun shining through the window. "I'm a PI. When I had a real badge, I never jammed anybody. I didn't do it then, I don't do it now."

Her eyes left his.

"They give you a bad time here?" he asked.

"I get time off from purgatory," she said. "Watch your ass, bub."

When he went outside, his Caddy was being hauled away by a wrecker. The desk sergeant was watching from the curb. "You were in a no-parking zone."

ALAFAIR WAS COMING out of Victor's Cafeteria when she saw Labiche. He was driving a cruiser, looking in the rearview mirror. When he saw her, he swung out of his lane, causing two other drivers to brake. He parked in the shade and got out. He had a gold-tipped cigarette in his mouth. He looked warily up and down the street. "Got a minute?"

"Not really," she said.

"It's important. About our last conversation. Misunderstandings that got to be cleared up."

"There's nothing to be cleared up, Detective."

He turned his face and exhaled the smoke into the wind, then dropped the cigarette onto the sidewalk and stepped on it. "Your father thought I was putting moves on you or something. Robey gets steamed up."

"Robey?"

"Whatever." He gazed down the street. "It's warming up. I hear this movie deal is coming together."

"News to me."

"Come on, Levon Broussard is hooking up with Tony Nemo. You're writing the script. It's all around town."

"Talk to Levon."

"Like I told you before, I know the locale. Or maybe they want to use some real cops."

"Could be."

"I was an extra in a *Miami Vice* episode. They didn't do the real story, though. You know the real story about Miami?"

"No, I don't."

"Jimmy Carter let all the boat people in. It took Reagan to stop it." He squinted across the street at the square and the sun glinting on the Teche. His forehead was shiny, his upper lip beaded. He cleaned the humidity out of his eyes with his fingers. "Don't look right now, but do you see a guy over there?"

"Which guy?"

"He's wearing red tennis shoes."

"I'm sorry. I don't see anyone like that."

Labiche turned slowly, his arms over his chest. He stared at the square, his lips a tight button. "There're a lot of weirdos around. This guy looked like a perv."

"Are you talking about the man who stole the ice cream truck and killed Maximo Soza?"

His face blanched. "Yeah. We got an all-points on him."

"I don't see anybody in red tennis shoes."

"Let's go inside. I'll buy you something cool to drink. Or maybe you want something stronger."

"There're some people down by the bayou. You don't want to check them out?"

He put a fresh cigarette into his mouth and lit it. He shook the front of his shirt with his fingers as though ridding it of the heat rising from the sidewalk. "I got to quit these. No, there's nothing down by the bayou. About the movie—"

"Two things," she said. "Don't be giving my father nicknames. I'm surprised he hasn't broken your jaw by this time. Second, stay away from me. It's not your fault that you're ignorant and stupid. In fact, you give the lie to the notion of white racial superiority, and for that reason, society owes you a debt. But please stop bothering me."

He stepped into the shade. He widened his eyes, his profile as jagged as broken glass, his teeth showing. "Maybe you'll need a friend down the track. That friend could be me. But I won't be there. Think about that."

"You'd better rephrase your words, trash."

Two people walking by looked over their shoulders.

"I might put something in that smart-ass mouth you're not expecting," he said.

"What did you say?"

He opened the door of his cruiser. Before he shut it, he turned toward her and squeezed his phallus, his lust and iniquity undisguised.

That evening she told me what had happened.

Chapter
25

THE SUNSET WAS like pools of fire inside clouds that were turning into rain. The crowd at the bar-and-grill up the bayou was a happy one. Before going inside, I stood at the deck railing and gazed at the live oaks on the lawn of the old convent, the people of color who were pole-fishing on the bank, the raindrops chaining the bayou's surface. Then I went inside. People who knew me glanced away, either out of embarrassment or in fear.

Babette, the young Cajun woman who had told me she'd seen La-biche with Kevin Penny, was working behind the bar. She was serving a highball to Spade Labiche. In the shadows at the end of the bar, Clete Purcel was eating a bowl of étouffée and drinking from a mug of beer caked with ice. He looked straight into my eyes but didn't stop eating.

"Hi, Miss Babette," I said.

"Hello, Mr. Dave," she replied. "You want to order some food, suh? If that's what you're having, I mean."

"Not right now. Just a diet drink. Any kind is fine."

"You here to talk to me, Robicheaux?" Labiche said. "If you are, that's a mistake."

"Why is that?"

"You got a beef, do it by the numbers, at the office. That's what offices are for."

I took a glass of iced Diet Coke and lime slices and cherries from

Babette's hand. I had not asked for the lime and the cherries, but she had put them in just the same. I sat down next to Clete.

"Care to tell me why you're in here?" he said.

"Thought you might be here," I lied.

He looked at Labiche but spoke to me. "You want to eat?"

"Nope."

"You just like slop chutes? Like memories of past boom-boom?"

I glanced up at the TV screen. "I want to watch the ball game."

"Yeah? Who's playing?"

I placed my hand on his shoulder. It felt like concrete. "Think we're too old for this?"

"Old for what?"

"All this crap."

"Don't buy in to that. Most people are dead inside at forty." He snapped his fingers. "Look at me."

"I am looking at you."

"You're looking at Labiche. What gives?"

"Nothing," I said.

"Are you trying to have another slip? Because if you are, I'm leaving."

"You worry too much. Miss Babette, can I have another one of these, please?" I handed her my empty glass.

But I could not say liquor wasn't on my mind. I could not only smell it, I was drawn to it the way a bee is drawn to flowers. The bottles on the back counter rang with light. I could almost taste the foam and brassy bead of the beer splashing from the spigot into a big ice-crusted mug, the whiskey brimming on the edges of a shot glass, the Collins mix and shaved ice and mint leaves in tropical drinks made with vodka and rum and gin. I could not explain the metabolic craving that had brought me nothing but sickness and misery, not to mention a murderous rage that was often the surrogate for the booze I couldn't get enough of.

I looked at Labiche's profile and the way he positioned himself at the bar, one foot on the brass rail, shoulders back, half a head taller than those around him. He could see everyone coming in or leaving;

he could see down a woman's blouse, particularly the women behind the bar. He could see a tryst beginning in the parking lot. He could eyeball a parolee who wasn't allowed to keep company with other ex-felons or enter establishments where alcohol was sold. He was Polonius eavesdropping on the rest of the world.

I saw Babette bend over to pick up a napkin from the duckboards. I saw Labiche's eyes follow her breasts down.

"Where you going?" Clete said.

"To tell Spade whom he reminds me of."

"*Whom?*"

I stood behind Labiche but couldn't bring myself to touch him. I remember seeing Babette look at me, her brow furrowed. I remember Labiche turning around as though he heard the bell at a rail crossing.

"Want something?" he asked.

"Repeat what you said to my daughter earlier today."

"I didn't say anything to her. 'Top of the morning' or something like that. You drunk?"

"Think carefully. You asked her if she saw a guy in red tennis shoes. Then you said something else."

"You're a sick man, Robicheaux. Everybody knows it except you. In regard to your daughter, I wouldn't wipe my ass with her."

A quietness settled on the bar.

"Did you hear me?" he said.

I nodded. I picked at my nails.

"You just going to stand there?" he said.

"You're not hard to read, Spade."

"Have a drink. I'll put it on my tab. I'll drive you home. You and your daughter quit your bullshit."

"You didn't make your case on the Dartez homicide. So you thought you'd go all in."

"I can't take this," he said to no one. He slipped a credit card from his wallet and dropped it onto the bar. "I'm heading out, hon," he said to Babette. "I'll pick you up at closing time."

Babette picked up the card, her face coloring.

"Look at me, Spade," I said.

"Jeez, what does it take?" he said, turning toward me.

I caught him with my right, putting my shoulder and hip into it, driving my fist straight into his mouth, snapping his face sideways as though he had been dropped from a hangman's rope. I saw blood fly against the back mirror and heard a stifled cry rise from his throat. I hooked him twice with my left hand and caught him again with my right, knocking his head against the bar as he went down.

I should have pulled the plug. But I knew I wasn't going to. The simian that had lived in me since I was a child was back in town. A cloud that was red and black and without shape seemed to explode inside my head and destroy my vision, although I was able to see my deeds from somewhere outside my body. Labiche was on the floor and I was stomping his face, hanging on to the bar for purchase, his blood stippling my loafers. The image reminded me of the blood on the grass where T. J. Dartez had been beaten to death. A woman was screaming. Someone was on a cell phone. Labiche's eyes were filled with terror. I kicked at his face and lost my balance. I felt the desire to kill him slip away from me, like ash dying on a dead fire.

Clete Purcel came out of nowhere and clenched me from behind and locked his hands on my chest and wrestled me out the door. We were out on the deck, the stars bright, the drawbridge at Burke Street lifting into the air. I pushed him away.

"He played you, big mon," Clete said. "Why'd you let him do it?"

I felt like I was coming off a drunk or getting off a ship without my sea legs. "What happened?"

"Who cares? It's done. Get in the Caddy."

"Where are we going?"

"How about another galaxy?" he said.

We walked into the parking lot and got into the car. He started the engine. "You got it together?"

"Tell me what happened."

He exhaled loudly. "You don't know?"

"He put his hand on me?"

"No, he didn't do anything. You laid him out."

We drove down the street and over the steel grid on the drawbridge.

"I didn't kill Dartez," I said.

He looked at me oddly, but I didn't try to explain.

AT SIX THE next morning, I put sardines on the spool table in the backyard for Mon Tee Coon, then showered and dressed and went to work as though nothing had happened the previous night. No one in the building treated me differently than they would have any other day. Helen seemed preoccupied with the paperwork on her desk. I made some calls to cops I knew in Fort Lauderdale and Miami. I drove to the convenience store and again interviewed the clerk who had sold Ding Dongs to the man in red tennis shoes. When I returned, my mailbox was full of messages, and at least half a dozen had been slipped under my door, all from my colleagues. Below is a sampling:

Way to go, Robicheaux.

Rip ass, big Dave.

Fucking A, Streakus.

Tell Purcel to finish the job.

Next time cap the cocksucker.

Helen tapped on my door.

"Come in," I said.

She sat sideways in a straight-back chair. She was wearing dark blue slacks and a white shirt with her gold badge on the pocket. I felt like I was in a filmstrip that had just shifted into slow motion. Her face was composed, her eyes neutral.

"Labiche isn't pressing charges," she said.

"I see."

"You're not surprised?" she said.

"He wants to look stand-up."

"Why'd you do it?"

I told her what he had said to Alafair.

"You should have come to me," she said. "I would have done something about it."

"How bad is Labiche hurt?"

"It's probably not felony assault. That doesn't mean it's acceptable."

She waited for me to say something. I didn't.

"I talked to the barmaid," she said.

"Babette?"

"She said you backed off. That Purcel didn't need to drag you outside."

"Could be."

"Were you drinking?"

"No, ma'am."

"You think Labiche set you up?"

"Probably."

"The prosecutor's office will be looking at you again. You know that, don't you?"

"Here's the rest of it," I said. "In front of Victor's, he told Alafair there was a guy wearing red tennis shoes down by the bayou. Alafair said Labiche seemed spooked, but he didn't want to check the guy out."

"Like he already knew who the guy was?" she said.

"That was Alafair's opinion."

Helen gazed into space. "What's your take on all this?"

"Labiche was probably on a pad for some dealers in Miami. He had ties there to Penny. I talked to a retired detective in Dade County. He said Penny got out of Raiford on appeal after some drugs disappeared from an evidence locker. The detective said Labiche was a suspect in the disappearance of the drugs."

"So maybe our man in the red tennis shoes is a hitter from Florida who knows Labiche?"

"Or Labiche knows him."

"But what's the agenda of the guy in the red shoes?" she asked.

"Pookie Domingue told Clete the guy's a cleaner."

"Pookie the Possum?"

"Clete said he was about to dump in his pants."

"Can I get a promise from you?" she said.

"What?"

She squeezed her eyes shut, then opened them again. "Forget it."

"What is it?"

She stood up to go. "Don't get into it with Labiche again. Got it, bwana? Bwana not have time to evolve. Bwana clean up brain with vacuum now or get thrown through window."

SURPRISES NEVER END. Just after work on Wednesday afternoon of the following week, Spade Labiche walked into my backyard while I was washing my boat. Mon Tee Coon was high up in a tree, looking down at us. Labiche was dressed like a sport in two-tone shoes and a panama hat and a tropical shirt that hung outside his slacks, as though he were trying to transform himself from one identity to another, like people do when they can no longer bear their own mistakes and the lives they lead. The swelling had gone out of his face, but the bruises and scrapes were still there. I never thought I could feel sorry for a guy like Labiche, but I did. There was another element in his face, namely, systemic fear, the kind that eats through your stomach and your entrails or the kind you see in people who know the Great Shade is waiting for them.

"Before you tell me to get lost, let me make my case," he said.

I squirted the hose on the boat's bow and ran a sponge along its surface. "I don't think we have much to talk about."

"Here's my situation," he continued, undaunted. "You don't work undercover in Miami without getting dirty. I crossed lines. I've been in situations where I had to either let a guy get smoked or get smoked myself. You ever have a gig like that?"

"Close."

"You let it play out? You let the guy go down?"

"I popped the guys who were going to pop him."

"I got it. Mr. Moral Superiority."

"Your meter is running, Spade."

"I know things nobody else knows. Something is going on that doesn't make sense. I got to have a deal."

"See Helen."

"She listens to you like she's got a thing."

"Lose it," I said.

"Screw that. I got the key to your head. I got the key to your soul."

"Are you crazy?"

He stepped closer to me, even though the spray from the hose drifted onto his clothes. He must have smeared himself with deodorant rather than taking a shower before coming to the house. "The guy who clipped the St. Mary deputy and cooked the guy in the ice cream truck probably has a list. But the list doesn't make sense. Maybe Tony Squid put out the contracts. I think this is political. That means Jimmy Nightingale."

"Who killed Penny?"

"With an electric drill? A sadist for hire."

"Maximo Soza was a sadist."

"I don't know who that is."

"The guy in the ice cream truck," I said.

"Ask me about Miami, I know all the names. I don't know all the names around here."

"I thought you were an expert on New Orleans."

His cheek, yellow and blue from my knuckles, quivered like jelly. "This is the deal I need. I keep my badge. Nothing goes in my jacket on this. You help me with Helen, I'll give you some information you can't get from anybody else."

How do you react to perps or corrupt cops who try to bargain? As Alafair once said about her dealings with venal people in the film industry: "It's easy. You hang up on them. They can't stand it."

"Did you hear me?" Labiche said.

"Sorry, I drifted off."

"What is it with you? I want to be friends. I didn't file charges."

"I think you wanted me to attack you."

He adjusted his tie and made a snuffing sound. "Who knows why anybody does anything?"

"Did you ever destroy evidence or steal it from an evidence locker?" I asked.

"Where'd you come up with that one? People are getting killed, and you're talking about evidence lockers."

"Everybody dies," I said.

His face drained as though he were aging before my eyes.

"You all right?" I said.

"Yeah, why wouldn't I be all right? Why'd you say that?"

"No reason, Spade. Have a good one."

I turned my back on him and resumed washing the boat. Mon Tee Coon jumped from one tree limb to the next, shaking leaves on my head. When I looked up, Labiche was gone.

JUST OUTSIDE LAFAYETTE, a man someone said looked like an egg with features painted on it turned off the service road in a Mazda and parked in front of a rental storage locker. He fitted a key into the lock and pulled up the door, waving to anyone nearby. He removed a cardboard box overflowing with folded clothes that still had price tags and placed the box into the trunk of the car. He did the same with a large and seemingly heavy rifle case. He was almost hairless and wore red tennis shoes that were caked with mud. While he loaded the car, he sucked on a lollipop.

A little boy wandered next to him. The man in tennis shoes patted him on the head. "What's your name, little fella?"

Before the child could answer, his mother jerked him away.

"Why'd you do that?" the man said to her.

"He's not supposed to talk to strangers."

The man took her measure, his face crumpling. "I don't think I like you."

She hurried to her car with the child, looking nervously over her shoulder. The man drove into a trailer court inside an oak grove on the far side of the service road, and ate a sack lunch on a picnic table with people from the trailers. Smoke drifted from barbecue grills into the trees. A ball game was being broadcast from a radio placed on a windowsill. The man in tennis shoes flagged down an ice cream truck and bought Popsicles for any kid who wanted one. Then he walked on his hands and did flips across the grass, filling the children with delight.

THAT EVENING, JUJU Ladrine and Pookie Domingue stopped at a fruit and watermelon stand located not far from the drawbridge at Nelson's Canal, a historical site that few cared about and where re-treating Confederates tried to stop Nathaniel Banks's invasion into southwestern Louisiana in the spring of 1863.

On the far side of the four-lane street were a drawbridge, a church, a pecan orchard, and a pasture with horses in it. The evening star was winking in the west, the light in the trees as bright as a flame, the wind smelling of distant rain. Pookie and JuJu ordered big bleeding slices of rattlesnake melon served on paper plates with plastic forks and a roll of paper towels for napkins. They sprinkled their melon with salt and dug in, chewing with their mouths open, enjoying the grandeur of the evening.

Opposite the stand was a huge sugarcane field where the cane was hardly more than green tentacles waving in the wind. In the distance, a solitary truck was parked on a dirt road.

"There was some kind of battle here?" JuJu said.

"Nothing like the battles at Vicksburg or places like that," Pookie said.

"That was in the Civil War?"

"Yeah, between the Nort' and the Sout'," Pookie said.

"Back in the 1960s, over civil rights and shit?"

Pookie stared at the side of JuJu's face. JuJu had been scratching at his scalp and was looking at his nails.

"Where'd you go to school?" Pookie asked.

"After the fourt' grade, I didn't go nowhere."

"You could fool me," Pookie said.

A black kid was unloading melons and cantaloupes from a flatbed trailer behind their table. Behind the truck on the dirt road, there was a flash of light and a puff of smoke, then a sound like the pop of a wet firecracker. JuJu touched his forehead. "What's with this?"

"What's what?" Pookie said.

"I got watermelon in my hair."

Pookie looked over his shoulder. "The kid was t'rowing melons around. Hey, kid! Ease up on t'rowing them melons."

"I wasn't t'rowing no melons," the kid said.

"Then why is slop running down your pile?" Pookie said to JuJu.

"Is there somewhere around here we can get laid?" JuJu said.

"Your friend Maximo gets clipped by a guy with a birdcage for a brain and you're talking about cooze?"

"I got the creeps," JuJu said.

"What you got is a walking nervous breakdown you came out of the womb wit'."

The wind changed, and Pookie thought he heard another solitary pop. He felt something wet on his face. JuJu's head was teetering on his shoulders, then it sank in his plate. Pookie stared across the field at the truck and at the early cane bending in the wind and at the amber-tinged twilight glinting on the train tracks, as though he were being drawn against his will into a historical photograph that would have no importance to anyone except him. For a brief moment, he wanted desperately to relive his life and change every thought and deed and event in it, even the ones that were good, in order to alter the sequence of events that had placed him near a site where ragged specters in gray and butternut took their revenge upon the quick.

Chapter 26

THE SUN WAS low in the west, flooding the crime scene with a red glow, when I arrived. Helen arrived minutes later. Someone had pulled a polyethylene tarp over the two bodies that sat slumped at the picnic table. An ambulance, three cruisers, and a fire truck had pulled onto the grass. The crime scene tape was already up. Cars were slowing at the intersection, people gawking from the windows. Spade Labiche was waiting for us. "Better take a look," he said.

I lifted up a corner of the tarp, high enough to see both victims without exposing their state to people on the other side of the tape.

"Jesus," Helen said.

I lowered the tarp. "The entry wounds are in the front."

"There's splatter on the flatbed behind them," Labiche said. "One guy says he thought he heard a backfire. A woman says she heard firecrackers."

"From where?" I said.

"Across the road," he said.

The sugarcane field was empty, the sky lavender and full of birds. A dust devil spun across the rows, wobbling, then broke apart.

I walked over to the trailer where a black kid had been stacking or unloading melons. Three melons were cored or broken. There was no bullet hole in the trailer that I could see. Farther down the street were houses and small businesses. I talked with the black kid, who was still

287

shaken by what he had witnessed. "One guy was wiping melon out of his hair, then his whole head blowed off. Man, I ain't up for dis."

"Did you see anyone out there in the field?" I asked.

"No, suh. Wait. I seen a truck."

"Did you see the truck go somewhere?"

"No, suh, I ain't."

"You see anything else? Think about it."

"Maybe a flash behind the truck."

"You see a man?"

"I cain't remember."

"That's all right," I said. "Let's talk again later." I gave him my card and joined Helen.

"Want me to start knocking on doors?" Labiche said.

"Yeah, while we have daylight," Helen said. "Good job."

"We'll get this guy," he said. "Right, Dave?"

I didn't answer. He shrugged and walked off.

"Good job?" I said to Helen.

"Give the devil his due," she said.

"Remind me to keep my own counsel."

A Jeff Davis Parish sheriff's cruiser, its flasher rippling, pulled onto the grass and stopped at the tape. Sherry Picard got out, her badge on her belt. "Mind if I get in on this?"

"What's this got to do with Jeff Davis?" Helen said.

"This is probably connected to the hit on Kevin Penny," she said. "Penny is my case."

"Help yourself," Helen said.

"Who's the vic?" Sherry said.

"Vics," Helen said. "Pookie Domingue and JuJu Ladrine."

"Can I?" she said, holding the corner of the tarp.

Helen nodded.

Sherry pulled up the tarp, her face impassive. She lowered it again and looked over her shoulder at the field. "The shots came from out there?" she said.

"That's the way it looks," I said.

"It was probably done with a fifty-caliber. I'm thinking an M107 sniper rifle."

"Where'd you come up with that?" Helen said.

"I used one," Sherry said.

"Pardon?" Helen said.

"In Afghanistan."

"Let's take a walk," I said to both of them.

We crossed the road and walked several hundred yards to a spot where a heavy vehicle had parked and then backed in a semicircle and driven away on its own tire marks. The ground was soft and moist, the impressions sharply stenciled. There were shoeprints by the tire tracks.

Helen got on her radio. "We need some tape in the field."

"This is my guess," Sherry said. "The shooter set up a bipod on his vehicle and fired through a space in the traffic. That means he's very good. The first shot was high. The second and third were on the mark. The M107 is a semi-auto. Unless he fired from inside the truck, the brass must have hit the ground."

But there was no brass on the ground. If the shooter used a semi-auto outside the truck, he had picked up his spent cartridges, which only cops and professional hitters do.

"You got any idea who this guy is?" Helen said to Sherry.

"Somebody who doesn't care if he drills a hole in a house one mile away and kills a child in a high chair," Sherry answered.

OUR LITTLE TOWN was not emotionally equipped to deal with the presence of a contract killer. Oh, yes, we're a libertine and atavistic people with a patina of Christianity, but by and large, our self-indulgence is that of children and perhaps even an expansion of Christ's recommendation to abide Caesar. Fear spread throughout the town, and Bobby Earl tried to insert himself into the mix, appearing on local television, speculating that Islamic terrorism was at the root of things. But Earl was an amateur, a race-baiter who had faded away with the Klan and the sweaty redneck demagogues shouting through megaphones on the bed of a cotton wagon.

Jimmy Nightingale, however, had found his voice. He, too, appeared on television, usually with police officials or a respected politician at his side. He was avuncular and assuring. He praised law enforcement, the Constitution, our way of life, our people in uniform overseas. As I looked at him on the screen, I believed Jimmy's time had come around.

Another figure showed up prominently, as is usual when we lose faith in ourselves and reach out for the worst members of our species. Tony Nemo was back in town, in a chauffeured steel-gray limo with charcoaled windows that hid the identities of either celebrities or individuals who would make small-town souls uncomfortable. He reserved the old Evangeline Theater, built on Main Street in 1929, for what he told *The Daily Iberian* was "a screening" of his work. The two films were *The Attack of the Worm People* and *Ninja Surf Vixens*.

After the screening, he threw a grand party in City Park, with barbecue and dirty rice and kegs of beer and crawfish boiling in caldrons filled with artichokes and corn on the cob. The oaks were strung with Japanese lanterns; a Cajun band played "La Jolie Blon" and "Allons à Lafayette" and Clifton Chenier's signature song, "Ay-Te Te Fee." I sat in my backyard and watched it from across the bayou. A few feet away, I could see the hooded eyes of an alligator among the cattails. Mon Tee Coon was eating from a can of cat food on the picnic table. The band played "La Jolie Blon" a second time. For me, there is no more haunting ballad in the world. Its origins go back to the eighteenth century, but the rendition by Harry Choates is the one that never leaves you.

Harry was born in either Rayne, Louisiana, or New Iberia, no one ever knew. He composed and sang in French but didn't know how to speak it. He sold his song for a hundred dollars and a bottle of booze and died drunk or was beaten to death by cops in the Austin city jail. The oddity of Harry's song is that you don't have to speak French to understand it. You know immediately it's about mortality and a lost way of life. Cajun culture is parodied and ridiculed; it is also treated as quaint and commercially exploited and vulgarized. But the travail of the Acadians was real, and so was the love affair of Evangeline on the banks of Bayou Teche, written about by Longfellow. Whenever someone asks me what southern Louisiana used to look like, and what has been despoiled by industrial polluters and Louisiana's corrupt politicians, I suggest they listen to Harry's lament. In my opinion, anyone who can be indifferent to this song has a spiritual affliction.

I heard Alafair behind me. Mon Tee Coon glanced up and went back to eating. Alafair picked up a pecan that was still in the husk and tossed it at the alligator's head. He ducked under the lily pads, his tail slapping water on the bank.

"What's the haps, Baby Squanto?" I said.

"We have Visigoths in the driveway."

I waited, dreading the rest of it.

"Tony Nemo," she said.

"Who's with him?"

"Levon Broussard."

"Are you going to work with these guys, Alf?"

"I'll do the adaptation with Levon. I won't be on the set."

Ouch, I thought. "What's Nemo want?"

"I didn't ask. They're drinking champagne in the back of the limo. You want me to blow them off?"

I got up from my deck chair. "Nope." I walked into the front yard. The limo was the color of a shark. The back door was open. Levon was standing on the grass, his tie pulled loose, a dark green bottle in his hand. "I've got a table by the band. I thought you might like to sit with Rowena and me."

I could see Tony's dark massivity piled in the backseat. "No, thanks."

"I owe you an amends. Isn't that what you twelve-step people call it?"

"You don't owe me anything."

"You're an intelligent, educated man, Dave. But you don't listen. Jimmy Nightingale is going to cause a lot of harm in the world."

"You should know. The guy in the backseat gave him his start in politics."

"Well, Tony doesn't feel that way now."

"Quit lying to yourself," I said. "Lie to yourself and you're never the same again."

"Say anything of me you wish. I'm going to bring Nightingale down."

"What you're doing is serving a diseased fat slob with a penis for a brain."

"What was that?" Tony said.

"I'm glad you dropped by," I replied. "I've had a problem of conscience about you."

His face looked like a bowl of mashed potatoes. He took a hit from his oxygen cup. Rowena sat next to him, obviously embarrassed. A movie star whose name I won't use sat in the shadows, a champagne glass balanced on his knee. He was handsome in the way that superficial people are, his jaw firm, his teeth capped, his manner easy and detached, as though a greater world awaited his presence.

"What's this about conscience?" Tony said.

"I think you're in danger," I said. "I think the guy who took out Maximo and JuJu and Pookie Domingue has you on his list."

"People love me. Why's this guy want to hurt me?"

"Why'd he want to clip Maximo and JuJu?" I said.

"They had enemies. I'm not the only guy they worked for."

"The killer has a fifty-caliber sniper rifle, Tony. It has a box magazine that holds ten rounds. It's accurate for a mile. I'd stay indoors if I were you."

"Hey, Levon, let's get out of here," Tony said. "This guy is nuts."

"Nightingale is behind this, Dave," Levon said.

"Yeah, I heard he invented original sin, too," I replied.

"Good line," he said. "Check with you later."

"Alafair made a choice against my wishes," I said. "Treat her right."

Levon tried to smile and let the remark pass, but there was no hiding the injury in his eyes.

One hour later, he was back in our yard on foot, drunk, his coat gone, his sleeves rolled. "You don't think I'd treat Alafair right?" he said. "Where do you get off with that?"

I turned on the gallery light and went down the steps. Alafair stood in the doorway.

"Lose the attitude," I said.

"You're accusing me of dishonorable conduct."

"This isn't about you. It's about my daughter."

"She's a grown woman."

"Not for me. Not for any father. This isn't 1865. Pull your head out of your ass."

"You're wrong," he said.

"Wrong about what?"

"It is 1865. You never quit the field. The battle is never over."

"You're going to defeat the forces of evil by joining up with Tony Nemo? Stop being a fool."

"A pox on you, Dave Robicheaux. You're the one person who should know better."

And that's the way he left it, stumbling down the street, tripping where the sidewalk had been wedged up by giant live oaks, talking to himself. Then he did something I will never understand, nor do I wish to understand, because it truly scared me. He stopped in front of the Shadows and stared through its piked fence as though having a conversation with people, perhaps comrades in arms, whom no one else could see. I do not believe it was an illusion on my part. Nor do I believe he was deranged. I believed Levon was who he was, and that was what scared me about him.

Chapter
27

Two months passed. The man in red tennis shoes seemed to have disappeared. The days were long and hot, the palm fronds and banana plants rattling dryly when the wind blew. Years ago, during the summer, rain showers fell throughout southern Louisiana at almost exactly three o'clock every afternoon. Now the gumbo soil in the sugarcane field was baked as hard as ceramic and cracked just as easily.

Most people believe that law enforcement and the solving of crimes and the apprehension and prosecution of criminals proceed in a systematic, linear fashion. The opposite is true. A successful outcome is usually produced by informants and dumb luck. The waiting, the missed opportunities, the bureaucracy, the tainted or lost evidence, the witnesses who change their accounts are endless. Lassitude, frustration, and anger become a way of life.

Mrs. Dartez continued to tell anyone who would listen that I was the murderer of her husband. The prosecution of Levon Broussard for the murder of Kevin Penny crept forward in Jefferson Davis Parish. Location scouts and line producers working for Levon and Tony Nine Ball began arriving in town, with all the attendant excitement. Homer was taken away from Clete and placed in a foster home, but he ran away and crawled through a window in Clete's cottage and hid there for two days until Clete returned from his office in New Orleans. So far, the social welfare agency had not tried to take him back. Alafair finished her initial adaptation of Levon's book, then consented to do the polish and to stay on the set after production began. Levon was drunk a lot. I went to meetings. Spade Labiche stayed in the background and said little, although I still believed that every day was his Ides of March. And no one talked anymore about the Jeff Davis Eight.

But while the rest of us were absorbed with our minutiae, Jimmy Nightingale was on the move. He appeared on network morning shows. He was the emissary of the New South, urbane and humble and jocular, a self-deprecating glint of the rogue in his eye. The host or hostess threw him softball questions about his casinos, his oligarchical history, his association with scum like Tony the Squid. He was the aviator who flew biplanes under bridges, an oilman who warned about global warming, an advocate for rural blacks whose neighborhoods were dumping ponds for petroleum waste. One host compared him to the young Bill Clinton, another to the young John F. Kennedy. When Jimmy got finished with an interview, the audience had one reaction: thunderous heartfelt applause.

On a dark night, the clouds crackling with dry lightning, Clete Purcel was knocking back shots in an end-of-the-line mixed-race joint in North Lafayette, the kind that had a pine-plank bar and red bulbs above the mirrors and where the clientele copulated in their cars without embarrassment. It was set back from the highway in a black neighborhood where some of the streets were still unpaved and desiccated privies still stood in backyards. Clete had a shot glass and a small pitcher of beer in front of him, and he stood rather than sat at the bar so he could watch the door. The air was thick was smoke, the restroom door open and stinking of urine and ammonia and weed. He could only guess at the race of the people around him.

A woman in jeans and boots and a western shirt came through the front door, her black hair tied up with a bandana. He had to rub his eyes with the backs of his wrist to make sure his vision wasn't failing him. She stood next to him and looked around. "This is where you hang out?"

"I'm supposed to meet a skip," he replied.

"What'd he skip on?"

"Felony assault, a fifty-grand bond. Were you looking for me?"

"I went by the motor court. Homer was alone. He said you were here."

He felt his face burn. "I check on him every thirty minutes."

"He's a nice kid."

"I know that, Miss Sherry. You want a drink?"

"Just a glass." She tinked a fingernail against the pitcher. "Let's go over in the corner. God, what a dump."

They sat at a table by a painted-over window, a wood-bladed fan turning overhead. She had carried a clean glass from the bar. He poured it full, the foam running over the edge. He kept his eyes on the door, waiting for a skip who was probably a no-show.

"I've got a bad feeling about the Penny investigation," she said.

"Levon Broussard is going down for it, right?"

"Too many people think Penny got what he deserved. Tony Nine Ball's influences aren't to be taken lightly, either."

"Tony got to somebody?" Clete said.

"That's why squids have tentacles."

"Dave Robicheaux thought the guy in red tennis shoes was going to clip Tony."

"Why?" she said.

"The guy's a cleaner."

"Somebody bigger than Tony Nemo is pulling the strings?"

"Or the agenda is bigger than Nemo's," he said. "Do you know who was the only guy to deal successfully with the Mafia?"

"No," she said.

"Mussolini. I grew up in the Irish Channel with those guys. I worked for some of them. In Vegas and Reno and Montana."

Her eyes searched his. "Yeah?"

"They broke my hand with a car door. Later, some of them went off-line," he said.

"You're a funny guy. I don't mean like strange. You're just a different kind of guy."

Once again Clete felt his old enemy come back. As a boy, he'd hated delivering milk off his father's truck to the back doors of the rich in the Garden District. He'd hated the welfare store where the clothes he was given were generic and ill-fitting; he'd hated the cops who'd hauled his parents out of the house when they were drunk and fighting; he'd hated his father for beating him with a razor strop and making him kneel all night on grains of rice; he'd hated a nun who'd told him he was unwashed, and a priest who'd shut the confessional window in his face when he was twelve years old. These moments should have disappeared long ago, but every time Clete looked into the eyes of a normal person, the dead coals he had carried for decades burst alight, giving life to every dark memory in his unconscious, telling him once again he was worthless in the sight of God and man.

"I don't like to talk much about myself," he said. "Not because I'm humble. On my best day, I never got more than a C-minus. That includes time in the Crotch."

"I checked you out. You have the Navy Cross."

"I got it while I was running in the wrong direction. How about we ditch yesterday's box score?"

He tilted the pitcher to fill her glass, but she covered it with her hand.

"Sometimes I get the blues," she said. "That's when I know I shouldn't drink too much. If I do, I really get the blues. I like Emmylou Harris's line: 'I got the rhythm, and I don't need the blues.'"

"You're talking about your husband?"

"He was a West Point graduate. He could have been an academic, but he went to Ranger school. He loved the army. He was killed by friendly fire."

"I'm sorry."

He stole a look at her eyes. She was looking at the bar. A man was telling a dirty joke to two women, both of them disheveled, grinning. "You know what I'm saying, don't you?" she asked.

"I'm not too smart about these things. I'm old, too."

"So is the earth. Is your guy going to show?"

Clete glanced at his watch, the same one he'd owned since the Corps. The hands had a soft green luminosity. "Probably not."

"I'll buy you a fish sandwich and a cup of coffee at McDonald's," she said.

"I don't want to leave Homer alone too long."

"Sure," she said.

"Another thing. I was involved with this lady. I'm not now, but it wasn't long ago, and she's a nice lady."

"The social worker?" she said.

"Yeah."

She nodded.

"You're beautiful, Miss Sherry. You got guts, too. I mean, working with some of those assholes in your department."

"I got you. Lay off the personal inventory."

"I don't want to walk out of here feeling bad," he said. Had he just said that? Why did he never have the words that accurately described his feelings? "I didn't mean—"

"I've got to pee," she said.

When she returned from the women's room, she filled her glass with beer and drank it. "I'd better get going."

"How about that fish sandwich?" he said.

She followed him to McDonald's in her car. They ate in a booth. Heat lightning flared in the clouds and died somewhere over the Gulf. She said little. He wondered about the images she had seen through the telescopic sight on a sniper's rifle, images she had created with the slow squeeze of a trigger.

"You go somewhere in your own head sometimes?" she said.

"On occasion."

"You know what they say."

"No, I don't."

"Don't go into a bad neighborhood by yourself."

"It's the only neighborhood I have," he replied.

She finished her sandwich and wiped her mouth. There was lipstick on the paper napkin when she crumpled it in her hand.

"There's a lady who stays over with Homer when I go out of town," he said.

"It's your call," she said.

He cupped his cell phone. "I'll be outside."

The motel was halfway to Opelousas on the four-lane. There was a piney woods behind it and a fountain in front that glittered with pink and blue lights. She followed him there and went into the lobby by his side.

DURING THE NIGHT he dreamed of a ville burning, the sparks spinning into the sky. Then the dream changed and he heard the 105s coming in short on his position, a whistling sound like truck tires on a wet highway. When he woke, the ceiling was shaking with thunder. He went into the bathroom in his skivvies and opened the window. The only sound he heard was the wind in the pines, their needles orange with drought and blight.

When he went back to bed, he took his snub-nose out of its holster and slipped it under his pillow for reasons he didn't understand. Audie Murphy did it. And probably thousands of other guys who never told anybody about it. Why not Clete Purcel? He lay awake most of the night, trying to provide himself explanations that had eluded him all his life.

ON A SATURDAY morning, Alafair came back early from filming outside St. Martinville. She went into the kitchen and took one of my diet Dr Peppers out of the icebox and drank it from the can.

"Something happen with the Hollywood crowd?" I said.

"They're midlevel pond scum. Neither good nor bad. Just run-of-the-mill scum."

"So what's the problem?"

"Levon Broussard."

"What's wrong with Levon?"

"He's a closet elitist. Rather than work with conventional film people, he signed on with a bunch of simian throwbacks who hide behind sunglasses and are afraid to talk at the table because they sound like they have throat cancer and a vocabulary of fewer than a dozen words. In the meantime, he pretends."

"Pretends what?"

"That he's on a mission. He insists on hiring only union people. The food has to be of a certain organic quality. The actors should be included in our script meetings. The black actors have to be given more lines. I think this is all a cover-up for what's really in his head."

"What's in his head?"

"Guilt. Hatred of the truth about his ancestors."

"You knew this, Alf," I said.

"I didn't know Levon would show up every morning unshaven with booze on his breath and crazy changes in the script."

"Maybe it's time to cut loose from these guys," I said.

"I don't want to lose my work."

"Then don't worry about it."

"Levon claims he didn't kill Kevin Penny. I think he's capable of it. I also think he's capable of doing Jimmy Nightingale harm."

"You're suggesting Levon might want to kill him?"

"Levon says Nightingale airdropped explosives on an Indian village in South America and killed women and children. That's not true, is it?"

"I'm afraid it is, Alf. Jimmy told me about it."

She couldn't hide the look on her face. At age five she had survived an army massacre of her Salvadoran village. The soldiers had used machetes to hack open the bodies of pregnant Indian women.

"Why doesn't the media say something about it?" she said.

"If people don't care about eight poor women murdered in Jefferson Davis Parish, why would they care about some oilmen bombing Indians in Latin America?"

"Maybe Nightingale deserves a bullet in the face," she said.

"I think he's remorseful."

"After the fact," she said. "What a piece of shit."

"Have another diet Doc with me," I said.

"At least I had one laugh this morning."

"At what?" I said, glad that we were through with the subject of Jimmy Nightingale and Tony Nemo and Levon Broussard.

"This cute little man was behind the cordon when we were filming a scene in St. Martinville. He had on a pale blue baseball cap and clothes out of the box from Penny's. The tags were still on. He looked like a big ceramic doll. He'd read two of my novels."

"Oh yeah?" I said, my interest fading.

"He was eating a fudge bar. He made me think of Truman Capote without the blubber."

Mon Tee Coon was waddling through the backyard, side by side with our old warrior cat, Snuggs.

"Are you listening?" Alafair asked.

"Sure."

"I'd love to use him as a character. He was such a cuddly little guy. He said his nickname was Smiley."

"Cuddly?" I popped a Dr Pepper and went outside.

CHESTER DROVE A compact he had stolen down the bayou road, until he saw the refurbished antebellum home of the Nightingales. He passed the driveway and the tunnel of oaks that led to the spacious porch and the second-story balconies and dormers and floor-to-ceiling windows that gave the main house the look of a baroque paddle wheeler on the Mississippi. He crossed a drawbridge and parked by a canebrake and lifted the sniper rifle from the trunk and entered an empty boathouse that had a walkway built along one wall. Across the Teche, he could see the sloping green yard of the Nightingale home and a swimming pool and a bathhouse spangled with sunlight sifting like spiritual grace through the oak limbs and Spanish moss.

Chester also carried a hand-crafted leather folder with pockets and braided borders and a bucking horse and cowboy rider stenciled on it. The folder had been given to him years ago by a friend he'd met at a state mental hygiene clinic. The friend had told Chester he'd murdered three people while hitchhiking across the country; the friend had considered Chester a man who would understand.

"You shouldn't hurt people who give you a free car ride," Chester had said.

"I needed their car," the friend had said.

"Did you hurt a child? If you lie, you know what will happen."

"I'm sorry, Chester. Don't be mad. I didn't hurt no kids."

"Let's have no more ugly talk."

"No more. I promise."

"That's a good boy," Chester had said. His nostrils were flaring, his breath out of control.

In the pouches of his folder were his index cards wrapped with a rubber band. The cards were in numerical order. Each one had a drawing on it depicting the stages of the job he had been assigned. The system never failed him. If you had no connection to the target, and if the target deserved his fate—which they all did—it was easy to walk up on the target with a smile on your face and click the off switch on the side of the target's head and walk away. He'd done it with an ice pick to a rapist on a subway in New York City, and had covered the dead man's face with a raincoat and sat in the next car until the train pulled in to the station and the body tumbled out of the seat.

Of course there were occasions when he did it in self-defense, when people decided he was a half-grown man they could tease and torment, like the two drug dealers in Algiers or the deputy who gave him a bad time for simply walking down a backroad by the bayou. Chester didn't like to think about those kinds of people. They made him grind his teeth, which were as small and rounded as pearls and loose in his gums because of the untreated abscesses that were his constant companions in the orphanage. When a dentist warned him about grinding his teeth in his sleep and his obvious need to wear a guard during the nocturnal hours, Chester told the dentist he ground his teeth in the daylight, and the dentist had better watch his greedy mouth and concentrate on keeping his fingernails clean and washing his hands after he went to the bathroom.

Chester sat down on a rolled tarp and rested the rifle across his thighs. The sun was white in the sky, the bayou a dirty chocolate color, dragonflies hanging over the cattails. A dead catfish floated upside down past the boathouse, its stomach as bloated as a softball. Then he saw a woman emerge from the back of the house. She was wearing a bathing suit that was as black as her hair; it fit her as tightly and smoothly as molded rubber. He released the box magazine from the rifle's frame and lifted the telescopic sight to his eye. Suddenly, the face of the woman was a few feet from his. Her body was an artwork, a landscape of valleys and hills and mysterious places that yearned to be discovered and touched. He felt an erection tightening against his underwear.

She walked slowly down the tile steps into the pool, one hand gliding along the hardness of a chromium rail, the water slipping over her knees and thighs and the secret place he knew it was wrong to think about. Through the telescopic sight, he could see the sweat on her neck and the tops of her breasts, and he had to rest the rifle butt-down and clench the stock and kiss the barrel to stop his hands from shaking.

He closed his eyes and began counting backward from a hundred to make his erection go down. Inside his head, he saw himself strapped to a bed, his underwear soaked with urine, his bare chest and legs crisscrossed with welts from a switch the operators of the orphanage had made him cut for himself. Then the kindly face of someone not much older than he was appeared above him. Her loving hands un-buckled the straps and removed his soiled underwear and washed his body and stroked his forehead.

He forced himself to breathe slowly until he regained control. He wiped his saliva off the gun barrel, his desire reduced to little more than a guttering flame. He must not have impure thoughts, he told himself. They made him want to hurt people. Others enjoyed forbidden things, and he could not. The thoughts followed him around, and the more he tried to keep them out of his head, the more they enticed him. When nothing else worked, he wanted to hurt someone the way his friend the hitchhiker did, and he never wanted to be like the hitchhiker.

He waited for the quivering in his shorts to subside completely, then he dared look at the swimming pool again.

A man in a yellow bikini and flip-flops emerged from the house and walked toward the pool. A towel hung around his neck. Chester lifted the telescopic sight to his eye again. The man's hair was peroxided, his artificially tanned torso plated with muscle, his phallus shaped like a fat banana inside the bikini. Chester put the crosshairs on the man's face. There was something wrong with it. It was sunken in the center, the eyes and nose and mouth too small. It was a stupid face. Chester did not like people with stupid faces. He felt himself grinding his teeth again.

Naughty boy, he thought gleefully.

The man with the perfect body and stupid face dove into the pool and swam on his back. The woman joined him, then the two of them rested by the gutter in the deep end, closer than they should have been, perhaps their legs or stomachs touching. Chester fantasized about parking a big one at the base of the man's brain. It would leave his head floating in chunks, dissolving like red smoke in the turquoise depths. Chester ran his tongue across his lips at the thought.

The woman pulled herself up on the ladder and got out of the pool, her rump dripping. She seemed very angry and shook her finger at the man clinging to the pool gutter, his face turned up to hers.

Chester wondered if the man with the stupid face had tried to put his hand somewhere he shouldn't have. If that was true, Chester wanted to kill him. And not all at once. Bad men deserved bad things, and Chester knew how to do all of them. He began to breathe heavily again, frustrated with himself and with the restraints placed upon him. He shouldn't have come here. Or wheeled his suitcase down the two-lane road by the bayou, thereby drawing the attention of the deputy he was forced to kill. The job and the places were always on the cards. There were no cards that showed him in a boathouse, gripping an M107 with both hands.

But these were things he had to do, whether others liked them or not. He had survived at the orphanage and on the streets of Mexican border towns where children were rented by the hour. Today he had power that he wanted to take back in time and use on all those who had exploited his little body. But that was not the way it worked.

Time did not take away the pain; nor did it allow him to use his skills on people out of the past who waited for him in his sleep.

Chester got up and realized there was a wet spot the size of a quarter in his underwear. Although no one was in sight, he felt his face burning as he walked back to the car and dropped the rifle into the trunk. He drove straight to a Dairy Queen in Franklin and cleaned himself in a restroom, then sat at a wooden table in the shade and began eating a paper plate full of ice cream sandwiches.

Three teenagers sat in an SUV ten feet away, the doors open, the panels throbbing with rap.

"Turn that down, please," Chester said.

A kid lowered the volume. "What was that?"

"That music. It hurts my ears," Chester said.

"It grows on you," the kid said. He turned the volume up full-blast.

Chester walked to the door of the SUV. The three kids were looking at one another and grinning, as though they intuitively knew a lifelong object of ridicule had wandered into their midst and they were free to do anything they wished to him.

"Why do you want to act smart-alecky?" Chester shouted above the roar.

"You like Dilly Bars?" said the kid in the passenger seat. "Strap on your kneepads in the restroom. I'll bring you one."

"Don't talk like that."

"My father owns half this town. Now get out of here, freak."

Chester rested one hand on the door like a lump of dough. "You shouldn't say that to me."

"Oh, he's all mad now," the kid said, forming his mouth into a pout. "He messed himself. He's starting to cry."

"He's a retard," the driver said. "Leave him alone."

"He's cute," said the kid in the passenger seat. "We like you, little buddy. Want to meet some girls?"

"You're very mean," Chester said.

"We're finished here," the driver said. He leaned toward the passenger window. "You hear me? Get your hand off the door."

When Chester didn't move, the driver smashed his hand.

"Owie," Chester said.

The three kids laughed.

Chester got behind the wheel of his vehicle. He started the engine but could not hear its sound and had to rest his hand on the dashboard to make sure it was running. He had entered one of those soundproof moments in his life that belonged to neither the past nor the present. The catalyst and the consequence were always the same. Contempt, ridicule, public shame, followed by his eardrums swelling so tightly he couldn't hear, and his optical nerves popping loose from the backs of his eyes, deconstructing the external world piece by piece.

For perhaps thirty seconds, the backs of his eyelids were a red veil on the other side of which stick figures performed gross acts and fought one another with staves and staffs like the caricatures in tarot cards. It was funny how life replicated the tarot rather than the other way around. Maybe that was how thought worked. You had the thought, then the thought became the thing. That was why bad thoughts were to be avoided.

The moment passed, and the world reassembled itself, and Chester drove into the street and down to the intersection. Ten minutes later, the three boys in the SUV pulled out and drove in the opposite direction. They stopped at a girl's house, a filling station to gas up, a street corner in a black neighborhood to score some weed, a drive-through window for daiquiris, a gun-and-ammo store to buy .22 shells. They parked by a swampy woods used as an illegal dump and took turns pocking holes in a rusted-out car body that had no engine and no glass in the windows. When they were out of shells, they got back into the SUV and Bic-fired a bong.

Chester estimated the range at eight hundred yards. With his gloves on, he loaded nine armor-piercing rounds into the box magazine, then wet the tenth round with his mouth and inserted it with the others. He braced the bipod on the car hood and sighted through the scope. Inside the SUV, the silhouettes of the boys moved back and forth like cutouts on a moving clothesline. He felt a flame lick at his loins, a hardening again in his manhood, a desire that went so deep he knew he would never satisfy it. His ears whirred with sound, his heart pounded, and just as he squeezed the trigger, he felt a dam break inside him and an orgasmic sensation flood through his body, so strong and warm and encompassing that his legs went weak.

There was no movement inside the SUV, nor any sound. The round had punched a hole just below the rear window and probably gone through the seats and the radio. Chester kept the rifle aimed at the same level and delivered four more rounds, blowing pieces of the seats and upholstery and dashboard and windshield onto the hood.

His last shot was into the gas tank. He picked up his brass and dropped it into the pockets of his baggy trousers. Before he pulled onto the asphalt, he glanced through the rear window. One of the kids had spilled onto the ground. One was running through the woods. Chester didn't know where the third had gone. He turned up the air-conditioning until the inside of the car was frigid and the sweat on his face turned to ice. He thumbed a CD of Brahms into the stereo and took a deep breath through his nose, as though inhaling air off a glacier on the first day of creation, long before a thick-legged quadruped with fins and gills and lungs waddled out of the surf and began its agenda.

Chapter 28

Helen came into my office on Tuesday morning. She had just gotten back from the sheriff's department in St. Mary Parish. She told me of the shooting.

"None of the boys were hit?" I said.

"That's what's peculiar," she said. "The shooter clustered five rounds below the rear window and put one in the gas tank. Why didn't he riddle the whole vehicle if he was out to do maximum damage?"

"How far away was he?"

"Far enough that the boys never saw him. By the way, 'boys' isn't a good term for these guys. They're walking promotions for Planned Parenthood."

"No brass?"

"Just tire tracks," she said. "They may belong to a stolen car that was found in Des Allemands."

"You think this is our guy?" I asked.

"He was obviously using a high-powered military rifle and probably firing armor-piercing rounds."

"The kids don't have any idea who was shooting at them or why?"

"They say a weirdo guy was yelling at them at the DQ."

"About what?"

"Their radio was playing rap. That was a couple of hours before the shooting. I don't think they were just playing rap, either."

309

"They wised off?"

"Who knows? They'd drown in their own shit if they ever left St. Mary Parish," she said.

"What kind of car was the guy at the DQ driving?"

"They just remembered it was green. Like the stolen one in Des Allemands."

"Any latents?"

"The owner's," she said. "You think the shooter just wanted to scare the hell out of them?"

"He parked one in the tank."

"Maybe he didn't want them coming after him," she said.

"Or he wanted to burn them alive," I said.

"No, I think our boy lost control and went outside his parameters. Like somebody rolling the dice and shutting his eyes. Charlie Manson claims he never killed anyone. That's because he got somebody else to do it."

I said earlier that Clete Purcel was the best investigative detective I ever knew—but Helen Soileau was a close second.

"What did the guy at the DQ look like?" I asked.

"Chubby buttocks. A lisp. The kind of guy who hangs around playgrounds."

"I think these kids have sexual problems of their own," I said.

"Before they got into it, they said the guy was smiling at everybody in the DQ, particularly at children."

"The kind of guy somebody might call Smiley?"

"I think this baby is back in town and ready to rock," she replied.

SOMETIMES IT IS hard to explain to outsiders the culture of southern Louisiana and the quandary of many of its people. The world in which they grew up is now a decaying memory, but many of them have no place in the present. I know Cajuns who have never been farther than two parishes from their birthplace. There are people here who cannot add and subtract, cannot read a newspaper, and do not know what the term "9/11" means. Over forty percent of children are born to an unwed mother. In terms of heart and kidney disease, infant mortality, fatal highway accidents, and contaminated drinking water, we are ranked among the worst in the nation. Our politicians are an embarrassment and give avarice and mendacity a bad name.

So how do you get angry at someone who was born poor, speaks English so badly that she's unintelligible to outsiders, has the world-view and religious beliefs of a medieval peasant, cleans houses for a living if she's lucky, and is obese because of the fat-laced bulk food she feels thankful for?

The temperature had hit ninety-eight degrees at four in the afternoon. The humidity was eye-watering and as bright as spun glass, as tangible as lines of insects crawling on your torso and thighs. At sunset, lightning pulsed in the clouds over the Gulf, but no rain fell, and the wind was dry and hot and smelled of road tar and diesel fuel. I walked down to the bayou and watched the sun shrink into an ember between two black clouds and disappear. Then the wind died and the trees stood still, and the surface of the bayou quivered in the sun's afterglow, as though a molecular change were taking place in the water.

It's a phenomenon that seems unique to South Louisiana, like a sea change, as if the natural world is reversing itself and correcting an oversight. The barometer will drop unexpectedly, the bayou will swell and remain placid at the same time, and suddenly, rain rings will dimple the surface from one bank to the other. Fish sense the change in barometric pressure and begin feeding on the surface in anticipation of the rain that will wash food from the trees into the stream or swamp.

The wind sprang to life just as a solitary raindrop struck my face. I went back into the house to get Alafair. "Come outside."

"What's going on?" she said.

"It's actually raining. Let's walk down to Clementine's for dessert."

She was writing in longhand at her worktable, a flat-sided oak door I had nailed onto sawhorses. She looked out the window. The light was almost gone, and leaves were scattering across the yard, and Mon Tee Coon was standing stiff-legged on top of Tripod's hutch, his nose pointed into the wind. "Wonderful," Alafair said, and capped her pen.

As we stepped out onto the gallery, we saw a short, stocky woman in a dark dress walk at an angle across Main, carrying a hand-lettered sign, undaunted by the whir of the automobile tires whizzing past her. Her shoulders were humped, the muscles in her calves shaped like upside-down bowling pins, her expression as angry as an uprooted rock. The sign read "D. Robicheaux killed my husbon and was let free. How my family going to live?"

"Let me talk to her, Dave," Alafair said.

"I'll do it," I said.

My expression of confidence was vanity. There in the dying light, trapped in her own rage and madness and the heat radiating through the soles of her cheap shoes, her hair tangled wetly on her face, raindrops spinning down from the stars above oak trees planted by slaves, dredged out of a sixteenth-century mob armed with pitchforks and rakes, Mrs. T. J. Dartez had persevered through time and history and the elements and brought her war to my doorstep and, worse, confronted me again with the bête noire I could not exorcize from my life. I tried to place my hand on her arm.

"Don't touch me, you," she said. "Liar. Killer. *Fite putin.*"

"Don't be talking about my mother, Ms. Dartez," I said.

"I seen the preacher at our church. He said I got to forgive. 'Not Detective Robicheaux, I don't.' That's what I tole him, yeah. Ain't nothing in the Bible say we got to forgive evil. And that's what you are."

"I didn't kill your husband."

"How you know that if you say you was so drunk you didn't know what world you was in. My man was sick. He didn't have no money for his prescriptions. He couldn't protect hisself."

"What prescriptions?"

"For his epilepsy. His truck was ruint, and he couldn't work 'cause of the accident and 'cause the insurance company wouldn't give him no money."

"That's not true, Ms. Dartez," Alafair said.

"You stay out of it, you."

"Let us drive you home," I said.

"I ain't taking no favors from y'all. God gonna get you, Mr. Robicheaux. I'm gonna stay out here all night. Then I'm gonna stay out here all day tomorrow."

"No, you will not," I said.

"You ain't gonna boss me, no."

"I wouldn't try to do that," I said. "I think you're a good lady, Ms. Dartez. I think someone used your husband to bring me harm."

"It was you," she said. "It's all been you."

"No, ma'am, it's not me," I said.

A raindrop struck her forehead and ran through one eyebrow and across her nose like silver thread. But she never blinked, and she did not try to wipe the water from her face. "Why you done this to me? I ain't got nothing except two hungry kids, me."

I put a hand on each of her shoulders, whether she liked it or not. "My wife Annie was murdered. So was my mother. My father was killed by an oil-well blowout that shouldn't have happened. I know what it feels like to be treated badly by the world. That is why I would never deliberately hurt you or your husband. Look into my face and tell me I'm lying."

"I ain't got to do nothing you say."

"No, you don't. But what does your conscience tell you? Forget about the preacher at your church, good man that he might be; forget about me; forget about every other person in the world except you and your children and your own idea of God. What does your conscience tell you?"

She faltered. "I ain't sho'."

"No, tell me, Ms. Dartez. Tell me now." I squeezed her shoulders tighter. Tears were welling in her eyes. She shook her head.

"Say it."

"You're telling the troot'."

"Thank you," I said.

She dropped the sign on the grass. "What am I gonna do, suh?"

"Whatever it is, Alafair and I will help you with it."

She buried her face into my chest, her hands at her sides. I could feel the wetness coming through my shirt.

"I'll be inside," Alafair said.

"You okay, Ms. Dartez?" I said.

"No, suh, I ain't. I ain't never gonna be okay. Never, never, never." She ground her forehead deeper into my chest, into the bone.

Considering the hand she'd been dealt, who would take her to task?

AT NOON ON Wednesday, Clete was about to go across the street to Victor's Cafeteria when a midnight-blue Buick with tinted windows pulled to the curb and a chauffeur in gray livery got out and looked across the roof at Clete and said, "Got a minute, Mr. Purcel?"

Peroxide hair, dented-in face, shades, flat stomach, concrete deltoids, scar tissue around the eyes, a half cup of brains. Where had he seen him before?

"You're Swede Jensen. You parked cars at the casino."

"You got a good memory," the chauffeur said. "I work for Ms. Nightingale now."

"I'm closed till one."

"She gave me orders. I told her you probably didn't want to be bothered. She pissed in the swimming pool about it. How about cutting me a break?"

Clete tried to process what he'd just heard. It was impossible. "Come in and make it fast." He went back into the office and closed the blinds. His secretary had already gone to lunch; the waiting area was empty. He sat behind his desk and opened a drawer and took out a roll of mints and put one into his mouth. He left the drawer open. A .25-caliber semi-auto lay under a notepad. Swede took a chair.

"She wants to hire you," he said.

"So why doesn't she come in?"

"She's shy."

"I'll believe that in a minute."

"I told her we go back."

"We don't go back, Swede. I remember you. That's a long way from 'we go back.'"

"This is my meal ticket, Purcel."

"Before Tony Nine Ball got you a job parking cars, you were a porn actor in that studio out on Airline Highway."

Swede took off his shades and pinched the bridge of his nose. His eyes were blue, one of them defective, as if there were an ice chip in the lens. "I took a pinch for a lewd act with a minor. I had to wait eight months in jail to go to court. The charges got dropped. You want me to leave, that's fine with me."

"What's on Ms. Nightingale's mind?"

"She thinks Levon Broussard's lawyers are going to put the Kevin Penny torture/murder on her brother."

"Why would they want to do that?" Clete asked.

"What do you think? To break his sticks."

"So he can't get elected to the U.S. Senate?"

"The Senate is just the rosin box," Swede said. "Jimmy Nightingale is the man for our times."

"I knew a mobbed-up guy from Jersey who knew Nightingale in the casino business. He's doing life for tying a guy to a tree and shooting him in the balls. He said Nightingale was a Murphy artist without the virtues."

"Go to one of his rallies. All those people are wrong?"

Clete looked at Swede again. His eyebrows were irregular in shape, like earthworms that had been stepped on. "You were in the ring?"

"Ham-and-egg stuff. Nothing to write *Ring* magazine about."

"Where'd you learn to fight?"

"Inside. When I was eighteen. The Nightingales gave me a break, like they have a lot of people. Here's the gig. Two thousand a month retainer, probably for a year."

"Retainer to do what?"

"To swat flies. This place is Bum Fuck on acid. You know the kind of dirt that people are trying to dig up on Mr. Nightingale?"

"Tell Ms. Nightingale to call me."

"She's waiting for you now."

"Where?"

"You got a problem with food from Popeyes?"

"No."

"She's in the park."

Don't do it, a voice said.

"I'll follow you," Clete said.

HE DROVE HIS Caddy onto the grass by a concrete boat ramp and a row of camellia bushes on the water's edge. Emmeline was sitting under the roof of a picnic shelter, wearing a sundress and a wide-brimmed straw hat with silk flowers sewn on it, like one from the plantation era. She and Swede had spread a checked cloth on the table and placed there a bucket of fried chicken and one of fried crawfish and a box of buttermilk biscuits with a container of milk gravy. Clete removed his porkpie hat and sat down. "How do you do, ma'am?" he said.

"You're as big as they say," she said.

"My stomach?"

"A big guy is a big guy," she said.

"Swede says you want some help."

"I don't want Jimmy stabbed in the back."

"Who wants to do that?"

"Levon Broussard, the savior of humanity," she said. She pushed the bucket of fried crawfish toward him.

"Got a soft drink?" he asked.

"You don't want a long-neck?" Swede asked.

Emmeline's eyes drilled a hole in Swede.

"Coca-Cola coming up," he said.

"So you want Levon Broussard off your case?" Clete asked Emmeline.

"Or tied to an anchor and thrown in the Gulf," she said. "That's a joke."

"I don't think the guy's got a lot of arrows in his quiver."

"What do you call an abomination like Tony Nemo?" she asked.

"I don't like to say this, but Fat Tony poured most of your brother's concrete."

"Nemo poured half the concrete in New Orleans," she replied.

Clete took a long sip from his Coke, his eyes veiled. What was she after? Now she was talking about oil companies, their mistreatment of Jimmy, the unfair role they'd placed him in in South America, the stupidity of the media, the hypocrisy of Levon, the vile nature of his wife.

"How's Broussard a hypocrite?" Clete asked. "He did a lot of good down in Latin America, didn't he? With Amnesty International and that kind of stuff."

"He can't write or talk enough about his glorious ancestors, who happened to be slave owners; then he bleeds all over the television screen about the suffering people in Guatemala. In the meantime, his Aborigine wife tells everybody who'll listen that Jimmy raped her."

"She's an Aborigine?" Clete said.

"She looks like one."

"You're not going to go jogging with her?" he said.

"Did I misjudge you?"

"Do you mean am I dumb instead of smart? Yeah, probably."

"That's not clever, Mr. Purcel. You have a good reputation as a private investigator. But I don't think you understand how vicious Jimmy's enemies are. You also don't know how good a man he is."

Right, Clete thought. He took another sip from his Coke. How far should he take it?

"Swede mentioned a retainer of two grand a month," he said. "That's a lot of money for what sounds like doing nothing."

"There would be a few duties," she said.

"Like what?"

"Security, maybe."

He picked up a biscuit and dipped it in the gravy and put it into his mouth, his cheek pouching. His eyes remained empty, as though he were detached from the conversation. "Has Dave Robicheaux got anything to do with this?"

"No. Why would he be involved in anything regarding Jimmy? Actually, I don't care for Mr. Robicheaux."

"Don't take this personal, Ms. Nightingale. When a guy like Tony the Squid can't get a cop on a pad, he goes to a friend of the cop. Maybe he wines and dines the cop, then lends him money. The issue is information. Any place there's vice, extortion, blackmail, union corruption, insider trading, jury-rigging, highway contracting, the issue is always information. The rest of it doesn't mean diddly-squat on a rock. Outside of the scut work I do for bail bondsmen, I make my living off information. I'm not proud of it."

"Your perception is correct," she said.

"About what?"

"I want to retain you to keep me informed about people who want to hurt my brother," she said. "Got it?"

"I don't do wiretaps, I don't do videos through windows, and I don't deliberately mess people up, not even the lowlifes."

"I don't expect you to," she said.

"Let me think on it."

"You've taken up this much of my time, and you'll think on it?"

Clete looked at the glare of the sun on the water. It resembled a yellow flame, dancing under the chop from a passing boat. "I've got a big enemy. My own head. So I got to think through things before I make choices. Then I usually make the wrong choice anyway. Then I got to think my way back through it a second time, and it's not only a drag, I get a bad headache."

She gazed into space as though she had been listening to someone speaking Sanskrit.

"Hello?" he said.

"Yes?"

"Could I have a couple of these crawfish for the road?" he asked.

"I can't believe I've had this conversation," she said.

ONE HOUR LATER, Clete looked out the back window of his office and saw Swede Jensen on his patio, where Clete kept a reclining chair and a spool table outfitted with a beach umbrella. Swede was tossing his chauffeur's cap into the air and catching it. Clete opened the French doors and stepped out into the heat. "You trying to creep my office?"

"Ms. Nightingale is picking up her Lexus at the dealership. I got a question. Are you on the inside with the Robicheaux girl?"

"Time to use your words carefully, Swede."

"You got me wrong. You said something about me working in a porn studio. Maybe there was some porn made there, but I wasn't part of it."

"I'll contact the Vatican so they can get started with your early canonization."

"I was in two independent films; they made it into a few legitimate theaters."

"Yeah?" Clete said.

"I'll tell you something else. The porn guy on Airline? He almost nailed the hijackers before 9/11. He tried to get ahold of somebody at the FBI. He said the ragheads buying dirty films from him weren't religious fanatics, they were degenerates and rod floggers, like most of his clientele. The message got lost or delayed or something. A few days later the Towers and the Pentagon got hit. True story. So how about it?"

"How about what?"

"Will you put in a word for me with Robicheaux's daughter? She's the screenwriter for this Civil War film. I'm a pretty good actor. I just want a shot."

"I'll ask her."

"No kidding?"

"I'll tell her you're available."

"You're okay, Purcel. Not like what I'm always hearing."

"Do me a favor?"

"Anything," Swede said.

"Keep the Nightingales away from me. And don't give Alafair any trouble. Think of me as her uncle."

"I owe you a solid, man."

Clete watched him walk away whistling, flipping his hat into the air and catching it on his head. He turned around and gave Clete a thumbs-up.

Chapter 29

FEW PEOPLE UNDERSTOOD Clete. As simple-minded people are wont to do, they put him into categories. He was a compulsive gambler, a disgraced cop who'd flushed his career with weed and booze, a mercenary who should be considered a traitor, a lover of women who belonged in straitjackets, a human wrecking ball, a child in a man's body, a rum-dum living on yesterday's box score, a former leg-breaker for the Mob, and most realistically, a dangerous, war-damaged man whose unpredictable moods could lay waste to half a city.

But as with all simple-minded and dismissive people, they were wrong. And not only were his detractors wrong, none of them could shine his shoes. Clete was one of the most intelligent people I ever knew, and one of the most humble, less out of virtue than his inability to understand his own goodness. He was so brave that he didn't know how to be afraid. In the same fashion, he was generous because he cared little about money or social status or ownership, except for his Caddy convertibles. His physical appetites were enormous. So was his capacity for self-destruction. His father the milkman had taught Clete to hate himself, and Clete had spent a lifetime trying to unlearn the lesson.

The people who understood him best were usually in the life. Grifters, hookers, money washers at the track, street dips, Murphy artists, and shylocks respected him. So did uptown house creeps and old-time petemen. Button men avoided him. So did strong-arm robbers and child molesters; men who abused women or animals were terrified of him. When Clete's anger was unleashed, he transformed into someone larger than himself. His fists seemed as big as cantaloupes, his pocked neck as hard as a fire hydrant; his arms and shoulders would split his clothes. He dropped a New Jersey hit man off a roof through the top of a greenhouse. He hooked his hand into a Teamster official's mouth and slung him from a balcony into a dry swimming pool. He almost drowned a NOPD vice cop in a toilet bowl. He burned down a plantation home on Bayou Teche, fire-hosed a gangster across the restroom floor in a casino, pushed a sadist off the rim of a canyon in Montana, filled a mobbed-up politician's antique convertible with concrete, went berserk in a St. Martinville pool hall and piled five unconscious outlaw bikers in a corner and would have doubled the number with a baseball bat if Helen Soileau hadn't talked him into cuffing himself.

He was the trickster from folk mythology who flung scat at respectability. But he was a far more complicated man, in essence a Greek tragedy, a Promethean figure no one recognized as such, a member of the just men in Jewish legend who suffered for the rest of us. If there are angels among us, as St. Paul suggests, I believed Clete was one of them, his wings auraed with smoke, his cloak rolled in blood, his sword broken in battle but unsurrendered and unsheathed, a protector whose genus went back to Thermopylae and Masada.

He pulled to the curb as I was walking home from work. He was eating a spearmint sno'ball, the top of the Caddy down. "I had a talk with Emmeline Nightingale in the park today."

"Not interested," I said.

"Is Alafair home?"

"Probably."

"Ms. Nightingale's chauffeur would like a part in her picture."

"What are you up to, Clete?"

"I thought that would get your attention. Get in."

That's how it worked. Clete would roll the dice, and I would get stuck with the math. I opened the door and sat back in the seat. He was wearing aviator shades and a Hawaiian shirt with hula girls on it. The sunlight through the trees was as red as a ruby on his skin. He pulled away from the curb, driving with the heel of his hand, like a 1950s lowrider.

"What's this about the chauffeur?" I said.

"I just wanted to get you in the car. Ms. Nightingale wants to hire me."

"Hire you?"

"She says it's to keep Levon Broussard off her back."

"That's not it?"

"I think she knows I might be in a relationship with Sherry Picard." We bounced into my driveway. "A relationship?" I said.

"Yeah, we got it on. I'm seeing her tonight."

"Leave out the particulars. What in God's name are you doing?"

"There you go again."

"I just asked a question. You can't take care of yourself."

"That's it. No matter what I say, you're on my case. I'm too old. I should put my stiff one-eye in a safe-deposit box. I drink too much. I eat the wrong food. How about respecting my space for a change?"

"I'm sorry," I said. "You're the best guy I've ever known. I worry about you."

"Remember how you used to bounce your stick on the curb in the Quarter? Everyone thought you were signaling me about a crime in progress. You were telling me to meet you at the Acme for a dozen on the half shell."

"We'll do it again, too," I said.

He swallowed the rest of his sno'ball, a green ribbon running from the corner of his mouth when he smiled. "The Bobbsey Twins from Homicide are forever."

"You really offered to help the Nightingale chauffeur with Alafair?"

"He doesn't seem like a bad guy, although I got the feeling he's porking Ms. N., the way they look at each other and all."

"Why do you think she's interested in your relationship with Sherry Picard?" I said.

"Maybe she wants to make sure Broussard goes down for the Kevin Penny homicide."

"You think she could have done Penny?" I said.

"Ever look into her eyes? Two inkwells, midnight blue. She has antifreeze for blood."

"You didn't answer my question."

"I think Jimmy Nightingale killed Penny or had it done."

"I don't think you're entirely objective, Cletus."

"You're right. I'd love to bust a cap on that guy."

"Why does he get to you?"

"He scares me. I can't shake the feeling."

EVER HAVE CONFLICT with the concept of mercy? I'm talking about those challenges to our Judeo-Christian ethos that require us to forgive or at least not to judge and to surrender the situation to a Higher Authority. That's badly put. The challenge is not the venerable tradition. The real issue lies in the possibility that the person to whom you're extending mercy will repay your trust by cutting you from your liver to your lights.

That's why I hated to be in the proximity of Spade Labiche. There was an accusatory neediness in his face, a baleful light in his eyes, as though others were responsible for his lack of success and the monetary gain and happiness that should have been his. Friday morning, he opened my door without knocking. "Can I throw up on your rug for a minute?"

How about that for humor?

"I'm pretty busy, Spade."

He looked over his shoulder. "I got to talk to somebody. How about it, Robicheaux? You know the score, man. Not many people around here do."

"Come in."

"Thanks," he said. He sat down in front of my desk and lit a cigarette.

"Not in the building, partner."

"I forgot." He mashed out the cigarette on the inside of my trash basket and let the butt fall on top of my wastepaper. There was a razor nick on his jawline and one under his left nostril. I could smell cloves on his breath. "What's the update on this guy with the cannon that blows heads off at eight hundred yards?"

"There isn't any."

His face looked like a white prune. "No prints, no brass, no feds involved, no guesses about the identity of the shooter?"

"Nope."

"Look, I knew people in Miami who had a couple of hotels rigged to set up congressmen and business types out for a good time. The skanks would be in the bar and get these guys juiced up and in front of a hidden camera that would film stuff you couldn't buy in Tijuana. They'd squeeze these poor bastards for years. They had a perv working them, a guy they called Smiley. He never took a pinch, not for anything."

"What kind of perv?"

"He gets off on splattering brain matter, that kind of perv."

"Why are you telling me this?"

"I think my number is up," he said. He swallowed and cleared his throat. "It's a feeling you get. It's like malaria or rheumatic fever. You feel sick all over and can't shake it. I tried to tell you this before, man. You wouldn't listen."

"The first time I went down a night trail, I couldn't stop my teeth from clicking," I said. "A kid on point hit a trip wire and was screaming in the dark. We had to go after him. There were toe poppers all over the place. I didn't think I could make myself walk through them. Then an old-time line sergeant whispered something to me I never forgot: 'Don't think about it before you do it, Loot, and don't think about it after it's over.' What's this dog shit about a sex sting in Miami?"

He pressed a hand against his stomach, grimacing. "I think I got an ulcer."

I opened my drawer and threw him a roll of TUMS. "Catch."

"You're a coldhearted man."

"This perv named Smiley is going to take you out?"

"People think I know things I don't. I was in vice. You know what that means. I dealt with twenty-dollar whores and dime-bag black pukes. The average IQ was minus-ten."

"You took juice from Tony Nine Ball?"

"Not juice. Tony's associates had some stuff on me. So I cut their guys some slack a couple of times. Possession charges, nothing else. In Miami, not here."

"What stuff?"

"Those cameras I mentioned in the hotels? There was this one working girl I thought was on the square. They got me good on the video. I was married."

"Why is it I feel like you're telling half of something?"

"I want to be a good cop. I'm seeing this Cajun girl, Babette. You know her. At the bar-and-grill. She's a nice girl."

"You'd better treat her as one."

"Lay off it. I'm hurting enough. I've been hitting the sauce a little too hard. I know you're A.A. I thought I could go to a meeting with you."

I brushed at my nose. "You don't need me to do that."

"Like get lost?"

"The hotline is in the phone book. Dial them up."

"Forget I came in here. That guy out there. I got a funny feeling about why he's here. I mean the real issue."

I leaned back in my chair and spun my ballpoint on the ink blotter. "What feeling is that?"

He squeezed his temples, his eyes crossing. "He's got a list of people to pop. Jimmy Nightingale is one of them."

"What do you base that on?"

"Nightingale is too smart, and he knows too much. He's also got a reputation for shitcanning his friends after he gets what he wants. Don't you get it? These people are like a bunch of scorpions in a matchbox. They kill each other all the time. Why should they care about us? They use us and throw us away."

I had never seen a man more tortured by his own thoughts.

"You're just going to stare at me and not say anything?" he asked.

"I think you need to talk to a minister or a psychiatrist, Spade."

"I could have been your friend. Except you don't want friends. You're a hardnose. You think everybody has to cut it on their own."

"Take it somewhere else, partner."

He stood up. His skin was gray, the way people's faces look when they see the grave. "I need help."

I hated what I had to do. I wrote my cell phone number on a memo slip and handed it to him. "There's a meeting at seven o'clock. I can pick you up."

He crunched the memo slip and bounced it on my desk. "I'll stick with drinking. I may get popped, but I'm not going to crawl. I'll still be me, for good or bad. What will you be? A big fish in a dirty pond."

"You said Jimmy Nightingale knows too much. Too much about what?"

"How Frankenstein works," he replied. "What'd you think?"

I THOUGHT THAT, ONE way or another, my life was moving away from the night T. J. Dartez died. I was wrong. Sleep is a mercurial mistress. She caresses and absolves and gives light and rest to the soul in our darkest hours. Or she fills us with fear and doubt and disjointed images that seem dredged out of the Abyss. If you're a drunk, she can instill memories in you that may be manufactured. Or not. And clicking on a bedside lamp will not rid you of them; nor will the coming of the dawn. They take on their own existence and feed at the heart the way a succubus would.

In the dream, I saw the face of Dartez behind the window of his truck, illuminated by the passing headlights of a vehicle on the two-lane. His mouth was red and twisted out of shape, a rubbery hole trying to make sound. His forehead struck the glass. Then I was grabbing him and pulling him through the window, his body thrashing. I came down on him with all my weight, reaching with my fingers for his face. Was I trying to gouge his eyes, to drive a thumb deep into a socket, to break his windpipe?

I woke shaking and sat on the side of the bed in the moonlight. I had never had such a bad dream except for the ones I'd brought back from overseas. Alafair stood in the doorway, backlit by a red light on a clock flashing in the hallway.

"I heard you talking," she said.

"What was I saying?"

"'Don't fight.' Then you said something in French. Maybe *'Que t'a pre faire? Arrêt!'*"

"'What are you doing? Quit!'"

"I can't be sure." Her eyes were full of sorrow. "It's almost dawn. You want me to fix you something to eat?"

"I think I'll go back to sleep. It was just a dream."

"About the war?"

"I don't remember."

"Don't lie to the only people you can count on."

"Okay, Alf."

"I'm going to get back on my manuscript. Try to sleep."

"Don't get close to Tony Nemo."

"He comes around the set. Nobody pays attention to him."

I lay back down on the pillow. "See you later, Alfenheimer."

She closed the door. I stared at the ceiling, afraid to sleep again.

I KNEW IT WOULD happen. Sunday morning, I saw Babette Latiolais outside the church I attended. The church was located in a mixed-race neighborhood, one of windmill palms and small frame houses with tin roofs and yards that had no fences. She was wearing a pillbox hat that looked dug out of an attic, and a pink suit that probably came from a secondhand store. She saw me out of the corner of her eye and quickened her step in the opposite direction.

I caught up with her. "You're not going to say hello, Miss Babette?"

"Hi," she said, not slowing.

"You in a hurry?"

"My li'l girl is by herself. I got to get some cereal, then we going to church."

"You belong to St. Edward's?"

"I go to Assembly of God. Why you axing me this?" She kept her face at an angle so that one side was covered with shadow.

"Can you look at me, Miss Babette?"

"What you t'ink I'm doing?"

"Look at me."

"I got to go, Mr. Dave."

"Who hit you?"

"Suh, please don't be doing this. It was an accident."

"Spade did this?"

"He was drunk. I fussed at him."

"A man who strikes a woman is a moral and physical coward. A cop who hits a woman is the bottom of the barrel. Is Labiche at your house?"

"I don't know where he's at."

"You need to file charges. We don't want a man like this representing the sheriff's department."

"I ain't going near that building. Ain't nobody there gonna he'p me. I already taken care of it."

"How?"

"My cousin used to be a landscaper for Jimmy Nightingale. He called Mr. Jimmy and tole him what happened. Mr. Jimmy sent a lawyer and a doctor to my house. That's a good man, yeah."

"Jimmy Nightingale doesn't have any authority over the sheriff's department."

"He's on our side. Ain't nobody else ever he'ped us. Not since Huey Long ain't nobody he'ped us."

What do you say to that? "It was good seeing you, Babette. If I can do anything for you, you have my card."

"I said somet'ing wrong, huh?"

"Not you. But the rest of us have. *Je vot' voir plus tarde, petite chère.*"

But she belonged to a generation who no longer spoke French of any kind, even what we called *français creole* or *français neg,* and she had no idea what I was saying in either French or English.

*   *   *

JIMMY NIGHTINGALE WAS holding a rally that night at the Cajun
Dome in Lafayette, and I talked Clete into going with me. The
American South has a long history of demagoguery. Budd Schul-
berg coined the term "demagogue in denim" for his character
Lonesome Rhodes, portrayed by Andy Griffith in the film adaptation *A Face in the Crowd*. Robert Penn Warren, who taught
at LSU, won the Pulitzer for his creation of a fictionalized Huey
Long in *All the King's Men*. But it would be a serious mistake in
perception to join Jimmy at the hip with a collection of sweaty
peckerwoods and white minstrel performers who majored in getting drunk, race-baiting, quoting from the Bible, and screwing the
maid.

The Cajun Dome was overflowing. Jimmy walked onto the stage
ten minutes late in a white suit and cordovan boots and a dark blue
shirt open at the collar, a short-brim pearl-gray Stetson gripped in his
hand, as though he hadn't had time to hang it. The crowd went wild.
In front, some rose to their feet. Then the entire auditorium rose,
stomping their feet and pounding the backs of the seats with such
violence that the walls shook.

I thought of Hitler's arrivals, the deliberate delay, the trimo-
tor silver-sided Junkers droning in the distance from afar and then
appearing in the searchlights like a mythic winged creature descend-
ing from Olympus.

Clete took a flask from inside his coat, unscrewed the cap with
his thumb, letting it swing loose from its tiny chain. He took a hit of
Jack. "I think I'm going to start my own country and secede from the
Union."

"Quiet," I whispered.

"Fuck it," he replied.

"There's ladies here," a man in front of us said.

Clete looked steadily at the back of the man's head. "Excuse me."

The man turned his head halfway and nodded.

Jimmy was a master. He seemed to float like a dove on a rosy glow of love and warmth that radiated from the people below. He belonged to them, and they belonged to him, like Plotinian emanations of each other. He gave voice to those who had none, and to those who had lost their jobs because of bankers and Wall Street stockbrokers and the NAFTA politicians who had made a sieve of our borders and allowed millions of illegals into our towns and cities. He never mentioned his political opponents; he didn't have to. One boyish grin from Jimmy Nightingale could have people laughing at his challengers without knowing why, as though they and Jimmy were one mind and one heart.

Was he race-baiting or appealing to the xenophobia and nativism that goes back to the Irish immigration of the 1840s? Not in the mind of his audience. Jimmy was telling it like it is.

His adherents wore baseball caps and T-shirts and tennis shoes and dresses made in Thailand. They were the bravest people on earth, bar none. They got incinerated in oil-well blowouts, crippled by tongs and chains on the drill floor, and hit by lightning laying pipe in a swamp in the middle of an electric storm, and they did it all without compliant. If you wanted to win a revolution, this was the bunch to get on your side. The same could be said if you wanted to throw the Constitution into the trash can.

Clete took a small pair of binoculars out of his coat pocket and scanned the audience. He handed the binoculars to me. "Check out the top row, straight across."

I adjusted the lenses. Bobby Earl was sitting against the wall, scrunched between a fat man and a woman with a barrel of popcorn propped between her thighs, the spotlights above him smoking in the haze gathering under the roof. The sloped shoulders and wan expression and crooked necktie and distended stomach were a study in despair and failure. His attention was fixed on the audience, not the stage, as though the people around him didn't realize he was in their midst, ready to reclaim the glorious vision that was his invention, not this pretender's.

I handed the binoculars back to Clete. "Scott Fitzgerald said there are no second acts in America."

"Richard Nixon must not have heard him," Clete said.

The air-conditioning wasn't working properly. People began fanning themselves, getting up for water or cold drinks, blotting their foreheads. I'd had enough of Jimmy Nightingale and wanted to leave, but Clete had found another object of interest with his binoculars. He stared through them at a spot by the rafters, in a corner bright and hot with humidity and motes of shiny dust.

"You got a number for security?"

"No," I said. "What do you see?"

"A guy who looks like a smiling dildo. He's carrying a box about four feet long and four inches wide."

The man in front of us turned around again. He was Clete's height, well groomed, thick-shouldered, a flag pin in his lapel, indignation branded on his face. "I'm about to have you removed."

Clete's eyes were round green stones. "What for?"

"You used a word about a certain female instrument."

"How about this? Shut your fucking mouth." Clete handed me the binoculars. "In the corner, ten o'clock."

I looked but saw nothing. Clete took back the binoculars and looked again. "He's gone."

"We'll tell security on the way out."

The shots were rapid, two pops, then nothing. One blew apart a vase full of flowers by Jimmy's foot; the other hit the staff of an American flag, cutting it in half, toppling the flag on a plastic bush. Hundreds of people ducked under the seats; some ran. Jimmy didn't move. Instead, he detached the microphone from the stand and raised his left hand in calming fashion. "It's all right, friends. Do not panic. I'm fine. Look at me. They can't stop us. Do you hear me? Sit down. We're the people. Neither death nor life, neither angels nor principalities, nor powers, nor things present, nor things to come can separate us from the love of God."

The response was thunderous, on the level of an earthquake, an exorcism of fear and even mortality itself, an affirmation that the man they had chosen was indeed the apotheosis of all that was good.

I opened my badge and held it high above my head and, with Clete behind me, began working my way up the stairs on the far side of the building. The entire audience was on its feet and shouting incoherently. Down below, the spotlights glowed on Jimmy's white suit with an iridescence just this side of ethereal.

Chapter
30

THIS TIME, THE shooter had left his brass, a pair of .223 casings that were probably from a scoped rifle modeled on the old M1 carbine. I picked them up with a pencil and put them into an empty candy box I found on the floor and turned them over to a Lafayette police detective. Clete described the man he had seen with the elongated cardboard carton, and that was the end of our official participation in the attempted assassination of Jimmy Nightingale.

Clete was silent most of the way to New Iberia. We were in the Caddy, the top up. He turned on the radio, then clicked it off and huffed air out his nose.

"What's eating you?" I said.

"I don't buy what we saw."

I knew what he was going to say. But I didn't want to taint his perceptions by speaking first.

"Sociopaths are all the same," he said. "Every one of them is vain. They'll go to the injection table rather than admit an imperfection."

"Are you talking about the shooter or Nightingale?"

"Our .223 man put one round in a glass vase that was no more than five inches across. The second clipped the flagstaff dead center. He hit two small objects three seconds apart from seventy yards but couldn't nail Nightingale? Who's kidding who?"

"I think you're right."

"You think Lafayette PD or the state police will pick up on that?"

"People believe what they want to."

"Nightingale is a hypocrite. He brought immigrants from Costa Rica to work in his casinos and hotels."

"You're preaching to the choir, Cletus."

"No, I'm not. You're always making excuses for this guy."

"Heroes are hard to find these days. That's why we have the bargain-basement variety."

"What is that supposed to mean?"

"How about Levon Broussard? I always respected him. Now he's making a film with Tony Nine Ball, and Alafair is working with them."

Clete took out his flask and chugged it to the bottom. "I don't like to drink in front of you, Streak, but sometimes that's the only way I can put up with this crap."

I HAD A PROFESSIONAL and ethical problem Monday morning. The previous day, in front of St. Edward's Church, Babette Latiolais had in effect told me that Spade Labiche had struck her in the face. She also had told me that she would not file charges. If I reported Labiche to Helen, she would take him to task, and he would lie and later slap Babette all over her house.

I went into his cubbyhole of an office. "I'm going to a noon meeting. How about joining me?"

He was drinking coffee, one leg resting across the trash can. "I'm boxed in today."

"You'd be doing me a big favor, Spade."

"How am I doing you a favor by going to an A.A. meeting?"

"It's called the ninth step. Making amends to people we've hurt. I attacked you. I have to make up for it."

"All sins are forgiven. I hear you were at the Cajun Dome when someone tried to grease Nightingale."

"Clete Purcel and I were there."

"I called it, didn't I? I knew somebody would try to knock him off."

"You knew what you were talking about. How about the meeting? Be a sport. It's like prayer. What's to lose?"

"You've got a brick for a head. Let me take a piss."

The meeting was in the back of an electrical shop by one of the drawbridges, the windows painted over. The attendees were mostly working people. The room smelled of dust and old rags and machine oil that had soaked into workbenches. Before Labiche sat down, he flicked his handkerchief several times on the seat of the chair.

When the leader of the meeting asked newcomers to introduce themselves by first name only and not to put anything into the basket, Labiche did as requested and then began clipping his nails. It wasn't long before I noticed something wrong. Two black women who were regulars and spoke often at meetings were silent, their eyes turned inward, their bodies shrunken, as though they were trying to make themselves smaller. Labiche reset his watch, sucked his teeth, and looked sleepily into space while an elderly man spoke of his wife's death. Then Labiche went to the restroom, tucking in his shirt with his thumbs as he walked. One of the silent black women left in a hurry through a side door. The other bent deeper into herself, her eyes lidded. When Labiche returned, he stank of cigarette smoke.

After the "Our Father," he helped stack a couple of chairs and followed me outside. The heat was ferocious, the wind like a blowtorch.

"How'd you like it?" I asked.

"Good stuff, but I don't think it's for me, Robo. I know I got kind of screwed up and depressed for a while and was talking a little crazy, but I'm okay now."

"You and Miss Babette are okay, too?"

"Peaches and cream. What makes you think otherwise?"

"No reason. She's probably had a hard life. She deserves a break."

"You trying to tell me something?"

"No," I said. "Did you know any of the people in the meeting?"

"You talking about those black whores? I think I busted one of them."

"There're no whores in A.A. Whatever people did before they came in doesn't count."

"Yeah, and all God's chil'en got shoes, too," he said. "This heat stinks. I need to get back to Florida. There's nothing like that blue and green water down in the Keys." He lit up, letting the smoke drift in my face.

"You're done worrying about somebody clipping you?" I said.

The tropical vision that gave him a brief respite from his problems left his eyes. "What the fuck, man? You get me here to mess with my head?"

Something like that, I thought.

THAT EVENING CLETE and I went to City Park and watched Homer play softball under the lights. Homer was still awkward with the bat, but he usually got a chunk of the ball and made it to first base. Once there, he was a greased laser beam on the bases. He came in under the tag on his face, like a human plowshare burrowing through the dirt. When the second baseman thought it was over, Homer was on his feet and headed for third. He got caught in the hotbox once, then scampered between the shortstop's legs and went around third and almost sanded his face off sliding across home plate.

"What's Homer's status with the social welfare people?" I said.

"I think they want the situation to go away. It doesn't matter, though. I'm not giving him back."

"You and Sherry Picard getting along?"

"Sure, I dig her."

Of course, that was not what I'd asked. "I took Spade Labiche to a meeting today."

"I bet he was a big hit."

"I think he's been working for Tony Squid from the jump. I think he sent Penny after me the night T. J. Dartez died. In so many words, he's told me he has the key to my soul, meaning he knows what happened when Dartez cashed in."

"I can make a midnight visit on this guy. He'll be in a cooperative mood, I guarantee it."

"That stuff is for the other guys," I said. "We don't do it."

Clete took a beer out of a sack by his foot and cracked the tab. "Better look around, noble mon. There's some bad shit going down. My stomach clenches up when I think about it."

"Jimmy Nightingale?"

"I know how assassins feel."

"Don't ever give these guys that kind of power," I said.

Homer was in the batter's box. He smacked a Texas-leaguer into short center.

"Look at that kid go," Clete said.

WAY LEADS ON to way.

After the game, we strolled with Homer back to Clete's Caddy, down by the concrete boat ramp. Not far away, Levon Broussard and Tony Nemo's film crew were winding up for the day. In the twilight, I saw Alafair standing by Nemo's limo. The back door was open. Alafair was shouting at someone in the backseat.

"I'd better check this out," I said.

"Stay out of it, Streak," Clete said.

"I've had it with Nemo."

"Alafair isn't going to like it."

"I'm her father."

"Homer and I will wait here."

"Maybe we should go with him," Homer said, looking up at Clete.

"Dave's got it covered," Clete said, patting him on the back.

I walked toward the limo just as Alafair flung the clipboard inside.

"Make your own damn changes!" she said. "You're an idiot! You have no business in a movie theater, much less on a set!"

She stormed past me.

"Whoa, what's the deal?" I said.

"Spermo thinks he's D. W. Griffith."

"Spermo is Tony?"

"Duh." She kept walking, furious, wiping her hair out of her face.

I looked inside the limo. Tony was spread across the backseat like a dirigible with a bad leak.

"Tony, baby. What's the haps?" I said.

"I think your daughter is the product of a busted rubber."

"I couldn't say. She's adopted."

His portable oxygen bottle was propped on his groin; his face was mottled and sweaty, a piece of dried mucus at the corner of his mouth, his breathing arduous, like a strand of piano wire sawing on a hole in a tin can. "Fuck both y'all, you arrogant cocksucker."

"A cleaner's out there, Tony. I think you're next in line."

"I shot craps in Reno with Jimmy Fratianno. I ate dinner with Meyer Lansky. A leg-breaker for a certain celebrity gave me trouble once, and I kicked a baseball bat up his ass. I'm making a movie Jimmy Nightingale thought he was gonna make. I got Levon Broussard jumping through hoops. What's that tell you, wise guy? I got a broomstick up the ass of every one of y'all."

"Hear that sucking sound?" I said.

"What sucking sound?"

"It's the ground pulling on you."

"Yeah? Guys like me live a hundred years and get hanged for rape. Play your mind-fuck games with somebody else."

I looked up and down his person. "Your fly is unzipped."

I left him staring down at his lap and walked along the bank in the gloaming of the day, then onto the drawbridge. The air was full of birds, the sky mauve, the bayou bladed by the wind. Far down the Teche, a solitary streak of lightning split the sky and quivered as brightly as gold in the water.

I HEARD FROM LAFAYETTE PD that the .223 shell casings I'd picked up in the Cajun Dome were clean. If the shooter was the same as the killer of the St. Mary Parish deputy and JuJu and Pookie, he probably had an arsenal at his disposal. Whether he'd tried to hit Jimmy Nightingale was debatable. The consequence wasn't. The story was on the wire services, CNN, FOX, all the networks, and the front pages of newspapers across America as well as overseas. Jimmy was a star, a populist in whom everyone could find something to like. I had to hand it to him.

SPADE LABICHE LIVED in a rented two-story small house with a balcony and ironwork in the shadow of the drawbridge. At high tide, the bayou was almost in his front yard. He had no neighbors. The flower beds were planted with banana plants and windmill palms and caladiums and hydrangeas. The plaster on the bricks, the rain-washed lavender paint, and the trumpet vine on the balcony's railing reminded him of his boyhood in New Orleans or, rather, the boyhood he wished he'd had.

Spade had grown up in the Iberville Project on a diet of welfare commodities and a drunk man's breath. The Quarter was for tourists and homosexual artists. The Iberville playgrounds were the St. Louis Cemetery and Louis Armstrong Park, where Spade and his friends jackrolled any fool who wandered in at night. The Garden District was the other side of the universe.

Spade felt secure in his rented home. Through the front windows, he could see the bayou, the old convent on the far side, the green and red lights smudged in the fog. Behind him, the slope rose to the backside of buildings that were over a century old, the bricks fissured, the wooden storm shutters hanging askew on rusted hinges. No one could approach his house without being detected by his surveillance cameras and motion-activated floodlamps. This was Fortress Labiche. Let the world have at it.

On a muggy Saturday evening, he made a salad and grilled a chicken on his patio and ate dinner inside, first locking all the doors. The light was golden in the sky, a few raindrops striking the windows. He had never seen weather like this. The days were superheated, the nights flickering with heat lightning that promised relief but gave none, the sunrise as swampy as an egg yolk. After he washed his dishes, he turned on the television and took a touch of nose candy and a few hits of reefer and a sip of Scotch on ice. But his chemical accessories didn't work like they used to. His worries and bad dreams and paranoia seemed to intensify to the point where he feared both solitude and the company of others. He feigned composure during the day and fell apart at night. People wondered why a cop would eat his gun. Try waking up with snakes every morning not because you're loaded but because you're not.

After sunset, Spade walked to the bar-and-grill for a drink. But he couldn't put up with the crowd, at least not tonight. He returned home in the dark and went inside and locked the door, his heart a lump of ice. Maybe he should quit the department on Monday and go back to the Keys, hang out at Sloppy Joe's and the other joints on Duval, fish for marlin, screw all this Cajun bullshit. Yeah, kick the addictions, live on orange juice and sunshine and lobster tail and get it on with hippie girls who loved sugar daddies with a badge and a gun.

He went upstairs and lay down on top of the sheets in his skivvies. As he closed his eyes, he heard the rain clicking on the roof. Tomorrow would be a better day. Yes, he would quit Monday and eighty-six his woes and rock on down to his old haunts.

In the early A.M., he woke to an odor that made no sense: mayonnaise and ham and tomatoes and onions and bread. Was he dreaming? He sat up in bed, an erection dying inside his shorts. In the red glow of the clock on the nightstand, a man was eating a sandwich, the juice running down his chin. He was wearing cotton gloves and a baseball cap. His limbs looked composed of sourdough. His smile made Spade think of an open wound.

"Hi. My name is Chester," the man said.

Spade pushed himself up on his elbows. "How'd you get in here?"

"You invited me."

"I invited you when? Who are you?"

"When people do bad things, they invite me in. I just told you who I am."

"Is that a gun?"

"A .357."

"You're the cleaner, aren't you."

Chester didn't answer.

"I'm not tied up with anybody," Spade said. "You got no beef with me."

"You've done bad things."

"Who sent you? Just tell me. I'll square it."

"You sent me."

"You're talking in riddles. I didn't do anything to anybody. You're operating on wrong information."

Chester set his sandwich on the nightstand with a napkin or magazine under it. "These index cards have drawings on them. They show what you made the colored ladies do."

"What colored ladies?" Spade said.

"The ones you were cruel to."

"Somebody's been lying. Look, we've got to talk this out."

"I have to give you the chance."

"Chance for what?"

"To say you're sorry."

"I didn't do anything."

"So you don't want to say you're sorry?"

"I'm ready to work with you on that. Don't point that at me, man. Come on, you got the wrong guy. I get along with black people. I was undercover in Liberty City."

"You made one of the ladies put her baby in the freezer. You left him in there till she agreed to do that bad thing."

"I never did any such thing. Put down the piece."

"You're sure about that? Think hard. Don't make a mistake."

"I smoked some skunk with angel dust on it. It makes you crazy. Don't cock that. Please."

"Take the pillowcase off the pillow."

"Do what?"

"Put the pillowcase over your head."

"I'm forgetting this ever happened. I'm leaving town. I already made up my mind before you came in. Nobody will ever see me again."

"I'm going to shoot you in the stomach unless you do what you're told," Chester said.

"I got a feeling you had a bad childhood, kind of like me. I grew up in the Iberville. That's in New Orleans. My old man was a guard with the Big Stripes in Angola. He was meaner than hell to us kids."

"I was born in New Or-yuns. The boys in the Iberville made fun of me."

"That's not me. I wasn't like that."

"I know all the things you're going to say. They won't change anything."

Chester stood up and aimed. The shot was deafening inside the room. Matting flew from the hole in the mattress just below Spade's genitalia.

Spade's bowels melted. He had to force the bile back down his throat to speak. "I got the pillowcase. I'm putting it on. Where we going? My cuffs are on the dresser. You want to hook me up?"

"On the dresser? I don't see them."

"I'll show you. Can I take off the pillowcase?"

There was no answer. Spade could hear himself breathing, smell the sourness of his breath, feel two wet lines running from his eyes. He'd never thought he could be this afraid. "Say something. Please."

But there was no reply.

"I got some cash and gold cuff links. I took them off a guy in the Medellín Cartel. Anything you want here is yours. Take my watch, too." Then he realized what his tormentor was doing. "You're eating a fucking sandwich?"

"Not now. I'm finished."

Spade remembered a prayer from his childhood. How did it go? He always said it before he went to bed. Somehow it removed the sounds of his father yelling, his mother laughing even when he hit her, a baby crying in the other room. *Now I lay me down to sleep.* Was that how it went? It was too simple. He needed something heavier, a magical or metaphysical way to block off what was about to happen. Where were the words? Why were they denied him?

"Chester?" he said.

"What?"

"I used to say a prayer called 'Now I Lay Me Down to Sleep' when I was a kid."

"But you've been very bad, haven't you?" Chester said.

"Yes, I've been a bad man."

"Do you feel better now?"

Spade could feel the last drops of his self-respect sliding from his armpits. "You creepy little snerd, who do you think you are?"

Spade reached for the top of the pillowcase. Then the world became a snow-covered mountain slope cracking loose from its fastenings, grinding up trees and rocks in its path, boulders as big as cars bouncing over his head, the sky an immaculate blue, the air pristine, the flecks of ice on his skin as cool and gentle as a lover's fingers. He closed his eyes and extended his arms by his sides and waited for the roar to engulf him, to lift him into a place where rage and fear and need were but rags ripped away in the wind, the soul as bright as a burnished shield, the landscape down below one of blue and green waters and coral reefs and sea horses that frolicked in the waves.

Then he realized he was already there. Safe. The book written. The covers closed.

Chapter
31

Helen called at 3:16 Sunday morning. "I'm in Lafayette. We got a shots-fired at Spade Labiche's house. Can you get over there?"

"Yeah," I said. I was barefoot and in my skivvies in the kitchen. "Who called it in?"

"A guy walking across the bridge. He heard a pop and saw a flash through the upstairs window. A patrolman just kicked open the door. He says it's a mess. We ROA there."

"Labiche is dead?"

"His place is a fortress. I don't know how anyone could get in. Maybe he ate his gun."

I rubbed water on my face and brushed my teeth, put on a pair of khakis, and hung my badge around my neck and hooked my nine-millimeter on my belt.

"Where you going?" Alafair said from her bedroom door.

"It's Spade Labiche."

"Somebody caught up with him?"

"Maybe."

I felt her studying my face. "I'll lock you in," I said. "Maybe this guy Smiley is back in town."

"That's not what's on your mind. Labiche is the only guy who knows what happened the night T. J. Dartez died."

"That sums it up."

I drove down East Main and turned onto the side street that led to Labiche's house. Someone had turned on the lights inside. A cruiser was parked in front. There had been a six-car pileup on the four-lane, and the paramedics had not arrived. I went through the broken door and up the stairs. A red-haired, barrel-chested patrolman nicknamed Top met me at the entrance to the bedroom. "I left everything alone. The pillowcase was half off his face when I got here."

There was blood splatter on the headboard, the wall, and the window glass. There were three bullet holes in the headboard and a tear in a sheet with powder burns around it and a long bloody swath down the side of the mattress and the bed frame that dead-ended at the body on the floor.

Through the French doors, I saw the lights of emergency vehicles turning off Main. I knelt on one knee and lifted up the edge of the pillowcase with my ballpoint. There was an entry wound high up on Labiche's left cheek, a graze that had taken off most of one ear, and another entry wound on his neck. His left eye had turned to milk. Half of his body was painted with blood. I let the pillowcase drop and looked around the floor, then shook out the sheets and a bedcover on the foot of the bed.

"You see a gun?" I said.

"No," Top said.

"Casings?"

"Nope. You think he shot himself four times?"

"I was hoping our shooter dropped his weapon."

The truth was, I hadn't precluded the possibility of suicide. I've seen victims who had to take a run at it several times before they pulled it off, particularly when they were filled with rage at others and couldn't let go of this world.

I looked under the bed and the nightstand. The recoil in a suicide can put a firearm in strange places. But there was no gun. I opened the drawer on the nightstand. There was a five-shot holstered titanium .38 Special inside, the Velcro strap in place. Then I realized the enormity of the presumption I had been operating on. Labiche's left hand twitched, as though a tiny electric current had touched it. I knelt again and peeled the pillowcase off his head. The clotted hair in one nostril moved almost imperceptibly.

"Get the medics up here, Top."

I STAYED IN THE emergency room with Labiche until sunrise, then walked along beside the gurney to the ICU. The neurologist said the bullet in the cheek had been fired at a downward angle and had tunneled through the temporal lobe and cerebellum, destroying Labiche's hearing and sensory transmitters and muscular control. There was a chance that other areas of his brain were impaired as well. His face was sunken, his breathing little more than a rasp, the rectal catheter leaking. I rested my hand on the rail of the gurney and pushed a door open to help one of nurses. I felt Labiche touch my hand.

"Stop," I said. "He's trying to tell me something."

The nurse smiled kindly and shook her head and made the word "no" with her lips.

"What is it, Spade?" I said.

One eye had eight-balled. It stared into my face. His other eye was caved, the lid black.

"Wait out here, Detective," the nurse said.

"Sure," I said.

I looked through the glass in the door as three nurses wheeled him into a room. I wondered what images lay in his head. Was the touch of his finger the result of a muscular spasm, a bump of the gurney, or a signal that the only man who knew the fate of T. J. Dartez was taking flight forever?

I drove back home and slept for three hours. When I woke, Sherry Picard's cruiser was parked in my driveway.

I OPENED THE SCREEN door and stepped into the yard. She got out of the cruiser and looked at me across the roof, her hair blowing, leaves drifting on her clothes. "Your daughter said you were asleep. I told her I'd wait."

"Where'd she go?" I said, half asleep.

"To the movie set."

"They're union," I said. "They're not supposed to work Sundays."

"Tony Nine Ball keeps the Sabbath, does he?"

"What's up, Detective?" I said.

She walked toward me. Her jeans were high up on her hips. She was wearing her gun and badge, her eyes locked on mine. There was an aggressiveness in her body language that was hard to deal with.

"You got a beef, don't you?" she said.

"Me?"

"You don't think I'm good for Clete."

"It's his life."

"His image of himself has a lot to do with your opinion of him."

"Young women feel safe in his company. Then they start feeling better about their situation and dump him."

"I look like a dependent woman? That's what you're saying?"

"Clete's my friend. I worry about him. Sometimes unnecessarily."

"What's the status on Labiche?" she asked.

"One step this side of a vegetable."

"The cleaner did it?"

"We don't know. Four rounds fired, one into the mattress. Large-caliber. It could be a .357."

"Same caliber used on the deputy in St. Mary?" she said.

"Yes."

"You think he did Penny?"

"Spade is a mean motor scooter, but torturing a man to death with an electric drill is on another level."

"What kind of level?"

"Sexual vengeance comes to mind."

"Levon Broussard for the rape of his wife?"

"That's a hard fit." I looked at my watch. "I was going to church at St. Edward's."

She looked down the street. Leaves were scudding along the sidewalk. "There's something you're not saying."

"When you figure out what it is, tell me."

"I hear Labiche is paranoid and fanatical about security systems," she said.

"That's Spade."

"How'd the shooter get in?"

"He spray-painted the cameras, jumped the wiring, and probably turned a dead bolt with fishing line. He may have used a microcontroller to steal the pad code. Our guy is a total pro."

"But you're in doubt about who he is?"

"My money is on Smiley," I said.

"But there's something wrong, isn't there? Cleaners don't fire four rounds and leave their victims alive."

"Want to come inside?"

"No. You think Labiche got to the shooter? Sent him off in a rage?"

"Psychotic people are psychotic for a reason," I said. "They don't deal well with confrontation."

"Clete isn't answering his cell. You know where he is?"

"He probably took Homer fishing."

I saw the light fade in her eyes.

"What is it?" I said.

"Some guys in the department have a hard-on about Clete meddling in the Jeff Davis Eight case. They're going to go through Homer to fuck him up."

I KNEW WHERE TO find him. It was an emblematic postage stamp out of the past on the southwestern side of the Atchafalaya Swamp, a reminder that our connection to the Caribbean and our neocolonial origins was only one hour away.

On the edge of the bay was a flooded woods strung with moss and dotted with hollow tupelos that reverberated like conga drums when you knocked on them, the lichen on the water undulating like a milky-green blanket in the wake of a passing boat. In a hummock that had been part of a plantation built in the late eighteenth century were former slave quarters made of cypress and roofed with corrugated tin that had been eaten into orange lace. There were palm trees in the hummock and depressions back in the trees where people born in Africa were buried, their names and histories lost. Supposedly, Jean Lafitte moored his boats here when he and James Bowie were transporting slaves from the West Indies to the United States in violation of the 1808 embargo. The story of the Mid-Atlantic Passage was here, as well as the story of the auction houses in New York, Jamestown, Charleston, and New Orleans, all of it now bleached by sun and rain and washed clean of memories that steal into your sleep, the scattered planks and logs as weightless and innocuous as balsa wood and the whitish-brown cylindrical stain in the soil that supposedly was the remnant of a whipping post.

I cut my outboard and drifted onto the bank. Fifty yards away, Clete and Homer were anchored in a channel that flowed out of a bay between two narrow islands thick with gum and willow trees. They were casting their lures at the edges of the lily pads on the shady side of the islands. The time of day was equally wrong for big-mouth bass and sacalait and goggle-eye perch and bream, but catching fish wasn't the issue for Clete. He had become Homer's father, and I didn't want to think about the travail and injury that awaited both of them.

The sun was white in the sky, the surface of the bay gold and brown and wobbling with light, the breeze out of the south, smelling of salt and distant rain. I went into the shade and propped an air cushion under my head and went to sleep. I dreamed of a scene out of T. E. Lawrence's *The Seven Pillars of Wisdom*, though I don't know why. Bedouins on camels and in open-air motorcars were charging down a sand dune, the early-morning sun at their backs. Down below was a hospital train that had been dynamited and jacked off the tracks. The motorcars were equipped with Vickers machine guns, the muzzles flashing, sand rilling from the balloon tires. The train cars were filled with typhoid victims. The cries and moans of the dying were louder than the Vickers.

I woke with a jerk, a weight like an anvil on my chest, pushing me into a dark pool.

"Hey," Clete said. "You're having a dream. Wake up."

I held my head. I looked at my watch. I'd been asleep fifteen minutes. I didn't know where I was.

"Must have been a whameroo," Clete said.

I looked at Homer and tried to shake the train from my mind. He had put on weight, the right kind. His hair was long and straight, mahogany-colored like an Indian's, his skin coppery, his eyes blue. I had the feeling he would be a tall boy, maybe a soldier, an underwater welder, a chopper pilot flying out to the rigs, but something out of the ordinary, something that required courage and paying dues. The restoration of his life was due to one man only, and that was Clete Purcel.

Homer was holding a huge mud cat on a stringer that was wrapped around his wrist.

"Is that yours or Clete's?" I said.

"I caught it on a throw line with a piece of liver," he said.

"You know how to skin one without getting spiked?"

"Yes, sir."

I opened my Swiss Army knife and handed it to him backward.

"I don't have no pliers," he said.

"Any pliers," Clete said.

"Any pliers," Homer repeated.

"They're in the tackle box," Clete said. "There's a nail on that gum tree by the water."

We waited until Homer was out of earshot.

"Something happen?" Clete said.

I told him about the shooting at Labiche's house. He listened quietly, showing no expression. Then he said, "It sounds like our guy lost his Kool-Aid. That is, if it's the nutcase who steals ice cream trucks."

"It's got to be the same guy. He just got sloppy."

"Like he's losing control?" Clete said.

"That's my guess. Sherry Picard was at the house this morning."

"What for?"

"She didn't know where you were. She also said some cops in Jeff Davis want to screw you over."

"With the adoption?"

I nodded.

"Maybe this isn't just about some pinheads wanting to do pay-back," he said. "I've been making some calls about Nightingale. That bombing down in South America he told you about? Did he give you specifics?"

"He said he didn't see the aftermath," I replied.

"I bet. There were more than three dozen people maimed and blinded and killed. The government burned and bulldozed their vil-lage and moved them two hundred miles away. Nightingale's family owned the company. Did he tell you that?"

"No."

"I'm going to fix him. I mean legit. I know a couple of wire-service guys in New Orleans."

I didn't reply.

"That's not going to slide down the pipe?" he said.

"How many people cared about the things you saw in El Sal?"

He went to his boat and opened his cooler and took out two cans. He sat down next to me on the mound of compacted dirt and broken bricks. "You were dreaming about 'Nam?"

"Not directly."

He looked around at the cabins, the pools of heat in the corrugated roofs that had been added during Reconstruction, when the former Confederate colonel who owned Angola Plantation turned it into a rental convict farm to replace the slaves set free by the Emancipation Proclamation.

"It's still with us, isn't it?" he said.

"What do I know?"

He put a cold can of Dr Pepper in my hand. "Drink up, big mon. Let's take it to these motherfuckers. Whoever they are."

High above us, a burnt-orange pontoon plane was working against a headwind, frozen against a satin-blue sky, droning like an angry bee.

* * *

WE GOT THE ballistics back late Monday afternoon. The rounds fired in Labiche's home came from the same .357 used to kill the St. Mary deputy and the two drug dealers in Algiers.

The same afternoon Alafair came home in a huff from filming in the backyard of a plantation east of Jeanerette. "I quit."

"Because of Nemo?" I said.

"Along with his skanks and his lowlife hangers-on."

"Good for you."

"But it's Levon who disappoints me," she said.

"You have to leave people to their own destiny, Alf."

We were in the kitchen. She hadn't noticed Mon Tee Coon sitting on the counter. "When did this happen?"

"I fed him in the house a couple of times. Now he pops right in, just like Tripod."

Snuggs, our short-haired, thick-necked white cat, walked across the floor and joined Mon Tee Coon on the counter with a thump. Snuggs's body rippled with muscle when he walked, his tail springing back and forth. His badges of honor were his chewed ears and the pink scars embedded in his fur.

Alafair picked up Snuggs and cradled him in her arms. She looked down into his face. "Want to be a screenwriter? That's what I thought. You wouldn't touch Hollywood with your bare seat."

"You told Tony Nemo or Levon you were through?" I asked.

"Both of them."

"Nemo said something to you?"

"It's not important."

"Yes, it is."

"He said I'm lucky I'm beautiful because my books stink."

She focused her attention on Snuggs and jiggled his tail.

"What else did he say?"

"Nothing. He's a fat idiot."

"Tell me, Alafair."

"He said, 'I bet you give good head.'"

I gazed out the window at the bayou, the shadows and spangled reflections of the sun that were like gold coins in the branches, the smoke from a barbecue pit in the park, the children playing among the camellia bushes.

"I need to pick up some milk at the store," I said. "Were y'all filming at Albania Plantation today?"

"Why?"

"I just wondered. Is all the gang still there?"

"Leave it alone, Dave."

"There's an open can of sardines in the icebox," I said. "Why don't you treat these guys to a fine meal?"

JEANERETTE WAS A fifteen-minute ride back into the antebellum era, if that's what you wanted to look for. Albania Plantation was a magnificent place. The live oaks surrounding it were so large that the main house stayed in shadow throughout the brightest and hottest of days. Some of the original slave quarters, constructed of logs, were still standing. I parked my truck and walked around the side of the house. The backyard sloped down to the bayou. The film crew had turned the yard into the setting of a French cotillion when the year was 1862 and the Yankees had been whipped at both First and Second Manassas and the Lost Cause was not lost at all.

The trees were strung with paper lanterns. The actresses wore hoop dresses, and the actors wore the tailored steel-gray uniforms of the Army of Northern Virginia, many with silk sashes, and the band played the songs of Stephen Foster. The dying sun seemed to conspire with an Islamic moon and light the sky like a scene from *One Thousand and One Nights*. The food and punch on the tables were real. Imaginary or not, the evening had become a tribute to a moment in history that would not come aborning again. The people on the lawn seemed delighted with their departure from the twenty-first century.

Tony Nemo was eating from a plastic bucket of potato salad at a picnic table behind the cameras and lights. He was talking to two women in their twenties, both with tats that covered the entire shoulder and trailed away like snakes down the arm. Their midriffs were exposed, their jeans form-fitting, although the denim looked soaked in black grease.

Even before I went to Vietnam, there was a disorder in my head that I never understood. The catalyst, I suspect, lay in the unconscious. For me, the trigger always had to do with degradation of the body and the spirit, cruelty to animals or children, sexual assault, a man beating a woman, betrayal, lies that stole the faith of another.

I would see colors rather than people or the environment around me. My words contained little meaning, as though they were written on water and not meant to be understood. My intentions, however, were obvious. Without warning, I would try to tear someone apart, and I mean break bones and teeth and sling blood onto the walls and leave the object of my rage with a reservoir of fear he would never forget.

I never used a drop, but I owned half a dozen of them, taken from pimps, jackrollers, and smash-and-grabbers who turned over pawnshops. The serial numbers were acid-burned or ground off on an emery wheel, sometimes the trigger and handles reverse-taped so latents couldn't be lifted from the frame. They were a cop's get-out-of-jail card. They could have another purpose also.

Tony never saw it coming. He looked up from his potato salad and started to smile, then realized who I was. The drop was a .22 revolver. The sight had been filed off; the metal was pitted; one wood handle was cracked in half. I held it behind my back, then shoved it into his mouth and cocked the hammer. I stared into his eyes without speaking. He was choking on his own saliva and the food he hadn't swallowed. The people sitting around him stared in horror.

"Verbal abuse on the wrong young woman, Tony," I said.

He gagged and tried to push away my arm. I pulled the trigger. His eyes almost came out of his head. I screwed the barrel deeper into his mouth and cocked the hammer again. I snapped it on another empty chamber. His throat was gurgling, his jowls trembling. The blubber on his chest and stomach was shaking like whale sperm. A woman was screaming.

"Your odds are one in four, Tony. Unless I put two rounds in the cylinder instead of one. I can't remember."

I pulled the trigger a third time. In the silence, a terrible whimpering sound rose from his throat. I removed the pistol from his mouth. Blood and saliva ran down his chin. He fumbled for his oxygen mask. I flipped out the cylinder and showed it to him. "No bullets, Tony. Here, see for yourself."

His gaze lifted to my face; he looked like a man who realized a sea change had just taken place in his life, in full view of others, and he would never be able to erase the moment.

I splashed the gun into his bowl of potato salad and walked back to my truck. I drove back down the highway and passed a trailer slum and crossed the Teche on a drawbridge and continued past another oak-shaded plantation within one hundred yards of the slum property by the bridge. The juxtaposition of the two images could have been extrapolated from a Marxist propaganda film. I felt strange driving through the twilight by myself, as though I had deliberately severed my connection with the rational world and given up all pretense of normalcy and, in so doing, had set myself free.

Chapter
32

I WASN'T DONE. I went to Levon Broussard's home on Loreauville Road. His wife's car was in the garage, but his was not. I parked in front and waited. A few minutes later, his SUV turned off the road and came up the driveway. He got out and walked toward me, his engine still running. I could see Rowena watching from the gallery.

"You crazy fuck," he said to me.

"Problem?"

"I saw it all. Approximately a hundred and fifty other people did, too."

"My daughter took the screenwriting job because she respects you and your work. Her faith was repaid by Nemo's insults and his attempt to degrade her. To my knowledge, you didn't do a damn thing about it."

"I didn't know about it."

"You do now."

"I'm supposed to kick him off the set? He's the goddamn producer."

I could feel my anger returning, my palms tingling, a dryness in my mouth, a flame inching its way across the lining of my stomach. "What's wrong with you, Levon? You've devoted your entire life to good causes. How could you hook up with a guy like Tony Nine Ball?"

"It's what the situation demanded."

"You want him to rig a jury for you? He'll end up owning your soul."

"I didn't kill Kevin Penny. A lot of people believe I did. Some have even congratulated me."

I stepped closer to him. I saw Rowena walk into the yard, a flowering tree in bloom behind her.

"Look me straight in the face and tell me you didn't do it," I said. "Your prints were on the drill only because you tried to save his life. Tell me that."

"It's as you say." There was not a flutter of emotion in his face or his eyes.

"He raped your wife. He put his mouth all over her body. He put his seed in her."

"You want me to knock you down?"

"You don't like the imagery? What do you think your trial is going to be like?"

"Tell Alafair I'm sorry. Ask her to come back on the set."

"Dream on."

"What can I say?"

"The truth."

"*White Doves at Morning* is one of my best books and one of the least read. I wanted to see it on the screen. Nemo obtained the funding. If I had gotten it myself, I would have ended up dealing with the same Hollywood people he deals with. When you get off the phone with them, you want to clean your ear with baby wipes."

"Who killed Penny?"

"I didn't."

"There's something you're hiding. I don't buy your story about the drill. It's too coincidental that you show up just after someone turns him into Swiss cheese."

"You never mention Jimmy Nightingale or his sister," he said. "He's headed for the Senate and maybe even bigger things. He's a fascist who's lying to all these poor people who think he's going to make their lives better. But you're worried about justice for the guy who raped my wife and maybe killed some of the Jeff Davis Eight."

"Seen any good movies?" I said.

"Fuck you."

"I'll remember that," I said.

But it wasn't over. Rowena walked across the grass to the edge of the driveway, wearing jeans and a beige T-shirt with paint on it and no bra. "Don't talk to him like that, Levon. Come in, Mr. Robicheaux. Have some tea with us."

She lived up to her name, right out of Sir Walter Scott. "You're a grand lady, madam," I said. "All the best to both of you."

On the way home, my cell phone vibrated in my pocket. I flipped it open. The caller was Melvin LeBlanc, the physician.

"What's the haps, Mel?" I said.

"I'm at Iberia General. The head nurse thinks you should get over here."

"Regarding what?"

"Spade Labiche. She says he keeps repeating the word 'Robo.' Mean anything?"

I PARKED UNDER THE oaks in front of the hospital and went inside. A nurse walked with me to the ICU. "Is he a friend of yours, Detective?"

"We work together."

"I wondered if he had any immediate family in the area."

"Maybe in New Orleans."

"I see."

"Why do you ask?"

"If he belongs to a church, this would be an appropriate time for his pastor to visit."

I went inside the room. The left side of his face was encased in bandages, except for the eye. He was breathing through his mouth, his lips formed in a cone as though he had eaten hot food and was trying to cool his tongue.

"It's me, Spade," I said. "Dave Robicheaux."

He seemed not to hear me. The fingers of his right hand twitched.

"I'm sorry this happened to you, partner," I said. "You got a bad deal." No reply, no reaction. I looked over my shoulder. The nurse had gone. "You want to tell me something?"

His fingers moved again, up and down, as though he were beckoning. I leaned over, my ear close to his mouth. "Tell me what it is."

His breath contained a stench like decomposition in a shallow burial or a body bag in a tropical country. "You."

"You what?" I said.

"You want save . . ." His voice trailed off.

The neurologist had told me his hearing was destroyed. But maybe that wasn't the case.

"Give it another try," I said.

"Dartez . . . Seizure."

I took a Kleenex from a box on the nightstand and wiped his spittle from my cheek. I eased my hand under his and held it. "If you can't do it, Spade, you can't do it. In your mind, just tell the Man Upstairs you're sorry for the mistakes you made. Don't worry about anything else."

I thought his left eye had been blinded. But it looked straight into mine. His voice was hoarse and coated with phlegm, the words rising from his throat like bubbles of foul air. "Epilepsy . . . he was strangling . . . something was in his throat . . . you tried to save him."

"Go on."

I felt his hand go limp in mine. "Hang in there, Spade. Come on, bud. Don't slip loose."

If you have attended the dying, you know what their last moments are like. They anticipate the separation of themselves from the world of the living before you do, and they accept it with dignity and without complaint, and for just a moment they seem to recede from your vision and somehow become lighter, as though the soul has departed or perhaps because they have surrendered a burden they told no one of.

I had brought nothing to record his words, but I didn't care. I owed Spade a debt and wanted to repay it. I removed my religious medal and silver chain from my neck and poured it into his palm and folded his fingers on it and placed his hand and arm on his chest.

I walked down the corridor and ran into the nurse by the elevator.

"Is everything all right, Detective Robicheaux?"

"Just fine," I said.

"Is he resting all right? It's time for his sponge bath. Then we'll be transferring him to hospice."

"I think Spade will be okay," I said.

"I'm sure he appreciated your visit. The poor man. What a horrible fate. It's funny the things they say to you, isn't it?"

"Pardon?"

"At the end, men usually ask for their mothers. But he asked for you. You must be very close."

I drove home and fixed a cup of café au lait in a big mug and sat on the back steps. Snuggs flopped down on my lap, then sharpened his claws on the inside of my thigh. I set him down next to me, and like two old gentlemen, we watched a rainstorm march across the wetlands and let loose a torrent of hailstones that danced like mothballs all over the yard.

Chapter 33

THE STORM CONTINUED through the night, filling our rain gutters with pine needles and leaves, flooding the yard and most of East Main. The Teche was high and yellow at dawn, lapping into the cane-brakes and cypress knees along the banks, the sun pink and the sky strung with white clouds and patches of blue. The trees were dripping audibly and throbbing with birds. It was a grand way to start the day, in spite of all that had happened.

Helen caught me at 8:06 A.M. in the corridor outside her office. "Inside, bwana."

"Tony Nine Ball is upset?"

"No, half of St. Mary Parish is."

I walked ahead of her. She slammed the door behind us. "What the hell were you thinking?"

"He told Alafair she probably gave good head."

Her face went dead. Her early days at NOPD were not easy. She was not only a woman, she was a bisexual woman. The cruelty and abuse by a detective named Nate Baxter set new standards. He ended up facedown in a plate of linguini in a family restaurant on Canal.

"I'd do it over if I had to," I said. "Fire me if you want. Nemo is a bucket of shit who should have been poured down the honey hole a long time ago."

She sat behind her desk and picked at a thumbnail.

"This isn't about Nemo?" I said.

"Labiche died last night. The head nurse says you were there."

"I was."

"And you knew he died?"

"Yes, he died with his hand in mine."

"And you didn't bother to call in? Or say what you were doing there? Or what he might have said before he caught the bus?"

"What he told me won't change anything," I said. "I didn't have my recorder."

"What did he say?"

"Dartez was having an epileptic seizure, and I tried to save him. There was something in his throat. That's about it."

"Jesus Christ, that's why you dragged him out the window," she said. "He had the plastic filter of a cigar lodged in his throat."

"That's it. Then I think Penny came up behind me and hit me with a rock or a chunk of concrete."

"Labiche mentioned Penny?"

"No."

"Nothing to suggest who might have sent Penny after you?"

"I believe it was Nemo."

"You're probably right. This won't get you off the hook, though, will it?"

"I don't care what anyone else thinks."

She opened her desk drawer and took out my medal and silver chain and set them on the corner of her desk. "A nurse brought this by about fifteen minutes ago. She said you must have left it in Labiche's hand, because nobody else was in the room with him."

I picked up the chain and put it around my neck and dropped the medal inside my shirt. "Thanks."

"You're a piece of work, Pops."

In a seedy motel north of the Four Corners area of Lafayette, Chester Wimple sat on the side of his bed and stared at the window shade. The bottoms of his tennis shoes barely touched the floor. He wore a white painter's cap with a long bill and a high square top, and brand-new pants that fitted his legs like buckets, and a stiff short-sleeved checked shirt, and a clip-on bow tie. When he tried to rethink the events in the Labiche house, his mouth and jaw contorted as though a puppeteer were playing a joke with his face.

He had never messed up a hit, or left loose ends, or allowed emotion to sully the virtuous nature of his work. Tidiness and cleanliness were his hallmarks. The left hand of God could not be otherwise. The words "creepy little snerd" crawled like worms in his ears.

On the bedspread were his .357, a scoped .223 carbine, a Beretta nine-millimeter—the earlier model with the fourteen-round magazine—and a World War II British commando knife, the blade double-edged, narrow, shining with an oily-blue liquidity, tapering into a dagger point. The steel was cold and hard when he picked it up and closed his palm on the handle, his lips parting, his phallus tingling inside his boxer shorts. This was the only weapon in his possession that had the personal touch, that brought him into eye contact with the target and allowed him a guilty pleasure not unlike the impure thoughts he was not supposed to have.

Yesterday he had received a new set of index cards at the general-delivery window. The drawings on each card and the names of the next targets caused him no difficulty. He did not know them or why they needed to be removed from the landscape, which, for Chester, was an antediluvian world governed by raptors and pterodactyls. The flowing calligraphy on the first card was the issue. The words seemed to contain a trap, the way words were used to trap him when he was a child. They made his eyes jitter and the window shade change from a warm yellow to a dull red that pulsed as though a fire were burning on the other side.

The note read:

My dearest Chester,

You have been a good boy. Don't ever let anyone say you are not. But I have the feeling you have been spying on me. You mustn't do this. We cannot be together again until our work is

*over. Please don't be offended. You know how much I love and
care for you. You are the light of my life. Had we not had each
other, we would not have survived.*

*We'll be together soon. Just keep being the sweet boy you
are and stop these evil people from preying on our friends and
children who cannot defend themselves.*

She had not signed the note or even used an initial. He wanted to
cry. Not out of joy, either. She did not want to see him.

He pushed the point of the commando knife into the skin behind
his chin, forcing his head back until his neck ached. What if he shoved
the blade to the hilt? Would it reach the brain? What was the poem
she used to read to him? He could remember only pieces. *Tiger! tiger!
burning bright. In the forests of the night . . . What the hammer?
What the chain? In what furnace was thy brain?*

He had thought she was talking about him and why he was different from other children.

"Oh, no, no," she said. "You're a good boy, Chester. This poem is
about bad people, the kind who have hurt us."

At that moment, he knew no power on earth would ever separate
them.

He replaced the rubber band around the index cards and flipped
through the images with his thumb. Two more targets, people he
knew nothing about. What had they done? Actually, he didn't care. If
they were on the cards, there was good reason. They knew it, too. He
saw the regret in their eyes before he sent them to that place where
they couldn't hurt people anymore, and he felt no guilt about their
passing. He gave ice cream to children with a glad heart. That's who
Chester Wimple was.

But something else was bothering him. He was losing his objectiv-
ity, and his motivations were becoming impure. For personal reasons,
he wanted to do the man with the convex face and the peroxided
shoe-brush haircut and the muscles that glistened with suntan oil. The
man in the pool with Emmeline Nightingale, the man whose body
fluids floated in the water and touched hers. He wanted to do this

man on his own, up close with the commando knife, or with a rifle from afar so the soft-nosed, jacketed round would be toppling when it keyholed through the face, all of it caught inside the cylindrical simplicity of the telescopic sight.

Chester turned on the television set and stared at cartoons for the next two hours, sitting on the side of the bed, his mouth open, his face as insentient as a bowl of porridge.

CLETE WAS NOT only a member of our family, he would lay down his life for Alafair or me. Which also meant he inserted himself into situations without consulting anyone. On Tuesday, he and Homer went fishing in St. Mary Parish, then drove top-down to the movie set behind Albania Plantation. Levon and Rowena Broussard were standing behind a camera down the bayou. The actors and the crew were just breaking for lunch. Tony Nine Ball was nowhere in sight. Clete removed his porkpie hat. "My name is Clete Purcel, Mr. Broussard. Got a minute?"

"You don't have to tell me who you are," Levon said.

Clete put his hat back on and looked at the bayou and the hundreds of robins in the trees. "This is my pal Homer."

"Homer Penny?" Levon said.

Homer looked at his feet.

"I'm his guardian," Clete said. "Unofficial but guardian just the same. He's never seen a movie set."

Clete could hear the wind in the silence.

"How are you, Homer?" Rowena said, and extended her hand. The scars where she'd cut herself were red and as thick as night crawlers.

"Dave and Alafair Robicheaux don't know I'm here," Clete said.

"You're on a mission of mercy?" Levon said.

"I was an extra and did security on a couple of films but didn't have my name on the credits. I didn't think you'd mind. I mean us being here and all."

"Welcome," Levon said.

"I wanted to ask a favor, too."

"I never would have guessed," Levon said.

"I have a Frisbee over there on the table, Homer," Rowena said. "Why don't you and I toss a couple?"

Homer looked down the slope at a row of cannons and actors in kepis and butternut uniforms. "That'd be great," he said.

Levon waited until they were out of earshot. "You're here about Alafair?"

"She worked hard on the script," Clete said. "It wasn't for the money, either."

"What do you want me to do about it?"

"Tell her you want her back."

"She can come back any time she likes."

"That's not the same as apologizing for what happened and telling her you appreciate her work."

Levon took out his cell phone and found a number in his contacts. His call to Alafair went straight to voicemail. "This is Levon. Tony is a jerk. I need you here, Alafair. Your script is beautiful. I don't want amateurs messing it up. I sent you two e-mails. Call me." He closed his cell. "Anything else?"

"I sent the Nightingale chauffeur to you. A guy named Swede Jensen. I hope you didn't mind."

"He's a Confederate soldier. He's down by the bayou now."

"No kidding?" Clete said.

"I'd like to eat lunch and get back to work."

"Sure," Clete said.

"Do you and Homer want to join us?"

Clete saw a red Frisbee sail over the cannon and Homer jump in the air to catch it, his face split with a smile. "That'd be nice."

THAT NIGHT THE rain came again, mixed with hail and bursts of tree-lashing wind. Clete ordered in a pizza, and he and Homer watched *My Darling Clementine* on Clete's television set. At the end of the film, when Henry Fonda leaves the woman by the side of the road and rides away into the Arizona wastelands, Homer's eyes turned wet, and he looked at Clete for an explanation, either for the film or for his emotions.

"See, it's about the fact that a guy like Wyatt Earp wouldn't ever be able to enjoy a normal life," Clete said.

"Clementine is so beautiful," Homer said. "You can see the love in her eyes. It's not right to leave her just standing by the road."

"See, John Ford directed that film, Homer. He was always experimenting with light and shadow. The story is about good and evil. Even though all the Clantons are killed, Wyatt knows more of them are waiting out there in the wastelands. He's the guy who has to keep the rest of us safe."

"So maybe he'll come back and see Clementine again?"

"You never can tell."

LATER, AS CLETE lay in the dark with the rain clattering on the roof, his own words brought him to conclusions about himself that he didn't want to face. He had two kinds of dreams, one in color, one in black and white. Sometimes in his sleep, he returned to the French Quarter of the old days, when Sam Butera and Louis Prima were blowing out the walls at Sharkey Bonano's Dream Room on Bourbon, the balconies dripping with flowers along streets that seemed about to collapse in on themselves, the street bands playing for coins and the sidewalk artists setting up their easels in Jackson Square, the black kids dancing with taps as big as horseshoes clamped on their feet, the smell of beignets and café au lait in the Café du Monde, the palms and banana fronds ticking inside the gated courtyards, the arched entranceways dank and cool-smelling, the stone stained with lichen and ponded with water that resembled spilled burgundy in the shadows.

The dreams in black and white went back to an Asian country where, out there in the sweltering dark, beyond the concertina wire and the claymores and the flicker of an offshore battery, Bedcheck Charlie launched grenades randomly with a captured blooker, blowing mud, foliage, and even a sit-down shitter into the air, the detritus raining down on Clete's poncho and steel pot. Occasionally, Bedcheck

Charlie got lucky, and after the explosion, a grunt down the line would scream words at the stars that Clete did not want to attach to an image.

Sleep came to Clete only by way of surrender to a fantasy. Before he went overseas, he saw a black-and-white news film in an art theater in San Fran that showed Vietminh sappers crawling through barbed wire strung by French Legionnaires. The Vietminh wore sandals cut out of rubber tires and sweat-soaked black pajamas that looked like black oil on their skeletal frames. Their only possessions and weapons were a rice ball, a piece of fish tied in a sling on their waist, and a bamboo cylinder packed with explosives tied on their back. Without flinching, they crawled across anti-personnel mines that blew them into dog food; yet they kept coming, undaunted. Clete wondered how desperate a person would have to be in order to become so brave.

At about 0400, he would surrender to his fatigue, the eggs of a malarial mosquito humming in his blood, the sour stench of his body, the jungle ulcers on his skin, the squishiness of trench foot inside his boots, the insects that got into his socks and up his legs, the cut on his nose where his steel pot had scissored down on his face. In surrendering, he put the faces of the sappers on Bedcheck Charlie and, for a brief time, did not think of him as an enemy. Clete gave himself over to a mental opiate, and Bedcheck disappeared into a box.

Clete never spoke to others of the private universe in which he lived; nor did he share his belief that the world was mad, that most politicians were liars who served the interests of corporations, that populists were con artists, and that the poor were kept poor and uneducated as long as possible.

Sunrise brought heat and humidity that felt like fire ants crawling inside his utilities. The dawn also meant rice paddies filled with human feces and trails with poisonous snakes looped around tree branches and booby-trapped 105 duds and Vietnamese knockoffs of our M14 mines and Bouncing Betties that would steal your limbs and eyes or simply take you off at the waist and leave half of you to whisper your last words. In his dreams he saw all of this in black and white, never in color, and he believed the phenomenon had something to do with the distinction between good and evil. The irony was that he had never learned where the difference lay.

He woke with a start at 3:06 A.M., unsure where he was. He saw lightning outside and the silvery-green slashing of an oak limb across the window. But it was not the storm that woke him. Just before waking, he had seen an image in his mind, an incandescent wormlike creature whose heat was so bright and intense that it evaporated the rain and the darkness surrounding it.

He took his snub-nose from under his pillow and put on his slippers and unbolted and unchained the door and stepped out on the stoop in his pajamas, ignoring the rain. "Who's out there?"

An electric light burned in a boathouse across the bayou. His Caddy was parked in the cul-de-sac, the hood and cloth top sprinkled with leaves and pine needles, the hand-waxed paint job beaded with water. In the corner of his eye, he thought he saw a figure moving through the trees, away from the motor court. Clete walked out on the gravel, rain running into his face, his pajamas sticking to his skin, the snub-nose hanging from his hand. "I saw you, pal. Come out or you might catch one in the brisket."

No response.

"Hey, shit for brains, I know who you are," he said.

No answer or any movement in the trees.

"You're the guy they call Smiley," he said. "My daughter is Gretchen Horowitz. A fuck like you is lucky to do hundred-dollar hits in Little Havana."

None of it worked, and Clete felt foolish talking to the rain. He walked through the trees to the water's edge, his slippers sinking in the loam. The bayou was the color of café au lait, wrinkling in the wind like shriveled skin. His hand was squeezed tight on the grips of the .38. Maybe he had imagined it all. There was no wormlike creature anywhere except in his mind, which for years had been a repository of weed and alcohol.

He walked back to the cul-de-sac and his Caddy, then saw the slim-jim stuck solidly and abandoned between the driver's window and the door. Clete reached under the back fender and removed the

magnetized metal box that held his spare key, and unlocked the passenger door and removed a small flashlight from the glove box. He
went to the driver's side and shined the light on a few footprints that
seemed inconsequential, then opened the car door with the key and
searched the floor.

Nothing.

He pulled the slim-jim from the window and began searching the
ground. Again nothing. Or almost nothing. Just as he clicked off the
light, he saw a glimmer in the grass. He clicked the light on again and
stooped down and touched a small glass tube with the flashlight's
case. It was a mercury tilt switch, probably homemade.

He went back into the cottage and pulled off his pajamas and dried
off with a towel and put on clean clothes and wrote a note for Homer.
Then he tore up the note and sat in a stuffed chair and stared out
the window until daylight, when the rain thinned into rings on the
bayou and fog bumping in thick clouds amid the tree trunks. When
he thought of the glass tube's implications, his shingles flared like a
nest of heated wires between his shoulder blades, and the remnants
of his undigested supper spilled into his mouth.

Chapter
34

He pulled in to my driveway at seven a.m., when I was feeding Snuggs and Mon Tee Coon on top of Tripod's hutch. I fixed a pot of coffee and took it and two tin cups out to the redwood table in the backyard and filled our cups, waiting for him to explain why he had come to my door.

Clete's face was a complex study, particularly during times of crisis or decision. The more intense the emotion, the more silent and withdrawn he became. The pattern never changed. He breathed evenly through his nose, his green eyes fixed on a hologram no one else saw. The crow's-feet at the corners of his eyes flattened and turned the color of papier-mâché, his forehead turning as cool as marble, the blood settling in his cheeks because it had nowhere else to go.

"Had an early visitor this morning," he said. "In the middle of the storm." He hooked a finger through the handle on the cup. The coffee was black and scalding hot, a wisp rising from it like a trail of cigarette smoke. He drank from the cup a sip at a time, then swilled half of it, swallowing with no discomfort.

"What happened?" I said.

"Somebody tried to put a bomb in my car."

"You saw somebody around your car with a bomb?"

"I went outside before he could finish jimmying the window. He ran off."

"How do you know he had a bomb?"

"I found a tilt switch in the grass next to the driver's door." He saw the confusion in my face. "It's a glass tube that's got mercury in it. It's attached to the brake pedal or the accelerator. When the driver presses down on the pedal, the tube tilts and creates the electrical connection that detonates the charge."

"You saw the guy?"

"He took off. If I hadn't woken up, he probably would have killed me and Homer. We go down to McDonald's in the morning for biscuits and eggs."

"Do you have the tube?"

He nodded. "I think it's this guy Smiley. I told him that."

"We'll get everything to the lab."

"Waste of time. The guy's a pro. One of two guys sent him."

I knew where we were going. "You don't know it was Smiley. Don't start making connections."

"He's out-of-town talent. He's working for Fat Tony or Jimmy Nightingale. They both have the same motivation."

"Like what?"

"Tony thinks he's hit the big time in Hollywood. Nightingale is about to become an international figure. They're leaving their baggage in the depot."

But I knew Clete's thought processes had not reached their destination.

"It's Nightingale," he said. "His shit-prints are on all of this."

"Okay, he's the Antichrist of St. Mary Parish," I said. "You made your point. But the evidence that he's hired a killer isn't there. Tony Nemo hires killers. Rich guys like Jimmy hire lawyers."

"Jimmy?"

"Nightingale," I said.

"Right." Clete refilled his cup and wrapped his hand around it and lifted it to his lips, then set it down without drinking. "I didn't come here to tell you about my suspicions. You're my friend, and I got to be up front with you about something."

I felt the moisture in my mouth dry up, even the taste of the coffee disappear.

"The guy who sent the bomber after me didn't care if he killed Homer or not," Clete said. "It doesn't matter if it's Tony Nine Ball or that punk in St. Mary Parish, the guy behind this is going off the board."

"I didn't hear that. You didn't say it. That thought never crossed your mind."

"I'm going to cap him, Streak."

I took the tin cup from his hand and threw the coffee on the ground. "We're done."

"What would you do if it was Alafair?" he said. "Think about it. What would you do?"

LATE THAT NIGHT, a pizza scooter pulled in to the driveway of a rented nineteenth-century home outside Jeanerette, and a short man in a stiff hat with a big bill got out with a pie box and looked around as though unsure of the address. The house was set back from the street and dark with shadow except for a light in the bathroom. A tall figure walked out of the driveway and confronted the delivery man. There was a brief exchange, then the tall figure disappeared and the delivery man climbed the steps to the gallery and twisted the bell.

The man who answered was wearing a brocaded royal blue silk robe. His body was shaped like a pile of inner tubes. "What's this?"

"Your pizza."

"I didn't order a pizza."

The deliveryman looked at the bill in his hand. "Anthony Nemo?"

"The name is Tony. I didn't order a pizza. Where's Robert?"

"Who?"

"My chauffeur."

"He's sleeping."

"You leave your flying saucer on the lawn?"

"He was tired. He went to sleep. Like you." The deliveryman raised a stun gun and touched it to the center of Tony Nine Ball's face. Tony hit the floor like a cargo net loaded with salami.

When tony awoke, all the curtains were closed, the air-conditioning blasting out arctic levels of cold air. A toy man with lips as red as a clown's was sitting on a chair two feet from him, staring at him with a silly smile. Tony's arms were pulled behind him.

"Hi, sleepyhead," the man said. "My name is Chester. Do you want some pizza?"

"I can't move."

"You have ligatures on. So you won't hurt yourself."

"You almost knocked my head off. I can't breathe. I got emphysema."

Chester went into the bedroom and came back with a pillow. He put it under Tony's head. "Better?"

Tony's eyes were small and black and buried deep in his face. "You sound like Elmer Fudd."

"Don't be impolite. I can make you go back to sleep."

"You're the wack job everybody is talking about."

Chester removed a rolled comic book from his back pocket and tapped it on Tony's nose. "Bad, bad, bad."

"You're nuts. You belong in a gerbil cage. Tell me what you want."

"Don't make me mad."

"My dick in your mouth, jerk-off. I got guys out there gonna take you apart no matter what happens in here."

"No nasty talk. Not one word." Chester tightened the comic in his grip and hammered the butt end on Tony's nose. Tony's face went out of shape, his eyes watering. A sound like a punctured tire wheezed from his throat. "I got to have my tank."

"Bad boys don't get what they want. I did some research on you. You have been very bad."

"What the fuck is this?"

"Did Kevin Penny work for you?"

"So what?"

"He was cruel to his little boy. You knew about it. You didn't stop it."

"I didn't know nothing about his personal life. You're here from Boys Town?"

Chester's head was throbbing like wooden blocks falling down a staircase. "I wasn't in Boys Town. I was in a place where bad things were done to me."

"From what I hear, you already fucked up two hits. One with the cop in New Iberia, one with Clete Purcel. Kevin Penny's kid is living with Purcel. You were supposed to blow up the kid, too? You looking for child abusers? Go look in the mirror, gerbil boy."

Chester's mouth had shrunk to a stitch, his nostrils no more than tiny holes, white around the rims. He unrolled his comic book and stared at the cover. Wonder Woman was leaping across a canyon undaunted, her gold and red bodice pushing up her breasts, her blue star-spangled shorts skintight, the message in her face unmistakable. *I will,* Chester said inside his head.

"You'll do what?" Tony said.

"What Wonder Woman tells me to. If I don't, I'll have bad thoughts and do bad things."

"Bad thoughts? You're an assassin who talks to a comic book. You're a meltdown. I can get you help for that."

Chester rolled the comic into a tight cylinder again and jammed it as hard as a stick into Tony's eye. "You will not talk back anymore."

Tony's face quivered with shock. His wounded eye was watering and rimmed with a red ring.

"I never did anything to you. Somebody is using you. I'm a businessman, a movie producer. Check me out. You want to be in a movie? I'll put you in a movie."

"You need to be punished."

"What do you call this?"

"Nothing," Chester said.

He went outside and returned with a black leather bag, the kind physicians once carried. He removed a pair of needle-nose pliers and a plastic container. Tony's face seemed to shrink and become miniaturized. "Don't."

Chester unscrewed the cap and fitted the pliers on Tony's nose and squeezed. "Open wide."

Then he poured the container of Drano down Tony's throat, making sure not to get any on his clothes or hands.

THE NEXT MORNING Helen called half a dozen plainclothes into her office. She was looking out the window at the Teche as we filed in. When she turned around, it was obvious that she planned to be brief and deliver a message that cops understand but don't talk about.

"The coroner says Nemo went out about as hard as it gets. His chauffeur is still in a coma. A passerby said he saw a man in a box-like hat get out of the delivery wagon and talk to someone in the driveway. The 'someone' was probably the chauffeur: He got his eggs scrambled with a stun gun. The pizza wagon was stolen. Maybe it's our man Smiley. Maybe not. The homicide is under the jurisdiction of St. Mary Parish."

"That's it?" someone said.

"It's my belief that the same guy tried to put a bomb in Clete Purcel's car," she replied. "Or maybe we've got a tag team at work. Whoever it is, we need to cool them out. Everybody hearing me on this? We don't get hurt. Civilians don't get hurt. Bad guys go out of business. Everybody copy?"

There was a collective "Yes, ma'am!"

"You stay, Dave," she said.

She waited until everyone else had gone. There was a solitary red rose in a slender glass vase on her desk. "This is eating my lunch."

"Don't let it," I said.

"We've got a guy killing people all over Acadiana, and we don't know his name. We don't have prints or weapons; all we have is two casings from the Cajun Dome that were wiped clean. Nobody is that good."

"Nothing more from the feds?"

"They've heard of a guy working out of Miami named Smiley. They don't know any more than we do."

"Maybe we're all looking in the wrong place," I said. "Maybe he's from overseas. The Mob used to bring hitters in from Sicily. They'd stay with a local family, wash the dishes, do the hit, and go back home."

She tried to straighten the rose in the vase, then picked up a petal that had fallen on the desk and dropped it into the wastebasket. Her eyes seemed out of focus.

"That's a pretty flower," I said.

"A fellow gave it to me for my birthday. A fellow I might start seeing."

I had no idea why she was behaving the way she was. "You okay, Helen?"

"There was a worm right in the middle of the rose. Funny, huh?"

I knew better than to say anything.

"It's like Smiley," she said. "He's out there, invisible, always ready to do harm."

"He's just a guy, nothing more."

She sat back in her chair, her gaze receding. "You know better."

I wasn't going to pursue the subject. I had known Red Cross personnel and American soldiers who had been at the liberation of Ravensbrück and Dachau. None of them was ever the same again. They also spent the rest of their lives trying to explain the nature and sources of evil. Cops fall easily into the same trap. A day comes when you see something that you never talk about again, and it lives with you the rest of your days.

"We'll get him," I said.

"I'm not talking about Smiley or whatever his name is. It's something else. And I say 'it' deliberately."

"Keep it simple, Helen."

"Jimmy Nightingale is involved in this."

"That's not what the evidence indicates."

"Maybe he didn't rape Rowena Broussard, but I think he knew Kevin Penny did. Maybe he even sicced him on her."

"We'll never prove that, Helen. Let it go."

"I saw him at the Winn-Dixie yesterday. People were lining up to shake his hand. He put his arm over my shoulders. I felt like I'd been molested."

I had never heard her talk like this. "You think he's the third Antichrist in Nostradamus?"

"No, I think he's Huey Long on a national scale, and that scares the shit out of me."

THAT NIGHT I drifted off to sleep while watching the local news. When I woke, I realized I was listening to the voice of Jimmy Nightingale. He was confessing to the satchel bombing of the Indian village in South America. There were tears in his eyes. He could have been a character actor in a medieval Everyman play. Out on the salt, he had told me the same story; I believed then and I believe now that he was at least partially contrite. But the man I saw on television that night was a man who could sell snow to Eskimos and electric blankets to the damned.

I DROVE TO BARON'S Health Club in New Iberia at five-thirty the next morning and went to work on the speed bag.

"I'm glad that's not my face you're hitting," a voice behind me said.

I turned around. "Visiting with the lumpen proletariat?"

"I'll buy you breakfast at Victor's," Jimmy said.

"Forget it."

"What'd I do now?"

"I caught your performance on the news last night."

"Performance?"

I let my hands hang at my sides, my bag gloves tight on my knuckles, the blood hammering in my wrists. I could smell my own odor. "You and I talked about that situation in South America. I thought you were genuinely sorry for the bad choice you made."

"I like that terminology. Yeah, bad choice. It's the kind of crap you hear in Hollywood."

"I didn't finish. I think you're using the suffering of the people you maimed and killed to further your career. That takes a special kind of guy."

"That's pretty strong, Dave." He rested one hand on my shoulder, even though my T-shirt was gray with sweat.

"I don't like people touching me."

He lowered his hand. "Take a shower. We'll eat breakfast and talk. I always looked up to you. You know that."

"I have to go to work."

A kid was hitting the heavy bag, hard enough to make it jump on the chain.

"Can you give us a minute?" Jimmy said.

"Sure," the kid replied awkwardly, as though he had done something wrong.

"Hang on, podna," I said. "Mr. Jimmy and I are going outside."

"I got to get to class at UL," the kid said. "It's all right."

After we were alone, Jimmy said, "You look like you want to drop me."

"You know the chief sign of narcissism, don't you? Entitlement. That's another word for self-important jerk."

"I want to offer you a job. Maybe Purcel, too."

"Doing security?"

"That's part of it."

"What's the other part?"

"Arguing with me and telling me when I'm wrong. You know what LBJ said to Eric Sevareid when the two of them were watching Nixon's inauguration on the tube?"

"No."

"'He's made a mistake. He's taken amateurs with him.' I don't want amateurs on my team."

"I'll start now, free of charge. Stop lying."

"Liars own up on television to murdering defenseless Indians?"

"Hump your own pack, Jimmy. How'd you know where I was?"

"Your daughter was up. She's back on the set, huh?"

"What about it?"

"I wish I was on it," he said. "Hollywood is a magical place. I don't care what people say about it."

"Don't tell that to your constituency," I said.

"You think they don't like movies? Who do you think has filled the theaters for the last hundred and sixteen years?"

He clenched his hand on the back of my neck, his fingers sinking into the flesh, fusing with the oil and sweat running out of my hair, his eyes next to mine, his breath on my skin. One of his feet stepped on top of mine. "Work with me. You can have power you never guessed at. We'll turn the world into the Garden of Eden."

As he walked away, I picked up a towel and wiped my face and neck and arms and hands, trying to cleanse his touch and the wetness of his mouth from my body and mind.

Chapter
35

ALL DAY I was troubled by thoughts about Jimmy Nightingale. And Levon Broussard. And the way Kevin Penny and Tony Nine Ball and Spade Labiche had gone out. I have always believed there is no mystery to human behavior. We're the sum total of our deeds. But that wasn't the way things had been working out.

I was fairly certain Labiche had been on a pad for Tony and was told to set up a situation with T. J. Dartez that would put me either in prison or on the injection table. Other than that, I had no idea who'd killed Penny or who was pulling the strings on the surreal hit man known only as Smiley.

At the center of it all were Jimmy Nightingale and his foil, Levon Broussard. I suspected an analyst would say both of them had borderline personality disorder. Or maybe a dissociative personality disorder. Unfortunately, those terms would apply to most drunks, addicts, fiction writers, and actors.

Both men descended from prominent families in a state where Shintoism in its most totalitarian form was not only a given but most obvious in its sad influence on the poor and uneducated, who accepted their self-abasing roles with the humility of serfs. But there was an existential difference between the two families. For the Nightingales, manners and morality were interchangeable. For Levon Broussard

and his ancestors, honor was a religion, more pagan than Christian
in concept, the kind of mind-set associated with a Templar Knight or
pilots in the Japanese air force.

For the Broussards, honor was a virtue that, once tarnished, could
never be restored. They may have been aristocrats and slave owners
who lived inside a fable, but they still heard the horns blowing along
the road to Roncevaux and accepted genteel poverty and isolation if
necessary but would be no more capable of changing their vision of
the world and themselves than Robert E. Lee could have become a
used-car salesman.

That was why I had a hard time believing that Levon could have
tortured and murdered Kevin Penny. I had even greater difficulty believing he would throw in his lot with Tony Nemo in order to weigh
the balance in his upcoming trial in Jefferson Davis Parish.

On Monday morning, I got a call at my office from Sherry Picard.
"I need your help," she said.

"What can I do for you?" I asked, trying to suppress my feelings
about Clete's involvement with younger women in general and this
one in particular.

"Catch you at the wrong time?"

"Not at all."

"I still have prints from the Penny homicide scene that I believe
are significant. The fast-food trash. Penny kept the area around his
motorcycle clean. That means the person who left it there was on the
property the day Penny died."

"What does this have to do with me?" I said.

"I want to fingerprint the Nightingale employees. I'm not getting
anywhere."

"St. Mary Parish was teleported from the fourteenth century. His-
torians come from far away to study it."

"Did I do something to offend you?"

"I can't help you in St. Mary."

"How about with Levon Broussard?"

"What about him?"

"I want to fingerprint his wife. I think she may have been an accomplice."

"I'm not convinced Levon is guilty, much less his wife." I could feel her resentment coming through the phone. I tried again. "What makes you suspicious about his wife?"

"Her general attitude. I think she needs a flashlight shined up her ass."

How about that?

"Did you hear me?" she said.

"Absolutely."

"Absolutely what?"

"That I heard you," I said.

"What's your problem?"

"I don't have one."

"Are you pissed off because of Clete and me?"

"I don't know what you're talking about."

"We called it off. That's why you've got your tally whacker in the hay baler?"

"I'll talk with Levon, Ms. Picard."

"Detective Picard."

I softly replaced the receiver in the cradle.

THE PHONE RANG three minutes later. I thought she was calling back. I felt embarrassed as I picked up the receiver and wished I hadn't hung up on her. Surprise time.

"I heard you used to live in New Or-yuns," a voice said. "You were a police officer in the Quarter."

I sat up in my chair. "That's right."

"I had an artist friend who knew you. He painted people's pictures in Jackson Square. He said you were an honest police officer."

I waved my arm at a cop in uniform passing in the hallway. He looked through the glass. I pointed at the receiver. He nodded and disappeared down the hallway.

"What's your name?" I said. "I'll help you if I can."

"I think you know who I am."

"Not for sure. Are you visiting in New Iberia?"

"Some people call me Smiley."

"That doesn't ring bells."

"I want to ask you a question."

"Yes, sir, go right ahead."

Helen was at the glass in my door now. I mouthed the word "Smiley."

"Does the man named Purcel have a boy?"

"You mean Clete Purcel?"

"A boy lives with him?" he said.

"Clete doesn't have a birth son, but he takes care of an orphan. Is that the boy you're talking about?"

He cleared his throat but didn't speak.

"You there, Smiley?"

"Yes."

"Did you want to tell me something?"

"What's the boy's name?"

"Homer."

"What's the rest of it?"

"Homer Penny is his full name."

I waited in the silence. I had given up information I normally wouldn't. But this situation was outside the parameters of any in my career.

"Did you try to hurt Clete, Smiley?"

"This call is a relay. It won't help you to trace it."

"I figured. That means we can talk as long as you want. Where'd you get your nickname?"

No answer.

"Know who your accent reminds me of?" I said. "Tennessee Williams. He said 'New Or-yuns' just like you. I knew him when he lived in the Quarter."

I could hear him breathing against the mouthpiece, as though deciding whether or not to hang up. "I don't care about him."

"Have you been to Algiers?" I said. "A couple of bad black dudes got their grits splattered over there."

"What do you know about it?"

"Between you and me, I think they probably had it coming. You hear anything about that?"

"They were bad to a colored lady. Her name was Miss Birdie."

"Did you smoke these dudes?"

"Maybe," he said. "If you're bad or treacherous with me, I'll smoke you, too."

"I believe you. But I'd rather be friends with you."

"I wouldn't hurt a child," he said, his voice downshifting.

"I know what you mean. There's nothing worse than the abuse of children or animals. That's why Clete takes care of Homer. Clete had a hard upbringing."

"I'm sorry. Tell him that."

"Tell Clete?"

"Yes. I didn't know about the boy."

"I read you loud and clear, partner. Know anything about Kevin Penny, Smiley?"

"He was a bad man."

"You didn't help him do the Big Exit, did you?"

"You're trying to trick me."

"Not me. I'm not that smart. You're like a shadow. You come and go, and nobody has a clue. Who was your artist friend?"

"He was my friend for a while. Then he wasn't my friend anymore."

"Could we work out a way to communicate when both of us have more time? I'm pretty tied up right now."

"I can come by your house."

He had me. I could almost see him grinning. "You're calling the shots. Did you ever hear Louie Prima and Sam Butera play at the Dream Room on Bourbon?"

"You want to know how old I am? Remember fifteen years ago when a house was torn down on Calliope and a body fell out of the wall? It had been in there long enough not to smell anymore. This man was bad to somebody who trusted him and got walled up with his paintbrushes stuffed in his mouth. He was a very bad boy. Bye-bye."

The line went dead. I looked blankly at Helen through the glass. I had witnessed two deaths by electrocution in the Red Hat House at Angola. On both occasions I'd felt that I was watching an element in the human gene pool for which there was no remedy, and I mean the desire to kill, either on the part of individuals or the state. I took a Kleenex from a drawer in my desk and cleared my throat and spat in it, then dropped it into the waste can.

AT NOON, I took Clete to lunch at Bon Creole out on East St. Peter Street. We ordered fried-oyster po'boys and sat at a table under a blue-and-silver marlin mounted on the wall.

"You couldn't make the trace?" he said.

"The signal was probably relayed off two or three towers," I said.

"You checked out the story about the artist in the wall?"

"His name was Pierre Louviere. Evidently, he was an eccentric guy who hung out with a weird crowd in the Quarter."

"How'd he go out?"

"Not easy."

"You think Smiley did Penny?"

"No."

"Why not?"

"He would have said so. He doesn't have any guilt about the people he kills."

"Psychopaths lie for the sake of lying," Clete said.

"He was obviously bothered about putting a bomb in a car that would kill a child."

The waitress put our food on the table. She looked uncomfortable, obviously having overheard our conversation.

"Don't pay attention to us," I said.

She tried to smile but had a hard time with it. She walked away, blinking.

"Go on," Clete said to me.

"I think Smiley feels he got set up."

"No idea who he's working for?"

"None. Sherry Picard called."

Clete looked at a place six inches from the side of my face. "Yeah?"

"She said y'all aren't hanging out anymore."

"It's more like she flushed me. No big deal."

Right. I avoided looking at his eyes. He put a cracker into his mouth and chewed. He hadn't touched his sandwich.

"She's off the wall, Clete."

"I'm old, she's young. You warned me. End of subject."

"Age is not a factor. She has the grace of a chain saw."

Wrong choice. Three things about Clete Purcel: Since I'd first met him, he'd never once used God's name in vain; referred to a woman in a profane way; or criticized a woman who'd dumped him, unless you counted the postcard he sent me from El Sal when he skipped the country on a murder beef and asked me to tell his ex, who'd cheated on him, that he wanted her to have the toothbrush he'd left in the bathroom.

He wadded up a napkin and lobbed it into a trash can by the cold-drink dispenser. "Smiley say anything about Jimmy Nightingale?"

"No. But I had a strange experience with Jimmy at Baron's Health Club."

"Like what?"

"I was hitting the speed bag and pretty sweaty and dirty. He squeezed the back of my neck and whispered in my ear. He was standing on my foot."

Clete's gaze went away from mine, then came back. "He's AC/DC?"

"He was talking about making the world into the Garden of Eden."

"You're making this up?"

"Jimmy isn't the same guy I used to know," I said. "But that's not what bothers me. I couldn't scrub his touch off my skin. Helen said the same thing about him."

Clete looked into space. "I think I'm going back to the Big Sleazy for a few days. Start putting junk in my arm, hanging out at bottomless clubs, go to a Crisco party at a steam room, do something healthy for a change."

"It's not funny, Clete."

"None of this is," he replied. "I didn't give you the whole gen on Sherry. She called one of her sniper targets a sand nigger. She tried to take it back, but it made me think about her relationship to Kevin Penny."

"She might have decided to get rough?"

"Sherry wouldn't make a good Maryknoll."

CLETE WENT TO Walmart that afternoon. On the way out, he ran into Swede Jensen, the Nightingale chauffeur, whom he'd helped get a job as an extra in Levon's film adaptation. Swede was wearing white Bermuda shorts with bananas on them and a sleeveless golf shirt, his tan as dark as saddle leather, his armpit hair stiff and bleached by the sun. His concave face always reminded Clete of a hominid replica he had seen in a natural history museum.

"What's the haps, Swede?" Clete said.

Swede looked around but kept walking.

"Wait up," Clete said.

"Oh, hey, what say, Purcel?" Swede replied, studying his watch. "How's it hanging?"

"I saw you on the set behind Albania Plantation. You were wearing a Confederate uniform."

"Yeah, it's a lot of fun."

"They paying you okay?"

"Yeah, union scale, all that stuff."

Clete waited for Swede to thank him. It didn't happen. "You don't have a conflict with your chauffeur job?"

"The Nightingales are flexible. Sorry, I got to boogie."

"Yeah, the sky's about to fall. Look at me."

"Like I said—" Swede began.

"No, you didn't say anything. Your eyes are going everywhere except my face. In the meantime, you're blowing me off. It's called rude."

"Thanks for what you did. I got a ton of things to do. Nice seeing you."

Clete stepped in his way. "Don't talk shit to me, Swede."

Swede looked like an animal with a limb caught in a trap.

"Did you know fear smells like soiled cat litter?" Clete said.

Swede almost ran through the door.

THAT WEEKEND, SOUTHERN Louisiana was sweltering, thunder cracking as loud as cannons in the night sky; at sunrise, the storm drains clogged with dead beetles that had shells as hard as pecans. It was the kind of weather we associated with hurricanes and tidal surges and winds that ripped tin roofs off houses and bounced them across sugarcane fields like crushed beer cans; it was the kind of weather that gave the lie to the sleepy Southern culture whose normalcy we so fiercely nursed and protected from generation to generation.

I could not sleep Sunday night, and on Monday I woke with a taste like pennies in my mouth and a sense that my life was unspooling before me, that the world in which I lived was a fabrication, that the charity abiding in the human breast was a collective self-delusion, and that the bestial elements we supposedly exorcised from civilized society were not only still with us but had come to define us, although we sanitized them as drones and offshore missiles marked "occupant" and land mines that killed children decades after they were set.

These are signs of clinical depression or maybe a realistic vision of the era in which we live. During moments like these, no matter the time of day or night, I had found release only in a saloon. The long bar and brass foot rail, the wood-bladed fans, the jars of cracklings and pickled eggs and sausages, the coldness of bottled beer or ice-sheathed mugs, the wink in the barmaid's eye and the shine on the tops of her breasts, the tumblers of whiskey that glowed with an amber radiance that seemed almost ethereal, the spectral bartender without a last name, the ringing of the pinball machine, all these things became my cathedral, a home beneath the sea, and just as deadly.

Thoughts like these are probably a form of alcoholic insanity. But on that particular Monday morning, I preferred my own madness to what I had begun to feel, as Helen and Clete did—namely, that an inchoate sickness was in our midst, and it was as palpable in the hot wetness of the dawn as the smell of lions in the street at high noon.

At 9:33 A.M., I received another call from Sherry Picard.

"I need to talk to you or Clete," she said. "Since he's not in his office and not answering his cell phone, I called you."

"Thanks," I replied.

"I was warned about you two."

"This is a business line," I said. "If you have a personal issue, call me at home."

"My ass. Did you try to dime me with the FBI?"

"That's probably one of the craziest things I've heard in a while."

"Because an agent just left my office. I have the distinct feeling that I'm being looked at for the Penny homicide."

"Talk to the U.S. Justice Department," I said. "The feds hate Clete's guts. I don't have contact with them. Most of them wouldn't take the time to spit on us."

"Don't give me that. They're in contact with your boss, which means they're in contact with you."

"Why would either Clete or I dime you, Detective?" I said.

"Because I told him we're not right for each other. It was fun and now we move on. It was nothing personal. I thought he was a sweet guy."

"Rejection is not personal. That's wonderful."

"You'd better stay out of my life and my career," she said.

"Be assured I will."

"I have a second reason for calling. Levon Broussard just came into the prosecutor's office and confessed to torturing Penny to death. What do you think of that, slick?"

Chapter 36

THAT WAS NOT all Levon did. After confessing to an ADA in the Jeff Davis courthouse, he went out the side door, drove to a low-bottom joint north of Four Corners in Lafayette, got plowed out of his head, and at sunset drove across his lawn to the gallery on the front of his house and announced to his wife, "Hi, honey, I'm home."

Helen called me on my cell. "Get over to Levon Broussard's place. It looks like he's lost it."

"What's he doing?"

"Who knows? His wife called in the 911. He's in the yard with a Confederate flag and a sword, ranting at the sky. He fired a flare pistol across the bayou and asked some people in a boat to come in for a drink. I think they're still emptying out their shoes."

I drove to his house. The sky was a red-and-black ink wash, the oaks he had named for Confederate officers chattering with birds. A patrol car was parked in the neighbor's drive; another was parked by the tennis courts across the two-lane highway. I got out of my pickup and walked around the side of the house and through a line of camellia bushes into the backyard. He was sitting at a folding table under a huge oak by the bayou, the faded battle flag he had kept encased in glass hanging from an overhead branch. It looked like cheesecloth against the sunset. The dried blood of the drummer boy reminded me of the coppery stains on the Shroud of Turin.

Levon lifted a bottle of Cold Duck above his head. "Welcome to Chaucer's blue-collar good knight. Or is it Everyman I see? Wrong evening for bromides, Davey."

His face was oily and dissolute with booze. He had stabbed his great-grandfather's sword into the sod by his foot. His teeth were stained with wine.

"Looks like you've had quite a day," I said.

"How's that, Davey?"

"Confessing to an ADA in Jennings. Scaring your friends in New Iberia."

"Not so about scaring my friends."

I nodded at the flag lifting in the breeze above us. "That should be in a controlled environment, shouldn't? Protected from dust and humidity?"

"It survived Yankee artillery at Owl Creek. That's where the Eighteenth Louisiana got torn to pieces. In fifteen minutes, forty percent were casualties."

"You can't win on yesterday's box score. Why lose because of it?"

"That one zipped by me."

"The past has no reality. The world belongs to the living."

"You know better. You see them in the mists out at Spanish Lake."

"See whom?"

"I love you for your diction, if nothing else. The boys in butternut. You see them slogging through the cypresses."

"Who told you that?"

"They did," he replied.

I wanted to believe he was mad. Unfortunately, I no longer knew what madness was.

"Why did you confess to a crime you didn't commit?" I asked.

"You don't believe me capable of killing the man who raped my wife?"

"You didn't try to kill the black guys who raped her in Wichita."

"I'm making up for lost time."

"Not with toggle bolts and an electric drill."

"I thought that was an inventive touch."

"Quit lying, Levon." I pulled the sword from the ground and stuck the brass guard in his face. "Look at the names on there: Cemetery Hill, Sharpsburg, Gaines's Mill, Chancellorsville. Would the soldier who was at these places torture a man to death, even a piece of shit like Kevin Penny?"

"No, he would not. But that doesn't mean I wouldn't."

"Good show. No cigar," I said. "Let's go."

I placed my hand lightly on his upper arm. He shook his head and sucked in his cheeks. "Don't underestimate the situation, Davey."

"Call me Davey again, and I'll break your jaw."

He grinned up at me. "You're a good guy. Butt out of this. Let others do their job."

"You want one of our guys to cap you because you can't do it yourself?"

"Maybe."

"Get a card in the Screen Actors Guild. Come on. I'll take you down to City Hall. Your lawyer will work out something. Helen isn't going to let the guys in Jeff Davis cannibalize you."

I heard the French doors open on the back porch, which was built of brick, high off the ground, and hung with ceiling fans. "Leave him alone," Rowena said.

"It doesn't work that way," I said.

"He's sick," she said. "He doesn't know what he's saying."

I looked at her hands. They were empty. I walked toward her. "Don't be a problem for me, Miss Rowena. Go back inside. We'll take good care of him. You have my word."

"He's innocent."

"I believe that."

"So leave him here. Talk to him when he's sober."

"There's a bigger question we need to deal with. Why is he confessing to a crime he's not capable of committing?" There was a shine in his eyes. I looked at her a long time. "The question stands, Miss Rowena."

"I'll bring him to City Hall with our attorney in the morning."

"You can bring yourself, but he's going to jail. Right now."

"Hold up there, Dave," Levon said behind me. "No need for this." He lifted the flag off the tree with the tip of his great-grandfather's sword. "Let me put this away and we'll be toggling off," he said.

I looked back at Rowena. For the first time in the case involving the Jeff Davis Eight and Tony Nine Ball and Jimmy Nightingale and Levon Broussard and Kevin Penny, I knew what had happened.

Clete Purcel believed in straight lines. "Bust 'em or dust 'em" was his mantra. But there was a caveat. Clete was never what the Mob called a cowboy. He could be a violent man, but with few exceptions, his violence was committed in defense of others. Consequently, his greatest virtue became his greatest vulnerability, and his enemies knew it.

He told me about his encounter with Swede Jensen at Walmart, and about Jensen's guilt and fear, or at least Clete's perception of it. Then Clete stopped answering my calls. I should have known what was coming next.

Clete kept a custom-made extra-long foot locker in the garret above his office. In it were a cut-down Mossberg semi-auto twelve-gauge he'd taken off a hit man in Las Vegas, a Glock, two Berettas, a .44 Magnum, a derringer a deranged prostitute had pulled on him during a vice raid, a sap and a blackjack and a baton, a slim-jim, brass knuckles, a gun that fired a bean bag, Mace, a tear gas pen, a carton of flash grenades, handcuffs, wrist and waist chains, and the most unusual drop I'd ever seen, an engraved snub-nose gold-over-silver Colt Police .32 with ivory grips that only a collector or a rich man would own.

The drop came from the safe of a mobster who operated a lodge and casino above Lake Tahoe. Because the gun was a collectible, its serial numbers, all of them intact, were obviously registered, and the discovery of the pistol at a crime scene would lead the authorities back to the mobster, long dead, and more important, to the casino culture he represented.

Tuesday afternoon, Clete showered and shaved and put on fresh sport clothes and had his hair cut and drove to the Nightingale plantation outside Franklin. He carried the drop in an ankle holster and a scoped 1903 Springfield rifle in the trunk. The azaleas were still in bloom when he turned in to the driveway, the St. Augustine grass a deep blue-green, the four-o'clocks open in the shade of the oak trees. He could feel a surge of adrenaline come alive in his chest and wrists and hands, not unlike the high of going up the Mekong in a swift boat behind twin fifty-calibers, the stern dipping and swaying in the trough.

HE DIDN'T GET far. Security came out of the carriage house, from the patio, and a state police car and a parked SUV with tinted windows. The men in suits were wearing shades. As Clete slowed the Caddy, he unstrapped the ankle holster and let it fall to the floor, then braked and lowered the window. A close-cropped man wearing shades stared into his face. "This is a security area."

"Y'all got the nuclear codes inside?" Clete said, the corners of his eyes crinkling.

"Is there someone in particular you're looking for?"

"Jimmy Nightingale. I'm Clete Purcel. I'm a PI out of New Orleans and New Iberia."

"I'm afraid you're not on our visitors list for today."

"How about telling Mr. Nightingale I'm here, and then we'll take it from there?"

The man at Clete's window looked over his shoulder. "You can turn your vehicle around in front of the house. Then get back on the road, please."

"That doesn't sound too cool," Clete said.

"Is that a firearm inside your jacket?"

"I'm licensed to carry."

"You need to leave, sir."

"No, I don't."

"Step out of your vehicle, please."

With the back of his foot, Clete pushed the drop under the seat. "I'm at your service." He got out of the Caddy and lifted his hands and smiled. He towered over most of the security personnel. "What's next?"

"I'm going to reach inside your jacket for your piece," the man in the suit said. "Are you comfortable with that?"

"As long as you give it back."

The man in shades removed the snub-nose from Clete's shoulder holster and handed it to a St. Mary's Parish sheriff's deputy. "Could I have your keys?"

Clete pulled the keys from the ignition and dropped them into the security man's palm. The St. Mary deputy popped the trunk with them. "He's got a scoped rifle and an M1 in here."

"They're legal," Clete said. "I shoot at a target range. How about giving this stuff a rest?"

"Stop dancing around with this guy," a voice in the background said.

The voice belonged to a tall man wearing western-cut pants and a tight cowboy shirt and mirror-shined, needle-nosed Tony Lamas and a straw cowboy hat with a thin black bejeweled band around the crown. His gray mustache was clipped and as stiff as a toothbrush. "Remember me?"

"No," Clete said.

"Angola in the eighties. I herded some of the Big Stripes."

Clete saw a hazy image in his mind, a gunbull mounted on horse-back atop the Mississippi levee, silhouetted against a dull red sun, his expression lost in the shadow of his hat. A sweat-soaked black convict was mule-jerking a stump from the silt, ripping it loose in a shower of dirt.

"Wooster," Clete said.

"Good memory."

"You shot a kid."

"I made a Christian out of a nigger."

"You went to work for Tony Squid," Clete said.

"Who?" Wooster said.

"Is Nightingale here or not?" Clete said.

"It's none of your goddamn business," Wooster said.

Clete blew air out of one nostril and looked sideways. "How y'all think this is going to play out?"

"With you hauling your ass out of here," Wooster said.

Clete opened and closed his hands at his sides. They felt stiff and thick, the veins in his forearms cording. "You guys deal the play."

Then Jimmy Nightingale came around the side of the house in tennis clothes, a racquet over his shoulder, his skin shiny, not a strand of his bronze-colored hair out of place. "Hey, slow down out there."

"We've got it under control, Mr. Nightingale," Wooster said.

"Clete's my friend. What are you doing out here, big fellow?"

"Long time no see. Not since I ran into you and Bobby Earl at the casino."

"How could I forget? You took a drain in poor Bobby's car."

"I called you a cunt, and you had me taken out in handcuffs."

"We all have our off nights," Nightingale said.

"You've got quite a place here."

"Why don't you join us out back for a drink?"

Clete wondered how the buried images of the Indians dying in the explosions of the satchel charges did not crack through the perfection of Nightingale's perfect egg-shaped face, and leave it like pieces of porcelain at his feet.

"Somebody tried to blow up my shit," Clete said.

"I didn't know about that."

"If he'd pulled it off, he would have killed a young boy I take care of. That's a big problem for me."

"Let me know if I can help. A little influence never hurts."

"The authorities usually see me as the problem. They're often right. See, I'm going to square this on my own."

"Give 'em heck," Nightingale said.

"I love that kind of language. 'Give 'em heck.' 'You betcha.' It's folksy."

"Let me take him out of here, Mr. Nightingale," Wooster said.

"I want to be your friend, Clete," Nightingale said.

"You know that old expression 'I don't have an enemy in the world'? As long as I'm alive, you'll always have one."

Nightingale laughed. "God, you've got the guts of a beer-glass brawl, Purcel. Come work for me."

"I need my piece back."

"Give it to him," Nightingale said to the security man.

"Mr. Nightingale, I think you should let us handle this."

"There will be none of that," Nightingale said.

The security man handed Clete his snub-nose. Clete dropped it into his shoulder holster. A freshly waxed purple Lincoln with chrome-spoked whitewalls came out of the carriage house with Emmeline Nightingale in the back and Swede Jensen in livery behind the wheel.

"You're behind that geek from Florida, Jimmy," Clete said.

"Which geek is that?"

"Goes by the tag Smiley. You're dirty. You know it and I know it, and I'm going to prove it."

"The peace of the Lord be with you."

"Stay indoors during lightning storms," Clete said. He got into the Caddy.

Nightingale leaned down to the window. "I always liked you, Clete."

"Watch your foot," Clete said. He backed in a semicircle, breaking the flowers off the camellia bushes, and drove toward the highway, the sunlight splintering in the oak limbs above his head.

How do you get to a guy like Nightingale? he wondered. More important, who was he? A master of illusion or a guy with a genius IQ who was brain-dead when it came to morality?

Clete looked in the rearview mirror. The security men had gone back to their posts, but Nightingale still stood in the middle of the driveway, one hand lifted in farewell, as though he were saying good-bye to a friend from a previous life.

CLETE CALLED ME and told me to meet him at Clementine's at seven.

"What for?" I said.

"I think Nightingale got inside my head."

"Come by the house."

"It might be bugged," he said.

"You've been thinking too much."

"Yeah, I imagined the mercury tilt switch I found by my automobile."

After supper I walked down to the restaurant. Clete was at the bar. He knocked back the whiskey in his shot glass and pointed at a table by the brick wall in the back of the dining room.

"Where's Homer?" I said.

"Playing softball in the park." He caught the waiter. "What are you having, Dave?"

"Nothing."

Clete ordered a plate of étouffée and half a dozen raw oysters and a bottle of Danish beer. "I'm so dry I'm a fire hazard. Don't get on my case because I've got to have a hit of this or that."

"Lose the Mouseketeer routine, will you?"

"I got the willies." He told me what had happened in front of Jimmy Nightingale's home. "You think he's just an actor? Nothing rattles him. For a minute he made me feel like we were old friends."

"That's Jimmy. He can be humble because he already owns what everyone else wants. What were you doing out there?"

"What I said I was going to do." Clete kept his eyes on mine.

There was no one within earshot of our table. "You were actually going to bust a cap on him?"

"If I was sure he put the hit on Homer and me."

"In his front yard?"

"I was going to take down the chauffeur, too. I was going to give them a fair chance, then smoke them."

"This is madness, Clete."

The waiter brought the Danish beer. Clete took a long swig, looking at me with a protruding eye. He set the bottle on the tablecloth. "Madness is when you let an innocent boy get maimed or blown apart, the way Nightingale did those Indians. Don't give me any doo-dah, Streak."

"Who'll take care of Homer if you're in Angola?"

"Thanks for the help. You really know how to say it."

"I'll talk to you in the morning," I said. I flicked my fingernail on the neck of the Danish beer. "No more of this tonight."

Clete picked up the bottle and chugged it dry. I got up from the table and squeezed his shoulder, then kept going out the door and down the sidewalk in the summer night, the air heavy with the smell of jasmine, the water high and yellow and coursing with organic debris under the drawbridge. For just a fleeting moment, I wished the year were 1862.

Chapter
37

LEVON BROUSSARD WAS transferred from custody in Iberia Parish to Jefferson Davis Parish. I did not believe he was guilty of the Kevin Penny homicide, but nonetheless I was glad he was gone, and I hoped that I would not be entangled with him and his wife for a while.

That wasn't the way it worked out. Sherry Picard was in my office Thursday morning. I rose from my chair when she entered, but it was hard. "Good morning," I said. "How are you? What brings you to town? Nice day."

"You speak like you're constipated," she said.

"I have a tumor on my vocal cords," I said. "It comes and goes. I've never understood it."

"What's with Levon Broussard? Why do you think he confessed?"

"Haven't a clue," I said, my face empty.

"Good try."

"He's in your jurisdiction, he's your problem."

"I thought he was your friend."

"Right now I'm worried about Clete Purcel. He has a terrible character defect. He's a bad judge of people."

I saw the color climb in her face. "I want to speak to Sheriff Soileau."

"Bang on her door."

"Listen—"

Then I saw her blink, the breath go out of her throat, a tremble in her chin.

I lowered my voice. "Look at me, Detective."

"Look at you?" she said.

"Sometimes I get my head on sideways. I'm reactive. I don't mean it."

"I'm tired of getting fucked over," she said.

I dropped my eyes. It was an unpleasant moment. Her need was obvious. There is no organizational injustice worse than putting a misogynistic cop or military officer in charge of female personnel. The abuse that follows is immediate, egregious, and cruel to the bone.

"Can I ask you something?" I said. "I heard that you called one of your targets in Iraq or Afghanistan a sand nigger."

"I was mad at Clete. He kept talking about the mamasan he killed by accident. I told him to let it go. I was deliberately crude about my own history. You think I'm a racist?"

"No."

"You want to have lunch?" she said.

I opened the bottom drawer in my desk and lifted up a brown paper bag that was folded neatly across the top. Inside I kept a spare rain jacket and hood. "Brought my own."

"I didn't intend to hurt Clete. He's a good guy."

"So are you," I said.

"Oh, yeah?" She touched at a mole on her chin and looked at the ball of her finger. "See you around, hotshot. Keep it in your pants."

I watched her walk out the door. I had a feeling that Sherry Picard cast a large net. Maybe that was just my imagination.

ON A PENINSULA that extended into the Gulf of Mexico, Chester Wimple followed the Lincoln driven by the chauffeur with peroxided hair that reminded him of popcorn butter. The wind was blowing hard out of the south, the flags on the boathouses and the elevated camps snapping, waves breaking against the chunks of concrete that had been dumped along the banks to keep the peninsula from eroding away. Chester could see Emmeline in the backseat of the Lincoln, in sunglasses, a scarf on her head.

The Lincoln turned in to a camp at the end of the peninsula, and Emmeline and the chauffeur went inside, laughing.

At what? Had Chester set the bomb in the Cadillac owned by the fat man, he might have killed a child. That was something to laugh at? No, Emmeline couldn't hurt a child. Not after what she and Chester had suffered in the orphanage in Mexico City.

Chester parked his rented car on a lot that had been left deserted after Hurricane Rita wiped out the structure and left little except clusters of banana plants and windmill palms and persimmon trees. Because it was a weekday with a forecast of storms and lightning, few of the other camps were occupied. He got out of his car with his binoculars and scoped .223 carbine and worked his way along the bank until he had a good view of the Lincoln and the camp to the south, backdropped by waves that were swelling higher and higher.

The camp had a rustic exterior with a peaked metal roof and walls made of heavy dark-stained timbers, but the satellite dishes and the propane crab boiler and barbecue pit on the fantail and the sliding glass and gold trim on the doors hinted of the luxury and level of comfort inside.

Chester focused his binoculars through the sliding door on the living room. Emmeline was brushing out her hair in front of a mirror. The chauffeur had put on boxer swim trunks and was sitting in a black leather chair, his legs crossed. A clipboard was propped on his knee. He was writing on an index card. He tilted his head one way, then another. No, he was not writing. He was sketching something on the same kind of cards that told Chester who and where his target was.

Chester removed the binoculars from his eyes and watched the seagulls dipping out of the wind into the froth, scooping up tiny fish with their beaks. The sky was gray, the clouds torn in strips like a ruined flag. Out on the horizon, he saw a sailboat trying to tack against the storm, the mast bending into the waves.

He sat on a block of concrete that knifed into his buttocks, his fists propped on his thighs, his head bowed. He stared at the camp without aid of the binoculars. The building looked like a harmless photo snipped out of a newspaper, without depth or meaning, glued on cardboard. Then he used the binoculars again and saw the face of the chauffeur in the reflection of a desk lamp. The chauffeur was grinning, perhaps laughing at a joke, perhaps laughing at Chester. Emmeline sat in his lap.

Chester pulled back the bolt on the carbine and snapped a round into the chamber.

"What you doin', mister?" a voice said.

The flesh jumped off his back. He turned and saw a little black girl, no more than ten. She had her pigtails tied on top of her head with a pink ribbon. She wore tennis shoes and floppy shorts and a T-shirt with a laughing octopus on it.

"Hi," Chester said, his face like stretched rubber.

"Is that an air gun?" she asked.

"Yes."

"You ain't shooting the gulls, are you?"

"No, I wouldn't do that."

"You just target-practicing?"

"Yes. Who are you?"

"Loretta. My mama work for the Vidrines. Up the road there."

"Do they know where you are?"

"My mama do. Ain't nobody else there."

"You should go back home. There's a storm coming."

"Then I'll go inside. What's your name?"

"Smiley."

"Hi, Smiley. Do you know somebody here?"

"I have a friend named Miss Emmeline."

"Look, there's a flying fish," she said.

He watched it glide above the waves, its fins extended, its scaled body as sleek as a spear blade. It disappeared, then rose again, defying the laws of nature.

"How come it can fly?" the girl asked.

"It was probably born in a place full of sharks. The sharks were eating all the little fish. So a magic lady who lives under the sea gave them wings. From that day on, they sailed above the water and got away from sharks."

"Where's the magic lady?"

"She's still down there, taking care of little fish that don't have a mommy or a daddy."

"I bet you made that up."

"Not me."

"You're smiling."

"You make me smile," he said.

"What's that can on the end of your gun?"

"It stops the sound so when I'm target shooting, I don't scare people."

"I got to go now. It was nice to meet you."

"Good-bye, Loretta."

She looked back. "Don't get caught in the rain, no."

He watched her walk away, then stepped carefully among the chunks of concrete and placed himself on an embankment by a cluster of banana stalks with a clear view of the camp.

Fifteen minutes passed. A line of black clouds veined with lightning had formed on the southern horizon. The chauffeur came out on the deck and propped his arms on the rail, his unbuttoned shirt swelling around him. Chester sighted and pulled the trigger.

The chauffeur seemed to stiffen as though someone had touched him unexpectedly between the shoulder blades. A red flower bloomed against his shirt. He turned in a circle, his fingers splayed across his breastbone, and walked with the concentration of a tightrope performer toward the sliding door.

Chester picked up the ejected shell and drove to the camp and knocked on the door. The carbine hung from his hand.

Emmeline pulled the door open. Her mouth was twitching, her fingers slick with blood that was as thick as paint. "What have you done?"

"Could I have a sandwich, please? I didn't eat lunch. I need to pee-pee, too."

He walked past her. She was speechless, her eyelids fluttering, as translucent as a moth's wings.

THROUGH A DOOR off the living room, he could see a double bed with the coverlet and pillows and sheets in disarray. The chauffeur was sitting on the rug by the sliding doors, one arm hooked over the end of the couch, breathing through his mouth as though he had run up a hill. Emmeline washed her hands in the kitchen sink, looking over her shoulder. The chauffeur began to moan.

"Get the towels out of the bathroom," she said to Chester. "There's a first-aid kit in the closet. I have to think."

"I want a snack, Em."

"A snack?"

"My tummy is hurting."

"Why did you shoot Swede?" she said, her voice pulling loose from her throat.

"Who's Swede?"

"The man you just shot, you stupid shit."

"I have to talk to you about what I was told to do," Chester said. "To the man with the convertible."

The chauffeur moaned again.

"Shut up," Chester said to Swede.

"Chester, please do what I say. Close the curtains. Get some bandages. I didn't mean to call you a bad word. I have to plan for us. I always took care of us, didn't I?"

"Did you know about the boy who lives with the fat man in the motor court?"

"What boy? What are you talking about?"

"The man named Purcel. He has a little boy living with him."

"I don't know anything about that. Get the kit out of the bathroom. I'll have to call 911, and you'll need to get out of here. Did anyone see you?"

The chauffeur coughed blood on the carpet and began gesturing and making unintelligible sounds. Emmeline was looking out the window at the road.

"I'll be right back," Chester said. He went into the living room and pulled up his trouser leg and removed the British commando knife strapped to his calf. A moment later, he came back into the kitchen and rinsed it in the sink and wiped it with a dish towel. Emmeline stared at him. "What did you just do?"

"Not much. Asked him why he was writing on my cards. He didn't answer. Now he can't."

Chester opened the refrigerator and removed a carton of orange juice and drank from it. He heard her go into the living room. "Oh my God," she said.

He sat down at the breakfast table, a great fatigue draining through his chest and limbs, the fragmented pieces of his life assembling and reassembling before his eyes. He remembered the music of a calliope in Mexico City, the slap of a teacher's hand, a punishment closet that had no light, a mattress pad soaked with urine.

"Snap out of it, Chester," Emmeline said. "You have to leave. I'll call 911 and tell them we had a home invasion. They'll believe me. They think a killer is after Jimmy. Did anyone see you?"

"Maybe," he replied.

"Maybe isn't good enough."

"A little colored girl named Loretta."

"She saw you with the gun?"

"I told her it was an air gun. I told a lie."

"Where does she live?"

"With a family named Vidrine."

Her eyes burned into his face. "She saw your car?"

"Yes."

"Did you give her your name?"

"Just Smiley. Not my real name." He looked at a thought inside his mind, a memory, a dark cloud that shouldn't have been there. He blanched with guilt. "I said I had a friend named Miss Emmeline."

A twisted cough came out of her chest. "You gave her my name?"

"She asked me, so I told her. I had already told one lie."

"You know what you have to do now, don't you, Chester?"

"No. Not what you're thinking, Em. No."

"Yes. And anyone with her. You shouldn't have done what you did. You've been a bad boy."

He hung his head and put his hands between his legs and clenched them with his thighs. She looked at her watch. "Take care of it, Chester. Now. Then call me. We'll get through this."

"The little girl and the people in the house?"

"We have to make sacrifices sometimes."

He nodded, then rose from the chair like a man in his sleep. He went into the living room and looked at the chauffeur curled in a ball on the carpet. He watched where he stepped and heard the first raindrops of the storm striking the windows and the metal roof and the glass doors, saw the rain denting the waves, swallowing the sky, probably thundering down on a sailboat and crew that were trying to reach the shore.

He wondered if flying fish could lift above the waves during a storm of such magnitude. He wished a whirlpool would form around him and this house and Emmeline and suck them under the sea. He hefted up the carbine he had propped by the front door and walked back into the kitchen and fired until the bolt locked open on an empty magazine, the brass dancing like little soldiers on the hardwood floor.

Chapter
38

WHEN HELEN AND I arrived at the crime scene, the rain was driving hard on the bay, turning it into mist, sweeping in sheets across the roof of the house and deck. The 911 call came from a neighbor named Vidrine who said the daughter of his maid had told him about a man carrying a rifle. The neighbor had gone to the Nightingale camp and discovered the bodies. A fireman in a yellow raincoat with a hood met us at the door. He looked like a bewhiskered monk staring out of a cave. Behind us I could see the headlights and flashers of several emergency vehicles streaming through the rain.

"The dead guy is by the couch," the fireman said. "One bullet wound through the back and out the chest. What looks like a double-edged puncture t'rew the throat."

"Where's the woman?" Helen said.

"In the kitchen," the fireman said. "Nothing's been touched or moved."

"Good job," she said. She went into the kitchen and came back out. "Emmeline Nightingale," she said. "What a mess."

"That's the chauffeur on the floor," I said. "His name is Swede Jensen. Clete got him a job as an extra in Levon's movie."

"Wrong place, wrong time?"

I nodded toward the bedroom. "Looks like they were getting it on."

I went to the kitchen door. I had latex on; so did Helen. There was

415

no brass on the floor or counters or table. It was impossible to count the number of wounds. Emmeline's expression was one I had seen before: It was devoid of emotion. The eyes were fixed on nothing. The heart-bursting level of fear and pain, the violent theft of life and soul, the desperate plea that never left the throat would remain un-recorded, written on the wind, in the memory of no one except the killer.

Helen flipped open her phone and called the dispatcher. "Find Jimmy Nightingale and tell him to call me immediately. Tell his peo-ple nothing, and don't take no from any of them. Out." She looked at me. "I'll take care of things here. Go up to the Vidrine place and talk to the little girl who saw the man with the rifle."

"Got it," I said.

"How do you figure this?"

"I don't get it at all."

"In what way?" she said.

"If the shooter is Smiley, I don't see the motivation."

"Sex," she said. "When somebody does a number like that on a woman, it's sex."

I drove to the camp up the road where the little girl was waiting for me with her mother on a screened-in gallery. Their clothes were damp from the mist blowing through the screen.

"Can we go inside?" I said.

"Yes, suh, we just didn't want to miss you," the mother said. She was overweight and wore a dress and a man's shirt with cutoff sleeves.

We went inside the small living room. The owners were gone.

"What happened to your employer?" I asked.

"Mr. Vidrine was upset," the woman replied. "He said this ain't suppose to be happening down here."

I asked the little girl her name, then asked her to describe the man who carried a gun.

"His mouth was real red," she said. "His name was Smiley."

"What did his rifle look like?"

"It had a telescope on top and a can on the front."

"What'd he say to you?"

"He told me the story of where flying fish come from. Sharks was always chasing and eating them, then a magic lady under the sea gave them wings so they could pop out of the waves and fly away."

"That's a pretty good story," I said.

"It wasn't him killed them people, huh?" she said.

"We're not sure, Loretta. Did Smiley tell you where he was going or where he lives?"

"No, suh."

"What kind of car did he have?"

"It was blue."

I asked about the license and the model, but these were not the kinds of things a child her age would take note of.

"Maybe the man in the car that passed him might know," she said.

"Which man? What car?"

"It was purple," she said. "What do you call them kind? The top is like canvas."

"A convertible."

"I seen Smiley drive up the road in his li'l blue car. The convertible drove down to the point. Then the convertible come back up the road and I didn't see it no more."

"Think hard, Loretta. What did the man in the convertible look like?"

"I couldn't see good. It was raining," she replied. "He was big and had on a li'l hat."

I stared at the mist and fog rolling off the bay, the bolts of lightning that flickered like snakes' tongues in the clouds. *What in God's name are you doing, Clete?* I thought.

"Can we go, suh?" the mother said. "I got to go home and fix supper."

"Yes, y'all have been very helpful. Thank you," I said.

The girl looked up at me. "I don't t'ink Smiley would hurt anyone. Would he, suh?"

I didn't answer and instead said good night and drove back to the crime scene. The paramedics were trundling the bodies on gurneys to an ambulance. Inside the house, Helen was talking on her cell phone to Jimmy Nightingale. Her face looked old when she hung up.

"Bad?" I said.

"He cried. I can never read that guy."

"The little girl told me a big guy wearing a small hat and driving a purple convertible passed Smiley on the road. Smiley was headed north, the convertible was headed south."

"Clete?" she said.

"Sounds like it."

"You get his butt in my office at oh-eight-hundred tomorrow."

I LEFT THREE MESSAGES for him that night and one the next morning. I went by his office. His secretary said she thought he was in New Orleans.

"When will he be back?" I said.

"It's Friday, Mr. Dave. In New Orleans. He'll be back when he gets back."

The double murder was the headline story in *The Daily Iberian*. I felt caught in a situation that was endless and had no good ending. The rain was unrelenting. We had gone from drought that had left the swamplands strung with dead vegetation to flooded fields and ditches and front yards and cemeteries in which caskets floated from the crypts. Levon Broussard was transferred to the jail in Jennings, then granted bail a second time. From all accounts, Jimmy Nightingale was devastated. I feared for Clete, because I believed he was becoming not only obsessed but irrational. I went to a noon meeting and passed when it was my turn to speak, primarily because I genuinely believed, as Clete and Helen did, that a shapeless and malevolent entity was in our midst. It was not the kind of stuff that improved a recovering drunk's day.

At one-thirty P.M. Saturday, Clete called me at home.

"Where are you?" I asked.

"In the Big Sleazy, where else? If you're worried about Homer, he's with the lady I hire."

"You were seen at the Nightingales' camp, Clete. Shortly after Smiley did a job on Swede Jensen and Emmeline Nightingale."

"So what?"

"What were you doing there?"

"I wanted to have another run at Jimmy Nightingale. A St. Mary deputy told me he was probably at the camp."

"You could end up a suspect."

"I was trying to be courteous and return your calls, big mon. How about getting off my case?"

"Don't shine me on."

"I'm going to bring that lying cocksucker down," he said. "Maybe I won't bust a cap on him, but one way or another I'm going to put a freight train up his ass. I mean that literally—in the bridal suite in Angola."

"How are you going to do that?"

"Nail him as a coconspirator in the death of the Jeff Davis Eight. One way or another, I'm going to get him. I've had a good life."

Then I remembered Jimmy Nightingale had a rally that night at the Superdome.

"I'll put you in handcuffs if I have to," I said.

He was already off the line.

I HEADED FOR NEW Orleans in my pickup, the rain twisting out of a gaseous-green sky. Just as I approached the bridge at Des Allemands, my cell phone vibrated on the seat. It was Sherry Picard.

"Clete left me a message," she said. "Something about him being sorry for his part in it, and if he didn't see me again, I was a great woman, blah-blah-blah."

"Clete isn't into blah-blah-blah."

"Whatever. He sounded like he was on a banzai mission."

"He says he's going to take down Jimmy Nightingale," I said. "In whatever fashion he can. Nightingale has a rally at the Superdome tonight."

"Shit," she said. "Clete's talking about capping him?"

"I didn't say that." I was atop the bridge now. I could see house-boats anchored at a wooded island, the bayou flowing into a chain of lakes, the rain denting the water. Somehow I knew what was coming, and I didn't want to hear it.

"Here's the gen," she said. "Remember the fast-food trash by Kevin Penny's motorcycle shed? I matched the prints. They belong to Rowena Broussard."

"I thought she wasn't in the system."

"She visited her husband when he was temporarily locked up. I gave her a cup of coffee in a Styrofoam cup."

"The match might put her at the scene, but not at the time of Penny's death."

"It gets worse, at least from a prosecutor's perspective. The prints of Herb Smith, a social worker, were at the scene."

"I don't remember the name," I said.

"It doesn't matter. His niece was one of the Jeff Davis Eight. Starting to get the picture?"

"You think Rowena did it, but there's no way she'll be convicted?"

"That's right."

"And Levon won't, either, because people around here think he walks on water?"

"You got it."

"What does this have to do with Clete?" I asked.

"He's convinced himself Jimmy Nightingale is partly responsible for the Jeff Davis Eight and for Penny's death and for the attempt to put a bomb in his car. I don't think Nightingale has anything to do with any of it."

"I wouldn't rule Nightingale out, Miss Sherry. At least not entirely."

"Lose the *Gone with the Wind* stuff, will you? I can't take that plantation cutesy talk."

"You know who else told me that?" I asked.

"No."

"Rowena Broussard," I said.

"See you at the Dome, hotshot."

*　　*　　*

FOR FIVE DAYS in August 2005, the Superdome had been shelter for more than thirty thousand people during and after Hurricane Katrina. Do not let the term "shelter" mislead you. The Dome became an introduction to hell on earth. The storm stripped off huge chunks of the roof; the power and water supply failed; toilets and urinals overflowed and layered the floors with feces. The food in the refrigerators rotted. The heat and humidity and stench caused television reporters to gag on-camera. Every inch of concrete surrounding the Dome was covered with garbage, clothing, and people sweltering under a white sun. Black people who tried to leave the area by crossing the Danziger Bridge were shot by people officers. One of those who died was a mentally disabled man.

But our excursion into the Garden of Gethsemane had slipped into history, the incompetence and cynicism and villainy of its perpetrators largely unpunished, the bravery and self-sacrifice of its heroes, such as the United States Coast Guard, largely unremembered. Jimmy's rally was more like Mardi Gras than a political event, even though most of the crowd knew about the murder of his sister. The purple and green columns of light surrounding the Dome were an ode to the ancient world, a pagan display presided over by a rotund and garlanded and sybaritic man who understood his constituency's love of shared power and empire and blood sports and the opportunity to participate and glory in them.

I called Clete and went directly to voicemail. Dixieland bands played outside and inside the Dome, the musicians in candy-striped jackets and straw boaters, their smiles frozen like ceramic dolls'. Tens of thousands filled the seats and aisles and corridors. The concession stands were heaped with Cajun and Creole cuisine; draft beer was ten dollars a cup, and a double-shot cocktail was fourteen-fifty. Jimmy Nightingale T-shirts and caps were everywhere. The ammonia smell of urinated beer bloomed from the men's rooms.

By the time Jimmy mounted the stage, the crowd had doubled, and the air was filled with an electric haze and a growing feral odor from the press of bodies in the corridors and aisles.

Jimmy was dressed in mourner's black. But through the tiny binoculars I carried, I could see a flag pin on his lapel and sequins that had been sprayed on his hand-tooled boots and his gold cuff links that were the size of quarters. His incarnations were endless, like Proteus rising from the sea. In this instance, he vulgarized his own image and yet did it with elegance.

His short-brim Stetson, one he never wore in Franklin, hung from his hand. His expression was neither somber nor celebratory. He gazed silently at the crowd, bathed in light, his posture and trim physique and resolute manner heartbreaking, considering the loss he had just incurred. All sound and motion in the Dome seemed to slow like a film winding down, then stop. Even the beer vendors in the aisles were motionless, their boxlike trays suspended painfully from their necks.

"I want to thank you," Jimmy said, a tremble in his voice. "I cannot express how much I appreciate your being here. You are the finest people I have ever known. God bless each and every one of you."

The stage lights were pointed up into his face, giving it the angular splendor of a Byzantine saint. One by one the audience members came to their feet, applauding lightly at first, then breaking into an ovation that shook the building.

Tears slid down both his cheeks. Then Jimmy did something I never saw coming. He went to the back of the platform and motioned for a man to join him. Even the audience seemed stunned. A gaunt figure whose plastic surgery had failed him was being raised from the dead, a modern Lazarus dragged against his will into the light, all his sins forgiven. Even he did not seem to understand his good fortune. He raised one hand timidly, as though afraid of the response.

The audience was transfixed and did not know what to do.

Jimmy lifted a microphone from a stand. "Many of us take different roads in our struggle to keep our country free and pure and unsullied by the millions crossing our borders. Bobby Earl loves his country and the traditions for which our brave fighting men and woman have shed their blood. We help the poor, the immigrant who honors our laws, the destitute and downtrodden, but we do not let others rob us of our heritage and birthright. Bobby Earl devoted his life to an honorable cause, and we will not be party to the political correctness that condemns a man because he speaks his mind and practices the freedoms guaranteed him by the First Amendment.

"Bobby is a good man, a Christian and a patriot. Let's give him the credit he deserves, and to hell with the people who don't like it. I'm proud to call Bobby Earl my friend."

One heartbeat later, someone let loose with a Rebel yell, and the entire place went crazy. That was when I saw Clete Purcel standing in a doorway that led to the concourse. He was eating a hot dog, wiping his mouth with a paper napkin as he chewed. My cell phone vibrated in my pocket. I looked at the caller ID and put the phone to my ear. "This is Dave."

"I'm in the Dome," Sherry Picard said. "Have you found Clete?"

"I just saw him. He went into the concourse. I'm walking there now. Before you hang up, I have to ask you a question."

"Go ahead."

"How does a woman the size of Rowena Broussard take down a guy like Penny?"

"Succinylcholine."

"Say again?"

"It paralyzes the muscles. Somebody shot a hypodermic load of it into his system. Rowena was a nurse in South America, wasn't she? Those lefties are a howl."

"Clete fought for the leftists in El Sal."

"I gave him a dispensation."

Stay away from this person, I thought.

Chapter
39

CLETE LEFT THE concourse and worked his way to the other side of the Dome, hoping to come up on the backside of the stage. If he could make it that far, he was going to walk onto the stage. It was undignified, self-abasing, and maybe the act of a public fool. What did it matter? He thought of the graves he had dug with an e-tool, the bodies hung in trees after the VC got finished with them, the people who had sat on scalding rooftops in the Lower Ninth Ward, waiting for the helicopters. This was the kind of world Clete believed Jimmy Nightingale would preside over. The man used people as he would a suppository. Clete wanted to print him on a wall.

But this was a fantasy, and he knew it. As a boy, Clete had never been a bully, although older and bigger boys had bullied him. He even forgave the kid from the Iberville Project who bashed him with the pipe that left the scar through his eyebrow. The kid had grown up no differently than Clete and later died at Khe Sanh. For Clete, the myth of Wyatt Earp was not a myth. You smoked them when they dealt the play but not before, even if you had to eat a bullet. And for that reason alone, Clete would always be at a disadvantage in dealing with a cunning man like Nightingale, who, minutes earlier, had incorporated the racism of Bobby Earl into his campaign while acting as the bestower of forgiveness.

Clete passed a restroom and a locked office, then found a door that opened onto a storage area under the stands. He opened a second door onto an entryway from which he could see the backside of Nightingale as he introduced a famous country singer wearing a thick-felt tall-crowned white cowboy hat and a pale blue western-cut suit stitched with flowers.

Clete also saw a beer vendor whose pants and shirt looked dipped in starch, the trousers stuffed inside rubber boots, a Nightingale baseball cap sitting on his eyebrows. He was a short, pudgy man with lips like red licorice.

Clete stared at the vendor but didn't move. What was he waiting for? He started again toward the aisle, his gaze riveted on the vendor's neck. *Let it play out,* a voice said.

His stomach was churning. *Maybe he's just an ordinary guy,* he thought. *What if you start something and security gets the wrong idea and the guy gets hurt just so Nightingale is safe?*

But he knew the real reason for his unwillingness to act. The weight on his heart was the size of an anvil.

"What are you doing here, asshole?" a voice said.

Clete turned around. Once again he was looking into the face that was one of many he could never rid himself of. The faces were out of a subculture that fed on need and dysfunction and systemic cruelty, in this case the face of an old-time gunbull whose measure of self-worth was the degree to which he could inspire terror in others. He wore tight gray slacks with high pockets and a shirt the color of tin and a bolo tie and a salt-and-pepper mustache as stiff as wire and a belt equipped with Mace, handcuffs, a slapjack, and a blue-black semi-auto with checkered grips.

"Birl Wooster is the full name, isn't it?" Clete said.

"When I woke up, it was. Answer my question."

"I just saw a beer vendor who might be the guy called Smiley."

"You're talking about this guy out of Florida?"

"He's down there."

"Where?"

Clete turned around and looked down the aisle. "I don't see him now."

"Because he was never there."

"A guy who fits his description was there."

"And you're a goddamn liar."

Clete's eyes searched the crowd again. "I think we blew an opportunity. But maybe not."

"You know why I don't like you, Purcel? One guy like you taints a whole department. It's like trying to launder the stink out of shit."

"You screwed the pooch, dickhead. By the way, that black kid you killed on the levee? He was nineteen."

"Until he stopped being nineteen," Wooster said. "I lost a lot of sleep over that."

"How's it feel?" Clete said.

"How's what feel?"

Clete shook his head. "Don't pay attention to me."

Wooster removed a toothpick from his shirt pocket and put it into his mouth. "I'm going to dial you up one of these days, Purcel."

The crowd began to drain from the Dome.

"I hear there's a reception at the casino," Clete said.

"Not for you, there isn't."

"See you around, Wooster. Don't beat up on any handicapped people."

Wooster elevated the toothpick with his teeth, his eyes veiled.

I FOUND SHERRY PICARD in the concourse and called Clete again. This time he answered.

"Where are you?" I asked.

"Behind the stage," he said. "I just got braced by an ex-gunbull from Angola. He blew away a black inmate for sassing him and put a shank on his body. A guy named Wooster."

"Who?"

"He does security for Nightingale."

"What does Wooster have to do with anything?" I said.

"Nothing. I think I saw Smiley. He's posing as a beer vendor. I was maybe forty feet from him when Wooster came down on me."

"You let a hump for Nightingale stop you from taking down Smiley?"

"Not exactly."

I couldn't put together what he was saying. Then it hit me. "You were going to let Smiley get to Nightingale?"

"The thought occurred to me."

"I'm with Sherry Picard. Wait for us."

"You brought her here?"

"No, she came on her own."

"Butt out on this, Dave. I got a handle on it."

"The way you handled Smiley?"

"You want the truth?" he said. "I was going to make sure both of them went off the board. Wooster screwed things up."

"Stay where you are."

"I'm going to the casino. My car is parked six blocks away. It'll take me a while to get there."

"What's at the casino?"

"A reception for Nightingale."

"I'll drop the dime on you, Cletus."

"No, you won't. Keep Sherry out of it. I'm copacetic and very cool and collected and totally in control of the situation. You're the best, big mon."

CLETE HAD TO walk to the other side of LaSalle to retrieve his Caddy. The sky was still dark, the rain blowing off the roofs of the few lighted buildings along the street. He cut through an alley lined with banana plants and garbage cans that had been knocked over by the wind. Twice he thought he heard footsteps behind him, but when he turned around, no one was there. The second time, he stepped between two buildings and waited. An elderly black man on a bicycle pedaled down the sidewalk at the end of the alley. Clete continued on.

He walked past a collapsed garage to the back of a deserted brick house where he had parked his vehicle. A tall man in a slicker and a wilted rain hat was standing by the driver's door. His face was dark with shadow. His shoulders were rectangular, his coat open, his hands invisible. "Beat you to it."

"You'd make a good bird dog," Clete said.

"Nice wheels," the tall man said.

"Am I going to have trouble with you?" Clete said.

"You hold grudges, Purcel. That nigger I popped had a shiv on him."

"After you planted it."

"You killed a federal witness."

"It was an accident."

"That's why you hid out in El Salvador. A lot of people go down there when they do something by accident."

Clete looked at his watch. "What's your problem, Wooster?"

"I don't have one. You do. The federal witness you killed was a friend of mine. You got your drop with you?"

"Why do you want to know?"

"Maybe I can make use of it."

"I'm not carrying."

"Doesn't matter. You're in the shitter." Wooster parted his coat and lifted a semi-auto into the light. He grinned. "We can do it standing up. Or you can kneel down."

"You're kidding."

"I don't like you. I put down seven people nobody knows about. What do you say to that?"

"Give your bullshit to somebody else."

"Look into the barrel and tell me it's bullshit."

"What do you get out of it?"

"Kicks."

"A guy like you does nothing for kicks. Except maybe standing in line to fuck your mother."

"Later tonight, after you're dead, I'm going to get laid. Think about that."

"Since I'm about to go out, tell me something. Who put the drill to Kevin Penny?"

"Maybe you're looking at him. Who cares? Bye-bye, asshole."

So this is how it comes, Clete thought. Not the Jolly Green caving in half when an RPG came through the bay, the frag he took in the carotid, the two rounds in the back while carrying his best friend down a fire escape, the burning roof that crashed on him when he ran through the flames with a little girl wrapped in a blanket.

"Fuck you, Wooster," he said.

Then he saw a flash at the entrance to the alley across the street, like a downed power line that had dropped onto a car roof, and heard a sound like *phifth* or someone spitting. Wooster heard and saw it also. He widened his eyes and stared into the darkness, his gun still pointed at Clete's chest. His jaw was hooked, his profile like a barracuda's.

Clete heard the sound twice again. The first round punched through Wooster's throat. Still holding the gun, he clenched one hand over the wound, blood congealing immediately between his fingers. He made a choking sound, as if he'd swallowed a fish bone. The second round made a hole less than the diameter of a pencil above his eyebrow, as though a bug had settled on it, and exited the back of his head cleanly and knocked out a window in a garage. He fell into a greasy pool of water, curled in an embryonic position, the rain falling in his eyes.

A cat meowed by a garbage can. The wind gusted, and a strip of tin on the roof of the deserted house swung on a nail. Clete slid behind the wheel of the Caddy and drove around the body into the street, hitting his brights, lighting up the alleyway where the shots had come from. His wipers were beating wildly, the windshield fogging. At the end of the alley, he saw a man in rubber boots running, a rifle cupped in his right hand, his skin as white as a slug's.

Clete picked up his cell phone from the seat and dialed a number with his thumb.

SHERRY PICARD AND I were inside the casino when I got his call. The casino was packed, the roar of noise deafening. "I can't hear you, Clete. You're not making sense."

"I went to get my car," he said. "Wooster, the gunbull, was waiting for me. He was going to kill me. He almost did."

"How would he know where your car was?"

"He was walking behind me, then got ahead of me and saw the Caddy," he replied. "I asked him if he did Kevin Penny. He said maybe. Then Smiley put two bullets in him."

"You're talking about the security guy?"

"Who do you think?"

"He killed Penny?"

"Maybe he was working my crank."

I worked my way into a corner, far from the drink and food tables where most of the crowd was concentrating. "Why would Smiley drop one of Nightingale's security people?"

"I don't know. It wasn't an accident. The guy is too good a shot."

"Smiley owes you?"

"Most of his victims were abused women or children or connected with people who abused women or children. Smiley tried to put a bomb in my car. He might have killed Homer. So maybe Smiley found out he got set up to kill a child and started cleaning the slate. Where's Nightingale?"

"Forget about Nightingale," I said.

"Like I can."

"Did you call 911 on the shooting?"

"In New Orleans? NOPD would have me on the injection table."

"Where are you now?"

"In a filling-station restroom, washing the splatter off me. I'll be there in fifteen minutes."

"Drop it, Clete. Let's go back to New Iberia."

"That's what you're always trying to do, Dave. You don't get it."

"Pardon?"

"The place you remember isn't there," he said. "There're no safe places anymore. Everyone knows that except you."

No, "EVERYONE" DID not. I had at least one partner in my grand illusion about the relativity of time and the melding together of the past and present and future and the possibility that the dead are still with us, like the boys in butternut marching through the flooded cypress at Spanish Lake, and the slaves who beckon us to remove the chains that bind them to the auction block, and all the wandering souls who want to scratch their names on a plaster wall so someone will remember their sacrifice, the struggle that began with the midwife's slap of life and their long day's journey into the grave.

I think madness is a matter of definition. But if you are afflicted by it, you thank God for those who share it with you. And that was why I was always drawn to Levon Broussard and, paradoxically, to Jimmy Nightingale. Neither accepted the world as it is, and neither was entirely rational. However, their difference lay elsewhere, and in this case the difference was critical not only to them but to us. Jimmy was a brilliant man who, of his own volition, chose to model himself on his benighted antecedents, demagogues who need no more mention. Conversely, Levon was the artist who enlisted in lost causes, flagellating himself because he could not change the nature of mankind.

After I finished talking to Clete, my cell phone throbbed again. It was Alafair.

"ROWENA AND LEVON Broussard just left our house," she said. "You won't believe this."

"I probably will," I replied.

"Rowena says she tortured and killed Kevin Penny."

"Yep."

"You're not surprised?"

"What do they plan to do now?"

"They didn't say. Rowena wanted to get it off her conscience. After Penny raped her, she thought he might be involved with the murder of the girls in Jeff Davis Parish. She thought she was going to get justice for them. And for herself."

"What did she find out from Penny?"

"Nothing."

"I'm not sure I believe her story. Maybe she's muddying the water so Levon can skate. Maybe neither of them is involved."

"Are you serious?" she said.

"A former hack at Angola named Wooster told Clete he did it."

"Told him when?"

"Tonight, just before Smiley killed him."

"Smiley just killed someone else? In New Orleans?"

"He gets around. Call Rowena and Levon and tell them what I said."

"You're trying to queer the DA's case, aren't you."

"All this would come up in discovery anyway. The former gunbull was going to kill Clete. Smiley saved his life."

"I bet he loves his mother, too," she said.

"I doubt it. Talk to you later, Alf."

I closed the cell phone.

Chapter 40

SHERRY PICARD AND I moved deeper into the crowd at the casino. The carpets were the color of a freshly sliced pomegranate, the gaming tables covered with lavender felt. Giant bronze replicas of palm trees looked down on the tables. Each gambling machine was outfitted with a padded leather-backed chair that gave the patron a sense of comfort and security. The ceilings were high and spacious and created the impression of a separate universe but one that allowed no view of the outside world.

Jimmy Nightingale was at the beverage tables, surrounded by hundreds of well-wishers, his security people around him but having a hard time of it.

"There's Clete," Sherry said.

"Where?"

"By the door."

I stood on my toes and tried to see over the heads of the crowd. "I don't see him."

"I'm almost sure it was him. He's gone now."

I pushed my way through the crowd. Many of them were drunk or on the edge of drunk. Over the heads I could see Bobby Earl with Nightingale. Somebody clamped me on the shoulder. "Robicheaux! You back on the hooch? Son of a bitch, I thought you were on the side of the tree huggers. You're one of us, you old bastard."

He was a big, sweaty, red-faced man whose skin oozed grease and whose rumpled suit smelled like a locker room. He threw a meaty arm over me, a well of stink rising from his armpit. I had no idea who he was. "Goddamn it, son, it's good to see you. This November we're gonna kick some ass. Who's this lady with you?"

Sherry opened her badge in his face. "On the job. Beat feet, fatso."

"What was that?" he said, releasing me. "What'd you call me?"

She pushed him in the chest. "You heard me."

"What do you think you're doing?" he said. "You can't push people around like that."

I was still forty feet from Nightingale. I felt like I was sinking in wet concrete.

"Somebody call security!" the fat man said. "There's a crazy woman here."

I thought I saw Clete on the edge of the crowd. I changed direction and headed toward him. I popped out on the back edge of the crowd and saw the men's room door open and smoke billow out. Clete was nowhere in sight. A short man in a panama hat and oversize white slacks and two-tone shoes and a dark blue shirt with bananas printed on it, worn outside the belt, was walking from the restroom through the banks of gambling machines and the throng that had come through a side entrance and was headed for the free booze and food.

"Smiley!" I shouted.

He did not turn around or change his stride. I went after him. A band up on a platform broke into "The Star-Spangled Banner."

WHEN CLETE SAW the smoke, he went straight to the restroom and watched the men flowing out the door. A young man in a security guard uniform, carrying a fire extinguisher, almost knocked him down.

"Sorry, sir," the guard said.

"You see a short guy with skin like an albino?" Clete said.

"No," the security guard said. "He have something to do with the fire?"

Clete looked through the doorway. Three wastebaskets packed with wet paper towels were burning. "His name is Smiley. He kills people."

"Sir, is that a weapon under your coat?"

"I'm a PI. I have a license to carry."

"Not in the casino, sir. Not under Louisiana law. That's a fact, sir."

"Take it easy," Clete said. "We're on the same side."

The security guard began spraying the fire with the extinguisher, glancing at Clete. "I got my hands full. You're not supposed to have a firearm in here, sir. I'll have to take it from you."

How do you fault a brave kid for doing his job? "Listen, there's a guy running loose in here who probably killed Jimmy Nightingale's sister. Don't give me a hard time. You *diggez-vous,* noble mon?"

"I don't speak French, sir."

"Look, you're stand-up and trying to do your job. But don't let your job get ahead of your brain."

The smoke had gathered on the ceiling, and eye-watering amounts of it were still rising from the cans.

"I have to ask for your gun, sir," the security guard said. He was not armed. He put his two-way to his ear.

"I'm sorry to do this," Clete said. He tore the radio from the security guard's hand; he wanted to smash it or throw it into the commode. He looked at the humiliation in the security guard's face. "What's your name?"

"Jody Weinberger."

"My name is Clete Purcel. You got moxie, Jody." Clete tossed him the two-way. "How about you forget my piece and cover my back? Do me a solid, kid. You won't regret it."

"I could do that."

"The bad guy I told you about is the real deal. His name is Smiley."

"What do we do when we find him?"

"We take him down," Clete said. But his words tasted bitter and insincere before they left his mouth.

* * *

CLETE PUSHED HIS way through the crowd. Once again he had thoughts of a kind he'd never had, a sense of foreboding that normally only de-ranged or messianic people were haunted by, as though only they saw the dark portent of the events taking place around them. In Clete's mind, Jimmy Nightingale had become the hooded figure that lives in our sleep, a memory passed on from the caves of ancient Albion and the pantheons of Philistines, the embodiment of guile and deception, a serpent cracking through its shell in a garden between the Tigris and the Euphrates.

Then Clete saw him, surrounded by his acolytes, Bobby Earl by his side. The band was playing "Under the Double Eagle." Amid the meretricious decor of the casino, Nightingale's face was suffused with the soft buttery glow of a gold coin. Bobby Earl's hand rested on his shoulder. Clete had never hated a man as much as Nightingale. He longed for the excuse to free his snub-nose from its holster and, in a blaze of bullets, free the world forever of the creature he was sure the Bible warned us about.

He looked over his shoulder. Jody Weinberger was right behind him, his youthful, trusting face expectant, his eyes fixed on Clete's.

"Shouldn't we warn Mr. Nightingale?" Jody said.

On the far side of a craps table, Clete saw a man in a panama hat and a loud shirt, his arms like rolls of sourdough, his head tilted down, his expression concealed.

"Can you answer me, Mr. Purcel?" the security guard said. "Maybe we should call it in. Sir, we've got to do something. Or I've got to call for help."

I FELT AS THOUGH I were in a mob of revelers at a public execution. The fat man who had clamped my shoulder was still with us, leading two security guards, pushing people out of his way. "There she is!" he shouted. "Impersonating a police officer! Lock that bitch up!"

A woman fell, and a man tripped over her. The brass horns in the band were ear-splitting. Someone with horrendous breath was yelling incoherently in my face. I had no idea who he was.

"What do you want?" I yelled.

"My wife is having a heart attack!" he said. He looked around desperately. "Help me get her out of here!"

"I'm sorry, I can't help you," I said.

Sherry grabbed my arm. "Look! On the other side of the craps table! The guy in the panama hat! Is that him?"

Smiley was standing alone, as though no one was in the building except him and Jimmy Nightingale. I saw him reach into his right-hand pocket. I began fighting my way toward him. It was like swimming with a bag of rocks strapped on my back.

CLETE SAW SMILEY moving toward Jimmy Nightingale and Bobby Earl, a hand in his pocket, a sweet look on his face. Clete reached inside his coat for his snub-nose. But he didn't pull it from its holster.

"Is that him, Mr. Purcel?" Jody said. "Is that him? What are you waiting on, sir?"

Let it happen, a voice said. *You're not God.*

"You've got to, Mr. Purcel," Jody said.

"Got to do what?" Clete replied, as though drugged.

"Stop whatever is happening."

"Get out of here, kid," Clete said.

"This is my job. I was trying to help you."

"That man up there is shit. Don't let him ruin your life. Now beat it before I knock you down."

Jody tried to get around him. Clete hit him in the chest with an elbow, then saw Smiley ease a small revolver from his pocket and lower it by his thigh and begin walking rapidly toward Nightingale.

Clete burst from the crowd and crashed through Jimmy Nightingale's security people, his gun falling from its holster. He tackled Jimmy and slammed him to the carpet just as Smiley fired one shot, then a second one. Clete could hear the breath wheeze out of Jimmy's chest and feel the spray of spittle on his cheek. When Jimmy tried to get up, Clete mashed his head into the carpet with a forearm. The casino turned into bedlam.

* * *

EVERYONE AROUND SHERRY and me either ran for the exits or cowered on the floor. Sherry squatted behind me, pulling a revolver from an ankle holster, trying to see beyond the beverage table where Clete and Jimmy Nightingale were. She pushed past me, touching my shoulder to steady herself, her face tight and pale, like that of someone looking into an arctic wind. I stood up next to her, my nine-millimeter in my hand. "You see him?" I asked.

"Who?" she said.

"Smiley."

"No."

"Circle to the left, I'll go right," I said.

"Roger that." Then she said, "Oh, fuck."

"What do you see?" I said.

"That kid. He's got a gun. He looks like he's about to piss his pants."

Amid the sea of people on the floor, we saw a young security guard walking toward the drink and food tables. He was pointing a white-handled snub-nose revolver, a .38, with both arms extended in front of him. The snub-nose looked exactly like Clete's.

Smiley was somewhere beyond a bronze palm tree and a fountain dancing with red and green and purple lights. Sherry and I closed on him from both sides. He began firing, then shucked his shells and used a speed loader and started firing again. Both of us huddled behind marble pillars and tried to get a clear shot, one that wouldn't hit a civilian. I could hear Smiley's rounds going long, breaking glass and ricocheting off metal and stone. I thought I heard a woman cry out. The kid who had the snub-nose was advancing on Smiley, snapping off three rounds, heedless of the people in the background.

CLETE RAISED HIMSELF on his elbows. He looked up at the young security guard. "Get down before you kill somebody."

"I'm gonna get him, Mr. Purcel."

"There's a dining room and a kitchen back there!"

Jimmy Nightingale crawled out from under Clete. He pressed his wrist against his nose and looked at it. "How much do you weigh?"

"Shut up," Clete said.

One of the food and beverage tables had been knocked over, and the carpet was soaked in booze and étouffée and shrimp and crawfish casserole.

"You saved my life," Jimmy said. "Maybe Bobby's, too."

"Shut your fucking mouth, Nightingale. I want to tear you up. You and Earl both. I want to keep you alive and hurt you every day of your worthless life. I don't care how this ends, but wherever you see me, you'd better cross the street."

Jimmy sat up and found a napkin and touched at his bloody nose, then wiped off his shirt. "You're a hell of a guy, Clete, whether you know it or not."

Clete fitted his hand on Jimmy's face like a starfish clamping a stone, mashing his nose, and shoved his head as hard as he could, almost snapping his neck.

I BOLTED FROM BEHIND the marble pillar and dove headlong behind a row of gambling machines. Sherry was running toward Smiley at the same time. The security guard went past me, firing Clete's revolver. People were flattened on the floor throughout the casino. Then I heard the revolver snap on an empty chamber. Sherry stood up, gripping her nine-millimeter with two hands, and fired until the bolt locked open.

The lights went out in the concourse that led to the front of the building. Smiley had disappeared. "Dave!" I heard Clete say.

I turned around. There was blood on his shirt. "Are you hit?" I asked.

"Nightingale had a nosebleed and got it on my shirt. I saved that pus-head's life. I'll never get over it. Where's Smiley?"

"He headed for the exit."

"Where's that security guard? Where's my piece? I'm going to kill that kid."

A semblance of order began to take place in the casino. My hands were trembling. The young security guard walked toward us. He handed Clete the snub-nose. "He got away. Some people in the concourse were wounded. Maybe flying glass or something."

I turned in a circle. "You see Sherry?"

"A minute ago," Clete said. "Out of the corner of my eye. She was putting another magazine in her nine-mike."

Medical personnel were coming through the portals of the building. The bandstand was a wreck. The fat man who'd wanted Sherry arrested was still yelling. The man whose wife had suffered a heart attack was weeping. I saw Sherry sitting in one of the leather-padded gambling machines, her back to me. She seemed to be staring at the five golden bells inside the machine's window. Her piece rested on her thigh.

I walked through the trash scattered on the floor and touched her on the back. "You good, Detective?"

"Lost my breath," she said. "Take my piece. I'm getting over the hill for this shit. Did you get him?"

"Smiley? It doesn't look like it."

"Too bad," she said. "Some fun, huh, boss?"

I stepped closer to her and rested my hand on her shoulder. Her head dipped forward. Then I saw the blood welling through her shirt, pooling in her slacks. The light was still in her eyes, like tiny chips of a diamond frozen in time. But there was no movement on her body except for the second hand on her watch.

Epilogue

I<small>T'S FALL NOW,</small> and the election is over, and Jimmy Nightingale is a member of the United States Senate, probably headed for an even grander career. The assassin nicknamed Smiley disappeared inside Mexico or the Caribbean Islands, depending on which law enforcement agency you talk to. For many legal reasons, neither Levon nor Rowena Broussard ever stood trial for the death of Kevin Penny. But the real reason was that nobody cared. In fact, Levon and Rowena adopted Homer. I knew the truth about Rowena's culpability, but I joined ranks with those who looked the other way. Perhaps I've become a cynic. Or better said, I've learned to let the season have its way, to not fight against the pull of the earth and the tidal movements of the oceans and the admonitions that the race is not to the swift and that the earth abides forever.

Clete had saved the life of a man he hated and may have contributed to the ascendancy of a man who would write his name on the clouds in the worst possible way. In the meantime, a brave woman lost her life from a bullet that ballistics proved to have ricocheted from Clete's snub-nose. Although exonerated, the boy who fired the round will probably live with guilt the rest of his life. Whenever Clete and I are in New Orleans, we ask him to dinner. He never accepts the invitation.

I visit Molly's grave, and I try to financially help the widow of T. J. Dartez. I sleep little, welcome each dawn, and bring Snuggs and

Mon Tee Coon into the house and feed them no matter how muddy they are. Through the summer, I watched the completion of Levon's film, and in December, Alafair and I went to see its screening in Los Angeles. I had a strange experience in the theater; to this day, I cannot explain it.

The scene was on Beauregard's left flank on a gray spring dawn outside the settlement know as Shiloh Church. The actors wore faded butternut, some with gold or blue piping, and were crouched among hemlock trees, looking up a hill where Yankee artillery was already in place, loaded with grape and chain and canister and exploding shells, the crews de-elevating in anticipation of the Confederate charge. There could be no doubt about the outcome. The commanding Confederate officer, a purple plume in his hat, rode his horse up and down a shallow creek with his sword drawn.

"No matter what happens, boys, form on me!" he said. "You're men of the South! Be not afraid! God and our people are with you! Drummer, begin your beat!"

The entire regiment rose to its feet, and a boy not over twelve, the one I'd seen splashing his way through the shallows at Spanish Lake, began a ragged cadence that set the regiment in motion like stick figures lurching unsteadily into a wind, their faces white, their equipment banging, some of them barefoot. Halfway up the hill, the artillery crews at the top of the slope fired in sequence down the line like a string of giant firecrackers, then reloaded and fired at will. The slaughter was immediate. The slope was blanketed with fog, the air filled with the Rebel yell, a fox call that sounded like "Woo, woo, woo," the green of the hillside and the wildflowers slick with gore.

The aggregate of smoke and dust and river mist seemed filled with bolts of lightning, as though a thunderstorm from heaven had lost its way and descended upon the earth. Inside the smoke, the battle flag of Granny Lee flipped back and forth on a staff, barely visible against a pale sun, its cloth rent with grapeshot. The commanding officer was still seated on his horse, his plumed hat on the point of his sword, shouting, "Don't falter, boys! We've got them, by God! Just a little farther! Form on me!"

The drummer boy and most of the others died or were wounded in under ten minutes. Was this magnificent and tragic ordeal, one that could compare to Golgotha, the manufacture of evil men who wanted to keep our brothers and sisters enslaved? I will never believe that. I think of each dawn as a gift, and I try to remember that the horns blowing along the road to Roncevaux save us from ourselves and the curse of mediocrity. But maybe that's just another way of saying fuck it. You've got me. I never figured out anything.

ACKNOWLEDGMENTS

Once again I would like to thank my editor, Ben Loehnen; my copy-editor, E. Beth Thomas; my daughter Pamala; and my wife, Pearl, for their help with the manuscript. I also wish to thank Jackie Seow for the many beautiful book jackets she has designed, and my thanks also to Amar Deol and the dozens of people at Simon & Schuster who have been so loyal to my work over the decades. Last, I'd like to express my gratitude to Philip Spitzer and Lukas Ortiz, my agents, who hung in there through the lean years before the good ones came along.

ABOUT THE AUTHOR

James Lee Burke, a rare winner of two Edgar Awards and named Grandmaster by the Mystery Writers of America, is the author of thirty-five previous novels and two collections of short stories, including such *New York Times* bestsellers as *The Jealous Kind, Creole Belle, Light of the World, The Glass Rainbow, Feast Day of Fools,* and *The Tin Roof Blowdown.* He lives in Missoula, Montana.